New York Times bestselling author **Sherrilyn Keny**
a life of extraordinary danger . . . as does a
three   husband
of sw

Writing as ▓▓▓▓ ▓▓ and Kinley MacGr▓▓▓ she is
an international phenomenon with more than twelve million
copies of her books in print, in twenty-eight countries. She's
the author of several series including: The Dark-Hunters, The
League and Lords of Avalon. Her books always appear at
the top of the *New York Times*, *Publishers Weekly* and *USA
Today* lists.

Visit Sherrilyn Kenyon's new UK website www.sherrilyn
kenyon.co.uk or follow her on Twitter at www.twitter.com/
kenyonsherrilyn

Night Pleasures

Sherrilyn Kenyon

piatkus

PIATKUS

First published in the US in 2002 by St. Martin's Press, New York
First published in Great Britain in 2005 by Piatkus Books
This paperback edition published in 2011 by Piatkus

A CIP catalogue record for this book
is available from the British Library.

ISBN 978-0-7499-5543-4

Typeset by Palimpsest Book Production Limited, Falkirk, Stirlingshire
Printed and bound by CPI Mackays, Chatham ME5 8TD

Papers used by Piatkus are from well-managed forests
and other responsible sources.

MIX
Paper from
responsible sources
FSC   FSC® C104740
www.fsc.org

Piatkus
An imprint of
Little, Brown Book Group
100 Victoria Embankment
London EC4Y 0DY

An Hachette UK Company
www.hachette.co.uk

www.piatkus.co.uk

For Kim Cardascia, who gives me the freedom to push past the boundaries of my imagination, and Nancy Yost, who keeps me sane while I do it.

To the Ladies of Sanctuary and the RBL Romanticans for all the laughs and support you guys have given me and the Dark Hunter series. I lub all of you. Thanks for just being you and for loving romance novels as much as I do!

For my friends without whom I would be eternally lost: Rickey, Lo, Janet, Cathy-Max, Deb, Rebecca and Kim Williamson.

To my husband and sons for your patience, your love and all the incredible happiness the four of you have added to my life. And last but never least, for my family for being an incredible source of support.

NIGHT
PLEASURES

AN ANCIENT GREEK LEGEND

Born to extreme wealth, Kyrian of Thrace wielded charm and charisma as powerfully as he wielded his sword. Courageous and bold, he ruled the world around him, and knew nothing save the very passionate side of his nature.

Ardent, wild, and restless, he lived his life recklessly. He knew no danger, no limitations. The world was his oyster and he vowed to feed fully from it.

With the strength of Ares, the body and face of Adonis, and the sensuous gifts of Aphrodite, he was sought by all women who saw him. They wanted him for their own, dreamed of possessing the proud warrior prince whose touch was said to be the closest a woman could ever come to paradise.

But he was not a man whose heart was easily tamed.

He was a man who lived for the moment, lived for his senses, and for the wild fulfillment of all his desires. He loved pleasure, both the giving and the receiving.

The few women who had claimed him for a night of ecstasy lorded it over those who could only dream of touching his exquisite body.

For he *was* passion. Desire. All things sensual and hot.

A born warrior, he was respected and feared by all who knew of him. And at a time when the Roman Empire was invincible, he, alone, beat the Romans back with a hero's glee, and brought riches and glory to his name and homeland.

For a while, 'twas said he would be ruler of the known world.

Until an act of brutal betrayal made him the Ruler of the Night.

Now he walks the shadowy realm between Life and the Underworld. Neither man nor beast, he is something else entirely.

He is Solitude. He is Darkness.

He is a shadow in the night.

A restless, lonely spirit whose destiny is to save the very mortals who despise and fear him. He will never know rest or peace until he can find the one woman who will not betray him. The one pure heart who can see past his dark side and bring him back into the light.

Chapter 1

'I say we should stake him to an anthill and throw little pickles at him.'

Amanda Devereaux laughed at Selena's suggestion. Leave it to her big sister to make her laugh, no matter the tragedy. Which was exactly what had her sitting at Selena's tarot card and palm-reading table in Jackson Square on a cold Sunday afternoon, instead of lying in bed with the covers pulled over her head.

Still smiling at the thought of a million ants biting Cliff's pasty, dough-boy body, Amanda glanced around at the tourists who were thronging the New Orleans landmark even on this drab November day.

The smell of warm chicory coffee and beignets floated from the Cafe Du Monde across the street, while cars zoomed past a few feet away. The clouds and the sky were an eerie gray that matched Amanda's dour mood.

Most of the Jackson Square peddlers didn't bother setting up booths during the winter season, but her sister Selena considered her psychic stand as much a New Orleans treasure as the St Louis Cathedral behind them.

And what a treasure Selena's stand was . . .

The cheap card table was disguised by a thick purple cloth their mother had sewn with 'special' incantations known only to their family.

Madam Selene, the Moon Mistress, as Selena was known, sat behind it wearing a flowing green suede skirt, purple knit sweater, and a large black and silver overcoat.

Her sister's strange outfit was quite a contrast to Amanda's faded jeans, pink cable-knit sweater, and tan ski jacket. But then, Amanda had always preferred to dress in an understated way. Unlike her flamboyant family, she hated to stand out. She much preferred to blend into the background.

'I'm through with men,' Amanda said. 'Cliff was the last stop on the bus to nowhere. I'm tired of wasting my time and energy on them. From now on, I'm going to focus all my attention on accounting.'

Selena curled her lips in distaste as she shuffled her tarot cards. 'Accounting? Are you sure you're not a changeling?'

Amanda gave a halfhearted laugh. 'Actually, I'm sure I am a changeling. I just wish my real family would come claim me before it's too late and some of the weirdness rubs off.'

Selena laughed at her while she set her tarot cards out in a game of psychic solitaire. 'You know what your problem is?'

'I'm too straitlaced and uptight,' Amanda said, using the words her mother and eight older sisters most often applied to her.

'Well, yeah, that too. But I'm thinking you need to branch out with your tastes. Stop going after these tie-wearing, hohum, cry-to-my-mama-'cause-I-have-no-life geeks. You, my baby sister, need a sexcapade with a man who can make your heart race. I'm talking truly reckless and wild.'

'Someone like Bill?' Amanda asked with a smile, thinking of Selena's husband, who was even more straitlaced than Amanda was.

Selena shook her head. 'Oh no, that's different. See, I'm the reckless and wild one who saves him from being boring. It's why we're perfect for each other. We balance. You have no balance. You and your boyfriends tip the scale way into Boredom City.'

'Hey, I like my men boring. They're reliable, and you don't have to worry about them having major testosterone moments. I'm a beta girl, all the way.'

Selena snorted as she played with her cards. 'Sounds to me like you need a few therapy sessions with Grace.'

Amanda scoffed. 'Right, like I need dating advice from a sex therapist who married a Greek sex slave she conjured out of a book. No, thanks.'

In spite of her words, Amanda really did like Grace Alexander. Unlike Selena's usual crew of insane friends, Grace had always been grounded, and blessedly normal. 'How's she doing, by the way?'

'Fine. Niklos started walking two days ago and now he's into everything.'

Amanda smiled as she imagined the adorable blond toddler and his twin sister. She loved it when Grace and Julian let her baby-sit for them. 'When's her new baby due?'

'March first.'

'I'll bet they're excited,' Amanda said, struck by a tiny stab of jealousy. She'd always wanted a house full of kids, but at twenty-six her prospects appeared bleak. Especially since she couldn't find any man willing to procreate with a woman whose entire family was certifiable.

'You know,' Selena said with that speculative look that made Amanda cringe. 'Julian has a brother who was cursed into a book, too. You could try—'

'Big no, thanks! Remember, I'm the one who hates all this paranormal junk. I want a nice, normal, *human* male, not some demon.'

'Priapus is a Greek god, not a demon.'

'Close enough in my book. Believe me, I had my fill while living at home with the nine of you casting spells and doing all that hocus-pocus. I want normality in my life.'

'Normality is boring.'

'Why don't you try it before you knock it?'

Selena laughed. 'One day, little sister, you're going to have to accept the other half of your blood.'

Amanda disregarded her words as her thoughts turned back to her ex-fiancé. She'd really thought Cliff was the one for her. A nice, quiet, average-looking data entry clerk, he had been just her cup of tea.

Until he had met her family.

Ugh! For the last six months, she had put off introducing him to them, knowing what would happen. But he had insisted and last night she had finally caved.

Closing her eyes, Amanda winced at the memory of her twin sister, Tabitha, meeting him at the door all decked out in the Goth clothes she used for stalking the undead. The outfit came complete with a crossbow Tabitha just had to show him, and her entire collection of throwing stars. *'This one is special. It can cleave the head off a vampire at three hundred yards.'*

If that wasn't bad enough, her mother and three of her older sisters had been conjuring a protection spell for Tabitha in the kitchen.

But the absolute worst had come when Cliff had mistakenly drunk from Tabitha's cup, which had been filled with her strength potion of curdled milk, Tabasco sauce, egg yolks, and tea leaves.

He had heaved for an hour.

Afterward, Cliff had driven her home. *'I can't marry a woman with a family like that,'* he'd said as she handed her engagement ring back to him. *'Good God, what if we had kids? Can you imagine what would happen if some of that rubbed off?'*

Leaning her head back, Amanda could still kill her family for the embarrassment. Was it too much for them to be normal for one dinner?

Why, oh why, couldn't she have been born to a regular family where no one believed in ghosts, goblins, demons, and witches?

Come to think of it, two of them still believed in Santa Claus!

How could her wonderfully normal father stand all their nonsense? He definitely deserved to be sainted for his patience.

'Hey, guys!'

Amanda opened her eyes to see Tabitha approaching. *Well now, isn't this just peachy keen?* What would happen next? Would a bus run her over?

This day just gets better and better.

She loved her identical twin, but not at this moment. At this moment, she wished very vile things on Tabitha's head. Painful nasty things.

As usual, Tabitha was dressed all in black. Black leather pants, turtleneck, and long black leather coat. Her thick, wavy dark auburn hair was pulled into a long ponytail, and her pale blue eyes glowed. Tabitha's cheeks were flushed and she had a chipper step.

Oh no, she was on a hunt!

Amanda sighed. How on earth could they have come from the same single egg?

Tabitha reached into her coat pocket and pulled out a scrap of paper, then placed it on the table in front of Selena. 'I need your expertise. It's Greek, isn't it?'

Without answering the question, Selena set her cards aside, and looked the paper over. She frowned. 'Where did you get this?'

'It was on a vampire we dusted last night. What does it say?'

'"The Dark-Hunter is close. Desiderius must prepare."'

Tabitha put her hands in her pockets as she considered the words. 'Any idea what that means?'

Selena shrugged as she handed the paper back to Tabitha. 'I've never heard of either this Dark-Hunter or Desiderius.'

'Eric said "Dark-Hunter" was a code name for one of us. What do you think?' Tabitha asked.

Amanda had heard enough. Ye gods, how she hated it when they began with the whole vampire-demon-occult garbage. Why couldn't they grow up and live in the regular world?

'Look,' Amanda said, rising. 'I'll catch you two later.'

Tabitha grabbed her hand as she started to walk off. 'Hey, you're not still sore about Cliff, are you?'

'Of course I am. I know you did all that on purpose.'

Completely unabashed about the fact she'd broken Amanda's engagement, Tabitha released her hand. 'We did it for your own good.'

'Oh yeah, right.' She beamed a false smile. 'Thank you so much for watching out for me. Wanna poke my eye out while you're at it, just for fun?'

'C'mon, Mandy,' Tabitha said with that cutesy face that made their dad forgive her anything. It didn't do anything to Amanda, except irritate her more. 'You might not like what we do, but you do love us. And you can't marry some uptight jerk who can't accept what all of us are.'

'Us?' Amanda asked incredulously. 'Don't include me in the madness. I'm the one with the recessive normal genes. You guys are the ones—'

'Tabby!'

Amanda broke off as Tabitha's Goth boyfriend ran up to them. Eric St. James was only an inch taller than the two of them, but since they were five-foot-ten, that wasn't unusual. His short black hair had a purple stripe in it and he wore it spiked. He would have been very cute if his nose wasn't pierced, and if he would actually find and keep a full-time job.

And lay off the vampire-hunting. Sheez!

'Gary got a lead on that vamp pack,' Eric said to Tabitha. 'We're going to try and get the vampires before it gets dark. You ready?'

If Amanda rolled her eyes any harder back into her head, she'd go blind from it. 'One day, you guys are going to inadvertently kill a human being acting this way. Remember that time you attacked the Anne Rice–Lestat reenactment group in the cemetery?'

Eric smirked at her. 'No one was hurt, and the tourists loved it.'

Tabitha looked back at Selena. 'Can you do some research for me, and see if you can find anything on this Desiderius and Dark-Hunter?'

'C'mon, Tabby, how many times do I have to tell you to lay off it?' Eric said irritably. 'The vamps are just playing with us. "Dark-Hunter" is just a bogeyman term that means nothing.'

Selena and Tabitha ignored him.

'Sure,' Selena said, 'but Gary would probably be your best bet.'

Eric let out a disgusted breath. 'He said he'd never heard of it, either' – Eric looked at Tabitha heatedly – 'which means it's nothing.'

Tabitha shrugged his hand off her shoulder, and continued to ignore him. 'Since it's written in Greek, I'm betting one of your college professor friends might be more up on it.'

Selena nodded. 'I'll ask Julian tonight when I go over to Grace's.'

'Thanks.' Tabitha looked back at Amanda. 'Don't worry about Cliff. I know just the guy for you. We met him a couple of weeks ago.'

'Oh Lord,' Amanda gasped. 'No more blind dates from

you. I still haven't recovered from the last one and that was four years ago.'

Selena laughed. 'Was that the alligator wrestler?'

'Yes,' Amanda said. 'Crocodile Mitch, who tried to feed me to his pet, Big Marthe.'

Tabitha snorted. 'He did not. He was just trying to show you what he did for a living.'

'Tell you what, the day you let Eric hold your head inside a live alligator, then you can make a comment. Until then, being the expert on alligator halitosis, I'll stick with my opinion that Mitch was just looking for a cheap Scooby snack.'

Tabitha stuck her tongue out at her before grabbing Eric's hand and dashing down the street with him in tow.

Amanda rubbed her head as she watched the two of them make goo-goo eyes at each other, thus proving that there was someone out there for everyone. No matter how bizarre the person.

Too bad she couldn't find someone for herself.

'I'm going home to sulk.'

'Listen,' Selena said before she could leave. 'Why don't I cancel with Grace tonight and the two of us can go do something? Have a symbolic itty-bitty weenie roast for Cliff?'

Amanda smiled in appreciation of the thought. No wonder she loved her family. In spite of the chaos, they were dear hearts who cared for her. 'No, thanks. I can roast the Vienna sausages on my own. Besides, Tabitha will stroke out and die if you don't ask Julian about her Dark-Hunter.'

'Okay, but if you change your mind, let me know. Oh, and while you're home, why not call Tiyana and have her do a penis-shrinking spell on Cliff?'

Amanda laughed. Okay, there were times when having a voodoo high priestess as an older sister came in handy. 'Trust me, he can't afford it.' She winked at Selena. 'Later.'

*

That evening, Amanda jumped as the phone rang, startling her out of her daydreams. Laying her book aside, she picked the phone up.

It was Tabitha.

'Hey, sis, can you go by my house and let Terminator out?'

Amanda ground her teeth at the familiar request that came at least twice a week. 'Oh, come on, Tabby. Why didn't you do it?'

'I didn't know we'd be gone so long. Please. He'll wet on my bed in protest if you don't.'

'You know, Tabby, I do have a life.'

'Yeah, right, like you're not sitting alone on the sofa, reading Kinley MacGregor's latest romance, and scarfing down chocolate truffles like there's no tomorrow.'

Amanda arched her brow as she looked at the multitude of truffle wrappers scattered on the coffee table in front of her, and her copy of *Claiming the Highlander* on the end table.

Damn, she hated it when her sisters did that.

'C'mon,' Tabitha begged. 'I promise I'll be nice to your next boyfriend.'

Sighing, Amanda knew she couldn't really say no to her sisters. It was her biggest weakness. 'It's a good thing you only live down the street or I'd have to kill you over this.'

'I know. I love you, too.'

Growling low in her throat, Amanda hung up. She cast a wistful look at her book. Doggone it, she was just starting to get into it.

She sighed. Oh well, at least Terminator would be company for a few minutes. He was one seriously ugly pit bull, but he was currently the only male she could stand.

She grabbed her tan ski jacket off her armchair and exited out the front door. Tabitha lived two blocks over, and though the night was extremely dark and cold, Amanda didn't feel like driving.

Pulling her gloves on, she headed down the sidewalk, wishing Cliff were here to do this chore. She couldn't count the times she had suckered him into letting Terminator out of Tabitha's house on his way home.

Amanda stumbled over a broken piece of the sidewalk as Cliff crossed her mind for the first time in hours. What really made her feel bad about their breakup was the fact she didn't miss him. Not really, anyway.

She missed having someone to talk to at night. She missed having a TV-watching buddy, but she couldn't honestly say she missed *him*.

And that was what depressed her most of all.

If not for her whacked-out family, she might have actually married him, and then found out too late that she didn't truly love him.

The thought chilled her more than the cold November winds.

Pushing Cliff out of her thoughts, she focused on her surroundings. At eight-thirty, the neighborhood was amazingly quiet, even for a Sunday night. Cars were parked along the street, and most of the houses were lit up as she walked down the old jagged sidewalk.

Everything was normal, but still it was eerie out. The partial moon hung high above, casting twisted shadows around her. Every now and again, she'd catch the faint sound of laughter or voices on the wind.

This was a perfect night for evil to—

'Get out of my head,' she said out loud.

Now Tabitha had *her* doing it! Jeez!

What next? Would she find herself walking the bayou with her sisters looking for weird voodoo plants and alligators?

Shivering at the thought, she finally reached the creepy old house Tabitha and her roommate rented on the corner. A garish purple color, it was one of the smallest houses on the street. Amanda was amazed no one in the neighborhood complained about the unsightly hue. Of course, Tabby loved it since it made giving directions easy.

'Just look for the little purple Victorian with the black iron fence. You can't miss it.'

Not unless you were blind.

After opening the low, wrought-iron gate, Amanda headed up the walkway to the porch where a huge, sinister stone gargoyle stood watch.

'Hi, Ted,' she said to the gargoyle Tabitha swore could read minds. 'I'm just letting the pooch out, okay?'

Amanda pulled the keys out of her coat pocket and opened the front door. Entering the foyer, she wrinkled her nose as she caught a whiff of a nasty-smelling something. One of Tabby's potions must have gone bad.

Either that, or her sister had tried to cook dinner again.

She heard Terminator barking in the bedroom.

'I'm coming,' she said to the dog as she closed the door, turned on the lights, and headed across the living room.

Amanda was one step away from the hallway when she heard the voice in her head telling her to run.

Before she could blink, the lights went out and someone grabbed her from behind.

'Well, well,' a silken voice said in her ear. 'At last I have you, little witch.' His hold tightened. 'Now it's time to make you suffer.'

Something hit her head a second before the floor rose up to meet her.

Chapter 2

Amanda came awake to an awful throbbing in her head. She felt terrible.

What had hap—

She tensed as she remembered the unseen man.

His words.

Terrified, she pushed herself up, and quickly learned she was on a cold concrete floor, in a very small, dust-covered room . . .

And *handcuffed* to an unknown blond man.

A scream wedged itself in her throat, but she held it back. *Don't panic. Not until you have all the facts.*

For all you know, Tabitha is making good her threat for a blind date – just like the time she 'accidentally' locked you in the supply closet with Randy Davis for three hours.

Or 'kidnapped' you in the trunk of her car with that weird musician.

Tabitha was always trying unorthodox ways to set her up with guys. Although, to be fair to her sister, Tabitha didn't usually knock the guy unconscious before she forced them together.

Still, with Tabitha there was a first time for just about

anything. And extreme blind-dating was very vintage T.

Forcing herself to remain calm until she had more information, Amanda took in her surroundings. The two of them were in a small room with no windows and one rusty iron door. A door she couldn't reach without dragging her 'friend' across the floor.

There was no furniture or anything else. The only light came from a small bulb in the center of the ceiling.

Okay, so she wasn't in immediate danger.

Still far from comforted, she looked at the body beside her. He lay with his back to her, and he was either dead or unconscious.

Preferring the latter, she inched toward him. He appeared rather tall, and he was positioned as if he had been dumped roughly onto the floor.

Her legs shaking, Amanda rose slowly to her knees and moved over him to keep his arm from being twisted any more.

He didn't move.

She trailed her gaze over his body. A long black leather coat, black jeans, and a black crew-neck shirt combined to give him an extremely dangerous appearance even while lying on the floor. His feet were covered by a pair of black biker boots with strange silver inlays in the heels.

His wavy blond hair fell over his face and met the collar of his coat, obscuring his features from her view.

'Excuse me?' she whispered, reaching out to touch his arm. 'Are you alive?'

As soon as her hand touched the hard, lean muscle of his biceps, her breath faltered. His prone body was like coiled steel. There wasn't a bit of a fleshy feel to him. He was all lithe, strong power.

Oh my, my.

Before she could stop herself, Amanda ran her hand down his arm. The feel of it!

She let out a slow, appreciative breath.

'Guy? Mister?' she tried again, shaking his hard, muscular shoulder. 'Mr. Goth man, would you please wake up so I can leave? I really don't want to hang out in a closet with a dead man any longer than I have to, okay? C'mon, please, don't make this a *Weekend at Bernie's* thing. There's only one of me and you're a really big, *big* guy.'

He didn't budge.

Okay, I'll have to try something else.

Biting her lip, Amanda rolled him onto his back. His hair fell away from his face at the same moment his collar did.

Her breath caught in her throat. Okay, now she was majorly impressed.

He was gorgeous. His jaw was strong and defined, his cheekbones high. His face was aristocratically boned, and he had just the tiniest hint of a cleft in his chin.

Oh baby, this man possessed that rare masculine beauty that only a few, *very* lucky women ever saw in the flesh.

Better still, he had the best looking lips she'd ever seen. Full and expressive, that mouth had been made for long, hot kisses.

In fact, the only flaw on his face was a hairline scar that ran across the lower edge of his jaw, from his ear to his chin.

He could easily rival Grace's husband for handsomeness. And Julian the Demigod was a hard man to compete with.

But then, Amanda had never been all that impressed with the way men looked. She preferred their minds over their bodies. Especially since most of the men she knew who looked even half this good generally had IQs that were smaller than her combined shoe size.

Unlike Tabitha, it took more than a cute butt and wide shoulders to turn her head.

Although . . .

Amanda ran her gaze over his lean, muscular body. In the case of this man, she might be willing to make an exception.

Provided he wasn't dead, anyway.

Hesitantly, she reached out and placed her hand against his tawny neck to check his pulse. A strong, heavy heartbeat thumped against her fingertips.

Relieved he was alive, she tried to shake him again. 'Hey, yummy leather guy? Can you hear me?'

He moaned low in his throat, then slowly blinked his eyes open. Amanda started at the sight of those eyes. They were so dark they appeared black, and when they focused on her, they dilated menacingly.

With a curse, he grabbed her by the shoulders.

Before she could move, he rolled over with her, pinning her against the floor beneath his body as he held her wrists above her head.

Those dark, captivating eyes searched hers suspiciously.

Amanda couldn't breathe. Every inch of him was pressed intimately against her and she became instantly aware of the fact that his arms weren't the only part of his body that was rock-hard and solid. The man was a wall of sleek, strong muscle.

His hips rested dead center between her legs while his hard, taut stomach leaned against her in a way that brought a flush to her cheeks. Made her feel hot and tingly. Breathless.

For the first time in her life, she wanted to lift her head and kiss a man whom she knew absolutely *nothing* about.

Who was he?

To her complete shock, he lowered his head down to the side of her face and took a deep breath in her hair.

Amanda went rigid. 'Are you *sniffing* me?'

A deep, melodious laugh rumbled through his body, sending an odd tingly surge through her.

'Only admiring your perfume, *ma fleur*,' he whispered

softly in her ear with a strange, provocative accent that melted her. His voice was so deep it reminded her of thunder and it rumbled through her with a devastating effect.

Okay, so the man was incredibly hot, and his breath on her neck sent thousands of needlelike chills over her body.

'You are not Tabitha Devereaux.' He whispered the words so softly that even with his mouth brushing her ear she had to strain to hear him.

She swallowed. 'You know T—'

'Shh,' he whispered in her ear as his thumbs caressed her captured wrists in a rhythm that sent electric surges through her. Her breasts drew tight as desire scorched her.

He moved his face against hers, scraping her cheek gently with his whiskers and causing another wave of chills to consume her. Never in her life had she felt anything more arousing than his weight on her or smelled anything more exciting than the spicy, manly scent of him.

'They are listening.' Kyrian drew a deep, appreciative breath.

Now that he was certain she posed no immediate threat, he knew he should move away from the woman beneath him, and yet . . .

It had been a long time since he'd lain between a woman's thighs. An eternity since he had dared be this close to a female. He had forgotten the warm softness of breasts pressed against his chest. The feel of hot, sweet breath on his neck.

But now that she was under him . . .

Oh yes, he remembered this. He remembered the way a woman's hands felt as they roamed his naked back. The way a woman felt as she writhed to his expert touch.

For a minute, Kyrian actually lost himself to the sensation of it as he imagined removing their clothes and exploring her curves more fully.

And *much* more intimately.

He closed his eyes at the thought of running his tongue over her breast, of toying with the swollen nipple while she buried her hands in his hair.

She squirmed beneath him, only adding to his fantasy.

Hmmm . . .

Of course, if she ever found out who and what he was, she would pale in terror. And if she were anything like her sister, she would attack until one of them was dead.

Such a pity, really. But then, he was used to people being terrified of him. It was the curse and the salvation of his breed.

'Who's listening?' she whispered.

Opening his eyes, he relished the sound of her gentle, lilting voice. How he loved a smooth Southern drawl, and this woman had one that rolled off her tongue like exquisite silk.

Against his iron will, his body stirred viciously in response to her. The need rose in him to taste those full, parted lips as he spread her thighs wide and buried himself deep inside her heat.

Oh yes, he could savor this woman.

All of her.

He pulled back slightly to better study her face. Her dark brown hair was liberally laced with auburn strands that caught the light. Her deep blue eyes showed her confusion, her anger, and her spirit. They were set in a beguiling face that had one tiny freckle just below her right eye. That mark alone distinguished her from her sister.

That and her scent.

Tabitha wore expensive perfumes that overwhelmed his highly developed senses, while this woman smelled of roses and softness.

Right then Kyrian wanted her with a need so demanding that it momentarily stunned him. It had been centuries since he last craved a woman this way.

Centuries since he had felt anything at all.

Amanda's face burned as his erection bulged disturbingly against her pelvis. The man might not be dead, but he was certainly stiff. And this had *nothing* to do with rigor mortis. 'Look, buster, I really think you need to find someplace else to rest.'

His gaze focused hungrily on her lips and she saw the raw longing in the depths of those midnight eyes. His jaw flexed rigidly as if he were fighting himself.

His masculine power and overt sexuality overwhelmed her.

As she lay there beneath him, she realized just how vulnerable she was to him. And how much she truly wanted a taste of those well-shaped lips.

That thought both scared and excited her.

He blinked and a veil came over his face, disguising his mood from her. He released her.

As he moved away, she saw the blood on her pink sweater. 'Oh, my God!' she gasped. 'You're bleeding?'

He took a deep breath as he sat next to her. 'The wound will heal.'

Amanda couldn't believe his nonchalant tone. Judging from the amount of blood on her clothes, she would say he was deeply injured and yet he showed no other signs of it. 'Where are you hurt?'

He didn't answer. Instead, he ran his left hand through his tawny hair. He paused to glare at the large silver handcuff on his right wrist, then he started pulling angrily at it.

By the deadly, cold light in his eyes, she could tell the handcuffs bothered him even more than they did her.

Now that he was awake and not on top of her, Amanda was struck by the dark moodiness of his features. There was something very romantic and compelling about his face.

Something heroic.

All too easily, she could see him dressed like a Regency

rake or medieval knight. His classical features held an indefinable quality that seemed oddly out of place in this modern world.

'Well, well,' a disembodied voice said. 'The Dark-Hunter is awake.'

Amanda recognized the evil voice as the one belonging to whoever had clobbered her at Tabitha's house.

'Desi, babe,' the man beside her said in a chiding tone as he looked about the brown walls. 'Still playing your little games, I see. Now why don't you be a good Daimon and show yourself to me?'

'All in good time, Dark-Hunter, all in good time. You see, I am not like the others who run and cower from the big, bad wolf. I am the big, bad woodsman who executes that wolf.'

The disembodied voice gave a dramatic pause. 'You and Tabitha Devereaux have been merciless in your pursuit of my brethren and the time has come for you to know fear. By the time I finish with the two of you, you will be begging me to let you die.'

The Dark-Hunter lowered his head and laughed. 'Desi dearest, I have never begged a day in my life, and the sun will surely splinter before I *ever* plead for anything from the likes of you.'

'Hubris,' Desi said. 'I so love punishing that crime.'

The Dark-Hunter pushed himself to his feet, and Amanda saw the wound in his side. His shirt was slightly torn and blood stained the floor where he had been sitting.

But he didn't seem to notice the injury.

'Tell me, do you like your handcuffs?' Desi asked. 'Those shackles are from the forge of Hephaestus. Only a god or a key fashioned by Hephaestus can open them. And since the gods have abandoned you . . .'

The Dark-Hunter glanced around the room. The fierce look on his face would have scared the devil himself. 'I am so going to enjoy killing you.'

Desiderius laughed. 'I doubt you'll get the chance once your little friend learns what you are.'

The Dark-Hunter cast a look at her that told her to keep her identity quiet. Not that he needed to. The last thing she would ever do was betray her sister.

'Is that why you chained us together?' the Dark-Hunter asked. 'You wanted to watch us fight?'

'Oh no,' Desiderius said. 'Not my plan at all. If you kill each other, that would be fine by me, but what I intend to do is release you come the dawn. You see, the Dark-Hunter is about to become the hunted and I am going to *thoroughly* enjoy tracking you down and making you suffer. There is no place you can hide where I won't find you.'

The Dark-Hunter smirked. 'You think you're capable of hunting me?'

'Oh yes. Yes, I do. You see, I know your weakness even better than you do.'

'I have no weakness.'

Desiderius laughed. 'Spoken like a true Dark-Hunter. But all of us have an Achilles' heel, especially those who serve Artemis. You are no exception.'

Amanda swore she could almost hear Desiderius lick his lips in satisfaction. 'Your greatest weakness is your nobility. That woman hates you, yet you won't kill her to be safe. While she tries to kill you, you'll guard her from me with your life.' Desiderius laughed evilly. 'You just can't resist a human in peril, can you?'

'Desi, Desi, Desi,' the Dark-Hunter tsked. 'What am I going to do with you?'

'Don't you *dare* take that flippant tone with me.'

'Why ever not?'

'Because I am not some scared little Daimon to run cringing from you. I am your worst nightmare.'

The Dark-Hunter scoffed. 'Must you resort to clichés? C'mon, Desidisastrous, couldn't you think of anything more original than that B-movie dialogue staple?'

A furious snarl echoed in the room. 'Stop mocking my name.'

'Sorry, you're right. The least I could do is show you respect before I expire you.'

'Oh, you won't *expire* me, Dark-Hunter. You are the one who will die this time. Have you given thought to how much she's going to slow you down? Not to mention the existence of her little friends. They will take you down like a pack of wild dogs. And if I were you, I'd pray for that. You have never known the suffering I will inflict upon you when next we meet.'

His lips in a tight, firm line, the Dark-Hunter smiled at Desiderius's threats. 'You seriously overestimate your abilities.'

'We shall see.'

Amanda heard a mike click off.

The Dark-Hunter jerked again at the cuffs. 'I am going to kill that horror-movie reject.'

'Hey, hey, hey!' she said as he flapped her arm around while trying to free himself. 'That arm *is* attached.'

He paused and looked down at her. His gaze softened. 'Twins. It never occurred to him. Have you any idea where your sister is?'

'I don't even know where *I* am or what time it is. For that matter, I don't know what's going on here. Who are you and who is that guy?' Then, she lowered her voice and added, 'Can he hear us?'

Kyrian shook his head. 'No, the mike channel is closed. For the moment, he's off plotting his Igoresque revenge. I don't know about you, but I have this image of him rubbing his hands together and laughing like Dexter from *Dexter's Laboratory*.'

Kyrian took a minute to study her. She didn't appear hysterical . . . yet, and he wanted to keep it that way. Telling her

Desiderius was a soul-sucking demon who was after her sister didn't seem like the best way to accomplish that.

Of course, given her sister's penchant for vampire-hunting, it shouldn't really come as a surprise to her, either.

Closing his eyes, he reached into her mind with his and found confirmation of his suspicions. There was a healthy dose of fear in her.

Unlike her sister Tabitha, she wasn't one to jump to conclusions, but she was curious and angry over their situation. It was possible he could tell her everything without freaking her out, but the Dark-Hunter in him operated on a need-to-know basis.

Right now all she needed to know was the bare minimum. With any luck he would be able to separate them without having to reveal anything more about himself to her.

'I am called Hunter,' he said solemnly. 'And *that guy* is a man out to harm your sister.'

'Thanks, but that much I already got.' Amanda frowned. She should be frightened by all this, but she wasn't. Her anger over it was too great. Leave it to her to get mixed up in her sister's crazy life.

In fact, she was glad they had captured her by mistake, since Tabitha would no doubt have pulled some kamikaze stunt and gotten herself killed.

She looked up at the Dark-Hunter and her frown deepened. How did he know about Tabitha? For that matter, how had he been able to tell them apart when even their own mother had trouble at times? 'Are you one of my sister's friends?'

He looked at her blankly, before pulling her to her feet. 'No,' he said as he patted his chest, hips, rear, and legs.

Amanda tried not to notice just how incredibly toned that body was as her hand was dragged in the wake of his. And when her hand brushed his hard inner thigh, she thought she would moan.

He was built for sex and for speed. Too bad he wasn't her type. In fact, he was the total antithesis to everything she found desirable in a man.

Wasn't he?

He cursed. 'Of course, he has my phone,' he muttered, before leading her to the door.

After trying the knob, he studied the hinges.

When he unbuckled his left boot and toed it off, Amanda arched a brow. 'What are you doing? Going for a swim?'

He gave her a cocky smirk before leaning down to pick the boot up off the floor. 'Trying to get us out of here. You?'

'I'm trying not to get irritated at you.'

Amusement flashed in his eyes, then he returned his attention to the door.

Amanda watched as he pressed one of the silver inlays on the boot heel and a vicious five-inch blade shot out of the toe. He was definitely Tabitha's type. She wondered if he had throwing stars inside his pockets, too.

'Oooo,' she commented dryly. *'Very scary.'*

He gave her an unamused look. 'Baby, you ain't seen scary yet.'

Amanda smirked at his Ford Fairlane, tough-guy demeanor and gave a very unfeminine snort.

He ignored her. Using the jagged blade, he tried to pry loose the rusted hinges.

'You're going to break that blade if you're not careful,' she warned him.

He gave her an arched look. 'Nothing on this earth could break this blade.' He ground his teeth while hammering the boot with his fist. 'Much like nothing on this earth appears able to move this hinge.' He tried for several more minutes.

'Damn,' he snarled when the hinge refused to budge. He retracted the blade, then bent over to put the boot back on. The back of his coat parted with his movements, gifting her with a nice view of him.

Oh yeah, *nice* butt.

Amanda's mouth went dry as he finally straightened to his full six-foot-five-inch height.

Oh my, my, my.

Okay, she took it back, he did have one feature she found irresistible. His height. She'd always been a sucker for any man taller than her. And with this guy, she could easily wear three-inch heels and not offend his male ego.

He towered over her.

And she liked it.

'How do you know my sister?' she asked, trying to keep her thoughts focused on the matter at hand and not on the matter of how much she wanted to taste those lips of his.

'I know her because she keeps getting in my way.' He snatched at the cuffs again. 'What is it with you humans that you feel this incessant need to delve into things you should leave alone?'

'I don't delve into . . .' Her voice trailed off as his words penetrated her mind. 'You *humans*? Why would you say that?'

He didn't answer.

'Look,' she said, holding up her arm to show the hand-cuff. 'I'm stuck with you right now, and I want an answer.'

'No you don't.'

That did it. She hated alpha men in the worst sort of way. Those domineering, I'm-the-man-baby-let-me-drive types nauseated her.

'All right, macho babe boy,' she said irritably. 'I'm not some little ditz to bat my eyelashes at the buff stud in black leather. Don't try your he-man tactics with me. I'll have you know, in my office I'm known as the ball-breaker.'

Kyrian frowned at her. 'Macho babe boy?' he repeated in disbelief.

There had never been a time in his extremely long life that anyone had had the mettle to stand up to him. As a mortal, he had made entire Roman armies flee in stark terror of his approach. Few men had ever dared meet him eye to eye.

As a Dark-Hunter, he made legions of Daimons and Apollites quake in his presence. His name was whispered in awe and with reverence, and this woman had called him . . .

'Buff stud in black leather,' he repeated out loud. 'I don't think I've ever been more insulted.'

'Then you must have been an only child.'

He laughed at that. In truth, he'd once had three younger sisters, but none of them had ever dared insult him.

He swept a look over her. She wasn't classically beautiful, but there was an exotic quality to her almond-shaped eyes that lent her a fey charm.

Her long, mahogany hair was loose, spilling about her slender shoulders. But it was her blue eyes that were captivating. Warm and intelligent, they were narrowed on him now with malice.

A faint blush stained her cheeks, making her eyes a full shade darker. In spite of the danger they were in, he wondered what she would look like after a full night of raw, exhausting sex. He could just see her eyes dark with passion, her hair mussed, her cheeks red from his whiskers, and her lips moist and swollen from his kisses.

The thought made his entire body burn.

Until Kyrian felt the familiar prickling on the back of his neck. 'It will be dawn soon.'

'How do you know?'

'I just do.' He pulled her to the left, then began examining the rust-covered walls for an escape. 'Once we're released, we'll have to find a way to break out of these cuffs.'

'Nice of you to state the obvious.' Amanda glanced down his body and saw the jagged wound through the torn material. 'You really need to tend that.'

'God forbid I should bleed to death, eh?' he asked sardonic-
ally. 'Then you'd have to cart around my rotting corpse.'

She wrinkled her nose in distaste. 'Could you be any more
morbid? Jeez. Who was your idol growing up? Boris Karloff?'

'Hannibal, actually.'

'You're trying to scare me, aren't you?' she asked. 'Well,
it won't work. I grew up in a house with an angry poltergeist
and two sisters who used to conjure demons just to fight
them. Buster, I've seen it all, and your gallows humor isn't
working on me.'

Before he realized what she was doing, she grabbed the
bottom of his shirt and lifted it.

Amanda froze at the sight of his bare stomach. It was lean,
hard, and flat, and he had a rippling six-pack of abs that any
gymnast would envy. But what made her gasp was the multitude of scars covering his flesh.

Worse, she saw the terrible gash in his side that ran along
his lowest rib.

'Good Lord, what happened to you?'

He jerked his shirt down and took a step back. 'If you
mean the scars, it would take me years to account for all of
them. If you mean the gash, it came from a thirteen-year-
old Apollite I mistook for a child in need of help.'

'You walked into a trap?'

He shrugged. 'It's not the first time.'

Amanda swallowed as she swept her gaze over him. An
aura of danger and death surrounded him. He moved like a
sleek, graceful predator, and those eyes . . .

They seemed to be able to take in more than just his basic
surroundings. Those wicked jet eyes held an indescribable
ethereal glint to them.

And they stole her breath every time he looked at her.

She'd never seen a blond man with eyes like that. Nor had
she seen any man so incredibly handsome. His features were
chiseled and perfect.

He oozed an almost unnatural masculine sexuality. She'd seen plenty of men who had tried their best to project what nature had dumped by the truckload onto this man.

'What is a Dark-Hunter?' she asked. 'Is it like *Buffy the Vampire Slayer*?'

He laughed at that. 'Yes, I'm a small, emaciated teenage girl who struts around fighting vampires in earrings they would rip out of my ears and shove up my—'

'I know you're not a girl. But what is a Dark-Hunter?'

He sighed as he led her around the room, looking at the walls as if searching for a secret door. 'In short, I execute the things that go bump in the night.'

A chill went up her spine at his words, and yet she sensed there was something more than just his simple explanation. He appeared deadly, but not twisted, or even cruel. 'Why do you want to kill Desiderius?'

He glanced at her before trying to open the steel door again. He wrenched the handle so forcefully, she was amazed he didn't rip the doorknob off. 'Because he not only kills humans, he steals their souls.'

She tensed at his words. 'Can he do that?'

'You said you've seen it all,' he said in a mocking tone. 'You tell me.'

Amanda wanted to choke him. Never in her life had she met a more arrogant, or infuriating man.

'Why do I always get sucked into this supernatural mumbo jumbo?' she muttered. 'Is it too much to ask that I have one average day?'

'Life is seldom what we want it to be.'

She frowned at his words, and at the odd note in his voice.

Kyrian tilted his head, and held his hand up to signal her for silence.

Out of nowhere, the doorknob clicked.

'Knock, knock,' Desiderius said. 'You have the day to hide. Come nightfall, we hunt.'

'Yeah, yeah,' Hunter said. 'You and your little dog, too.'

His blithe tone amazed her. The chilling words had absolutely no effect on him. 'You're not scared of his threats?'

He looked at her dryly. 'Chère, the day I fear something like him is the day I lie down at his feet and hand him the knife to cut my heart out. The only fear I have is getting you back to your sister and convincing High Queen Hardhead to leave off this matter until I can locate Desiderius and send his soul into oblivion where it belongs.'

In spite of herself and the danger they were in, Amanda laughed at his words. 'High Queen Hardhead? You know Tabitha well.'

He disregarded her comment as he carefully shielded her with his body, then opened the door slowly. He paused to look around.

Outside the door was a narrow hallway with large, dust-covered windows that showed the dawning sun.

'Damn,' Hunter snarled under his breath as he took a step back into the room.

'What?' she asked, her heart skipping a beat in terror. 'Is someone out there?'

'No.'

'Then let's go.' She started out the door.

He didn't budge.

Clenching his teeth, he looked down the hallway again and said something in a language she didn't know.

'What's the problem?' Amanda asked. 'It's dawn, and no one's out there. Let's leave.'

He took a deep, aggravated breath. 'The problem isn't the people. The problem is the sun.'

'And the problem with that is . . . ?'

He hesitated for a few heartbeats, then opened his mouth and ran his tongue over his long, *pointed* canine teeth.

Chapter 3

Mr. 'Do Me' Gorgeous Man is a vampire!

'Oh no, no, no.' Amanda's entire body shook from terror and it took every piece of self-control she possessed not to launch into a screaming fit. 'Are you going to suck my blood?'

He arched a sardonic brow. 'Do I look like a lawyer to you?'

She ignored his sarcasm. 'Are you going to kill me?'

His face completely unamused, Hunter sighed irritably. 'If I intended to kill you, don't you think you'd already be dead?'

He stepped closer to her and offered her a wry, evil grin she knew was meant to intimidate her. And boy howdy did it work.

He lifted his free hand up to stroke the skin of her neck where her jugular was. The feather-light touch sent chills over her. 'Come to think of it, I could just suck you dry, then gnaw your hand off with my fangs and be free.'

Her eyes widened in terror.

'But lucky you, I have no intention of doing that, either.'

'Don't be sarcastic, okay?' she breathed, her heart still

pounding because she wasn't sure if he was joking with her
or if he really would turn all grisly on her and start feeding
off her blood. 'I can't cope with it. Imagine if you were in
my shoes. I just went to let Tabitha's dog out so he wouldn't
mess on her bed. I went from that to being knocked on the
head, and chained to a vampire. Excuse *me* if I'm a little
freaky at the moment.'

To her amazement, he dropped his hand and backed off.
'You're right. I imagine you're not used to having people
attack you for no apparent reason.'

By his tone, she could tell he, on the other hand, was
rather experienced at finding himself in the middle of such
situations.

He offered her a tight-lipped smile that didn't quite reach
his eyes. 'If it makes you feel better, I don't feed on humans.'

For some reason, it did make her feel better to hear him
say that. Not that she believed it. But still, it was a little
reassuring. 'So, you're like Angel?'

He rolled his eyes at her. 'You watch way too much television,' he muttered. Then louder, he said, 'Angel has a soul.
I don't.'

'Now you're back to being scary again.'

The look on his face reiterated his earlier words: *Baby,
you ain't seen scary yet.*

He glanced back out the door. 'All right. We're going to
have to run for it before the sun rises any higher.'

Hunter gave her a penetrating stare. 'The main problem
is that I don't know where that hallway leads. In the event
it leads out into the open and I die a particularly agonizing
death where I spontaneously combust into flames, I need a
favor from you.'

'A favor?' she asked in disbelief. The man had one serious
set of cojones on him. He bullied her, threatened her, then
dared to ask a favor?

'Sure, why not?' she asked.

He took the ring off his right hand and gave it to her. 'I need you to take that and find a tree.'

Amanda frowned at the ring in her hand. The gold was scuffed and nicked in a number of places as if it had been seriously mistreated. Or rather the hand that bore it had been through a lot of damage.

The top of the ring was made of flat rubies and held the design of a sword of diamonds surrounded by emerald laurel leaves and topped with a sapphire crown. She could tell it was a valuable antique.

Why would he entrust it to her?

Unsure of what to make of him, she placed it in her jeans pocket. 'Any tree?' she asked.

'Any tree. Then say the words "Artemis, I summon you to human form."'

'Artemis—'

He put his hand over her mouth. 'For the love of Zeus, only say it once I'm gone. After you utter the words, wait until a very tall, red-haired woman appears and tell her you need protection from Desiderius.'

Amanda arched a brow. 'You want me to summon a goddess to protect me?'

'If you don't, he will get you and your sister.'

'Why do you care?'

'It's my job to protect the humans from the Daimons. That's what a Dark-Hunter does.' Though his face was harsh, there was a light in his eyes that told her there was much more to the story than that.

'What are Daimons?' she asked.

'They're vampires on steroids with a God complex. Now, promise me you'll do it.'

Why not? It was a strange request, but then, considering the fact she was handcuffed to a vampire, who was she to say what was or wasn't strange? 'Okay.'

'Good. Now, let's run for it.'

Before she could protest, he grabbed the handcuff over her wrist, and ran out the door to the right and down the hallway.

As they ran along the rusty floor, Amanda realized they were inside an abandoned factory of some sort.

At the end of the hallway were stairs that led down.

Hunter pulled her along after him until they reached the bottom of the stairs that opened into an enormous empty room with a cement floor. The old steel walls were cracked, with rays of the dawning sun streaming through.

The Dark-Hunter fell back into the shadows, away from the sunlight. His face looked a bit sunburned, but overall he didn't appear too much the worse from their mad dash.

'Now what?' she asked as she tried to catch her breath.

The Dark-Hunter wasn't even breathing hard. But his gaze was just a little too hot as he stared at her breasts with interest.

Amanda crossed her arms over her chest.

For the first time, she saw a real smile from him as she realized his hand was dangerously close to her breast. So close, his fingertips brushed the nipple, making fire rip through her veins.

She immediately dropped her hands to her sides while his smile taunted her. Though tight-lipped and devilish, it was still devastating. The amused gleam in his eyes was breathtaking, and his features softened into a boyish charm that could melt the heart of anything female.

He glanced around the empty factory. 'Now I wish we either had a cell phone or subway system. I knew I should have taken that open position in New York.'

Confused, Amanda looked up at him. 'Open position? What? Is hunting really a job?'

'Yes. They even pay me to do it.'

'*Who* pays you?'

Instead of answering, he held up a hand for silence in a

gesture that was starting to piss her off – the main reason being because it seemed to herald trouble. And she was tired of finding trouble meant for Tabitha.

Two seconds later, Amanda heard someone walking around outside. Hunter pulled her deeper into the shadows with him while they listened. He had his free arm draped over her shoulders, pinning her to his body.

Amanda went stock-still as her back connected fully with his chest and a wave of misplaced desire tore through her. The heat of him warmed her and that raw, masculine aura of power overwhelmed her. Even more disturbing, his welcoming scent of leather and sandalwood invaded her head.

She wanted this man.

What are you, nuts? The man's a vampire!

Yeah, but he's a really, really *sexy one.*

Kyrian couldn't breathe with her so close to him. His heightened senses felt her all the way through his entire body. He heard her heartbeat speed up, felt the dryness of her throat, but even worse, he could taste her desire.

It whetted his appetite for her even more. And it reminded him why he had made it his habit to avoid being around women as much as possible.

Damn you, Desiderius.

Because right then it was hard to remember he couldn't have her. And even harder to forget the way she smelled. The way she moved – like a confident dancer. Her lithe body was a symphony of grace and all too easily he could imagine her sitting on top of him as he showed her a sexual pleasure he was quite certain no other man had ever given her.

His loins tightened to the point of pain. He couldn't even remember the last time he had been this hard for a woman. And it took all his willpower not to kiss her. Not to bury his lips against her throat and inhale her warm sweetness as he . . . .

Kyrian flexed his hand on her shoulder as he realized all he had to do was lower his hand three inches and he would be cupping her breast.

Just three *tiny* inches . . .

Suddenly, the sound of a walkie-talkie broke the silence.

'It's a construction worker,' she whispered, bolting to a window.

Kyrian hissed as she pulled him into the sunlight. He jerked her back into the darkness.

'Sorry,' she whispered. She edged closer to the window, making sure to keep him out of the sun.

'Hey!' Amanda called as she saw the man a few feet away, poking around an old tractor.

The construction worker looked up at her and did a double-take. Scowling, he walked over to the window and looked inside. His eyes narrowed on them. 'What are you doing in there? This area is off-limits to the public.'

'It's a long story,' Amanda said. 'The short version is I got left here. You wouldn't happen to have a cell phone I could borrow, would you?'

Still scowling, he handed his cell phone to her through the open window.

Hunter immediately took it from her hand.

'Hey!' she snapped, reaching for it.

Moving it out of her reach, he ignored her while he dialed a number.

'Where are we?' Hunter asked the construction worker as he placed the phone to his ear.

'The old Olson Plant.'

'In Slidell?'

Amanda arched a brow that the Dark-Hunter would recognize it. She'd lived in New Orleans all her life and had no idea this place existed.

'Yeah,' the worker said.

Hunter nodded.

'Hey,' he said into the phone, 'it's me. I'm at the Olson Plant in Slidell. Do you know where it is?'

He paused as he listened to whoever was on the other end.

Amanda watched him closely. It amazed her that he was able to talk without showing his fangs, but he disguised them well.

And now that she thought about it, how could a vampire be so tanned and warm? How could he have a pulse and a heartbeat?

Weren't vampires supposed to be the cold, pale undead?

'Yes,' Hunter said. 'I need a ride out of here, preferably before the sun gets any higher.'

The Dark-Hunter turned the phone off and tossed it out the window to the construction worker.

'Hey!' she snapped, reaching out of the window to reclaim the phone. 'I need that.'

'Who are you going to call?' Hunter asked menacingly.

'None of your damn business.'

Hunter took the phone out of her hand. 'As long as we're attached, it is my business.'

She narrowed her eyes on him as she grabbed the phone. 'Mess with me, buster, and I'll take another two steps to my right.'

His heated glare sent a shiver over her. 'Don't you dare call your sister.'

The seething look on his face made her rethink pushing her luck. She handed the phone back to the worker. 'Thanks,' she said.

The construction worker clipped the phone to his belt and gave them a chiding stare. 'You know, you two need to get out of there. This b—'

The Dark-Hunter held his hand up and the man's eyes went blank, empty. 'There's no one in the building. Go do whatever you need to do.'

The man walked off without another word.

Mind control? Amanda gaped at Hunter.

Of course he had mind control. He was a vampire.

'You better not use that on me,' Amanda said.

'Don't worry. You're too strong-willed for it to work.'

'Good.'

'Not from where I'm standing, it isn't.'

Though the words were edged, there was an amused light in the depths of his eyes that said he wasn't as peeved as he sounded.

She looked askance at him. He was leaning nonchalantly against a post with his eyes closed, and yet she had the distinct impression that he was alert to everything around them, both inside the building and out.

'Why did you become a vampire?' she asked before she could think better of it. 'Did someone turn you against your will?'

He opened his eyes and cocked a brow at that. 'No one becomes a Dark-Hunter unless they are willing.'

'And you were willing to . . .' Her voice trailed off as she expectantly waited for him to explain.

'To sacrifice a nosy little human if she doesn't stop pestering me.'

She should be frightened of him and yet she kept hearing Desiderius's words in her mind telling her that he would never harm a human.

Was it true?

She ran her gaze over his scrumptious body wishing she knew for certain.

They stood without speaking for quite a bit, until Amanda couldn't stand it any longer.

'So,' she said, trying to break the awkward silence. 'How long do you think we'll have to wait?'

'I don't know.'

'Who did you call?' she tried again.

'No one.'

Amanda took a deep breath and fought the urge to strangle him. 'You don't like to answer questions, do you?'

'Honestly? I don't like to talk at all. I'd rather just stand here in silence.'

'And brood?'

'Yes.'

She blew her hair out of her face. 'Well, I happen to be bored and if I have to stand here waiting for your ride, I'd like to do something to pass the time.'

His gaze dropped to her lips, then slid slowly down to her breasts and hips. He shuttered his eyes, but even so she saw the raw hunger in the midnight depths. She felt it, hot and demanding.

'I can think of one way to pass time . . .'

She widened her eyes. 'You're not going to bite me, are you?'

He smiled wickedly. 'I don't want to bite you, *agapeemenee*. I want to nibble every inch of your bare flesh, especially your bre—'

She reached up and stopped his words by placing her hand over his lips. The softness of them contrasting with his whiskers stunned her. And the sensation of his skin under her hand jolted her with electricity. Swallowing hard, she dropped her hand. 'I didn't think vampires could have sex.'

He arched a taunting brow at her. 'Why don't you and I conduct a little experiment and see?'

Amanda knew she should be offended. She should be angry. She should be anything other than turned on by his words. But the idea actually appealed to her as she ran her gaze down his lean, perfect body.

Kyrian felt her confusion. She was actually considering his offer. Had the fire in his groin not been so fierce, he would have laughed. But as it was, he wasn't sure whether or not he was toying with her, or truly propositioning her.

All he knew was that the sight of her parted lips tempted him in a way he'd never been tempted before.

Not that he should be surprised by the way his body responded to her. She was just the type of woman who had always appealed to him. Intelligent. Brave.

And simply beguiling.

He glanced to the wall behind her, and imagined what it would feel like to press her against it while he took her hard, fast, and furious.

He swore he could feel himself already inside her. Could hear her moaning in his ear as he . . .

Kyrian shook his head to dispel the image. There were times when he hated his psychic abilities. Right now was definitely one of them.

Licking his dry lips, he remembered a time when he wouldn't have hesitated to take a woman such as this to his bed. A time when he would have peeled those safe, conservative clothes off her body and kissed every single inch of her bare flesh until she was wild with unbridled desire. Touched her until he brought her to the edge again and again as she clung to him and begged for more.

Kyrian clenched his teeth at the heat searing his blood. How he wished he could relive those days.

But that was a long time ago. And no matter how much he might want her, she was not his to take.

He would never know her body.

He would never know *her*. Period. It was why he hadn't asked her name or given her his. He had no intention of using it. She was nothing more than another nameless person he had sworn to protect. That was as close as he intended to get.

He was a Dark-Hunter, and she was an uninitiated human. The two were not to mix.

Kyrian looked up as he heard the faint sound of a siren approaching. Silently, he thanked Tate's timing.

Amanda glanced out the window as she heard an ambulance. Oddly enough, it stopped in front of the factory.

After a brief pause, the two front factory doors opened and the ambulance pulled inside.

'Your ride?' she asked.

The Dark-Hunter nodded.

Once the ambulance was deep enough inside the factory so that the sunlight didn't reach it, a tall African-American man got out and approached them. He gave a low whistle as he caught sight of Hunter's sunburned face. 'Man, you look like hell. Should I ask about the handcuffs?'

Hunter led her toward the driver. 'Not unless you want to die.'

'Okay,' the driver said good-naturedly. 'I can take a hint, but here's the next problem. You're not going to be inconspicuous in a body bag wearing those. People are definitely going to notice.'

'I already thought of that,' Hunter said. 'If anyone asks, tell them I died of a heart attack during a wild sexcapade with her.'

An eerie chill went up Amanda's spine as she recalled Selena's words the day before. 'I beg your pardon?'

Hunter cast an amused look to her that let her know he was thoroughly enjoying her torment. 'And she can't find the key.'

Tate laughed.

'I don't think so,' Amanda said heatedly.

Hunter gave her that devilish grin that warmed her all over, and the look he swept over her made her tingle. 'Look on the bright side; you'll have men lining up to date you.'

'You're not funny.'

Hunter shrugged. 'It's the only way out of here.'

'For you maybe,' she said. 'I can walk right out of here on my own, and dust you.'

He cocked a taunting brow at her. 'Try it.'

She did, and quickly learned that tall, dangerous vampires didn't budge unless they wanted to.

'Okay,' Amanda said, rubbing her wrist where the cuff was biting into it. 'We'll be getting in the ambulance, then.'

Hunter led the way.

When he got to the back of the ambulance, Hunter lifted her up with such ease that it startled her. She moved to the left, trying to make room for him, but he was so tall, he was doubled over. In one fluid motion, he lay down on the stretcher, inside the black body bag that was on top of it.

Without a word, Tate zipped it closed.

'You two do this a lot?' she asked.

Tate smiled in easygoing friendship. 'Every now and again.'

Amanda frowned as Tate adjusted the bag so that her hand was on the outside and Hunter's inside it. It seemed strange to her that Tate was so willing to help a vampire.

'How did you two meet?' she asked Tate.

'I was feeding off a body when he found me,' Hunter said from inside the bag.

Tate laughed as he straightened. 'One night while I was on call, I went to pick up a body that wasn't dead. If not for Hunter, I'd be the one in the body bag.'

'Shut up, Tate,' Hunter snapped, 'and drive.'

'I'm going,' Tate said as if completely unoffended by the high-handed way Hunter treated him.

'You know,' Amanda said to Hunter as Tate got up front and started the ambulance. 'You could try being nicer to people. Especially when they're helping you.'

She heard his aggravated sigh even through the plastic. 'Shouldn't that advice apply to you, as well?'

Amanda opened her mouth to respond, then closed it. He was right. She had been rather testy with him since all this started. 'I guess you're right. Maybe we should both try and make the best of this.'

If he responded, she didn't hear it since the siren blared again. Tate drove them to the hospital in record time, but the ride was far from smooth.

By the time they arrived, she felt as if she had been tossed around like sweatsocks in a dryer.

Tate pulled up to the rear of the hospital, under an awning that kept the sunlight from touching them. With a warning to her to remain quiet, he carefully pulled the stretcher out of the back so that he wouldn't hurt her arm as they descended out of the ambulance.

Once inside the hospital doors, Amanda held her jacket closed to hide the bloodstains on her sweater.

Hunter remained completely still and silent as Tate pushed the stretcher through the bustling areas. Amanda walked along beside them, and wanted to cringe and die given how obvious the handcuffs were.

Did they have to gleam so brightly under the fluorescent lights? Couldn't Desiderius have found nice, small police-sized cuffs?

Oh no, these had to be five inches thick with some kind of weird Greek design all over them. And a chain that ran a good four inches in length. Anyone who saw them would definitely think they came from one of Tabitha's weird sex catalogues.

The horror of it! Amanda had never even been inside a Frederick's of Hollywood. For that matter, she'd blushed profusely the handful of times she'd been in Victoria's Secret.

And everyone they passed turned to gawk at them.

'I haven't seen *that* in at least six months,' an orderly said as they passed the admissions desk.

'I heard that,' another orderly responded. 'Wonder how old the poor guy was?'

'I dunno, but by the looks of her, I'd say sign me up.'

Their laughter made her entire face burn. By the interested looks the men were raking over her body, she could surmise

Hunter's words about her having dates might not have been too far off the mark.

'Hey, Tate?' a young doctor asked as they drew near the elevators. 'Should I ask?'

Tate shook his head. 'You know all the weird shit comes through my office.'

The doctor laughed while Amanda covered her face with her hand.

As soon as the elevator doors closed behind them, Amanda whispered under her breath, 'Hunter, I swear, I'm going to kill you for this.'

'Dearie,' an elderly hospital volunteer said from beside her. 'It looks to me like you already did.' She patted Amanda lightly on the arm. 'The same thing happened to me and my Harvey. Poor thing. I sure do miss him, too.'

Tate choked on his laughter.

Amanda groaned and prayed for this ordeal to end.

Once they reached the morgue, Tate took them into a dim, metallic lab and locked the door. Hunter unzipped the bag from the inside.

'Thanks,' he said to Tate as he sat up and removed the bag from his body. He folded it and placed it on a table.

Tate opened a drawer in the small cabinet next to the door. 'No problem. Now, take your coat and shirt off and let me see what happened to you.'

'It will heal.'

Tate set his jaw stubbornly. 'What of infection?'

Kyrian laughed. 'Immortals don't die from infections. I am completely incapable of carrying *any* disease.'

'You may not die from it, but it doesn't mean it won't hurt and it'll heal faster if treated.' He gave Kyrian a look that said he would not be swayed. 'I'm not going to take no for an answer. Let me treat that wound.'

Kyrian opened his mouth to argue more, but if he knew anything about Tate, it was that the man was stubborn.

Deciding not to waste his time, Kyrian obeyed before he remembered the coat and shirt wouldn't come completely off, thanks to the handcuffs.

He gave an exasperated sigh and left his clothes to hang against his forearm, then got back on the stretcher and leaned back on his elbows to wait for Tate.

As he watched Tate gather supplies, he heard Amanda's heart pounding and her breathing speed up. Felt her keen interest as she raked her gaze over his body. She wanted him, and her hot desire played havoc with him.

Kyrian shifted and wished his jeans were a couple of sizes bigger, since the black denim started biting fiercely into his erection.

Damn, he'd forgotten what a literal and figurative pain his body could be when an attractive woman was around.

And she *was* attractive. What with that charming, elfish face and those big, blue eyes . . .

He'd always been a fool for blue eyes.

Even without looking at her, he knew she was licking those plump, full lips, and his throat went dry as he imagined the taste of them. The feel of her breath on his face and her tongue against his as he kissed her.

Dear gods, and he had thought the Romans had tortured him! Their best interrogator had been an amateur compared to the physical and mental agony her nearness caused him now.

Even more disturbing than her looks was the fact that she had been an amazingly good sport about all of this. Most women would have been screaming in terror of him or crying.

Or both.

But she had met the entire ordeal with a courage and strength of heart he'd not seen in a long time.

He actually liked her, and that surprised him most of all.

Amanda jumped when Hunter met her gaze. Those deep, black eyes bored into hers and made her hot and breathless.

He lay on the stretcher with one leg bent up and the other hanging over the edge. The black denim hugged his long, powerful body.

And those muscled arms . . .

Lean and defined, he was all masculine beauty. His biceps were flexed as he leaned back on his elbows. She wanted to reach out and touch him so badly that she ached from it. No doubt, he would be rock-hard and satiny underneath her hand.

His shoulders were incredibly broad, with sculpted muscles that promised strength, speed, and agility. His pecs and arms were every bit as well-formed and tight.

And his stomach, oh heaven! Those flat abs had been made for nibbling.

Unbidden, her gaze followed the thin trail of coffee-colored hairs that started at his navel and vanished under the tight denim. By the size of the bulge in his jeans, she could tell he was amply endowed, and more than passingly interested in her.

The thought made her even hotter.

The deep, golden tan of his flesh defied what she knew him to be. How could a vampire have skin so tawny and inviting?

But even more tantalizing than the lean muscles that beckoned for caresses were the multitude of scars that crossed his flesh. He looked as if he had been clawed by a huge tiger, or beaten within an inch of his life with a whip.

Or both.

Hunter lay down as Tate approached, and she saw a small double-bow-and-arrow symbol *branded* into his left shoulder. She cringed at the thought of how much such a thing must have hurt, and she wondered if he had agreed to it, or if someone had put it there against his will.

'I take it from your scars that your vampire friends don't think much of you,' she said.

'You think?' he retorted.

'Is he always this sarcastic?' she asked Tate.

'Actually, I thought he was being rather nice to you.' Tate cleansed the vicious-looking wound with alcohol. He prepared to give Hunter a local.

Hunter caught his hand before Tate could inject him. 'Don't bother.'

'Why?' Tate asked with a frown.

'I'm immune to it.'

Amanda's jaw dropped.

Tate just reached for the sutures.

'You can't do that,' she said, interrupting him. 'He'll feel it.'

'He needs that wound closed,' Tate insisted. 'Jeez, you can see his bones through it.'

'Go ahead,' Hunter said with a calmness that astounded her.

Stunned, she cringed while Tate made the first suture.

Hunter kept his jaw locked and said nothing.

Amanda watched Tate tend Hunter. Her heart wrenched at the thought of how much pain Hunter must be feeling.

'Doesn't that hurt?' she asked him.

'No,' Hunter said between clenched teeth.

Amanda could tell by the way the veins stood out on his neck and the way he clenched his fists that he was lying.

'Here,' she said, taking his hand in hers. 'Just hold tight.'

Kyrian started at the softness of her hand in his. He couldn't remember the last time someone had touched him like that. He'd been a Dark-Hunter for so long that he had all but forgotten simple kindness.

Tate acted out of gratitude and a sense of obligation.

But her . . .

There was no reason for her to hold his hand. He'd barely spoken a civil word to her, and yet she reached out to him when no one else would have. It made him feel strange toward her. Protective. Tender.

More than that, her simple touch scorched him all the way

to his caged heart. He swallowed, then stiffened. He couldn't let her close to him. She was a creature of light and he was one of darkness.

The two were not compatible.

'So, how long have you been a vampire?' she asked.

'I told you,' he said, his jaw tight, 'I'm not a vampire. I'm a Dark-Hunter.'

'What's the difference?'

Kyrian gave her a hard glare. 'The difference is I normally don't kill humans, but if you don't stop quizzing me, I might make an exception.'

'You are one seriously testy Creature of the Night.'

'I love you, too.'

Amanda dropped his hand. 'Oh, that's it,' she said. 'I was just trying to comfort you. God forbid, you should let anyone actually be nice to you.'

Irritated, she met Tate's surprised gaze. 'Can you just saw his arm off while we're here and get me loose?'

Tate snorted. 'I could do that, but he needs his more. I'd cut yours off before I did his.'

'Oh, great, what are you, his Igor?'

'Wrong movie,' Tate corrected. 'Igor was Frankenstein's flunky. Renfield is the one you're thinking of, and no, I'm not Renfield. Name's Tate Bennett. Parish coroner.'

'I'd already guessed the coroner part. Rather obvious since we're in a cold lab full of *dead* people.'

Tate arched a brow at her. 'And you call *him* sarcastic.'

Hunter jerked as Tate pulled too hard on the sutures.

'Sorry,' Amanda said. 'I won't distract him anymore.'

'I would appreciate it.'

Once Tate finished, Hunter put his shirt and coat back on. He slid off the stretcher with only the slightest hiss to reveal his side was sore.

Tate's pager went off. 'I'll be back in a few minutes. You kids need anything?'

'I'm fine,' Hunter said. 'But she probably needs breakfast and a phone.'

Amanda quirked a brow at his words. Why would he let her have a phone now?

Tate quickly cleaned up the mess. 'The phone is against the far wall, just dial nine to get out. I'll grab something in the cafeteria and be back as soon as I can. Stay in here and keep the door locked.'

As soon as they were alone, Hunter moved so that she could sit on the small stool by the phone.

Blinking, Hunter rubbed his hand over his eyes as if they were sensitive to the fluorescent lights. 'We need to make plans,' he said quietly. 'You wouldn't happen to know anyone in this city who might have a way to break handcuffs made by a Greek god?'

Getting used to his sarcasm, she smiled. 'Actually, I think I do.'

His face instantly lightened. Gracious, the man was gorgeous when not scowling or barking. 'One of your sisters?'

'One of their friends.'

He nodded. 'Good. We need to do that, preferably before sunset, or at least not long after it. You also have to call Tabitha and tell her to lie low for a few days.'

'You know, for the record, I hate to take orders. But!' Amanda said interrupting him before he could pull rank. 'I realize I'm in over my head. You have no idea how much I hate all this supernatural garbage. So I'm willing to listen to you, but you better start acting like I'm a person and not some mindless blow-up doll.'

She pulled his ring out of her pocket and returned it to him. 'And another thing, I really have to go to the bathroom.'

Hunter laughed out loud.

'It's not funny,' she snapped at him as he put the ring back on his finger. 'Any idea how we can do this without my dying of embarrassment?'

'More than that, any idea on how to do that without my getting arrested for being in the ladies' room?'

She cut a sharp glare at him. 'If you think I'm going into the men's room, forget it.'

'Then I hope you can hold it.'

'I am not going into the men's room!'

Five minutes later, she was in the men's room and cursing Hunter under her breath. 'You really get off on being a bully, don't you?'

'It's what I live for,' he said in a bored voice as he stood with his back to her. He had his arm bent behind his back to allow her more latitude with the handcuffs.

Amanda glared at him. Her bladder felt as if were going to burst, but she was having a very difficult time going with him sandwiched between her and the stall door.

And all because Tabitha couldn't remember to let her damn dog out! If she ever got out of this, she was going to kill her sister. Dead. Dismantled!

'What's taking so long?' he asked in an aggravated tone.

'I can't go with you standing there.'

'Would you just go?'

'Just you wait! Sooner or later, it'll be your turn and I'm going to enjoy watching you squirm.'

He went rigidly still at her words. 'Baby, you could never make me squirm.'

The coldness in his voice scared her.

It took her a few minutes, but she finally finished and her face was hotter than a summer afternoon at the equator. She washed her hands, all the while trying not to look at Hunter.

'You have toilet paper on your shoe,' he said, glancing down at her foot.

'Oh, of course,' she said. 'Anything to make this more embarrassing for me. Could you get any more personal?'

A devilish gleam entered his eyes. Then that dark, penetrating stare dropped to her lips. She swore she could feel his hunger, feel his inner need to touch her.

Before she knew what he was doing, he cupped her head with his free hand, brushed her bottom lip with his thumb, and bent his head down to capture her lips with his.

Stunned, Amanda couldn't think, couldn't move, as his warm lips parted hers.

The scent of leather and taste of vampire invaded her senses. Never in her life had she felt anything like his mouth on hers. His kiss was fierce and hot as he pulled her into his arms and ravished her mouth like a marauder.

Every hormone in her body fired. She moaned low in her throat. Oh heaven, the man could kiss. And the feel of his hard body against hers was so incredible that she clutched at his shoulders wanting desperately to taste more of him.

His tongue danced with hers as his honed muscles rippled under her hands, and when her tongue accidentally brushed against his fangs, an unexpected shudder of pleasure ran through her.

For the first time since she had learned what he was, the thought of him biting her neck actually appealed to her.

But not nearly as much as the thought of laying him down on the cold, hard floor and having her way with all that lean, mean strength until they were both hot, sweaty, and spent.

Kyrian tensed as he tasted the first bit of paradise he'd been allowed in over two thousand years. He was instantly aware of her soft, feminine curves pressing against his hardness. Aware of the way she smelled like flowers and sunshine – things that had been taken from him centuries before.

There was magic in her kiss. A raw, untapped passion. She might have been kissed before, but he could tell no man had ever made her feel like this.

His body on fire, he ran his hand down her back, pressing her closer to him. He wanted her in a way he'd not wanted a woman since his days as a mortal man. He ached to touch her all over, to gently scrape his fangs over her neck, her breasts.

To feel her writhing in his arms . . .

Closing his eyes, he breathed her sweet, feminine scent as his body throbbed and ached for her with a primitive need.

Amanda gasped as he slid his hand down the side of her breast to her waist, then down to cup her buttocks. She'd never been the kind of woman to let a man handle her this way, and yet there was something about the Dark-Hunter she couldn't resist.

When he pulled her heatedly toward the wall and pinned her to it, she thought she would literally melt.

His chest pressed against hers, making her even more aware of his lean, hard muscles. He separated her legs with his powerful thigh, and raised it to collide with the center of her body in a way that made her throb even more. Amanda hissed in pleasure as he deepened his fiery kiss.

She wrapped her free arm around his neck, pulling him closer as her head swam.

What would it be like to make love to such an untamed predator? To run her hands over all those sleek, taut muscles that rippled with every move he made?

He left her lips and seared a trail with his tongue from her mouth to her ear. She felt the barest scrape of his fangs on her neck.

Amanda shook all over in response to him as her breasts swelled, longing for his caress. And all the while his thigh stroked her between her legs, making her burn even more. Her knees weakened and she sank deeper onto him.

Suddenly, a knock sounded on the door. 'Hey, you two,' Tate said, cracking it open. 'Someone's coming.'

The Dark-Hunter pulled back with a growl. It was then she realized what she'd done.

'Oh God,' she breathed. 'I just kissed a vampire!'

'Oh gods, I just kissed a human!'

Amanda narrowed her eyes at him. 'Are you mocking me?'

'Guys!' Tate called again.

Hunter took her arm and led her out the door. The janitor gave them a strange look, but said nothing as he entered the bathroom behind them.

Tate led them to his small office outside the morgue.

An old wooden desk was set against the far wall, with two chairs in front of it. A sofa with a neatly folded blanket and pillow on top of it was to her right and a set of metal filing cabinets to her left. Tate showed her to the phone on the desk, then left them to attend his business.

Trying her best to forget what had just happened in the bathroom and how good Hunter had felt in her arms, Amanda called Tabitha while Hunter stood over her.

Of course, Tabitha immediately started in on her for not letting the dog out.

'Okay,' Amanda said irritably. 'I'm sorry Terminator scored on your new comforter.'

'Sure you are,' Tabitha said. 'So, what happened to you last night?'

'What? Are your psychic abilities failing you? I got waylaid in your house by one of your vampire buds.'

'What!' Tabitha shrieked. 'Are you okay?'

Amanda looked up at Hunter and wasn't sure how to answer. Physically, she was fine, but he did something strange to her that she couldn't even begin to define. 'I survived it. But they're looking for you, so you need to hide out some-place safe for a few days.'

'I don't think so.'

Hunter grabbed the phone from her hands. 'Listen to me, little girl. I have your sister with me, and if you don't leave your house and vanish for the next three days, I will make your sister wish you had listened to me.'

'You touch her and I'll stake you.'

He laughed bitterly. 'Been there, done that. Now get out of your house and let me handle this.'

'And Amanda?'

'She is safe as long as you listen to me.'

He handed the phone back to Amanda.

'Hey, Tabby,' Amanda said sheepishly.

'What has he done to you?' Tabitha demanded.

'Nothing,' she said, her face growing hot as she remembered his kiss. Nothing other than make her incredibly horny.

'Okay, listen,' Tabitha said. 'I'm going to Eric's, and we'll gather the gang, then head out to find you.'

'No!' Amanda said as she saw the dark, angry look descend on Hunter's face. Her heart stopped as she realized he could hear through the phone line.

You can hear her? she mouthed to him.

He nodded.

A chill went over her. 'Listen, Tabby, I'm safe. Just do what he wants. Okay?'

'I don't know.'

'Please trust me.'

'You, I trust. Him? Hell, I don't even know who he is.'

'I know,' Amanda said. 'You head over to Mom's and I'll stay in touch. Okay?'

'Okay,' Tabitha groused, 'but if I don't hear from you by eight o'clock tonight, I'm going hunting.'

'All right, I'll talk to you later. Love you.'

'You, too.'

Amanda hung up the phone. 'You heard all that?'

Hunter leaned over her, his body so close that she could feel his heat. His gaze bored into hers. 'All my senses are *highly* developed.'

His gaze dropped to her chest where her nipples drew tight from the intense stare. 'I can hear your heart beating faster, your blood flowing through your veins as you sit there wondering whether or not I would really hurt you.'

The man was truly frightening. 'Would you?' she whispered.

He locked gazes with her. 'What do you think?'

She stared at him, trying to get a reading on his mood and feelings, but the man was a brick wall. 'I honestly don't know.'

'You're smarter than I thought,' he said as he took a step back.

Amanda didn't know what to say to that. So she called work and told them she was sick for the day.

Hunter rubbed his eyes again.

'Do the lights bother you?' she asked.

He dropped his hand. 'Yes.'

She remembered what he said about his senses.

Before she could ask him anything else, he picked up the phone and dialed a number.

'Hola, Rosa. Cómo está?'

Spanish? she thought with a start. He spoke flawless Spanish?

Even more intriguing was the incredibly sexy sound of the words in that strange accent of his.

'Sí, bien. Necesito hablar con Nick, por favor.'

Hunter cradled the phone between his cheek and shoulder as he massaged the wrist where the cuff was making a red mark. She wondered if he realized the feral intensity that came into his eyes every time he saw the cuffs.

'Hey, Nick,' he said after a minute. 'I need you to retrieve my car from the corner of Iberville and Clay, and bring it to St. Claude. You can leave it in the doctors' lot.'

He let go of the cuff and took the phone back in his hand. 'Yeah, I know I'm a real asshole to work for, but you can't knock the pay and perks. Head out at three, and after you drop my car off, you can go home early.'

He paused as he listened for a few seconds. 'Also grab the backup case out of the cabinet . . . yeah, *that* one. I need you to bring it and my spare keys to the hospital and leave them for Dr. Tate Bennett.'

He stiffened as if Nick said something that irked him. 'Yes, you can take tomorrow off, but keep your beeper and phone on in case I need something.'

Hunter growled. 'Boy, don't make me change my tone with you. You forget, I know where you sleep.' Though the words were harsh, there was an underlying note of humor in his voice. 'All right, but don't burn out the clutch again. I'll see you later.'

Amanda arched a brow as he hung up the phone. 'So who's Nick?'

'My gofer.'

She gaped at him. 'My God, can it be you actually answered a question? Holy cow, we'd better call Tate in here quick before you keel over dead or undead or whatever it is you vampires do.'

'Ha, ha,' he said with a smile.

Good night, this is one sexy vampire when he smiles . . .

'Does Nick know what you are?' she asked.

'Only the people who need to know, know what I am.'

She thought about that for a minute. 'I guess I'm privileged, then.'

'"Cursed" would be more appropriate.'

'No,' she said as she thought more about it. 'When you're not being sarcastic, scary, or bullish, you're actually not bad to be around.' Impishly, she added, 'Of course, I've only been around you for about two minutes when you weren't one of those three things, so who am I to judge?'

His face softened. 'I don't know about you, but I have to sleep. I had a long night and I'm exhausted.'

She was rather tired, too. But as she slid her gaze to the fake leather sofa, she realized it would never fit both of them.

Hunter grinned at her. 'You take the couch, I'll sleep on the floor.'

'Can you do that?'

'I've slept in worse places.'

'Yeah, but don't you need a coffin?'

He gave her a droll stare, but said nothing as he led her to the sofa.

No sooner had Amanda lain down than she realized it wasn't going to work. 'This isn't comfortable. I can't sleep with my arm hanging over the edge and I'm twice as long as the couch is.'

'What do you suggest?'

She grabbed the blanket and pillow and lay down on the floor beside him.

Kyrian flinched as she lay so close to him that he could feel her body heat. Worse, the only way to comfortably sleep would be to drape his arm over her.

Like lovers.

The thought tore through him, lancing his heart so deep that for a minute, he couldn't breathe as he remembered the last time he had made the mistake of being with a woman and letting his guard down.

Unbidden, the sight of blood, and the memory of grueling, unrelenting pain ripped through him with such ferocity that it made him flinch.

That was the past, he told himself. Ancient history. Still, some things were impossible to forget. And not even a man with super psychic powers could bury them.

Don't think about it.

This wasn't the time for memories. It was a time to be practical.

Desiderius would be after him tonight and if he was to save her and her sister, he would have to be awake, and fully alert.

Closing his eyes, he made himself relax.

Until she shifted, and her buttocks collided with his groin.

Kyrian ground his teeth. He was on fire as he inhaled the

sweet rosy scent of her. It had been so incredibly long since he had last taken a woman. So long since he had dared close his eyes with one by his side.

Necessity was a bitch. But then he had learned that lesson the hard way when he had fought against the Romans.

Swallowing, he forced his mind to blankness. There was nothing in the past worth remembering. Nothing back there except pain so profound that even after two thousand years it could still bring him to his knees.

Focus, he told himself, relying on his staunch military training. *Now is the time to rest.*

Amanda tensed as he moved to spoon up against her spine. And when he put his arm over her, her heart pounded.

All that lean, hard strength was pressed against her back in a most distracting way.

She stared at his hand in front of her face. He had long, graceful fingers that looked as though they should belong to an artist or musician. Goodness, but it was hard to remember this man wasn't really a man.

You're lying with a vampire!

No, he's a Dark-Hunter. Not that she really understood the difference, yet.

But she would. One way or another.

Amanda lay for hours listening to Hunter breathe. She could tell when he had finally fallen asleep because his arm relaxed against her and the breath on her neck evened out.

Outside Tate's office, she heard people coming and going, the hospital paging system calling out for different doctors and orders.

A little after noon, Tate brought them lunch, but she wouldn't let him wake Hunter. She ate half of her sandwich and continued to lie there, all the while wondering how she could feel so strangely safe with a vampire she barely knew.

She rolled over slightly to look at him. He really was

scrumptious. His hair fell over his eyes as he slept and his relaxed features held a boyish charm to them.

As she stared at his perfect lips, she remembered the way they had tasted. The raw, powerful feel of them on her neck.

The remnants of that kiss made her lips burn, her body quiver.

She'd been kissed more times than she could count, but no man had ever made her feel the way he did. The touch of his mouth on hers had set her on fire.

How had he done it? What was it about Hunter that made her ache to have him in spite of herself?

Was it part of his immortal powers?

She wasn't a nymphomaniac. She had a normal, healthy sex drive that wasn't too low or too high. Yet every time she looked at him, she wanted to touch his skin, his lips, his hair.

What was wrong with her?

Put it out of your mind. Closing her eyes, she started counting backward from one hundred.

When she reached negative sixty, she realized it was futile.

Sighing, she absently reached out and toyed with the ring on his hand. Before she realized it, she was holding his hand in hers.

Hunter murmured dreamily as he snuggled closer. Amanda's eyes widened as his hot breath fell against her cheek and his erection pressed disturbingly against her hip. His grip tightened on her hand an instant before he gathered her in his arms and cradled her body protectively with his.

He whispered something in a foreign language, then settled again, still fast asleep.

Her heart hammered. No one had ever held her like this. So possessively. So completely. It felt as if she were cocooned by his strength. The weirdest part of all was that deep down she liked the feeling a whole lot more than she ever wanted to admit.

Nestled in his arms, she finally drifted to sleep.

Amanda came awake to a hard thigh wedged between her legs and to a hot hand beneath her sweater, skimming the flesh of her stomach. Hunter's arm held her so close to him that she could barely breathe.

'I've missed you,' he whispered tenderly an instant before he slid his hand under her bra and cupped her breast.

Amanda hissed in pleasure as his warm fingers brushed against her flesh in slow, simmering circles. That touch branded her with desire and it was all she could do not to turn her head to his and kiss him.

'Theone,' he breathed lovingly.

'Hey!' she snapped at him. It offended her to the core of her soul that he would dare call her by someone else's name. If he was going to grope, then he better damn well remember who it was he groped. 'What are you doing?'

Kyrian tensed as he came fully awake and opened his eyes wide. The first thing he felt was the warm, soft breast that overfilled his palm. The second was the throbbing ache in his body that demanded release.

Oh shit! He jerked his hand away as if it were on fire.

What the hell was he doing?

His job was to protect her, *not* touch her. Especially not when she felt this good in his arms. The last time he'd made that mistake with a woman, it had cost him his very soul.

Amanda saw the confusion on his face as he pulled away from her and sat up.

'Who's Theone?' she asked.

Hatred flared in his eyes. 'No one.'

Okay, he didn't like Theone while conscious, but there for a minute . . .

He rose slowly to his feet and helped her up. 'I slept longer than I meant to. The sun is already setting.'

'Is this some weird psychic thing you have with the sun?'

'Since I live and die by when it sets and rises, yes.' He pulled her toward the door. 'Now then, you said you know someone we can see about getting free?'

'Yeah, they should be home. Want me to call and make sure?'

'Yes.'

Amanda went to the desk, picked up the phone, then called Grace Alexander.

'Hey, Gracie,' she said as soon as Grace answered. 'This is Amanda. I was wondering if you guys would be home tonight? I have a bit of a favor to ask.'

'Sure. My in-laws are over for a bit, but that'll keep the babies occupied. You want to tell me—'

'Not over the phone. We'll be there as soon as we can.'

'We?' Grace asked.

'I have a friend in tow, if you don't mind.'

'No, not at all.'

'Thanks. I'll see you in a bit.' Amanda hung up the phone.

'Okay,' she said to Hunter. 'She lives off St. Charles. You know the way?'

Before he could answer, Tate came in with a black briefcase in his hand. 'Hey,' he said to Hunter, 'I figured you'd be getting up about now. A guy named Nick came by a couple of hours ago and left this for you.'

'Thanks,' Hunter said as he took the briefcase from him. He placed it on the desk and opened it.

Amanda's eyes bulged at the sight of two small handguns, a recoiling gun, a holster, a cell phone, three wicked-looking knives, and a pair of small, dark, round sunglasses.

'Tate,' Hunter said with a friendly note in his voice she wouldn't have thought him capable of. 'You're the man.'

'I just hope Nick didn't forget anything.'

'Nope, he nailed it.'

Amanda arched a brow at the strangeness of hearing

modern American slang coming out of a man with such a heavy, seductive accent.

Tate nodded to them, then left.

She watched as Hunter strapped the holster to his hips, then he slid the plate back to lock a bullet in the chamber of each gun. He flicked on the safety, twirled them around, then holstered them so that his coat concealed them.

Next, he picked up a butterfly knife and shoved it in his back pocket. The other two knives went into his coat pockets and he clipped the cell phone and his PDA to his belt.

Amanda arched a brow at his weapons. 'I thought only a wooden stake through the heart killed a vampire.'

'A wooden stake through the heart will kill just about anything. And if it doesn't, run like hell,' Hunter said blandly. 'Again, my lady, you watch too much television. Don't you have a life?'

'Yes, unlike you, I have a blessedly boring life where no one tries to kill me. And you know what? I like it, and I really want to get back to it.'

His eyes glowed with humor. 'All right, then, let's go find your friend to separate us so that you can get back to your boring life and I can lead my dangerous one.'

Raking her with a hot, lustful stare, he ran his tongue over his fangs. Then he placed the sunglasses on his face.

Amanda's pulse quickened. With those dark glasses on, he looked even more like a soulful poet than ever before. It was all she could do not to step back into his arms and demand he kiss her again.

He tucked her hand into his coat pocket with his to conceal the handcuffs, then led her out of Tate's office and through the hospital corridor.

As he walked, she noticed his smooth, predatorial gait. His air of refinement. The man was pure, fluid grace. And that was a seriously dangerous swagger he had developed. One that drew the attention of every woman they passed.

But Hunter didn't seem to notice as he headed out the back exit.

Once they reached the dark parking lot, Amanda gave a low whistle as she saw a Lamborghini Diablo in one of the employee spaces. The light above it glinted across the sleek black paint much like a halo. Normally, she didn't give a whit about cars, but the Lamborghini had always been her one exception.

It must belong to a surgeon.

Or so she thought until Hunter approached it.

'What are you doing?' she asked.

'I'm getting into my car.'

Her jaw dropped. 'You own this?'

'No,' he said sarcastically. 'I'm stealing it with the key in my hand.'

'Good Lord,' she gasped, 'you must be loaded!'

He pulled the sunglasses down the bridge of his nose to give her a peeved glare. 'It's amazing how much savings you can accumulate in two thousand years.'

Amanda blinked as his words registered. Could he honestly be . . .

'Is that *really* how old you are?' she asked skeptically.

He nodded. 'Two thousand one hundred and eighty-two years old last July, to be precise.'

She bit her bottom lip as she swept her gaze over his gorgeous body. 'You look good for an old man. I wouldn't have put you a day over three hundred myself.'

Laughing, he placed the key in the lock.

As Amanda waited for him to open the door, the imp in her couldn't resist teasing him. 'You know, they say men who drive cars like this are compensating for little' – she let her gaze roam meaningfully down the front of his body, pausing at the bulge in his jeans – 'packages.'

He cocked an eyebrow at her, then gave her a crooked smile that was teasing, warm, and wicked as he pulled the door up.

Before she knew what he was about, he stepped forward, overwhelming her with his masculine scent and power, then he took her hand that was cuffed to him and pressed it against his swollen groin.

Nope. No compensating there.

He dipped his head down to whisper in her ear. 'If you need more convincing . . .'

Her breath faltered at the incredible feel of him in her palm. That was *not* a tube sock in his jeans.

He stared at her lips and cupped her face with his free hand. She knew in that instant he was going to kiss her again.

Yes, please!

'Knock, knock,' Desiderius said from the darkness.

Chapter 4

'Now, ain't this a bitch,' Hunter said in an even tone as he pulled the sunglasses off and tucked them into his coat pocket. He moved with such deliberate slowness that Amanda knew it was his way of letting Desiderius know just how small of a threat the Dark-Hunter perceived him to be.

'Here I am, trying to kiss my girl, and you have to interrupt us. What, were you raised in a barn?'

With a calmness that astounded her, Hunter turned around to face Desiderius. 'By the way, touch the woman – or the Lamborghini – and you're a dead man.'

Desiderius came out of the shadows to stand beneath a circle of white moonlight. The contrasting buttery lamplight fell behind him at an odd angle, giving him a sinister appearance despite his angelic beauty.

'Nice car you have there, Dark-Hunter,' Desiderius said. 'It makes trailing it to you so much easier. As for your threat, I'm already a dead man.' His perfect lips twitched into a mocking smile. 'And so are you.'

Dressed in a fashionable blue pin-striped suit, Desiderius looked like a highly paid male model. His skin was golden and unblemished, his blond hair a shade lighter than the

Dark-Hunter's. His beauty was so flawless, it was almost surreal.

He didn't appear any older than his mid-twenties. A man at the height of his sexual appeal and strength.

Amanda swallowed as a shiver of fear went up her spine. There was something insidious about a man so evil looking so sublime. The only giveaway to his real nature was the long canine teeth he didn't bother to conceal when he spoke.

'I almost hate to kill you, Dark-Hunter. Unlike the others I've bested, you have such an amusing sense of humor.'

'Well, I try.' Hunter placed himself between them. 'Now, why don't you make this a bit more interesting and let the woman go?'

'No.'

Out of nowhere, they were attacked.

Amanda heard a sharp click.

Grabbing her hand that was bound to his so that he wouldn't hurt her during the fight, Hunter caught the first golden vampire with the toe of his boot. As the vampire vaporized into a cloud of dust, she realized the click had been the blade in his boot being released.

The blade instantly retracted.

With a move straight out of Hollywood, Hunter clipped another vampire with his elbow, then sent him flipping head over heels onto the ground. In one lightning-fast action, he knelt, twirled open a butterfly knife, embedded it into the Daimon's chest, then twirled it closed as the vampire evaporated.

Hunter rose to his feet.

A third one came from the shadows.

Acting on instinct, Amanda whirled and kicked him back with her leg. She caught him in the groin and sent him to the ground, whimpering.

Hunter arched a brow at her.

'Black belt in aikido,' she said.

'Any other time, I'd kiss you for that.' He smiled, then looked past her shoulder. 'Duck.'

She did and he tossed a knife straight into the chest of another vampire. The vampire vanished into black vapor.

Hunter pulled the gun out of its holster. 'Get in the car,' he ordered, pushing her toward the driver's seat.

Her entire body quaking from adrenaline, Amanda got in as fast as the handcuffs and his hold on her hand would allow. She climbed over the gearshift, into the passenger seat, while Hunter fired at the vampires.

He got in behind her, closed the door, and started the car.

Good Lord, Hunter was amazing, and perfectly calm. She'd never seen anything like it in her life. He was totally un-ruffled.

Another beautiful, blond vampire jumped on the hood as Hunter put the car in reverse and hit the gas. His fangs bared, the vampire tried to punch through the windshield.

'Didn't I tell you *not* to touch the Lamborghini?' Hunter groused an instant before he cut the wheel and sent the vampire flying through the air.

'And they told me you guys couldn't fly,' Hunter said, straightening out the car and heading for the street. 'I guess Acheron needs to update the handbook.'

Amanda realized there were two cars after them.

'Oh, my God,' she breathed, placing her hand on his thick, masculine wrist to allow him as much mobility as she could while he shifted gears. This was getting ugly and the last thing she wanted was to interfere with whatever he had to do to get her safely out of this.

'Hold tight,' Hunter said as he turned the radio on, and accelerated.

Lynyrd Skynyrd's 'That Smell' blared as they whipped out of the parking lot, into traffic.

Her entire body rigid, Amanda started praying the Rosary even though she wasn't Catholic.

'Lights!' Amanda shouted as she realized he was driving in total darkness and his windows were tinted far past the legal limit. 'Lights would be very good right now!'

'Since they hurt my eyes to the point I can barely see, no they wouldn't. Trust me.'

'Trust you, my left foot,' she snapped, using her free hand to hold on to the seat belt like a lifeline. 'I'm not immortal over here.'

He laughed at that. 'Yeah, well, in a bad enough car wreck, neither am I.'

Amanda gaped. 'I really hate your sense of humor.'

His smile widened.

They went speeding through the crowded New Orleans streets, weaving in and out of lanes until she thought she'd be sick with fear. Not to mention a couple of times when she was sure her hand would be wrenched off by his movements.

Swallowing, she did her best to keep her nausea at bay while she braced herself against the dash.

A huge black Chevy pulled up beside them and tried to run them into a tractor-trailer. Grinding her teeth, Amanda bit back a scream.

'Don't panic,' Hunter said over the music as he cut the wheel to move underneath the semi. He gunned the engine. 'I've done this a lot.'

Amanda couldn't breathe as they entered another lane where a red Firebird waited to try and ram them. The Dark-Hunter narrowly missed a parked car.

Amanda's panic was so severe all she could do was gape. And pray. She did lots and lots of praying.

By the time they reached the interstate, Amanda had seen her entire boring life flash before her eyes. And she didn't like what she saw.

It was way too brief. There were a lot of things she wanted to do before she died – including getting her hands on Tabitha and beating the snot out of her.

Suddenly, the black Chevy was back, trying to run them off the road. Hunter hit the brakes and jerked his car over. They skidded sideways.

Her stomach lurched.

'You know,' Hunter said calmly. 'I really hate Romans, but I have to say their descendants make one fine automobile.'

He shifted and accelerated again, flying past the Chevy. They jumped the median, drove across oncoming traffic, and went down an exit so fast that all she could see was a flashing blur of lights.

The sounds of horns and screaming brakes filled her ears. It was followed by grinding metal and a loud pop and crunch as the Firebird full of Daimons hit the black Chevy. The Firebird drove the other car of Daimons into the retaining wall where it flipped over the traffic.

Amanda still couldn't breathe as the Daimons' Chevy came to rest beside the highway without striking another car.

Hunter actually whooped as he cut the wheel to turn the Lamborghini around in the street to face the opposite direction. He slammed on the brakes and took a look at the chaos they had left in their wake.

Her entire body shaking, Amanda gaped.

Hunter turned the radio off and smiled triumphantly. 'And not a single mark on the Lamborghini. Ha! Eat steel, you soul-sucking bastards.'

Downshifting, he stomped the gas, turned a tight, squealing circle in the street, and headed back toward the Quarter.

Amanda sat in stunned disbelief as she did her best to take long, deep, soothing breaths. 'You actually enjoyed that, didn't you?'

'Oh, hell yes. Did you see the look on their faces?' He laughed. 'Man, I love this car.'

She looked up at the sky, and implored divine aid. 'Dear God, please separate me from this maniac before I die of fright.'

'Oh, c'mon,' he said, his voice teasing. 'Don't tell me that didn't get your blood pumping.'

'Yes, yes, it did. In fact, my blood is pumping so fast that I'm not really sure why my heart hasn't exploded.' She stared at him. 'You are one crazy human being.'

The laughter died instantly. 'I used to be, anyway.'

She swallowed at the hollowness of his voice. Without meaning to, she must have struck a nerve.

Their mood subdued, Amanda gave him directions to Grace's bungalow off St. Charles.

A few minutes later, they pulled into the driveway behind Julian Alexander's black Range Rover. The back fender was slightly crushed in from his latest collision with a lamppost.

Poor Julian, he really was a menace on the road. She slid a sideways glance to the Dark-Hunter. Then again, comparatively speaking, Julian wasn't so bad after all. At least he'd never given her a heart attack.

Hunter helped her out of his side of the car, then led the way to the door. The old-fashioned bungalow was completely lit up, and through the sheer curtains over the windows, Amanda could see Grace sitting in an armchair in the living room.

The petite brunette had her long hair in a ponytail, and her stomach was twice as round as it had been the last time Amanda had seen her. Even though the baby wasn't due for another nine weeks, poor Grace looked as if she could give birth at any moment.

Grace was laughing at something, but there was no sign of Julian or their guests.

Amanda paused to brush her hair with her hand, straighten her dirty clothes, and button her coat over the bloodstains. 'Grace said they have company, so I think we should try and be a little inconspicuous, okay?'

He nodded as she rang the bell.

After a brief wait, the door opened to show Julian Alexander in the foyer. At six three, Julian was every bit as striking as Hunter. He had hair the same shade of blond and the bluest eyes Amanda had ever seen. His face was perfectly sculpted, but considering that he was the son of the Greek goddess Aphrodite, it was to be expected.

The welcoming smile on Julian's face faded as he caught sight of Hunter.

His jaw went slack.

Amanda turned to see a very similar reaction from Hunter, who stood stock-still.

'Julian of Macedon?' Hunter asked in disbelief.

'Kyrian of Thrace?'

Before she could move, the two men grabbed each other like long-lost brothers. Her arm was snatched upward as Kyrian hugged him.

'Oh gods!' Julian gasped. 'Is it really you?'

'I can't believe it,' Hunter said as he pulled back and ran a shocked look up and down Julian's body. 'I thought you were dead.'

'Me?' Julian asked. 'What about you? I heard the Romans executed you. Dear Zeus, how can you be here?' Julian glanced down and saw the handcuffs. His frown deepened. 'What the . . . ?'

'That's why we're here,' Amanda said. 'We got latched together, and I was hoping you could separate us.'

'They were made by your stepfather,' Hunter added. 'Any chance you have a key lying around?'

Julian laughed. 'I guess I shouldn't be surprised. At least this time she's not an Amazon princess with an irate mother demanding parts of your body be removed.' Julian shook his head like a father scolding a son. 'Two thousand years later, and you're still getting into unbelievable messes.'

Hunter gave him a tight-lipped smile. 'Some things never change. Care to indebt me to you again?'

Julian cocked his head. 'Last time I counted, I was two favors down to you.'

'Oh yeah, I forgot about Prymaria.'

By the expression on Julian's face, Amanda could tell he hadn't and she was dying to know what had happened. But there would be time for that later.

First, she wanted her arm free. She jingled the chain, hinting.

Julian stepped back and let them enter his house. 'You're actually in luck,' he said as he led them into the living room.

Grace hadn't moved from her chair where she now held Vanessa on her lap while Julian's gorgeous, blond mother sat on the sofa teasing Niklos with a stuffed doll. A tall, dark-haired man sat beside Aphrodite, holding Niklos in his arms and laughing at the two of them.

The Dark-Hunter sucked his breath in sharply at the quaint family scene. Roughly, he pushed Amanda away from him an instant before Aphrodite looked up and cursed.

Before Amanda could process what was going on, Aphrodite threw her arm out and what appeared to be a bolt of lightning came out of her hand and struck Hunter. The blast knocked him off his feet and threw him to the floor, pulling her along with him.

Amanda landed on top of his chest. She saw the burn on his shoulder and smelled the smoldering leather and skin.

She knew his wound had to be excruciating, but he didn't even react to it. Instead, Hunter quickly removed his sunglasses, pushed her off his chest, and tried to get her as far away from him as he could.

Rising to his feet, he placed himself between her and Aphrodite.

'How dare you!' Aphrodite shrieked while fury contorted her beautiful face. Her eyes narrowed, she left the couch and stalked toward Hunter like a deadly beast of prey. 'You know you are not to be in our presence.'

Julian grabbed Aphrodite before she could reach them. 'Mother, stop! What are you doing?'

She glared at Julian. 'You dare bring a Dark-Hunter before me? You know it is forbidden!'

Frowning, Julian turned to look at Hunter. Disbelief was etched on his face.

Hunter glanced at Amanda over his shoulder. 'You're about to be free, little one,' he whispered.

Aphrodite raised her hand.

Terrified, Amanda realized Aphrodite meant to kill him. No! The word caught in her throat while her heart raced in panic.

Julian caught his mother's wrist before she could blast Hunter again.

'No, Mom,' Julian snapped. 'Dark-Hunter or not, he happens to be the only man who ever stood guard at my back while everyone else prayed for my death. You kill him, and I will *never* forgive you for it.'

Aphrodite's face turned to stone.

Julian let go of her hand. 'I have never, in my entire life, asked you for anything. But I'm asking you now, as your son, help him. Please.'

Aphrodite looked from Julian to Hunter. The indecision in her eyes was tangible.

'Hephaestus?' Julian asked the man on the couch. 'Will you free them?'

'It is forbidden,' he said gruffly, 'and you know it. Dark-Hunters are soulless and beyond us.'

'It's all right, Julian,' Hunter said quietly. 'Just ask her not to let the blast go through me and hit the woman.'

It was only then Aphrodite noticed Amanda. Her gaze fell to the cuffs.

'Mom?' Julian asked again.

Aphrodite snapped her fingers and the handcuffs disappeared.

'Thank you,' Julian said.

'I did it only to help the human female,' Aphrodite said grimly before returning to the sofa. 'The Dark-Hunter is on its own.'

Hunter said a quiet thanks to Julian. Then, he turned and started for the door.

'Kyrian, wait,' Julian said, stopping him. 'You can't go out there hurt.'

The Dark-Hunter's face was stoic. 'You know the Code, *adelfos*. I walk alone.'

'Not tonight, you don't.'

'If he stays,' Aphrodite said, 'we have to leave.'

Julian looked back at his mother and nodded. 'I know, Mom. Thanks again for helping him. I'll see you later.'

Aphrodite vanished in a flash of light. Hephaestus set Niklos down, then evaporated, too.

'Julian?' Grace called from her chair. 'Is it safe to let go of Vanessa now?'

'Yes,' he said.

Amanda watched the sad look on Hunter's face as the twins came running toward their father.

Niklos took a happy detour to her, jabbering as he held his arms out. Amanda picked him up and cuddled him close before kissing the top of his soft, blond curls.

Bouncing in her arms, he laughed and hugged her.

Vanessa made straight for Hunter in true Vanessa form. The little darling knew no strangers. She handed him the half-eaten cookie in her hand. 'Cook-ie?' she asked in her broken, baby speech.

Kneeling before her, Hunter smiled tenderly as he took it from her outstretched hand. He brushed a gentle palm over the toddler's dark hair.

'Thank you, sweeting,' he said softly before handing the cookie back to her. 'But I'm not hungry.'

Vanessa squealed and threw herself into his arms.

If Amanda lived an eternity, she would never forget the desperate, aching look on Hunter's face as he held Vanessa to his chest. It was one of such longing. Of pain. The look of a man who knew he held something precious in his arms that he never wanted to let go of.

He closed his eyes and leaned his cheek against the top of Vanessa's head as he balled his fist against her back and held her tight. 'Gods, Julian, you always made such beautiful babies.'

Julian didn't say anything as Grace came forward. But Amanda saw the anguish in Julian's eyes while he watched his friend and his daughter.

The two of them locked gazes.

Something passed between them, some shared nightmare Amanda knew nothing about.

Julian took Grace's hand. 'Grace, this is my friend Kyrian of Thrace. Kyrian, this is my wife.'

Like a graceful black panther coming out of its deadly crouch, Hunter rose to his feet with Vanessa cradled gently in his arms. 'I'm honored to meet you, Grace.'

'Thank you,' Grace said. 'I have to say the same about you. Julian's talked about you so much that I feel like I know you.'

Hunter narrowed his eyes on Julian. 'Considering how often he censured my behavior, I shudder to think what he's told you about me.'

Grace laughed. 'Nothing too bad. Is it true you once incited an entire bordello into—'

'Julian!' Hunter snapped. 'I can't believe you told her that.'

Completely unabashed, Julian shrugged Hunter's irritability off. 'Ingenuity under pressure was always your forte.'

Grace gasped, then put her hand against her distended stomach. Julian reached out and took her arm, watching her worriedly.

Taking deep breaths, Grace rubbed her stomach and offered them a tentative smile. 'Sorry, the baby kicks like a mule.'

Hunter stared at Grace's belly, and a strange light came into his eyes. For an instant, Amanda could swear they glowed.

'It's another boy,' he said quietly, his voice distant.

'How did you know?' Grace asked in surprise as she continued to run her hand over her stomach. 'I just found out yesterday.'

'He can feel the baby's soul,' Julian said quietly. 'It's one of the protective powers of a Dark-Hunter.'

Hunter looked to Julian. 'This one is going to be strong-willed. He's loving and giving, but completely reckless.'

'Reminds me of someone else I once knew,' Julian said.

The words seemed to haunt Hunter.

'C'mon,' Julian said, taking Vanessa from Hunter and setting her down even though she squealed in protest. 'I need to get you upstairs and tend that wound.'

Amanda stood in the hallway, unsure of what she should do. She had a million questions she wanted answered, and if not for Hunter's wound, she'd be on her way upstairs right now asking them all. But Julian was right. That vicious-looking wound needed tending.

With a wistful glance to the stairs, she turned back to Grace. 'You're amazingly calm given all this chaos. Gods poofing out, people coming in wearing bloody clothes, and getting blasted in your foyer. I would think by now you'd be freaking out, especially given your condition.'

Grace laughed as she herded the crying Vanessa back into the living room. 'Well, over the last few years, I've gotten rather used to Greek gods poofing in and out. As well as other things I don't want to think about. Being married to Julian has definitely been an education in staying calm.'

Amanda laughed halfheartedly as she glanced toward the stairs and again wondered about her enigmatic Dark-Hunter. 'Is Hunter – or Kyrian – a god, too?'

'I don't know. From the things Julian has said, I always

assumed Kyrian was a man, but I'm as much in the dark as you are.'

As Grace sat down, Amanda heard the men talking through the baby monitor.

Grace reached to turn it off.

'Please, wait.'

Amanda took a seat and played with Niklos while she listened to the men above.

'Damn, Kyrian,' Julian said as soon as Kyrian handed him his shirt. 'You've got more scars on you than my father had.'

Kyrian let out a deep breath while he gently probed the burn on his shoulder from Aphrodite's blast.

The two of them were alone in the twins' nursery at the end of the upstairs hallway. Kyrian squinted against the bright yellow teddy-bear wallpaper that hurt his light-sensitive eyes and reached for his sunglasses.

Julian must have remembered his ancient Greek mythology because he turned out the overhead lights and turned on the small nursery lamp that bathed the room in a soothing dull glow.

Weak from his pain, Kyrian noticed that his reflection in the mirror was only barely there. An inability to cast reflections was one of the camouflage benefits bestowed on all Dark-Hunters. The only way for them to have a reflection was to force it from within their own mind. Something that was hard to do when they were wounded or excessively tired.

He stepped back from the white-painted dresser and met Julian's curious gaze. 'Two thousand years of combat tend to take a toll on the body.'

'You always had more balls than brains.'

An eerie chill went up Kyrian's spine at those familiar words. He couldn't count the times Julian had said that to him in Classical Greek.

How he had missed his friend and mentor over the

centuries. Julian had been the only man he'd ever listened to. One of the few men he'd actually respected.

Kyrian rubbed his arm. 'I know, but the funny thing is I can always hear your voice in my head begging me for patience.' He deepened his tone and adopted Julian's rougher-edged Spartan accent. '"Damn, Kyrian, can't you ever think before you react?"'

Julian fell silent.

Kyrian knew what was going through Julian's mind. The same bittersweet memories that tugged at him at night whenever he paused long enough to dwell on the past.

They were images of a world that had long ago ceased to exist. Of people and family who were nothing more than vague memories and lost feelings.

Their world had been a special one. Its primitive grace a warmth in their hearts. Even now, Kyrian could smell the oil from the lamps that had once lit his home. Feel the cool, fragrant Mediterranean breeze blowing through his villa.

In an odd contrast to Kyrian's thoughts, Julian dug around the small first-aid kit for a modern ice pack.

Finding it, Julian popped the seal to release the cooling gel, then held it against Kyrian's shoulder.

Kyrian hissed as the ice touched his throbbing skin.

'I'm sorry about that blast,' Julian said. 'Had I known . . .'

'It's not your fault. You had no way of knowing I'd traded my soul. It's not exactly how I start out conversations. Hi, I'm Kyrian. I have no soul. What about you?'

'You're not funny.'

'Sure I am, you just never appreciated my sense of humor.'

'That's because you would only let it out when we were one step away from death.'

Kyrian shrugged, then wished he hadn't as pain sliced down his arm. 'What can I say? I live to tease old Apollyon.' Kyrian took the pack out of Julian's hand and stepped back.

'So what happened to you? I was told Scipio had you and your family assassinated.'

Julian scoffed. 'You know better. It was Priapus who killed my family. After I found them dead, I had a "Kyrian" moment where I went after him.'

Kyrian arched a brow at that. To his knowledge, Julian had never had an impulsive moment in his entire life. The man was forever calm and collected, no matter the turmoil. It had been one of the things Kyrian liked best about him. '*You* did something rash?'

'Yes, and I paid for it.' He folded his arms over his chest and he met Kyrian's gaze. 'Priapus cursed me into a scroll. I spent two thousand years as a sex slave before my wife freed me.'

Kyrian exhaled in disbelief. He had heard of such curses. The pain of them was excruciating and his proud friend must have had a hard time of it. Julian had never been one to let anyone rule his life. Not even the gods.

'And you called me insane,' Kyrian said. 'At least I only antagonized the Romans. You went after the pantheon.'

Julian handed him a tube of burn ointment. When he spoke, his voice was low and thick. 'I was wondering, after I left, what happened to . . .'

Kyrian looked up and saw the agony in Julian's eyes, and he knew what was too painful for his friend to even mention.

Even now, he could feel his own grief over the death of Julian's son and daughter. With blond hair and rosy cheeks, they had been beautiful and vivacious beyond description.

They alone had made Kyrian's heart ache with envy.

Gods, how he'd wanted his own children, his own family. Every time he'd seen Julian at home, he had yearned to have such a life.

It was all he'd ever truly wanted. A peaceful hearth, children to love, and a wife who loved him. Such simple things, really. Yet they had forever eluded his grasp.

Now, as a Dark-Hunter, such wishes were an impossibility.

Kyrian couldn't imagine the horror Julian must still feel every time he thought of his children. He doubted if any man had ever loved his children more than Julian had. Indeed, he remembered the time five-year-old Atolycus had replaced the horsehair in Julian's helm with feathers as a gift for his father before they rode out to battle.

Julian had been one of the most feared commanders of the Macedonian army, yet rather than hurt his son's feelings, he had proudly worn his son's gift in front of all his men.

No one had dared laugh. Not even Kyrian.

He cleared his throat and averted his gaze from Julian's. 'I buried Callista and Atolycus in the orchard overlooking the sea where they used to play. Penelope's family took care of her, and I sent Iason's body back to his father.'

'Thank you.'

Kyrian nodded. 'It was the least I could do. You were like a brother to me.'

Julian gave a halfhearted laugh. 'I guess that explains why you went out of your way to annoy me all the time.'

'Someone had to. Even at twenty-three, you were too serious and stern.'

'Unlike you.'

Kyrian could only vaguely remember being the man Julian had known all those centuries before. He'd been carefree and battle-ready. Hot-blooded and pigheaded.

It was a wonder Julian hadn't killed him. The man's patience knew no limits.

'My glorious days of misspent youth,' Kyrian said wistfully.

Looking at his shoulder, Kyrian spread the soothing salve over the burn. It stung, but he was used to physical pain, and he had suffered worse injuries than this tiny ache.

Julian leveled a probing stare at him. 'The Romans took you because of me, didn't they?'

Kyrian paused at the remorse in Julian's eyes. Then he returned to spreading the ointment over the burn. 'You were always too hard on yourself, Julian. It wasn't your fault. After you were gone, I went on a bloodthirsty crusade against their forces. I made my own destiny in that regard, and it had nothing to do with you.'

'But had I been there, I could have kept them from taking you.'

Kyrian snorted at that. 'You were good at pulling me out of trouble, no doubt about it. But not even you could have saved me from myself. Had you been there, the Romans would have just had another Macedonian commander to crucify. Trust me. You were much better off in that scroll than meeting the fate Scipio and Valerius had in mind for us.'

Still, Kyrian saw his friend's guilt and he wished he could give Julian absolution.

'What happened?' Julian asked. 'Historical accounts say Valerius captured you in battle. But I can't believe that. Not the way you fought.'

'And history says you were killed by Scipio's assassins. Victors make their own versions of truth.'

For the first time in centuries, Kyrian allowed his thoughts to turn to that fateful day in the past.

He clenched his teeth as a wave of rage and agony washed over him anew and he remembered all too well why he had banished those memories to the farthest corner of his mind. 'You know, the Fates are treacherous bitches. I wasn't taken by Valerius, I was handed over, gift-wrapped.'

Julian frowned. 'How?'

'My little Clytemnestra. While you and I were out fighting the Romans, my wife was at home welcoming them into her bed.'

Julian's face paled. 'I can't believe Theone would do that to you after all you did for her.'

'No good deed goes unpunished.'

Julian scowled at the bitterness he heard in Kyrian's voice. This wasn't the same man he'd known in Macedonia. Kyrian of Thrace had always been fun-loving and lighthearted.

The man before him now was jaded. Guarded. Suspicious and almost cold.

'Is her betrayal why you became a Dark-Hunter?' Julian asked.

'Yes.'

Julian closed his eyes as he felt compassion and anger for his friend. Over and over in his mind, he could see Kyrian the way he'd been all those centuries before. His human eyes had always been laughing, mischievous. Kyrian had loved life in a way very few people ever did.

Generous in spirit, kind in nature, and courageous of heart, Kyrian had even managed to win Julian over and he had truly wanted to hate the spoiled, arrogant brat.

But hating Kyrian had been impossible.

'What did Valerius do to you?' Julian asked.

Kyrian drew a deep breath. 'Trust me, you don't ever want the exact details.'

Julian saw Kyrian flinch as if some memory flashed in his mind. 'What?'

'Nothing,' Kyrian said sharply.

Julian's thoughts turned to Kyrian's wife. Small and blond, Theone had been more beautiful than Helen of Troy. Julian had seen her only once, and then at a distance. Even so, he had known instantly what attracted Kyrian to her. She had possessed an irresistible aura of grace and sexual expertise.

Barely twenty-two when he met her, Kyrian had fallen in love instantly with the woman who was eight years his senior. No matter what any of them said about her, Kyrian had never listened. He'd loved that woman with every fiber of his body and soul.

'What of Theone?' Julian asked. 'Did you ever find out why she did it?'

Kyrian tossed the salve back into the bag. 'She said she did it because she was afraid I couldn't protect her.'

Julian cursed.

'My thoughts were somewhat stronger,' Kyrian said quietly. 'You know, I lay there for weeks trying to figure out what it was about me she hated so much that she could hand me over to my worst enemy. I never knew I was *that* big an asshole.'

Kyrian clenched his teeth as he remembered the way his wife had looked when they had started his execution. She had met his gaze levelly, without even the tiniest bit of remorse.

It had been then he'd known that even though he had given her only the very best of himself, the whole of his heart and soul, she had never given him anything of her. Not even her kindness. If only she'd had one flash of regret in her eyes, one tiny bit of sorrow . . .

But only morbid curiosity had darkened her face.

It had torn his heart asunder. If she couldn't love him after all he had given, then he must truly be unlovable.

His father had been right all along.

'No woman can ever love a man of your standing and wealth. Face it. All you will ever be, boy, is a hefty purse.'

To this day, his heart wept from the truth of it. Never again would he allow a woman that much hold over him. He refused to let love or anything else blind him from what he needed to do. His duty was all that mattered.

Now more than ever before.

'I am so sorry,' Julian breathed.

Kyrian shrugged. 'We're all sorry for something.' He reached for his torn, bloodied shirt.

'Listen,' Julian said, stopping him, 'why don't you take a shower and let me loan you some clothes?'

'I have a hunt to finish.'

'No offense, Kyrian, but you look like hell. Granted it's been a long time since I fought, but I know how much easier it is with a full stomach and a hot bath.'

Kyrian hesitated.

'Fifteen minutes?'

'Make it quick.'

Kyrian let the soothing water slide over his battered body. The night was still young, but he was tired already. His shoulder throbbed and ached and his side wasn't much better.

Yet what held his attention was the woman downstairs.

Why was he so attracted to her? He had saved countless humans over the centuries. He had felt nothing for them other than a passing curiosity.

And yet this woman with open, honest eyes and a beguiling smile tugged at a heart he had banished centuries ago. He didn't need that. Dark-Hunters were forbidden to take steady lovers. Out of necessity, their sexual encounters were relegated to one-night stands.

They were reborn to walk alone through time. Each of them knew it. They had sworn themselves to it.

Never before had it bothered him.

There had only been one other time in his long life that he had felt this strange giddy feeling in the pit of his stomach when a woman smiled at him.

He cursed at the reminder.

'Oh, come on, Kyrian,' he said as he bathed himself. 'Get out of the house, kill Desiderius, and go home. Forget you ever saw her.'

Pain cut through him at the very thought of never seeing her again.

Still, he knew what he had to do. This was his life and he loved the night he was bound by oath to. His duties were his family. His loyal oath his heart.

His job was his love, and it would remain that way for eternity.

'Amanda?'

Forcing her thoughts away from her handsome Dark-Hunter, Amanda looked to where Grace was seated in the armchair.

'Would you mind going up to the babies' room and getting a diaper for me?' Grace asked. 'If I walk up those stairs again, I might not come back down.'

She laughed. 'Sure. Be right back.'

Amanda went up the stairs, then headed down the hallway. She passed the bathroom at the same time Hunter came out of it, wrapping a towel about his waist.

They collided. Hunter put his hands on her shoulders to steady her, his eyes widening a degree as he recognized her.

Amanda froze as she realized her silver charm bracelet had gotten tangled in one of the terry-cloth loops.

Worse, the sight of all that lush, tawny skin and the feel of his strong hands on her body made her mouth water for a taste of him.

Her heart hammered at the sight of all the lean power and strength. At the smell of his warm, clean skin. His wet hair was slicked back from a face so well sculpted that she doubted any man could ever be more handsome.

He fixed those dark eyes with sinfully long eyelashes on her. The raw hunger in them made her hot and shivery. He looked as if he could devour her, and in truth, she wanted to be devoured by him. Completely. Utterly.

And with relish.

'Now, this is interesting,' Hunter said with a hint of amusement in his voice.

Amanda didn't know what to do as she stood there with her wrist dangerously close to the sudden bulge under the towel. Why was it they kept getting attached?

Her gaze slid over the multitude of scars covering his body

and she couldn't help wondering how many of them were from the torture he'd mentioned to Julian.

'Most of them,' he whispered as he moved one hand over to cup her neck in his hand. She felt his fingers stroking her hair. His grip on her shoulder tightened ever so slightly.

'What?' she asked, looking up.

'Most of them are from the Romans.'

She frowned. 'How did you know what I was thinking?'

'I'm eavesdropping on your thoughts much the same way you listened to me and Julian.'

A chill went down her spine as she considered his psychic powers. 'You can do that?'

He nodded, but he wasn't looking at her, he was staring at his hand in her hair as if he were committing the texture and feel of it to memory.

His gaze returned to hers so fast it actually made her gasp. 'And in answer to the question you're too afraid to think, all you have to do is move your arm and you'll know.'

'Know what?'

'If I look as *yummy* without the towel as I do with it.'

Her face flamed at the way he used her own words to describe exactly what she was too terrified to think.

Before she could move, he released her and dropped the towel to hang from her bracelet.

Amanda gaped at the sight of him completely naked before her. His hard, well-toned body was perfectly sculpted. And she quickly learned that his skin was golden all over. It wasn't a tan, it was his natural skin color.

She wanted him with a desperate need.

All she could think of was taking him into the bedroom and pulling him on top of, over, and then under her for the rest of the night.

Oh, the things she wanted to do to this man.

A half-smile hovered on the edges of his lips, and by the light in his eyes, she knew he was reading her thoughts. Again.

He leaned forward, his face just to the side of hers. His hot breath fell against her neck, scorching her. 'Ancient Greeks never had a problem with public nudity,' he whispered in her ear.

Her breasts tightened.

Slowly, he lifted his hand so that he could tilt her chin up. His gaze held hers enthralled as he appeared to search her mind for something.

Before she could move, he lowered his lips to hers.

Amanda moaned at the contact. This kiss was different from his last one. This one was gentle. Tender.

And it made her burn.

He left her lips and trailed a blazing path down her jaw to her neck, his tongue laving her skin ever so lightly. She wrapped her arms around his bare shoulders and surrendered her weight to him.

'You are so very tempting,' he whispered, then traced the curve of her ear with his tongue. 'But I have a job to do and you hate all things not human. And *everything* paranormal.' He pulled back and gave her a wistful look. 'Pity.'

He freed his towel from her bracelet, tossed it over his shoulder, then headed to the bedroom. Amanda clenched her teeth at the sight of that luscious, gorgeous backside.

Her body on fire, she watched until he closed the door behind him.

Suddenly, she remembered the diaper.

No sooner had the thought crossed her mind than Hunter opened the door, tossed her one, then closed it again.

Kyrian leaned against the closed door as he fought the raging need inside him. It was raw and vicious, and it made him ache for things he knew he could never have.

Things that could only hurt him more. And he had been hurt enough to last ten thousand lifetimes.

He had to put her out of his thoughts.

But even as he stood there, the loneliness of his life settled down on him with a vengeance.

'*You let your heart lead you far too often, boy. One day, it's going to lead you to ruin.*' He winced at his father's warning in his head. Neither of them had any idea at that time just how true those words would one day prove.

I am a Dark-Hunter.

That was what he needed to focus on. He was the only thing standing between Amanda and annihilation.

Desiderius was out there and he must stop him.

But what he really wanted to do was go downstairs, scoop Amanda up in his arms, and carry her back to his house where he could spend the entire night exploring every inch of her body with his lips, his hands. His tongue.

'I am such a fool,' he snarled, forcing himself to dress in the clothes Julian had left for him.

He would think no more of her or of his past. He had a higher calling. One that couldn't be ignored.

He was a protector. And he would live and die as a protector, which meant that physical comforts such as a woman like Amanda were strictly off limits to him.

A few minutes later, dressed in Julian's jeans and a black V-neck sweater, he left the room with his leather coat over his arm, and went downstairs where Julian, Grace, Amanda, and the children were waiting.

Julian handed him a small paper sack.

'Gee,' Kyrian said as he took it, 'thanks, Dad. I promise to be a good boy and play nice with the other kids.'

Julian laughed. 'Smart-ass.'

'Better than a dumb-ass.' Kyrian sobered as he looked at Amanda and a burning wave of desire scorched him. What was it about her that made him unable to look at her without wanting to taste that mouth? Feel her warm body in his arms?

Kyrian cleared his throat. 'Make sure she stays here until morning. The Daimons can't enter without an invitation.'

'What about tomorrow night?' Grace asked.

'Desiderius should be dead by then.'

Julian nodded.

Kyrian turned to leave, but before he could reach the door, Amanda stopped him with a gentle hand on his arm.

'Thank you,' she said.

He inclined his head to her.

Leave. Because if he didn't, he just might yield to that demanding need inside him.

He looked past Amanda to Julian's wife. 'It was nice meeting you, Grace.'

'You too, Commander.'

As he started out the door, Amanda caught him again and turned him about. Before he knew what she was doing, she kissed him on the cheek.

'You be careful,' she whispered as she pulled away.

Stunned, he could do nothing more than blink. But what touched him most was the concern he saw in her crystal-blue eyes, the concern he felt in her heart. She really didn't want him hurt.

Desiderius is waiting.

The thought tore through his mind. He *had* to leave.

Yet walking away from her was the hardest thing he'd ever had to do.

'Have a nice life, Cupcake,' he said to her.

'Cupcake?' Amanda asked in an offended tone.

He smiled. 'After the "buff stud in black leather" remark, I figured I owed you one.' He patted her hand, then reluctantly removed it from his arm. 'It's almost eight, you better go call your sister.'

Kyrian let go of her hand and instantly felt the vacancy.

He exchanged a knowing look with Julian. This would be the last time they saw each other and they both knew it. 'Good-bye, *adelfos*.'

'Good-bye, little brother,' Julian said.

Kyrian turned around, opened the door, and made his solitary way to his car.

Once inside, he couldn't resist looking back. Though he couldn't see Amanda, he could feel her on the other side of the door, staring after him.

He couldn't remember the last time anyone had been sorry to see him go. Nor could he recall ever feeling this insane need to keep a woman with him at any cost.

Chapter 5

After Kyrian left, Amanda called Tabitha and reassured her she was safe, then took a quick shower and borrowed a pair of leggings and a sweatshirt from Grace. She sat on the couch with a plate of spaghetti while Grace and the babies retired for the night.

Julian came from the kitchen and handed her a Coke, then took a seat in the armchair. 'All right,' he said. 'Where shall I begin?'

She didn't even have to think about it. 'The beginning. I want to know exactly what Dark-Hunters and Daimons are. Where did the Apollites come from? And exactly how are the three of them related?'

Julian laughed. 'You cut right to the chase, don't you?' He turned his glass of iced tea around in his hands as he appeared to think about how best to answer her question. 'At times like this, I wish Homer's *Kynigostaia* had survived.'

'Cog-no-whatever that word is, is what?'

He laughed again, then took a drink of tea. 'It was the record of the birth of the *Kynigstosi*, the Dark-Hunters, and could have answered most questions you have about them.

It detailed the rise of the two races that once held dominion over the earth. The humans and Apollites.'

Amanda nodded. 'Okay, I know where humans come from, what about the Apollites?'

'Aeons ago, Apollo and Zeus were walking through Thebes when all of a sudden Zeus declared the greatness of the human race. He called humans the "earthly pinnacle of perfection." Apollo scoffed and said there was a lot of improving to be done. He boasted that he could easily create a superior race. Zeus told him to prove it. So Apollo found a nymph who agreed to bear his children.

'In three days the first four Apollites were born. Three days after that, those children grew into adulthood, and three days later, they were ready to be rulers of the earth.'

Amanda wiped her lips with her napkin. 'So the Apollites are the children of Apollo. Gotcha. Now what makes some of them Daimons?'

'Would you wait? I'm the one telling this story,' Julian said patiently in the voice she was sure he reserved for his college students. 'Because the Apollites were so superior to humans in intellect, beauty, and strength, Zeus banished them to the island of Atlantis where he hoped they would stay peacefully. I don't know if you've ever read Plato's Dialogues—'

'No offense, but I spent my entire college career avoiding liberal arts courses.'

Julian smiled. 'Anyway, most of what Plato wrote about Atlantis is true. They were an aggressive race who wanted to dominate the earth, and ultimately Olympus, as well. Apollo didn't mind since he would become the supreme god should they win.'

Amanda knew where this was headed. 'I'll bet that made old Zeus happy.'

'He was delighted,' Julian said sarcastically. 'But not half so much as the poor Greeks who were being hammered by the Apollites. Fed up with it, they realized they were fighting a lost cause. So they devised a scheme to seduce Apollo to their side. They chose the most beautiful woman ever born to them, Ryssa, to be his divine mistress.'

'More beautiful than Helen of Troy?'

'This was a *long* time before Helen, and yes, accounts claimed she was by far the most beautiful woman ever born. Anyway, Apollo, being Apollo, couldn't resist her. He fell in love with her and she ultimately bore him a son. When the Apollite queen heard of this, she became enraged and sent out a team of assassins to kill mother and child. The queen told her men to make it appear as if a wild animal had killed them so that Apollo wouldn't retaliate against the Apollites.'

Amanda whistled low as she guessed what happened after that. 'Apollo found out.'

'Yes, he did, and it got ugly. You see, Apollo is also the god of plagues. He destroyed Atlantis and would have destroyed every single Apollite as well had Artemis not stopped him.'

'Why did she do that?'

'Because the Apollites are part of his flesh and blood. To destroy them would be to destroy him and the world as we know it.'

'Oh,' Amanda said, her eyes wide. 'That's a big, bad thing. Glad she stopped him.'

'So were the rest of the pantheon. But still, Apollo wanted vengeance. He banished the Apollites from the sun so that he would never again have to see one of them and be reminded of their treachery. Since they had made it appear as if a wild beast had killed Ryssa, he gave them animal characteristics. Fangs, honed senses—'

'What about their strength and speed?'

'They already had that, along with psychic abilities that Apollo couldn't take from them.'

Amanda frowned at that. 'I thought gods could do anything they wanted to. Isn't that the point of being a god?'

'Not always. They have laws and such they abide by, same as us. But in the case of psychic powers, once that channel is opened, it can never be closed. That's why Apollo didn't take his gift of foresight from Cassandra when she spurned him, but rather made it so that no one would believe her prophecies.'

'Ah, that makes sense.' Amanda took a drink of her Coke. 'Okay, so the Apollites are psychic and strong, and can't come into contact with sunlight. What about drinking blood? Do they do that or not?'

'Yes, they drink blood, but only if it comes from another Apollite. In fact, because of Apollo's curse, they have to feed from each other every few days or they die.'

'Ew,' she said, wrinkling her nose. 'That's nasty.' She shivered at the thought of having to live that way. 'Some of them do drink from humans, right?'

Julian hedged a bit. 'Not exactly. If they turn Daimon, they will drain the blood from humans, but it's not the blood they're after so much as the human soul.'

She arched a brow as a tingle went down her spine. Kyrian hadn't been joking about that aspect of them. Great. 'Why do they need to steal our souls?'

'Apollites only live thrice nine years. On their twenty-seventh birthday, they die a very slow and painful death in which their bodies literally disintegrate into dust over a twenty-four-hour period.'

This time she cringed visibly at the thought. 'How horrible. I guess the moral of this story is not to tick off the god of plagues.'

'Yeah,' Julian said grimly. 'To avoid their fate, most Apollites kill themselves the day before their birthday. Others decide to go Daimon. As Daimons they cheat their sentence by taking human souls into their bodies. So long as they maintain the soul, they can live. But the problem is the human soul can't live in an Apollite body and it starts to die almost as soon as they take it. As a result, the Daimons are forced to continue preying on humans every few weeks to sustain themselves.'

Amanda couldn't imagine how horrible it must be for the people killed by the Apollites – to lose both their life and their soul. 'What happens to the souls that die?'

'They're lost forever. That's why we have Dark-Hunters. Their job is to try and find the Daimons and free the souls before they expire.'

'And they volunteer for this?'

'No, rather they're drafted.'

Her frown deepened. 'Drafted how?'

Julian took another drink of tea. His gaze fell to the floor and she saw a strange light in his eyes as if he were remembering something out of his own past. Something painful.

'When someone suffers a horrible injustice,' he said, his tone low, 'their soul makes a scream so loud that it resonates through the halls of Olympus. When Artemis hears it, she goes to the one who cried out and offers them a bargain. For a single Act of Vengeance against those who wronged them, they will swear allegiance to her and fight in her army against the Daimon predators.'

Amanda breathed deeply as all the information swam in her head. 'How do you know all this?'

Julian looked up and his gaze scorched her with its vivid intensity. 'Because my soul made that sound the day my children died.'

She swallowed at the hatred and pain she saw in his eyes. It was so raw, she hurt for him. 'Did Artemis come to you and offer you the bargain?'

'Yes, and I refused her.'

'Why?'

He looked away. 'I needed vengeance against another god and I knew she couldn't allow that.'

Amanda knew the story of Julian's entrapment inside the book all too well. But what interested her more was Kyrian. 'Kyrian traded his soul for vengeance against his wife, didn't he?'

He nodded. 'But don't judge him too harshly.'

'I'm not,' she said honestly. She didn't know what Kyrian had been through, but until she did, there was no way she would hold his decision over his head.

'Tell me, Julian, is there any way for Dark-Hunters to get their souls back?'

'Yes, but almost no one succeeds, and each test is unique to every Dark-Hunter.'

'Which means you can't tell me how Kyrian might be freed.'

'Which means *I* have no idea how he might be freed.'

Amanda nodded until her thoughts went to another matter. 'Do Dark-Hunters have to drink blood, too?'

'No. Since they began as humans, they don't *have* to. Plus, if they had to worry about finding blood, it would interfere with their ability to track the Daimons.'

'Then why do they have fangs?'

'In order to effectively track and kill the Daimons, they were given the same animal characteristics. The fangs are part and parcel of what goes with it.'

That made sense to her. 'Is that why the sunlight is deadly to Dark-Hunters too?'

'Sort of, but in the case of the Dark-Hunters it's more a matter that they serve Artemis, the goddess of the moon, and are an anathema to Apollo.'

'That doesn't seem fair.'

'The gods seldom are.'

Hours later, Kyrian sat in his car, damning his treacherous thoughts.

He could still see Amanda. Hear the sound of her soft,

gentle voice. Feel her body against his and her soft breast in his hand.

It had been so long since he'd wanted a woman like this. He thought he'd banished that part of himself the night he'd become a Dark-Hunter.

As the centuries passed, he'd felt only an occasional stirring for a woman, but he'd learned to control it. Learned to bury it.

Now those long-forgotten needs had been awakened by the touch of a temptress who was lethal to his well-being. Thoughts of her distracted him. Tormented him.

He wanted her in a way that bordered on desperate.

Why? What was it about her that he craved so much? He knew nothing about her except that she had a great sense of humor and held incredible grace under fire.

And yet he yearned for her as he had for no other woman. Not even his wife.

It made no sense.

Turning his car off, he got out and entered his house. He tossed the keys on the kitchen counter and paused. The house was completely silent except for a light, clicking noise coming from upstairs.

Kyrian walked through the dark rooms and up the ornate, mahogany staircase until he was upstairs, outside his office. Light spilled out from the closed door, across the Persian runner.

Silently, he turned the knob and opened the door.

'Nick, what the hell are you doing here?'

Cursing loudly, his Squire jumped out of his swivel desk chair.

Kyrian had to stifle a laugh at the sight of a six-foot-four human ready to kill him. Nick's blue eyes snapped fire as his jaw, which was badly in need of a shave, twitched. Nick brushed his hand through his shoulder-length dark brown hair. 'Jeez, Kyrian, would you learn to make some sound when you move? You scared the hell out of me.'

Kyrian shrugged nonchalantly. 'I thought you were going home early.'

Nick righted the chair and returned to sit in it, then scooted it back under the desk. 'I was, but I wanted to finish up the research into Desiderius for you.'

Kyrian smiled. Nick Gautier might be a hotheaded, smart-mouthed pain in the ass most of the time, but he was always reliable. It was why Kyrian had chosen him to be a Squire and had initiated him into the realm of the Dark-Hunters. 'Learn anything new?'

'You might say that. I've learned he's about two hundred and fifty years old.'

Amazed, Kyrian arched a brow. To his knowledge, no Daimon had ever lived so long. 'How is that possible?'

'I don't know. Dark-Hunters keep going after him and he keeps killing them. It seems your little Daimon friend likes to make you guys suffer.' Nick returned to the computer. 'There's nothing in Acheron's database about his exact modus operandi and when I talked to Ash earlier, he said he had no idea where Desiderius came from or who all of his targets have been. But we're looking into it.'

Kyrian nodded.

'Oh, by the way,' Nick said, glancing over his shoulder, 'you look like hell.'

'Obviously so, since everyone I've seen tonight has said that to me.'

Nick smiled until he saw what Kyrian was wearing. 'Why aren't you in your bad-ass, Daimon-killing clothes?'

Kyrian didn't feel like going there. 'Speaking of, I need you to buy me a new leather coat today.'

Suspicion clouded Nick's blue eyes. 'Why?'

'The old one has a hole in the shoulder.'

'Why?'

'I got attacked. Why else?'

Nick looked less than pleased by the news. 'You okay?'

'Don't I look okay?'

'No, you look like hell.'

There was no hiding from Nick. 'I'm fine. Now, why don't you go on and sleep in one of the guest rooms? It's four o'clock in the morning.'

'I will in a little bit. I want to finish this up first. Besides, I'm in the middle of finding out what Sundown did to piss off Ash.'

Kyrian heard the 'uh-oh' sound that alerted Nick he had a new instant message on the computer. 'Tell Jess to lay off taunting Ash before he gets toasted.'

Nick frowned. 'Jess?'

'Sundown's real name is William Jessup Brady. I thought you knew that.'

Nick laughed. 'Hell no. But I know a few Squires who would pay me lots of money to learn that.' His blue eyes turned speculative. 'Rogue isn't Rogue's real name either, is it?'

'No. It's Christopher "Kit" Baughy.'

Nick made a delighted noise. 'Now that one is really worth some serious cash.'

'No,' Kyrian corrected. 'It's worth some serious ass-kicking if Rogue finds out you know it.'

'Good point. I'll tuck that in my blackmail folder for when I need a Dark-Hunter favor.'

Kyrian shook his head. The boy was incorrigible. 'I'll see you tonight.'

'Yeah, night.'

Kyrian shut the door and headed down the long hallway to his bedroom. The large, lush room welcomed him with dark, peaceful colors that didn't hurt his light-sensitive eyes. Nick had lit the three candles in the small wall sconce and the dull glow flickered against the burgundy wallpaper.

This room was Kyrian's haven from the daylight.

He'd had the windows sealed and covered as soon as he bought the old neoclassical antebellum house. No Dark-Hunter ever willingly slept where daylight might accidentally find him.

Kyrian stripped off his clothes and lay down on the large bed he'd had since the fourteenth century, but his troubled thoughts spiraled through his mind.

Desiderius had eluded him and for the next few days, he would be out of Kyrian's reach.

Damn. But there was nothing to be done about it. Nothing, except to wait and be ready when Desiderius emerged. At least he had the comfort of knowing Desiderius would come after him first.

It would give him time to keep Amanda and Tabitha safe.

Amanda.

Her name hovered in his mind, along with a mental picture of her bright blue eyes. His groin tightened instantly against the cool silk sheets. He growled at the deep-seated ache that burned through him.

'She is not mine,' he whispered.

And by all the gods on Olympus, she never would be, no matter how much the corner of his heart that remained might wish otherwise.

Chapter 6

Amanda moaned as she felt a warm, strong hand sliding over her bare stomach to her hip. Instinctively, she turned into the caress, her body instantly on fire with need.

Kyrian rolled her over, onto her back, and captured her lips with his. Her head swam at the contact. At the feel of all his strength and power. Never in her life had she felt anything better than his tongue on hers. Or his exquisitely hard body sinuously sliding against her.

She burned even more.

His kiss was fierce and hot, yet strangely tender. Closing her eyes, she breathed in the spicy scent of his skin and tasted the heat of his mouth.

She ran her hands through the silk of his golden hair, delighting in the way the waves curled around her fingers.

He pulled back and stared down at her with a powerful hunger that made her burn as those gorgeous muscles of his shoulders bunched and flexed under her hands. 'I will have you,' he said fiercely, his voice possessive.

'And I will have you,' she said, smiling as she wrapped her legs around his narrow hips.

His devilish, fanged smile took her breath. With her cradled in his arms, he rolled onto his back and pulled her on top of him. Amanda bit her lip as she stared down at his handsome face while she felt his hard, masculine body between her thighs.

Needfully, she rubbed herself against his long, hard shaft. He growled in response to her caress.

He swept a famished look over her, then reached up and cupped her breasts in his warm hands. She covered his hands with her own as he squeezed them gently.

'I could stare at you all night,' he whispered.

She could definitely relate because nothing would please her more than watching him move around naked for the rest of eternity.

That walk . . . that body . . .

It was more than a mere mortal woman could handle.

He lifted his hips, sending her forward.

Amanda caught herself with her arms. She leaned over him, her hair falling around her face to form a dark canopy over them.

'Now that's what I want.' Kyrian reached up to cup her face and pulled her lips to his. His mouth teased hers as he gently sucked her bottom lip between his teeth.

Amanda moaned at the contact as he trailed his hand from her breast down her side and to the center of her body. 'And this is what I want most.' He plunged two fingers inside her.

Amanda hissed in pleasure as his fingers teased her relentlessly. In and out and around they swirled, making a hot fire to consume her.

He pulled back from her lips. 'Now tell me what you want.'

'You,' she breathed.

'Then you shall have me.' Kyrian moved his hands to her hips and pressed her body toward his erection.

Biting her lip expectantly, she longed to feel him inside

her. To have his fullness stretch her body while they shared the most intimate of experiences.

She felt the tip of his shaft pressing against her core.

Just as she was sure he'd slide inside, the alarm clock went off.

Amanda came awake with a start.

Dazed, she glanced around the unfamiliar room and it took a full minute before she remembered she was asleep in the nursery at Grace's house.

It had all been a dream?

But it had seemed so real. She swore she could still feel Kyrian's hands on her body, his breath against her neck.

'Oh, it's so not fair,' she groused as she got out of bed and turned off the alarm clock. It had just been getting *really* good.

How could it have been just a dream? Just a dream of a mysterious stranger who hid pain behind sarcastic quips and of eyes so dark and deadly they captivated her?

Trying her best to forget the intensity of her subconscious, Amanda wrapped Grace's thick robe around her, then headed for the bathroom.

'Where did it come from?' Grace asked.

Amanda paused in the hallway as she heard Grace and Julian talking below.

'I assume Kyrian left it,' Julian said.

Yawning, Amanda went downstairs and found the two of them in the living room surrounded by shopping bags and boxes. Julian was already dressed for work in a pair of khakis and a sweater. Grace wore a blue maternity nightgown while Niklos pulled and shredded paper from a sack beside her.

'What's all this?' Amanda asked.

Julian shrugged.

'You're right,' Grace said as she found a note in one bag. 'They're from Kyrian.' She read the note and laughed. 'All it says is, "Thanks for the Band-Aid."' She handed the note to Julian.

Julian let out an exaggerated breath as he read the note. 'It was customary in our time to bring gifts whenever you visited a friend. But I mean, damn, we didn't leave this many.' He ran a hand through his hair as he surveyed the mountain of gifts. 'Kyrian was always generous, but . . . damn,' he repeated. 'I guess he came back last night and dropped them off while we were sleeping.'

Amanda was amazed. It looked like Christmas . . . at the Rockefellers'. She watched as Grace pulled out dozens of toys for the twins. Dolls for Vanessa, building blocks for Niklos. A train and a toy horse.

Grace pulled a small box out of one bag. 'This one's for you,' she said, handing it to Julian.

Julian opened the box, then paled.

Grace looked over and gasped. 'It's your general's ring.'

They exchanged a stunned look.

'How did he get it?' Grace asked.

Amanda edged closer to take a look at the ring. Like Kyrian's, it had a sword of diamonds and emerald laurel leaves against a deep ruby background. 'It looks like the one Kyrian wears. Except his has a crown on it.'

Julian nodded. 'His is marked with a royal seal while mine is strictly military.'

Confused, Amanda looked up at him. 'Royal?'

'Kyrian was a prince,' he said simply. 'Sole heir to the throne of Thrace.'

Amanda's mouth dropped. 'The Romans crucified an heir? I didn't think they could do that.'

Julian's jaw ticced. 'Technically, they couldn't, but Kyrian's father disowned him the day he married Theone.'

'Why?' Amanda asked.

'She was a *hetaira*.' He saw the bemused scowl on her face and added, 'They were lower-class women who were trained to be entertainers and companions for wealthy men.'

'Ah,' she said, easily seeing how that could make his family angry. 'Was he looking for a companion when he met her?'

Julian shook his head. 'Kyrian met her at a friend's party and was enchanted by her. He swore it was love at first sight. All of us tried to tell him she was only after his wealth, but he refused to listen.'

Julian laughed bitterly. 'He did that a lot back then. His father adored him, but when Alkis found out Kyrian had broken his engagement to the Macedonian princess so that he could marry Theone, he was incensed. Alkis told him that a king couldn't rule with a whore by his side. They argued, and finally, Kyrian rode out of his father's palace, straight to Theone and married her within the hour. When Alkis found out, he told Kyrian he was dead to him.'

Her chest tightened at his words as sympathetic pain sliced through her heart. 'So, he gave up everything for her?'

Julian nodded grimly. 'The worst part is, Kyrian was never unfaithful to her. Neither one of you really appreciates what an accomplishment that was. In our day, there was no such thing as monogamy. It was completely unheard of for a man to be faithful to his wife, especially one of Kyrian's heritage and wealth. But once Kyrian married Theone, he never wanted anyone else. Never even looked at another woman.'

Julian's eyes flashed angrily. 'He really did live and die for her.'

Amanda's heart ached for Kyrian. The pain he must still have over it.

Grace handed Amanda three bags that held gift-wrapped boxes. 'These are for you.'

Amanda opened the largest box to find a thickly woven designer coatdress. She ran her hand over the soft, navy blue silk. She'd never felt anything like it. Looking in the bags, she found shoes, and other boxes marked with the Victoria's Secret logo. Blushing, she didn't dare open those around

Julian and Grace. Not unless she wanted to die of embarrassment.

'How did he know my size?' she asked as she checked the tags on the dress.

Julian shrugged.

Amanda paused as she found a note addressed to her. The handwriting was elegant and crisp.

Sorry about your sweater. Thanks for being such a good sport.

—Hunter

Amanda smiled, even though a tiny part of her was hurt by the fact he still refused to use his real name with her. No doubt it was his way of keeping a distance between them.

So be it. He had a right to his privacy. A right to live his dangerous immortal life without any kind of close entanglements with humans. If he wanted to remain Hunter to her, she would respect that.

Still, after all they had gone through last night . . .

In her heart, it didn't matter what name he used. She knew the truth of him.

Gathering her gifts, she headed back up the stairs to get ready for work, but what she really wanted to do was thank Hunter for his kindness.

After her shower, Amanda opened all her gifts to find a treasure of naughty lingerie. Hunter had bought her blue silk stockings with a matching garter belt. She'd never before owned or worn one, and it took her several minutes to figure out how to operate it. A matching silk bra and thong completed the outfit.

'Hmm . . .' For a man wanting to keep his distance, he certainly made some very personal choices for her. But then, he was nothing if not an enigma.

Amanda bit her lip as she reached for her dress. She felt so incredibly feminine and soft wearing her new lingerie, and a tiny shiver went up her spine as she thought about the fact that Hunter's hands had touched them.

It was incredibly erotic knowing his hand had probably traced the delicate lace of the thong that now rested intimately between her thighs. That his hand had touched inside the cup that cradled her breast.

How she wished to have him there to undress her. To touch her as intimately as the garments did.

She drew her breath in sharply between her teeth as she imagined the dark, hooded look on his face he would have as he took her into his arms and made love to her. Her breasts tingled and swelled at the very thought of it.

She picked up the dress from the bed and held it against her. For the merest instant, she thought she caught a whiff of Hunter's exotic scent. It sent stabs of desire through her.

As she dressed, the silk of the dress slid against her skin, reminding her of her dream. The feel of Hunter's hands on her body.

Oh, how she wished he were here. How she wished she could watch him unbutton her dress to discover the woman beneath it. But it would never happen. Kyrian was gone forever back to his dangerous life.

Her stabs of desire ended instantly, and were replaced by a profound pain in her heart. A pain that made no sense to her and yet it was there. Aching. Wanting. Needing.

Sighing, Amanda slid the shoes on and made her way downstairs where Julian was waiting to take her to work.

'I am so sorry about you and Cliff.'

Amanda looked up from her desk and counted to ten, Slowly. If one more person said that to her, she was going to go berserk, head down to Cliff's office, and carve him into little, bloody Cliff-kabob pieces.

He had told everyone in the office about their breakup and had arrogantly said she was too torn up by it to come in yesterday.

She could kill him!

'I'm fine, Tammy,' she said to their office manager with a forced smile.

'That's it,' Tammy said. 'You keep your spirits up.'

Amanda curled her lip as Tammy left. At least the day was over. Now she could go home and . . .

And dream of the tall, handsome man she'd never see again.

Why did that hurt more than the fact Cliff had broken up with her?

What was it about Hunter that made her miss him so . . . ?

But she knew. He was gorgeous and smart and heroic. He was mysterious and lethal. Better yet, he made her heart pound every time he flashed that dazzling smile at her.

And he was gone forever.

Depressed, she prepared to leave.

After putting her files in her briefcase, Amanda headed out of her office, to the elevator, and pushed the button to the lobby. She didn't want to keep Grace waiting outside with the twins. Besides, she was tired of the office.

This had been the longest day of her life.

Why had she ever wanted to be an accountant, anyway? Selena was right, her life was mind-shatteringly boring.

When the doors to the elevator opened to the glass-enclosed lobby, she stepped out and looked around. Even though it was dark outside, the parking-lot lights were so bright, she could tell Grace wasn't there yet. Damn! She was more than ready to go home.

Irritated, Amanda went to stand by the door.

As she shifted her briefcase, Cliff came out of the next elevator, surrounded by his friends.

Great, just great. Her day kept getting better and better.

Spotting her alone, Cliff preened like a peacock as he approached her. 'Is something wrong?' he asked as he stopped by her side.

'No. My ride isn't here yet,' she said curtly.

'Well, if you need a ride home . . .'

'I don't need anything from you, okay?' She headed out the doors to wait in the dark cold. Better to freeze in the winter chill than spend another minute around the last man on earth she wanted to see.

Cliff pulled her to a stop outside the building. The streetlights glinted dimly against his dark blond hair. 'Look, Mandy, there's no reason why we can't be friends.'

'Don't you dare be magnanimous about this after the stunt you pulled today. Who do you think you are, telling everyone about my family?'

'Oh, c'mon, Mandy—'

'Stop calling me Mandy when you know how much I hate it.'

He looked over his shoulder and she realized half the office was standing there, listening. 'Look, I'm not the one who had to stay home yesterday because I was so emotionally distraught over Saturday night.'

Her anger ignited. Emotionally distraught? Her?

Over *him*?

Amanda took a good look at him. And for the first time, she realized just what a weasel he was.

'Excuse me, but I wasn't home yesterday, either. In fact, you know where I was? I spent the entire day in the arms of a gorgeous blond god. I am so over you.'

He snorted. 'See, I knew it was just a matter of time before your family rubbed off on you. You're crazy like the rest of them. I bet you show up tomorrow decked out in black leather and talking about staking vampires.'

Never in her life had she wanted to slap anyone as much as she did him right then.

Why had she ever thought they were compatible? He was vile and rude. Worse, he was judgmental! Tabitha might be a nutcase, but she was her sister and no one not related to them had better insult her!

Suddenly, every flaw she had dismissed about Cliff came to the forefront. And to think she had spent a year of her life trying to please this jerk.

She was an idiot! And stupid, dumb . . .

Amanda felt the hairs on the back of her neck rise an instant before she heard the revving noise of a finely tuned engine in the distance.

Cliff turned his head toward the street and gaped.

She looked to see what had captured his attention and froze at the sight of a sleek black Lamborghini heading up the drive and stopping at the curb in front of them.

A smile broke across her face.

Surely not . . .

Her heart pounded as the door lifted and Hunter got out. Dressed in faded jeans, a gray and black V-neck sweater, and a black leather jacket, the man was drop-dead stunning.

And that deadly swagger of his made her weak in the knees.

'Oh baby,' she heard Tammy whisper as he came around the car.

Hunter stopped in front of Amanda and raked a hungry look over her body. 'Hi, luscious,' he said in that deep, evocative voice. 'Sorry I'm late.'

Before Amanda knew what he was doing, he pulled her into his arms and gave her a sizzling hot kiss. Her body burned in response to his tongue tasting hers as he fisted his hands against her back. Then, he dipped down and picked her up in his arms.

'Hunter!' she gasped as he carried her effortlessly toward the car.

He gave her that devilish tight-lipped smile. His midnight eyes were warm and alive with humor and hunger.

With the toe of his boot, he opened the passenger-side door and set her inside. He retrieved her briefcase and purse from the sidewalk where she had dropped them and handed them to her. Then, he turned and gave a knowing smile to Cliff. 'You really have to love a woman who lives to see you naked.'

The look on Cliff's face was priceless as Hunter closed the door, then gracefully walked over to the driver's side of the Lamborghini. In one fluid movement, he got inside the car and they were headed out of the lot.

A thousand emotions tore through Amanda. Gratitude, laughter, but most of all, happiness at seeing him again, especially after both Julian and her mind had convinced her that she never would.

She couldn't believe what he'd just done for her.

'What are you doing here?' she asked as he headed out of the parking lot.

'You have made me insane all day long,' he breathed. 'I could sense you in turmoil and pain, but I didn't know why. So, I called Grace and found out she was supposed to pick you up after work.'

'You still haven't told me why you're here.'

'I had to make sure you were okay.'

'Why?'

'I don't know. I just did.'

Warmed by his words, she toyed with her seat belt. 'Thank you for the clothes. And for what you did back there with Cliff.'

'My pleasure.'

Right now, it was all she could do not to reach out and touch him. To kiss her scrumptious champion.

Hunter shifted gears and headed away from the business district. 'I just have one question, why would a woman like you ever want to marry something like him?'

Amanda arched a brow. 'How did you—'

'I'm psychic, remember? Your true feelings for the "imbecilic jerk" are all over your mind at the moment.'

She cringed and wished she could shield her thoughts.

'I heard that, too,' Hunter teased, making her really wonder if he had.

'Is there anything I can do about your peeping into my head all the time? It really makes me uncomfortable.'

'If you like, I could relinquish that power over you.'

'Really? You can just drop a power anytime you want to?'

He snorted. 'Not exactly. The only power I can relinquish is the ability to see into someone's thoughts.'

'Once relinquished, can you get it back?'

'Yes, but it's not easy.'

'Then banish it, buster.'

Kyrian laughed and tried to focus on the road, but all he really noticed was the slit in her dress that bared a goodly portion of her silk-clad thigh. Worse, he knew what she wore beneath that dress. It was another image that had haunted him all day as he had tried to sleep.

The thought of her lush curves cupped by the garter belt and thong ... It made his mouth water. And all he wanted to do was slide his hand underneath that well-crafted hem until he felt the tiny strip of silk that shielded her most private place. Oh yeah, he could imagine moving it aside with his fingers until he had full access to her.

Or ripping that tiny, frail piece of silk away from her hips and burying himself deep inside her while her silk-clad legs wrapped around his.

Hunter shifted in his seat and remembered too late he should have bought himself a pair of baggy pants.

Touching her would be paradise.

If only paradise were a possibility for a creature like him. He tightened his grip on the gear shift as the thought tore through him.

'No woman will ever love you for anything other than your

money. Mark my words, boy. Men like us will never have that one basic need. The best you can hope for is a child to love you.'

His breath caught as the repressed memory flooded back to him with total clarity. And hard on its heels came the final words he'd spoken to his father.

'How could I ever love a heartless man like you? You mean nothing to me, old man. And you never will.'

The pain of it stole his breath. Words he'd spoken in anger that could never be retracted.

How could he have said them to the one person he had loved and respected most?

'So,' Amanda asked, distracting him, 'what happened with Desiderius last night? Did you get him?'

He shook his head to clear his thoughts and focus on the here and now. 'He went into a bolt-hole after our confrontation.'

'A what?'

'A bolt-hole. Sanctuary for the Daimons,' he explained. 'They're astral openings between dimensions. The Daimons can go in for a few days, but when the door opens, they have to leave again.'

Amanda was aghast at what he was describing. How could that be possible? 'I can't believe the powers that be would give the Daimons such a haven to escape justice.'

'They didn't. The Daimons discovered bolt-holes on their own.' He flashed a wicked smile at her. 'But I'm not complaining. It makes my job infinitely more interesting.'

'Well, just so long as you're not bored,' she said sarcastically. 'I would really hate for your job to *ever* get dull.'

He cast a glance at her that set her on fire. 'Chère, I have a feeling being bored around you would be an impossibility.'

His words struck a painful nerve in her. 'You're the only one who feels that way,' she said as she remembered her conversation with Selena. 'I've been told I tip the scales way into Boredom City.'

He stopped at a light and gave her a penetrating stare. 'I don't understand that comment since I've been nothing but amazed by you ever since the moment I woke up to you calling me "Mr. yummy leather guy."'

Her face on fire, she laughed at the memory.

'Besides,' Hunter continued, 'you can't blame people for saying that when you're the one who puts up the shield.'

'Excuse me?'

He shifted into first and headed down the street. 'It's true. You bury the part of you that craves excitement underneath a career guaranteed to one day replace tranquilizers. You wear drab colors and turtlenecks that hide the passion you keep harnessed.'

'I do not,' she said, bristling with indignation. 'You hardly know me well enough to say that. And you've only seen me in one outfit of *my* choosing.'

'True, but I know your type.'

'Yeah, right.' She mumbled her denial.

'And I've sampled your passion firsthand.'

Amanda's face flamed even more at that one. She couldn't deny the truth. However, it didn't mean she had to like the way he seemed to see straight into her heart.

'I think you're afraid of that other half of yourself,' he continued. 'You remind me of the ancient Greek nymph Lyta. She was two halves of one person. The two pieces warred with each other, making her – and anyone who knew her – miserable until one day a Greek soldier came upon the two halves and joined them. From that day forward she lived in harmony with herself and others.'

'What, are you saying I make you miserable?'

He laughed. 'No. I find you amusing, but I think you'd be much happier if you would accept your true nature and not try so hard to fight it.'

'This coming from a vampire who doesn't drink human blood? Tell me, aren't you fighting your nature, too?'

He smiled at that. 'Perhaps you're right. Perhaps I too would be happier if I turned the wild beast inside me loose.' He glanced askance at her. 'I wonder if you could handle that part of me.'

'Meaning?'

He didn't answer. 'Where do I need to take you? Julian's, your mother's, or your place?'

'Well, since you're headed toward my house, I suppose there. I live a few blocks over from Tulane.'

Kyrian did his best to stay focused on traffic, but over and over he kept seeing flashes of his dream in his mind. Damn, he couldn't remember the last time he'd had such a vivid dream. He'd awakened early in the morning, hard and aching for her. And he could have sworn her scent was on his pillows. His skin.

He'd spent the rest of the day trying his best to sleep, but it had been fitful at best. He wanted this woman with a need so profound that it made him shake just to be near her.

Never in his life had he wanted anything more than to do what she suggested: to turn himself loose on her and devour her.

If only he dared.

As soon as it had turned dark, he had gone hunting for *her*.

It was the first time in his Dark-Hunter life that he'd pursued a human.

'You know,' she said, that soft, lilting drawl sending an electric charge down his spine straight to his groin. 'You didn't have to pick me up. You could have just called the office and checked on me.'

Kyrian cleared his throat as he felt heat creep over his face. Dammit! She had him blushing? He hadn't blushed since he was a callow youth over two thousand one hundred and sixty years ago. 'I didn't have your number.'

'You could have gotten it from any phonebook or information. And of course, Grace has it.'

He felt her smiling at him.

'Heck, you could have probably picked it right out of my brain.' Her look turned devilish, suspicious. 'I bet you just wanted to see me again, didn't you?'

'No,' he said a little too quickly.

'Umm-hmmm.' Disbelief echoed in her tone. 'Why don't I believe that?'

'Probably because I never could lie worth a damn.'

They both laughed.

Amanda watched him while he drove. He had his small round sunglasses back on and looked more dashing than any man had a right to.

'Tell me something?' she asked.

He arched a brow expectantly, but didn't say anything as he kept looking straight ahead.

'Do you really like being a Dark-Hunter?'

He glanced at her and smiled a smile that actually showed his fangs. 'Tell me how many jobs are out there where you get to play hero every night. My pay is astronomical and I live forever. What is there *not* to love about this job?'

'But don't you ever get lonely?' she asked.

'You can be in a crowd and be lonely.'

'I guess so. Still . . .'

He looked sideways at her. 'Why don't you ask me what you want to know?'

'Since you can read my thoughts why don't you answer it?'

His smile widened hungrily like a wolf that had just found its next meal. 'Yes, sweeting, I think you're incredibly sexy. And I would love nothing more than to take you back to my place and make your toes curl.'

Heat consumed her face. 'I hate the way you do that. You're worse than Tabitha. Good Lord, do all Dark-Hunters have that kind of power?'

'No, baby, just me.' Then he added, 'Each one of us has our own set of abilities.'

'I have to say, I really wish you had a different one.'

'All right, love. For you, it's gone. No more mind reading.'

As Amanda watched him, she realized that even though he was blustery and macho, there was still a decent heart underneath it all. 'You're a good man, Hunter.'

'I'm a good vampire, you mean.'

'Yes, but you don't suck blood.'

One corner of his mouth quirked at that. 'So Julian told you that, did he?'

'Yes, he did. He said Dark-Hunters, unlike Apollites, were spared that part of Apollo's curse.'

'For the record,' he said ominously, 'we don't need blood to live, but there are some Dark-Hunters, called Feeders, who do drink it.' He shifted gears. 'I think you and Julian spent entirely too much time talking last night.'

'Perhaps.' But then Hunter had become her favorite topic. She'd kept poor Julian awake half the night asking things about Kyrian and the Dark-Hunters.

'Is it true Daimons only live twenty-seven years?'

He nodded. 'That's why they're so dangerous. Most Apollites will do *anything* to buy themselves another day.'

Which was why the Dark-Hunters, according to Julian, were soulless. It kept the Daimons from taking the most powerful souls of all. And the more powerful the soul the Daimons took, the longer they lived on borrowed time.

'Someone like you,' Kyrian said, 'is prime Daimon bait. When they take your soul, they take all your psychic powers with it.'

Amanda scoffed. 'I have no powers.'

'Whatever lie makes you happy.'

'It's not a lie,' she said defensively. 'I have no abilities whatsoever. At least not unless it involves crunching numbers.'

'All right, number-cruncher, I believe you.'

His words might say that, but his voice didn't. Narrowing her eyes on the stubborn man, she directed him toward her house.

As they drew near, she saw clouds of gray billowing smoke against the night sky. 'Is that a house fire?'

'Yeah, it looks like a big one, too.'

'Oh no,' she gasped as they got closer and she saw her house on fire.

But Hunter didn't stop there, he went down the street to Tabitha's where another blaze was roaring.

Tears filled her eyes as she fumbled for the door latch. 'Tabitha!' she screamed, terrified her sister might be inside the house.

Faster than she could blink, Hunter got out of the car and ran into the burning house.

Her heart hammering, Amanda scrambled from the car.

After kicking off her high heels, she ran to the porch, but didn't dare try to run inside with her bare feet.

'Hunter?' she called, trying to see through the flames. 'Tabitha!'

Please be okay, Tabby. Please still be at work!

As she waited for sight or sound of Kyrian, a motorcycle flew through Tabitha's yard and slid to a screeching halt next to the walkway.

Moving like lightning, a man pulled his black helmet off, tossed it to the ground, then ran toward the house so fast she couldn't even make out his features. He went around back at the same time Hunter came out the door, carrying Tabitha's roommate.

Amanda followed Hunter to the lawn where he laid Allison down on the grass.

'Tabitha isn't in there,' he said. He inclined his head to Allison's unconscious body. 'She inhaled a lot of smoke.' He scanned the street around them; several neighbors stood nearby, but none of them came forward. 'Where's the damned ambulance?' he snarled.

Terminator came running up to them. He licked Allison's face, then Amanda.

Patting the white and black dog, Amanda looked up to see the man who had arrived on the motorcycle. He was every bit as handsome as Hunter, yet there was something ethereal about him. Mystical.

His blond hair was cut short except for two long braids that fell from his left temple down to the middle of his chest. He wore a zipped-up black motorcycle jacket that had red and gold Celtic scrollwork painted all over it and a thick gold torc around his neck.

He knelt beside Hunter and passed his gloved hand over Allison's body about an inch above it.

'Her lungs are singed,' he said quietly.

'Can you help her, Talon?' Hunter asked.

Talon nodded. He removed his gloves, then placed his hands against Allison's ribs.

After a few seconds, Allison's breathing became slow and steady.

Talon met Amanda's gaze. She shivered as she saw that he had the exact same eyes as Kyrian.

There was something very unsettling and strange about this new Dark-Hunter.

He was stillness, she realized. Like some bottomless pond. There was a calm serenity to him that was both beguiling and frightening.

And it dawned on her that something really bad must be going on. Why else would another Dark-Hunter be here at the same time?

'Desiderius set the fires, didn't he?' she asked.

Both of the men shook their heads no.

Hunter looked to Talon. 'Your target?'

'My guess would be they've teamed up. Mine is trying to flush you out while yours is in hiding.'

At last the fire crews arrived. An EMT team took over with Allison while the three of them moved to stand to the side.

'Well, damn, Talon, this is new,' Hunter said as he raked a hand through his hair. 'It leaves us completely vulnerable.'

Talon inclined his head toward Tabitha's burning house. 'Yeah, I know. It sucks that they can combine their strengths while we can't.'

'Why can't you?' Amanda asked.

Talon turned to Hunter. 'How much does she know?'

'A lot more than she should.'

'Can we trust her?'

Hunter looked askance at her; the uncertainty in his eyes hurt her. She would never do anything to harm the man who had saved her life.

'I had a voice mail from Acheron this evening that said to give her whatever information she wanted.'

Talon frowned. 'That doesn't sound like T-Rex to me.'

'You know, Acheron really hates when you call him that.'

'Which is exactly why I use it. And I find it hard to believe T-Rex would give her carte blanche.'

'Yeah, but you know Acheron. There must be a purpose to it, and in his own, decrepit time, I'm sure he'll get around to enlightening us.'

'So tell me, then,' she prompted. 'Why can't you guys combine your strengths?'

'It's to keep us from cockfighting or using our powers against the humans or gods,' Hunter explained. 'As a result, as soon as we get together, we start draining each other's powers and dampening them. The longer we stay together, the weaker we become.'

Amanda gaped. 'That's not fair.'

'Life seldom is,' Talon said.

Hunter turned to Talon. 'Any idea where your target is?'

'I lost the tracking signal here. So I'm guessing there must be a bolt-hole close by.'

'Great,' Hunter said, 'just friggin' great.'

Talon concurred. 'I'm thinking we should call in Kattalakis to flush both of them out.'

'No,' Hunter said quickly. 'This isn't the typical Daimon we're dealing with and something tells me siccing a Were-Hunter on Desiderius would be like tossing a grenade on a keg of dynamite. The last thing we need is for him to grab one of their souls. Can you imagine the damage he could wreak with that?'

'Were-Hunter?' Amanda asked. 'Is that like a werewolf?'

Talon cleared his throat. 'Not exactly.'

'We protect the night,' Hunter said. 'Hence Dark-Hunter. And they . . .' He gave Talon a searching gaze.

Talon took up the explanation. 'Were-Hunters are . . .' He looked to Hunter as if seeking the right word, too.

Hunter shrugged. 'Sorcerers?'

'Works for me,' Talon said.

Well, it didn't work for Amanda, who had no idea what they were talking about. 'Sorcerers? Like Merlin?'

'Oh hell,' Talon muttered. He locked gazes with Hunter. 'You sure about what T-Rex said?'

Hunter unclipped his cell phone from his belt, scrolled through his saved messages, then handed it to Talon. 'Listen for yourself.'

Talon did. After a brief wait, he handed the phone back to Hunter and faced Amanda. 'All right, then, let's explain it this way. There are four basic kinds of Daimons or vampires: bloodsuckers, soulsuckers, energy/dreamsuckers, and slayers.'

Amanda nodded. That made sense to her. 'You guys are the slayers.'

Hunter snorted. 'What? Were you born with a remote in your hand?'

'No,' Talon corrected her while ignoring Hunter's sarcasm. 'Slayers are the nastiest of all the vampires because they don't want anything from their victims. They merely destroy for the sake of destruction. Not to mention, they are the strongest of the vampires.'

A shiver went down her spine. 'Is Desiderius one of them?'

Hunter shook his head negatively while Talon continued to explain it to her. 'To protect the world as we know it, there were three races of hunters created to police and destroy the Daimons. We are called "the Pyramid of Protection." Dark-Hunters pursue those who feed on human blood and souls. Dream-Hunters go after the energy- and dreamsuckers, and Were-Hunters stalk the slayers.'

Amanda frowned. 'I guess what I don't understand is why you don't have one group that does it all.'

'Because we can't,' Hunter said. 'If one person or group was strong enough to walk all four realms of existence, they would be able to enslave the world. Nothing and no one could stop them. And the gods would be greatly pissed.'

'What four realms?'

'Time, space, earth, and dreams,' Talon said.

Amanda let out a deep breath. 'Okay, now that is scary. Some of you guys walk through time?'

'And space and dreams.'

'Ah.' Amanda nodded. 'So Rod Serling was a Were-Hunter?'

They didn't look particularly amused.

'Okay,' she said. 'Bad attempt at humor. I'm just trying to figure all this out.'

Talon laughed. 'Don't. I've been trying to understand it all for over fifteen-hundred years and I'm still learning things.'

Hunter grimaced. 'You? Every time I think I have it pegged

someone like Desiderius comes along and completely alters the rules.'

'True,' Talon said with a short laugh. He rolled his shoulders. 'And speaking of scary things, I need to leave. My guides are fading even as we speak.'

Hunter faked a shiver. 'I hate when you commune with the dead in front of me.'

Talon gave him a droll, unamused stare. 'Are you the asshole who sent the "I See Dead People" T-shirt to me?'

Hunter laughed. 'That would be Wulf. I thought he was joking about it.'

'He wasn't. I got it three days ago. I am going to get him back for that.' Talon looked at Amanda. 'Keep her close.'

Hunter nodded.

Talon glanced over his shoulder at one of the fire crews. 'Is it just me or is the Apollite fireman behind me paying a little too much attention to us?'

'Yeah, I caught that, too. I think I should question him.'

'Not tonight. Secure her first. I'll interrogate the Apollite.'

Hunter cocked a brow in amusement. 'Don't you trust me?'

'Hell, no, Greek. I know you too well.' Talon headed back to his black Harley-Davidson and retrieved his helmet from the ground. 'I'll e-mail you later with the results.'

'E-mail?' Amanda asked. 'Should I ask?'

Hunter shrugged. 'We've come a long way. We used to pay runners to carry information between us.'

'Ah,' she said, then she noticed a solitary man standing across the street in the shadows. Instead of watching the fire, he seemed more concerned with Hunter and Talon.

Talon rejoined them.

'Question,' Amanda whispered as she studied the gorgeous blond shadow across the street. 'Are all Daimons blond?'

'Yes,' Hunter said. 'As are all Apollites.'

'Then how can you tell an Apollite from a Daimon?'

'Unless they have us blocked, we can sense them,' Talon said. 'But the only way for a human to tell is that when an Apollite crosses over, a black tattoo-looking symbol appears in the center of their chest where the human souls gather.'

'Ah,' she said again, still watching the man who was watching them. 'Tell me, do you think your targets are purposely putting the two of you together to drain your powers before they strike?'

The men gave her a puzzled look.

'Why do you say that?' Talon asked.

'Well, I'm no expert, but that guy behind you looks like a Daimon to me.'

The words barely left her lips before a flash of light hit Talon straight in his back and sent him to the ground.

Hunter cursed as he shoved her toward the car. He leapt over it, and ran straight at the Daimon who had attacked Talon. The two of them locked arms and fell to the ground in a fierce struggle.

Amanda made her way to Talon. He was covered in blood. Her heart pounding, she tried to help him up, but before she could another Daimon attacked them.

Reacting on instinct, she grabbed the Celtic dagger from Talon's belt and caught the Daimon across the chest. The man hissed, then shrank back.

Talon came to his feet. Grabbing his dagger from her hand, he sent it flying into the back of the Daimon as he fled. The Daimon vanished in a flash of light.

Hunter came out of the darkness, his breathing labored as he retrieved Talon's dagger from the ground, then returned it to the Celt. 'You all right?' he asked.

Talon grimaced as he flexed his arm. 'I've bled worse. You?'

'I've bled worse.'

Talon gave a curt nod to Amanda. 'Thanks for the assist.'

He rubbed the back of his shoulder with his hand. 'Secure your woman. We'll talk later.'

'All right.'

Amanda grimaced as she watched Talon sling his long leg over his motorcycle. His movements were slow and steady, and that alone was proof of the pain he must be in. 'Is he really okay?'

'We heal fast. Most wounds vanish in less than twenty-four hours.'

A siren sounded in the distance. Kyrian looked down the street where the lights were flashing. 'The police are coming. We need to head out before they arrive.'

'What about Allison?'

'She'll be all right once she wakes. Talon's touch can heal anything except death.'

'And Terminator?'

Hunter gave a whistle and opened the door to his car. He put Terminator in her seat. 'It'll be a tight squeeze, but I think we can manage.'

Amanda got in the car and adjusted Terminator in her lap as best she could. It wasn't until Hunter sat next to her that she saw the blood on his hand and arm. 'You're hurt?'

'Flesh wound on my forearm. It'll heal.'

'Jeez, Hunter. How can you stand doing what you do?'

He laughed. 'I've done it for so long, I honestly don't remember what life was like before I died.'

His words sent a chill over her. 'You're not really dead, are you? I'm kind of fuzzy on all this. You have a heartbeat and you bleed, not to mention that your skin is warm to the touch. That implies life, right?'

He started the car and headed down the street away from the police. 'Yes and no. Once a human dies, Artemis uses her powers to trap our souls. After the soul is contained, we are brought back to life.'

'How?'

'Since I was dead at the time, I have no idea. All I know is that I felt everything go black, then I woke up with powers and strengths I never knew before.'

Amanda thought about that as she stroked Terminator's ears and held the dog's head against her stomach to keep him quiet. 'Does that mean you can die again?'

'Yes.'

'Then what happens?'

Hunter took a deep breath. 'If we die before we reclaim our souls, we walk the earth eternally without powers. We are trapped as Shades in our corporeal bodies, but we have no real substance, which means we can't touch anything or be heard by anyone other than the Oracles. We crave food and water, but have no way to appease the hunger or thirst. It's a short trip from partial damnation to a total damnation.'

Amanda gaped at the horror of such a fate. She couldn't stand the thought of something like that happening to him. 'Does that happen even if a Daimon kills you?'

He nodded.

'That's not fair.'

He glanced over at her. 'What kind of life have you lived, little one, that everything seems to be a question of fair and unfair? Life and death just are. Fair has nothing to do with it.'

There was something very telling about that statement.

Just how many times had he suffered injustice to feel that way?

That thought was quickly followed by another. 'Julian said you can get your soul back.'

'In theory, yes.'

'In theory?' she asked as Terminator lifted his head to look at Hunter.

Hunter reached over and patted the dog's head until Terminator settled down again.

'We are given an out clause, but in the last two thousand

years, only a handful have succeeded. Most of the ones who tried ended up as Shades.'

Amanda frowned. How horrible. By his tone she could tell Hunter had resigned himself to the fact he would never even attempt it. Why?

'What would you have to do to get your soul back?'

He shrugged. 'I don't know. None of us do since the path to redemption is different for each Dark-Hunter. All I know is that when the moment of truth comes, the Dark-Hunter is either set free or damned for eternity.'

What Kyrian didn't tell her was that in order to be free, the Dark-Hunter must place his or her soul into the hands of someone who loved them. Having been burned so severely by his wife, he would never again trust anyone with his body or heart, never mind his immortal soul.

He had seen too many of his brethren trapped as Shades because the person they trusted had failed the test.

And in the back of his mind was the knowledge that no woman could ever love him. Not even a tiny bit. Let alone love him enough to set him free.

'Why did you agree to this life?' she asked.

He arched a brow. 'I told you, I have unlimited income and immortality. What's not to like?'

Still, Amanda didn't buy that. It was too easy and he didn't seem so superficial. 'You just don't seem the greedy sort to me.'

'No?'

'No. You're more grounded than that. More generous. Greedy people don't leave the kind of thoughtful gifts you left for Julian and his family.' She saw his jaw flex and she knew she'd pegged him perfectly. 'How did you get his ring back, anyway? Julian said he had sold it a few years ago.'

Hunter remained so quiet that she didn't think he would answer. Finally he spoke. 'I saved a man who was wearing it about a year ago from a Daimon attack. I couldn't believe my eyes when I saw it. I offered to buy it from him, but he let me have it for saving him.'

Amanda narrowed her eyes on him, wishing she could see into him the way he was able to see into her. 'Why did you want it?'

A veil fell over his face and she could tell just how much the topic bothered him.

'Well?' she prompted when it became evident he wouldn't answer.

'What do you want me to say?' he asked, his voice sharp and moody. 'That I had a moment of weakness when I saw it? That for an instant I felt the pang of being homesick? Yeah, I did. There, you now know the Dark-Hunter who has no soul has a heart. Are you happy?'

'I already knew you had a heart.'

He stopped at a red light and looked at her. A fierce frown creased his brow as if he were trying to figure her out.

'Believe it or not,' she continued, 'it shows in everything you do.'

He shook his head as if he couldn't believe her, then he looked back at the light. 'You know nothing about me.'

It was true and yet . . .

She was intrigued by him. Captivated. This man who wasn't a man called out to her and seduced her. All she had ever wanted in life was to be normal. To have a warm, loving home with children. A quiet life.

He could offer her none of that.

Yet when she looked at Kyrian, when she thought about him, the strangest things happened to her. It wasn't just lust.

There was something more.

Something undefinable that made her heart just a little happier, a little more tender. Something about being around him that made her soar.

She wondered if he felt that, too.

If he did, he kept it well hidden behind that tough exterior of his.

'Can I ask you something else?'

He sighed irritably. 'What the hell? You've asked me everything else.'

She disregarded his caustic words. 'Why did you become a Dark-Hunter?'

'I wanted vengeance at any cost.'

'Against Theone?'

This time there was no mistaking the pain on his face, the slight flaring of his nostrils. His hand was so tight on the steering wheel that she could see his knuckles protruding sharply against his skin.

Amanda took a deep breath as she stroked Terminator's ears. She couldn't fault him for wanting revenge against a woman who had been so cold-blooded as to turn him over to his enemies. 'Julian told me the gods give you twenty-four hours to exact revenge. What did you do to her?'

A tic started in his jaw and when he spoke, his tone was rife with anger. 'For her, I turned my back on my family. I gave up a kingdom and hurt the people who truly loved me. Because of Theone, the last words I spoke to my parents were hurtful and cruel. And when they delivered the news to my father that I had died, the grief of it drove him insane.

'He flung himself from the window of my childhood room onto the courtyard stones below, where he died a broken man, calling my name. My mother never spoke another word again until the day she died, and my youngest sister sheared her hair off to let the world know just how much she grieved.

'Without me to lead our forces, the Romans invaded and took over my homeland. My people lost their dignity, their nationality, and suffered for centuries under Roman occupation.'

Hunter glanced at her. 'Tell me, what would you have done to my wife?'

Tears welled in her eyes as she listened to the pain in his voice. How she ached for him. Dear Lord, no one deserved such punishment because they had mistakenly thought someone loved them.

But what struck her most was that there was no mention of what Theone had done to *him*. He was only sorry for what it had cost his family and country.

She wanted to touch him so badly that she wasn't sure how she refrained. Instead, she kept her attention on Terminator. Holding the dog the way she wanted to hold Hunter.

'I don't know,' she whispered past the stinging lump in her throat. 'I guess I would have killed her, too.'

'One would think that, anyway.'

A chill went up her spine. 'You didn't, did you?'

'No, I didn't. I had my hands wrapped around her neck and was about to end her life when she looked up at me with those weepy, fearful eyes. One minute I wanted to kill her and the next thing I knew, I wiped her tears away, kissed her trembling lips, and left her there in peace.'

He clenched his teeth. 'So, you see, you sit beside the greatest fool ever born. A man who traded his soul for a vengeance he never took.'

The *full* horror of his past hit her. After all he had suffered because of his wife, after all he had lost, he had still loved her. Greatly.

No matter what Theone had done to him, in the end he had forgiven her.

How could anyone have betrayed someone capable of so much love and loyalty?

Amanda couldn't fathom it. 'I'm sorry.'

'Don't be. As they say, I made my bed and I was crucified in it. I was the one who was blind and foolish. I realized too late that she had never, once, told me she loved me.'

The regret and sorrow in his voice tore at her. 'It wasn't

your fault,' she said as they headed into the Garden District. 'She had no right to betray you.'

'Theone never betrayed me. I betrayed myself.'

Good Lord, he was strong. She'd never known anyone who was so willing to shoulder such responsibility on his own shoulders. How she wished for a way to reach through that iron wall he kept around himself.

Her heart heavy, Amanda watched as they passed by the antebellum mansions where large oaks and pines were draped with tons of hanging Spanish moss.

Hunter pulled into a drive at the end of the street. Trees obscured her view to the house, and two large stone pedestals secured a heavy wrought-iron, twelve-foot-high gate. A tall redbrick wall surrounded the grounds and seemed to go on forever.

The place looked like a fortress.

He grabbed a remote out of the glove compartment, pressed the button, and the heavy gates swung wide.

Amanda's breath caught in her throat as he drove up the long, curving driveway and she could finally see where he lived.

Her jaw dropped. His house was huge! The neoclassical architecture was some of the best she'd seen. Tall columns ran all the way around the house and the upper balconies had ornate white iron scrollwork.

Hunter drove around to the back of the house and into a six-car garage where she saw he also owned a Mercedes, a Porsche, a vintage Jaguar, and a new Buick that looked strangely out of place.

Okay, the Lamborghini had clued her in that Hunter had a lot of money, but she'd never dreamed he lived like this.

Like royalty.

She winced at the thought. Of course he did, since that was what he was. A prince. A real-life prince of ancient Greece.

As the garage door closed behind them, Hunter helped her out of the car. He turned Terminator loose in his backyard, then led her inside the huge house. Her gaze tried to take in everything at once as they walked down a small hallway into a kitchen where a thin, elderly Hispanic woman was pulling something delectable out of the oven.

His kitchen was mammoth, with stainless-steel appliances and antiques lining the dark green walls and marble counter-tops.

'Rosa,' Hunter said in a chastising tone as he laid his keys down on the counter by the door. 'What are you doing here?'

Rosa jumped and patted her chest. 'Lord, *m'ijo*, you scared me out of ten years.'

'I'm going to scare you out of more than that if you don't do what the doctor said. You and I had an agreement. Do I have to call Miguel again?'

She narrowed her large brown eyes on him as she set her pan of chicken on the stove. 'Now, don't you go threatening me. I gave birth to that boy and I'm not about to let him go lecturing me on what I need to do. And that goes for you, too. I was minding my own home long before you were born. You hear me?'

'Yes, ma'am.'

Rosa paused as she caught sight of Amanda. A wide smile spread across her face. 'It's good to see you with a woman, *m'ijo.*'

Hunter passed a sheepish look to Amanda. He stepped over to the stove to inspect the food. 'This smells delicious, Rosa, *gracias.*'

Rosa smiled proudly as she watched him savor her work. 'I know; that's why I made it. I'm tired of seeing TV dinners and fast food bags in the garbage. You need to eat real food once in a while. That processed stuff will kill you.'

Hunter gave her a gentle, tight-lipped smile. 'I think I can handle it.'

Rosa snorted. 'We all think we can, and that's why I have to take heart medicine now.'

'And speaking of,' Hunter said, turning to her with a chiding stare, 'you are supposed to be home by now. You promised me.'

'I'm going. I put a salad for you in the refrigerator. There should be enough for both of you.'

Hunter took Rosa's coat from the back of the chair and helped her into it. 'You are taking tomorrow off.'

'But the gardener man, he comes.'

'Nick can let him in.'

'But—'

'Nick can handle it, Rosa.'

She patted his hand affectionately. 'You're a good boy, *m'ijo*. I'll see you Wednesday.'

'But not before noon.'

She smiled. 'Not before noon. Good night.'

'Adiós.'

'So,' Amanda teased as soon as they were alone. 'You actually do know how to be nice to someone.'

She saw the corners of his mouth twitch as he fought down the urge to smile at her. 'Only when the mood strikes me.'

He pulled a fork and knife out of a drawer and cut a small bite of chicken.

'Oh, this is good,' he said. He cut another piece. 'Here, you have to taste this.'

Before she realized what she was doing, Amanda allowed him to feed it to her. The spices filled her mouth at the same moment it dawned on her just how intimate a moment they were sharing.

By the look in his eyes, she would say it occurred to Hunter about two seconds after her.

'It's very good,' she said, stepping back from him.

Without another word, Hunter set about putting out plates

for them. As she watched him, the full horror of the night came crashing down on her.

'My house is gone,' she breathed. 'Completely gone.'

Kyrian set the plates aside as he felt her pain reaching out to him. It was a staggering wave of loss.

She looked up at him, her eyes swimming in grief. 'Why did he burn my house? Why?'

'At least you weren't in it.'

'But I could have been. Oh God, Hunter, Tabitha is normally home at that time! What if you hadn't been there? Allison would be dead. Tabitha could have been killed.' She sobbed as she looked about, panic-stricken. 'He's not going to stop until we're dead, is he?'

Without thinking, he pulled her into his arms and held her close. 'It's all right, Amanda, I've got you.' Kyrian froze as he realized what he'd done.

He'd used her name. And with it, he felt some inner barrier shatter.

Tears rolled down Amanda's cheeks. 'I know it's just a house, but all my things were in there. My favorite books, the blanket my grandmother crocheted for me before she died. Everything that was me was in there.'

'Not everything. You're still here.'

She wept against his chest. Kyrian closed his eyes and leaned his cheek against the top of her head as she clutched at him. It had been centuries since he'd comforted a woman. Centuries since he felt this way. And it shook him deeply.

'Can Desiderius get to Tabitha?'

'No,' he whispered against her hair, trying not to inhale the sweet rose scent. He failed and his body reacted instantly as his groin tightened and burned for her. 'As long as she stays in a private, human dwelling he can't get to her. It's one of the limitations Apollo put on them when he cursed them so that humans would have some protection.'

Amanda took a ragged breath and stepped away from him. 'I'm sorry,' she said, wiping the tears from her face.

He clenched his teeth as he noted the way her hand shook. He could kill Desiderius for hurting her like this.

'I don't normally cry in front of people.'

'Don't apologize,' he whispered, cupping her face in his hands. 'You're actually holding up a lot better than anyone should under the circumstances.'

She looked up at him from under those long, dark, wet eyelashes. His heart hammered at the vulnerability he saw. A vulnerability that touched him on a level he didn't want to think about.

He wanted her. Desperately.

He hadn't felt this in so long, no, he corrected himself, he had never felt this way about another woman, not even Theone. This wasn't just lust or love, he felt a bond with her. They were like two parts of a single heart.

But it was a lie. It had to be. He didn't believe in love anymore. Didn't believe in much of anything.

And yet . . .

She made him want to believe again. Made him long for things he had forgotten. Things like a tender hand in his hair when he woke up. The feel of a warm body lying next to him while he slept.

He was almost powerless before it.

His cell phone rang. Kyrian pulled it off his belt and answered it.

It was Talon.

'Is the woman with you?' Talon asked.

'Yes, why?'

'Because you have one big problem. The Apollite told me the fires were set from an electronic timer that was hidden inside the houses.'

Kyrian frowned, then went cold as he remembered something else Amanda had said to him yesterday. 'Amanda?' he asked, drawing her attention to him. 'Didn't you say Desiderius had captured you while you were inside Tabitha's house?'

She nodded. 'In her living room.'

His stomach settled into a cold knot of dread. 'Did you hear that?' he asked Talon.

Talon cursed. 'How is that possible?'

'Someone must have invited Desiderius in, which means there's a human running around working with or for him. My money says Tabitha wouldn't be so stupid.'

'Neither would Allison,' Amanda inserted. 'She knows to watch out for anyone suspicious.'

Kyrian thought it over. 'Any ideas?' he asked Talon.

'I don't know.'

'What does your guide say?'

'Ceara knows nothing. And the next tiny problem, my back isn't healing.'

If his stomach drew any tighter, it would make a diamond. 'Not healing how?'

'I was hit with an astral blast. The same kind a god wields.'

Kyrian went cold. 'I didn't kill a god, I killed a Daimon.'

'I know.'

Kyrian cursed under his breath. 'What have we gotten into?'

'Beats me, but until we know more, I suggest you sit tight on her. With the untapped powers she has, Desiderius will be after her full force. I'm sure by now he'd rather have her than her sister.'

Kyrian shifted the phone as he watched Amanda take a seat at his table. Gods, he couldn't stand the thought of her being hurt. The pain of the idea racked him. 'Do you need me to do anything for your back?'

'No. It just hurts like hell.'

Kyrian knew the feeling. His shoulder was still stinging from Aphrodite. 'I'm beginning to understand how Desiderius killed the last eight Dark-Hunters who went up against him.'

'Yeah,' Talon agreed. 'And I don't want us to be nine and ten.'

'Me, neither. Okay, I'll keep Amanda safe with me, but we still have the problem of her sister out there.'

'I can have Eric put a leash on Tabitha for the time being. You just make sure Amanda stays in touch with her or she's likely to make our lives even more difficult.'

'Will do.' Kyrian hung up and tossed his phone onto his counter.

'Is something wrong?' Amanda asked.

He laughed in spite of himself. 'I think a better question would be, is anything *not* wrong?'

'And that means?'

'It means your boring life has just ended. And for the next few days, it looks as if you're going to find out exactly how dangerous mine is.'

Chapter 7

'Oh no,' Amanda said, rising on her tiptoes to stand nose to nose with Kyrian. She arched a brow and dared him with her eyes to deny her words. As she spoke, each word was short and clipped. 'You are so wrong. I want my life back. I want it boring and I want it *long*.'

Her spirit amused him as she emphasized the last word. She was spectacular when riled and he wondered just how long he could keep that color high in her cheeks. The fire in those lush blue eyes.

Better still, as her breasts rose and fell with the weight of her conviction, images of other things that would make her breathless flashed though his mind.

He wanted to keep her breathless. Wanted to taste her passion fully.

Kyrian's lips itched to kiss hers, his hands ached to touch her body until she cried out with pleasure.

Gods, but this woman tempted him as he'd never been tempted before. And he had once loved temptation in a way that defied explanation. Over the centuries, he'd forgotten that small personality flaw, but ever since he had awakened with her next to him, he had been painfully reminded of the mortal man he used to be.

Slowly, bit by bit, he could feel her breaking down the barriers he had built around himself, the numbness. He had distanced himself from his feelings for centuries. And though he'd had mortals he cared about during that time, none of them had ever touched him as she did.

It was so strange to him.

Why her?

Why now? Now when he needed clarity of thought to deal with Desiderius.

The Fates were once again toying with him and he didn't like it in the least.

He could feel his blood pounding through his veins as he stared at those moist, full lips. Already he could taste them. Feel her. Dear gods, how he craved her.

She, alone, awoke the hungry beast in him. The part of him that wanted to growl and devour her body inch by slow, studied inch, all night long.

But Amanda was human and he could offer her nothing of himself. His soul and loyalty belonged to Artemis.

Besides, Amanda had a right to her dream of normality. Her dreams of a home and family with an average man.

After having his own dreams so cruelly, vengefully stripped from him, he refused to do that to her now.

She deserved to have her long, full, and boring life. Everyone deserved a chance to obtain their heart's wishes.

He swallowed the lump in his throat that ached with desire for her and knew, in that moment, he had to banish her from his thoughts.

She could never be his.

Her destiny was to return to a family who loved her and to find a mortal man who could . . .

He didn't finish that thought. It was too painful to even contemplate.

'For your sake,' he whispered, resisting the urge to touch her hair, 'I hope that's true, but I'm afraid with the raw, untapped powers you have and with the vampire-hunting Tabitha does, it's not going to be possible to live your boring life for the next few days.'

She broke eye contact with him. 'I have no powers.' Her voice was sharp, yet it lacked her earlier conviction.

He reached out and fingered her chin, seeking to comfort the trouble he saw on her face, the fears he didn't understand. Why wouldn't she acknowledge the gifts she had been given?

'You might not claim them, Amanda, but they're there. You have premonitions and telepathy. Projection and empathy. They're similar in many ways to Tabitha's, but your powers are a lot stronger than hers.'

The vivid sapphire returned to her eyes. 'You're lying to me.'

Her accusation surprised him. 'Why would I do that?'

She swallowed. 'I don't know. I just know that I have no powers.'

'Why are you so afraid of them?'

'Because . . .'

He cocked his head as her voice trailed off and she didn't finish her sentence.

'Because?' he prompted.

She looked up at him and the grief in her eyes took his breath. 'When I was fifteen,' she said in a hushed tone, 'I had a dream.' She blinked back tears as she gripped the counter beside her. 'I used to have a lot of them back then. They always came true. In this one, my best friend was killed in a car wreck. I saw her. I felt her panic and I heard the last thoughts that went through her mind before she died.'

Kyrian clenched his teeth at the pain he heard in her voice. Reaching out, he took her hand in his. Her icy fingers were shaking.

'When I saw her at school, I did everything I could to

keep her from going home that day with Bobby Thibideaux.
I even told her about my dream.' Tears fell again. 'She didn't
listen. She told me I was stupid and mean and jealous because
he liked her and not me.'

She shook her head as she relived that day. 'I wasn't
jealous, Hunter, I just didn't want her to die.'

He stroked her fingers, trying to warm her hand. 'I know,
Amanda.'

'She got in the car with me screaming at her to get out.
Everyone at school was staring at me, but I didn't care.
Tabitha pulled me away so they could leave and everyone
was laughing.'

She licked her dry lips. 'They weren't laughing the next
morning when they found out the two of them had died on
the way home. They called me a freak. For the next three
years, no one wanted to be near me. I was that weirdo girl
who saw things.'

Anger flashed in her eyes as she looked up at him. 'Tell
me, what good are these so-called powers when they make
people afraid of me? *Why can I see things I can't change?*
What good is that?'

Kyrian had no answer for her. All he could do was feel
her inner pain and turmoil.

'Don't you understand?' she continued. 'I don't want to
know the future when I can't stop it. I want to be normal,'
she insisted, her voice cracking on the last word. 'I don't
want to be like Talon or my grandmother and have dead
people talking to me. I don't want to know what you're
feeling. I just want to live my life like other people. Don't
you ever want that?'

Closing his eyes against the unfounded agony that clenched
his heart, Kyrian let go of the softness of her skin and stepped
back from her. 'It wouldn't matter if I did.'

Amanda started at the look on his face. She'd wounded
him somehow. 'I'm sorry, Hunter, I didn't mean—'

'It's okay,' he said slowly. He moved to stand by a chair and she watched the way he gripped the edge of it. Though he was trying hard to hide it, she could sense his pain.

'You're right,' he said at last. 'There are times when I do miss being able to feel the sunshine on my face. I miss so many things that I can't even begin to count them all. I have learned the best thing to do is to not torture myself with the memory of it.' He looked up at her and the heat in his eyes scorched her. 'But people like us have special gifts. We can't be normal.'

Amanda didn't want to hear that. Her heart couldn't take that news. 'Maybe you can't. But I can. I don't let myself feel those powers anymore. They are dead to me.'

He laughed bitterly. 'And you think I'm stubborn.'

'Hunter, please,' she said, hating the agony she heard in her tone. 'I just wish it were the day before yesterday. I wish I could wake up and have all this be a nightmare.'

In that moment, she felt something that scared her. It was just a quick twinge of the powers he referred to. And the sensation of it sliced through her as she heard his thoughts.

Wish you had never met me, you mean.

She moved toward him. 'Hunter . . .'

He dodged her touch and went to the counter where the phone was. He picked the phone up and handed it to her. 'Call Tabitha and tell her to stay at your mother's until Friday. She can come and go in the daytime, but after dark it is imperative that she stay indoors.'

'She won't like that.'

Aggravated fury smoldered in his midnight eyes. 'Then have your mother tie her down. We're not dealing with regular vampires here. These Daimons have unlocked some exceedingly dangerous powers, and until Talon and I figure out what we're dealing with, she needs to lie low.'

'Okay. I'll do my best.'

He nodded. 'While you talk to her, I'm going to change clothes.'

Amanda watched as he walked out of the kitchen, her heart heavy. She didn't want him to leave her even long enough to change. She felt a peculiar urge to follow after him and help him shed those clothes . . .

Instead, she dialed Tabitha's cell phone.

'Oh, thank God you're all right,' Tabitha said, her voice filled with tears. 'The police just told me about the houses and I knew it was past time for you to be home.'

Amanda's own eyes teared up, but she forced them back. Crying wouldn't accomplish anything. The houses were gone and all the tears in the world wouldn't bring them back. What she needed to focus on now was for all of them to survive Desiderius's wrath.

'How's Allison?' she asked, trying to distract herself from the fear.

'She's fine. Her mother's already at the hospital. I'm in the car on my way to see her even as we speak. No one knows what happened to Terminator.'

'I have him.'

Tabitha breathed a sigh of relief. 'Thank you, sis. I owe you big time. So, where are you now?'

It was the question Amanda dreaded answering. Tabitha was bound to go ballistic when she found out. 'I'd rather not say,' she hedged.

Silence.

It stretched for several minutes and all Amanda heard from the other end was the noise of traffic.

Tabitha was trying to read her.

Damn!

Tabitha said the word at the same moment Amanda thought it. 'You're with that vampire again, aren't you?'

Amanda cringed. How did someone tell her sister, the vampire hunter, that she had a crush on a vampire and planned on spending the night in his home?

There was no easy way around that one.

Sighing, she tried to think of some way to explain it. 'He's not a vampire . . . Exactly. He's more like you.'

'Uh-huh,' Tabitha said. 'Like me how? He has breasts? He has a boyfriend? Or he just likes to kill things?'

Amanda ground her teeth. 'Tabitha Lane Devereaux, don't be such a bitch. I know you don't like to kill things, either, and I don't want to play Twenty Questions with you. The guy who attacked me in your place is really scary, and not like the other scary things you play with. This is different. Hunter wants you to lie low and I agree.'

'Hunter? Is that the same bloodsucking ghoul who threatened your life to me earlier?'

'He didn't mean that.'

'Oh no? So you're willing to bet your life on it?'

'I'm willing to bet both our lives on it.'

'You're friggin' crazy, you know that?'

'Watch your mouth, little girl. Unlike you, I know what I'm doing. I trust Hunter. And this guy Desiderius is seriously evil. Like Hannibal Lecter evil.'

Amanda could just imagine Tabitha rolling her eyes as she made a disgusted snort. 'I'm not afraid of either one of them.'

'Maybe you need to learn a little fear. I for one am terrified.'

'Then why don't you come home where we can protect you?'

Because I want to stay with Hunter. Amanda didn't know where the thought came from. But there was no denying it. She felt safe and protected with him.

He had yet to offer to take her anywhere else. She had no doubt that if she asked, he would let her leave, and yet . . .

She didn't want to.

But she didn't dare tell Tabitha *that*. Things were bad enough between them, so she offered her sister the only excuse she could think of. 'I can't do that. Not while this thing is after me.'

Tabitha cursed again. 'How do I know this Hunter guy doesn't have you under some kind of mind spell?'

Amanda laughed at that as she recalled Hunter's words to her in the factory. 'Because, much like you, I'm too stubborn for it to work. Besides, he's a friend of Julian Alexander. You trust Julian and Grace, don't you?'

'Well, yeah. Of course.'

'Then trust their friend.'

'Okay,' Tabitha said reluctantly. 'But my trust is wearing thin. I want you safe.'

'And I want the same for you. Hunter said you're safe so long as it's daylight, but make sure you're in Mom's house once the sun sets and stay there. In fact, I don't think you should go to the hospital. You should probably go to Mom's right now.'

'Allison is my best friend, I need to see her.'

'What if you lead them to her? For all you know they're watching you already.'

Tabitha growled low in her throat. 'I don't like this. Not at all, but okay. You're right. I don't want to draw them to Allison. Mom can handle anything. I'll turn around at the next street and head to Mom's for the night. You call if you need me.'

'Will do.'

Amanda set the phone down and picked up her plate from the counter where Hunter had left it. She carried it to the small breakfast table that was set next to a large picture window. It looked out onto a beautiful, old-fashioned courtyard behind the house, complete with a rose trellis, Greek statuary, and sculpted shrubs. The area was lit by antique oil lamps that cast an eerie glow against the white stucco walls.

Amanda sat alone for several minutes until Hunter returned. He'd changed into a long-sleeved, black T-shirt that hugged his broad shoulders. He had the sleeves pulled up on his forearms and she saw the vicious cut that ran along his arm.

'Did the Daimon bite you or is that a knife wound?'

Hunter glanced at it as he sat down across from her. 'Bite wound.'

She went cold. 'You need that tended, don't you?'

'No, the entire wound will be gone by tomorrow.'

'Yeah, but don't such things turn you into a vampire?'

He laughed and gave her a droll stare. 'Technically, I already am a vampire. As for turning, it's impossible unless you're an Apollite.'

'So they can't bite humans and make them into vampires?'

'Bedtime story.'

She thought about that a minute. 'So where do all these misconceptions about vampires come from?'

He swallowed a bite of his food and took a drink. 'Scared villagers mostly. Since the day Atlantis was sucked into the ocean, Apollites and Daimons have been persecuted. At one time, all the Greek city-states knew about the Dark-Hunters and we were revered. But as time went on and the Dark-Hunters became more solitary, we were mostly forgotten except in myths and legends. Acheron and the others liked it that way. Ash even went so far as to collect and hide the ancient writings that referred to us.'

'Acheron?' she asked, cutting a piece of her chicken. 'You keep mentioning him. Who is he?'

'He was the first Dark-Hunter chosen by Artemis.'

'And he's still alive?'

'Oh yeah. I think he's in California this week.'

She arched a brow at him.

Hunter smiled. 'He travels to a new location every few days.'

'How? Why?'

He shrugged. 'I guess when you're eleven thousand years old, things get rather boring. As for how, he has a custom-built helicopter that can break the sound barrier.'

Amanda digested the news and tried to imagine what this

oldest Dark-Hunter must look like. For some reason, Yoda came to mind. Some small, gray-green-skinned ancient who walked around stooped over, spouting broken words of wisdom to the others.

'Have you ever met Acheron?' she asked.

Kyrian nodded. 'We all have. He trains all the new Dark-Hunters and in a way he is our unofficial leader. There's also the theory that he's the hit man the gods call in to execute us when we step over the line of propriety.'

She didn't like the sound of that at all. 'Step over how?'

'Preying on humans, for one. We have a Code of Conduct that has to be followed. No revealing of our powers before the masses, no association with Apollites or Daimons, et cetera.'

It was strangely comforting to know that they had such a thing, but also scary to think of one of these guys turning bad with the powers they possessed. 'If Dark-Hunters are forbidden to hurt each other and you drain one another's powers, how can Acheron be an executioner?'

'He doesn't drain our powers.' He took a drink of wine. 'Ash was the guinea pig Dark-Hunter. Since he was the first, the gods hadn't quite got the kinks out of the system. So he has some . . . peculiar, shall we say, side effects.'

Now she definitely pictured some mutant life-form. A little hunchback Dark-Hunter with a lisp.

'And just how many Dark-Hunters are there?' she asked.

'Thousands.'

Amanda's jaw went slack. 'Seriously?'

By the light in his eyes, she could see the answer.

'How often are new ones created?'

'Not often,' he said quietly. 'Most of us have been around for quite some time.'

'Wow,' she breathed. 'So if Acheron is the oldest, who is the youngest?'

Kyrian frowned as he thought about the answer. 'Offhand,

I would say Tristan, Diana, or Sundown, but I would have to check with Acheron on it.'

'Sundown? Nickname, or did his mother not like him very much?'

He laughed. 'He was a gunslinger and that was the name they used on his wanted posters. The authorities claimed he did his best work after dark.'

'Okay,' Amanda said slowly. Now she pictured some Wild Bill Hickok character. Complete with bowlegs and shaggy beard and a wad of tobacco in his cheek. 'I take it you Dark-Hunters weren't merchants or um . . .'

'Decent law-abiding folks?'

She smiled. 'I wasn't implying you were indecent, but you have the gist of what I was going for.'

Kyrian returned her smile. 'Indecent' would certainly describe the thoughts in his mind that concerned his guest. 'It takes a certain demeanor and passion to become a Dark-Hunter. Artemis doesn't want to waste her time or ours by picking someone incapable of hunting. I guess you could say we are all mad, bad, and immortal.'

Her smile widened, showing just a very tiny hint of a dimple in her right cheek. How odd he'd never noticed that before. 'Bad and immortal I will give you, but are you truly mad?'

'If by mad you mean insane, what then would you say?'

Her eyes flashed wickedly. 'That you are definitely mad. But you know, I think I like that about you. There's something to be said for unpredictability.'

Kyrian wasn't sure which of them was most surprised by her confession. She looked away quickly, her cheeks turning bright red.

She liked him . . . The words evoked a truly juvenile response inside him. He felt a peculiar urge to run tell someone, *'She likes me, she likes me.'*

Ye gods, what was that?

He was two thousand years old. *Long* past the age for such behavior.

Yet there was no denying the satisfaction and happiness he felt.

Awkward silence fell between them while they ate.

As she finished, Amanda did her best not to think about her house. All she'd lost. She would deal with that tomorrow. At the moment, she just wanted to get through the night.

'Tabitha is staying put,' she said as she watched Kyrian take his plate to the sink and rinse it off.

'Good.'

'You know,' she said quietly, 'you still haven't told me how you knew so much about my sister the night we met.'

He put the plate and silverware in the dishwasher. 'Talon and Tabitha have a mutual friend.'

Amanda's eyes widened at that. A mole . . . who would have thought. 'One of Tabitha's Zoo Crew?'

He nodded.

'Who?'

'Since this person spies for us, I'm not about to tell you who it is.'

She laughed at that, then narrowed her eyes, trying to divine who it was. 'I'll bet it's Gary.'

'I'm giving away nothing.'

It was intriguing, but not nearly as much as the Dark-Hunter before her. Sighing, Amanda continued to eat and glance around the richly appointed kitchen while Kyrian put the food away. There was a marble breakfast counter that vaguely resembled a Greek temple. It separated the table where she sat from the rest of the kitchen. Three tall bar stools were set before it.

Everything was crisp and clean and enormous.

'This is a big house for one person. How long have you lived here?'

'A little over a hundred years.'

She choked. 'Are you serious?'

'There's no need for me to move. I like New Orleans.'

She got up and took her plate to him. 'You put down some serious roots, don't you? Where did you live before here?'

'Paris for a while,' he said, putting the plate aside. 'Geneva. London, Barcelona, Hamburg, Athens. Before that I wandered around.'

She watched his face while he spoke. There was no tell-tale sign of his mood. He was hiding his feelings from her and she wondered if there was any way to draw him out. 'It sounds really lonely.'

'It was okay.' Still no facial clues.

'Did you ever have friends in any of those places?'

'No, not really. I've had a few Squires over the centuries, but for the most part, I prefer solitude.'

'Squires?' she asked. How strange. 'Like in the Middle Ages?'

'Something like that.' He looked at her, but didn't elaborate. 'What about you? Have you lived here all your life?'

'Born and raised. My mother's parents immigrated from Romania during the Depression and my father's people were backwoods Cajuns.'

He laughed at that. 'I've known a lot of those.'

'Living here for a hundred years, I'll bet you have.'

Amanda considered the life Hunter must have lived. All the centuries of solitude, of watching people he cared about die of old age while he never changed. It must have been hard for him.

But along with that, his life must have had a few really neat perks.

'What's it like knowing you're going to live forever?'

He shrugged. 'Honestly, I no longer think about it. Much like the rest of the world, I just get up, do my job, and go to bed.'

How simple he made it sound. Yet she sensed something

else from him. A deep-rooted sadness. Living without dreams must be excruciating. The human spirit needed goals to strive for, and killing Daimons just didn't seem like much of a goal to her.

She dropped her gaze to the counter and tried to imagine what Hunter had been like as a man. Julian had told her how they would drink after battle and how much Hunter had wanted children.

Worse, she remembered the way Hunter had looked holding Vanessa.

'Have you ever had any children?'

Intense pain flashed through his eyes for only an instant until he recovered his stoicism. 'No, Dark-Hunters are sterile.'

'So you *are* impotent.'

He gasped indignantly and looked at her. 'Hardly. I can have sex, I just can't procreate.'

'Oh.' She wrinkled her nose devilishly at him and tried to lighten the mood. 'That was really a nosy question. I'm sorry.'

'It's all right.'

Hunter started the dishwasher. 'Would you like a tour of the house?'

'House?' she asked, cocking a disbelieving brow. 'If this is a house, then I live in a two-room shanty.' Her breath caught as she remembered that she didn't live anywhere anymore. Clearing her throat, she pushed the thought aside. 'Yes,' she said quietly. 'I'd like to see it.'

Hunter led her through the doorway on her left, into a massively large living room. The walls, crown moldings, and medallions were absolutely gorgeous in their old-fashioned grace and elegance, but the furniture in the house was as modern as it could be.

The room was decorated for comfort, not to impress visitors. But then she imagined vampires didn't entertain guests too often.

A huge entertainment center lined one wall with a JVC

component system, big-screen TV, double-decker VCR and DVD player.

Though there were lamps all around, the room was lit only by candles from three ornate sconces.

'You don't like modern light bulbs, do you?' she asked as Hunter moved to light a candelabrum.

'No,' he said. 'They're too bright for my eyes.'

'Light hurts you?'

He nodded. 'Dark-Hunters have eyes made for darkness. Our pupils are larger than yours and they don't dilate the same way. As a result, our eyes let in a lot more light than human eyes.'

While he spoke, she noticed the floor-to-ceiling windows were covered with black shutters that would shield the house from daylight.

As she stepped around a black leather sofa, Amanda stopped dead in her tracks.

There was a coffin sitting in front of it.

'Is that . . .' She couldn't finish the sentence. Not while she held a gruesome image of Hunter lying asleep inside it every day.

Hunter glanced at it, then met her shocked gaze unblinkingly. 'Yes,' he said in a deadpan voice. 'Yes, it is. It's my . . . coffee table.'

He walked over to it, lifted the lid and pulled a remote out of it. 'For the TV if you want to watch it tomorrow.'

Amanda shook her head. Now that she noticed it, she saw there were all kinds of weird little vampire trinkets lying around. Miniature statues, small crossbows, even a vampire tarot deck on the mantel.

'Nick thinks it's funny,' Hunter said as she picked up the deck of tarot cards. 'Any time he finds something with a vampire in it or on it, he brings it here and leaves it for me to find.'

'Does it bother you?'

'No, he's a good kid most of the time.'

As he led her room by room through the old mansion, she began to get lost. 'Just how big is this place?' she asked as they entered a game room.

'There are twelve bedrooms and it's a little over seven thousand square feet.'

'Jeez, I've been inside smaller malls.'

He laughed.

An elaborate pool table was set in the middle of the game room, along with a collection of arcade games and a big-screen TV with an entire array of game consoles lined up on a low coffee table in front of it. But what she found most peculiar was a pair of baseball gloves and a baseball on a drop-leaf table in one corner of the room. Amanda went over to them.

'I toss the ball around with Nick some nights,' Hunter explained.

'Why?'

He shrugged. 'It clears my head when I'm trying to sort through things.'

'Nick doesn't mind?'

He laughed at that. 'Nick minds everything. I don't think I've ever asked him to do something he didn't complain about it.'

'Then why do you keep him around?'

'I'm a glutton for punishment.'

Now it was her turn to laugh. 'I would really like to meet this Nick.'

'No doubt you will tomorrow.'

'Really?'

He nodded. 'Anything you need, you tell him and he'll get it for you. If he offends you in any way, let me know and I'll kill him when I get up.'

There was a note in his voice that told her it might not be an empty threat.

Hunter opened the large French doors and led her into a glass-enclosed atrium. The ceiling was clear and showed a million stars flickering overhead and their shoes clicked idly on the tile floor.

'It's beautiful in here.'

'Thanks.'

She walked up to a large statue of three women in the center of the room. The piece was absolutely breathtaking. The youngest of them was lying on her side with a scroll while the other two were sitting with their backs to each other. One held a lyre while the other appeared to sing. But what amazed her most was the way they were painted. Each one looked real, and they bore a striking resemblance to Hunter.

'Is this from Greece?' she asked.

A painful look crossed his face as he nodded. 'They were my sisters.'

Her heart heavy, she studied them closely.

Hunter gently touched the arm of the one with a scroll. His brow furrowed ever so slightly while he gazed up at the life-sized statue of a girl in her late teens. The blue togalike dress matched her eyes perfectly.

'Althea was the youngest of us,' he said, his voice a full octave deeper. 'She was quiet and bashful, and she had a quaint stutter when she got nervous. Gods, how she hated it, but I thought it was sweet. Diana' – he indicated the one with a lyre who was dressed in red – 'was two years older than me and had the temperament of a shrew. My father said we were too much alike and that is why we could never get along. And Phaedra was a year younger than me and had the voice of an angel.'

Amanda looked up at the young woman dressed in yellow.

There was such delicate grace to his sisters. The sculptor had captured them as if they were in mid-movement. Even the folds of their clothes were realistic and dainty. She'd never seen such craftsmanship. They looked so real she half expected them to talk to her.

No wonder it hurt him so.

'You loved them a lot.'

He nodded.

'What happened to them?'

He moved away. 'They married and had long, happy lives. Diana named her first son after me.'

A tenuous smile curved her lips that the one who had fought most with him had done such a thing. It spoke a lot for their relationship. While she looked at the women, she remembered what he had said about Althea in the car. She had shorn off all her long, wavy blond hair when she learned her brother was gone. They must have loved him as much as he loved them.

'What did they think of your transition into a Dark-Hunter?'

He cleared his throat. 'They never knew. To them, I was dead.'

'Then how do you know so much about—'

'I could hear them while they lived. Feel them, the same way you can open your heart to Tabitha and tell when she's troubled.'

She stiffened at his words. 'How did you know about that?'

'I told you, I can feel your powers.'

A shiver went down her spine and she wondered if she could hide anything from him. 'You are one scary man.'

A strange light darkened his eyes. 'I'm not a man. I gave up my humanity when I crossed over.'

He said that, but she knew better. He might not have a soul, but the man had a good heart and was nothing if not humane. 'Why did you agree to be a Dark-Hunter even though you never took your revenge against Theone?'

'It seemed like a good idea at the time.'

With those few words something inside her melted. Perhaps

it was the loneliness in his voice, the calm acceptance of his fate in his eyes. She didn't know exactly what it was, but she knew she couldn't just walk back into her old life and forget this man.

She'd seen too much of his goodness. Too much of his pain. And God help her, the more she learned about him the more she wanted him.

Wanted him in a way that defied explanation. They'd barely met and yet there was something that bound them together.

Amanda looked up at those tormented eyes that studied her with hunger and heat. He was what her mother had called the 'missing half.' It was the term her mother used to describe her father. The term Selena used when she spoke of Bill.

For the first time in her life, Amanda understood. And having found it with him, she knew she couldn't just let it go.

Not without a fight.

Unaware of her thoughts, Hunter turned and led her back into the house. He showed her to a bedroom suite on the bottom floor. 'You can sleep in here. I'll bring you something more comfortable to wear.'

Amanda wandered around the lush bedroom. The king-sized plantation bed looked like something out of an old movie. The dark green paint would have made a small room look tiny, but in this massive space, it gave it a quaint, homey feel.

Hunter returned a few minutes later with a black T-shirt and a pair of sweatpants that would swallow her whole. 'Thanks,' she said, taking them from him.

He stood before her, his eyes searching hers.

To her surprise, he lifted his hand and ran his finger down her jaw. His short fingernail gently scraped her flesh, sending chills through her. She knew he wanted to kiss her, and she was amazed at how much she wanted his kiss.

But he didn't kiss her. He just stared at her with those dark hungry eyes.

Then he ran the pad of his thumb over her lips and she barely bit back a moan at how good he felt. How good he smelled. The air between them was rife with tension. With mutual desire and need. The force of it took her breath and made her both weak and strong at the same time.

Just when she was sure he'd kiss her, he pulled away. 'Good night, Amanda.'

Her heart pounding, she watched him go.

Kyrian cursed himself with every step he took toward his office. He should have kissed her. He should have . . .

No, he'd done the right thing. There would never be anything between them. Dark-Hunters could take women for a few nights, but they were forbidden to become seriously involved with them. The danger was just too great.

It made the women vulnerable to the Daimons, and it made the Dark-Hunter weak. Made him cautious, and in this line of work, caution got you killed.

It had never bothered him before.

Tonight, the pain was almost enough to break him.

He hated these feelings inside him. Hated needing her. He'd long ago banished his emotions and he preferred to live that way; in a safe cocoon free of turmoil.

'I have to get her out of my mind.' He entered his office and went to log on to the Dark-Hunter.com Web site.

His instant messenger program was blinking with incoming messages and as always, his e-mail was filled with notes from other Dark-Hunters. Technology was a wonderful thing. Being able to communicate with each other was a true godsend. It made dealing with the long nights more bearable and it allowed them to exchange important information.

Kyrian sat in his black leather chair and double-clicked the flashing icon. It was a note from Acheron.

Nick called, said Desiderius had kicked your butt. You okay?

Kyrian clenched his teeth, then typed in a response. 'I'm going to kill him for that. I'm fine. Desiderius is down a bolt-hole. What do you know of him?'

He's the one who took out Cromley a few years back, so you're dealing with a major power. I talked with Cromley's Squire and he said Desiderius took a tremendous amount of pleasure from messing with Cromley's head. D. ended up killing Cromley in a manner best not mentioned. Personally, I wish D. would come after me, I need a good dance partner. My Daimons have lame legs.

Kyrian laughed at Ash's dry wit. The man truly had no patience for lame Daimons. 'Talon said they're using astral blasts. Have you ever come across that?'

In eleven thousand years, I can honestly say . . . hell, no. This is a first. I've called in the Oracles and they are communing with the Fates. But you know how they are. I'm sure it'll come back as 'When the sky is green, and the earth turns black, the Daimons will give you lots of flack. To kill the great awful one you seek, you'll have to find something unique.' Or some bullshit like that. I really hate Oracles. If I wanted to play mind games, I'd buy a Rubik's Cube.

'I don't know, Ash, you're pretty good at that. Sure you don't want to take up an Oracle position?'

Picture this, General, my middle finger is extended all the way up, and aimed right at you. Now let me work. I have Daimons to track, Dark-Hunters to antagonize, and women to seduce. Talk to you later.

No longer in the mood to talk, Kyrian logged off the Dark-Hunter site. He opened his e-mail, but he didn't really want to read it, either.

What he wanted was beyond his ability to claim.

Against his will, he wandered down the hallway, then down the stairs.

Before he realized what he was doing, he found himself outside Amanda's room. He pressed his hand against the dark wood door and splayed his fingers. Closing his eyes, he could see her sitting in bed, her long legs bare beneath his T-shirt.

Fire pounded through his blood. He could feel her pain at the loss of her house. Feel her fear as she thought of Desiderius hurting her sister, and her worry over Tabitha's roommate.

Worse, he could sense the tears she was holding back. She was so strong. So capable. He'd never known a woman like her before.

His dream from the morning tore through him. He could still feel her in his arms.

'I want you.'

He'd give anything to hear her say those words for real. To see her look at him as if she could devour him.

Right now, the only thing he wanted to do was to kick open the door and make love to her. To have her touch him Hold him.

Welcome him.

But it wasn't meant to be.

His heart heavy, he forced himself to leave her.

He had work to do.

Amanda glanced at the clock. Twelve-thirty. Normally she would be fast asleep by now. But to Hunter the night would still be young.

She wondered what he did during the wee hours. Surely he didn't kill Daimons every night. There weren't that many of them, were there?

Before she realized what she was doing, she got out of bed and wandered through the enormous house. She didn't know where Hunter was. He hadn't bothered to show her his room while he had given her the tour.

But her instinct told her his room would be upstairs. Probably as far away from hers as possible.

She was halfway up the stairs when she heard something odd outside. It was a strange whooshing noise.

Backtracking, she found her way to the dark game room. There was no light, but the moon and stars were so bright outside that she could see a shadowy figure in the atrium. Her first impulse was to call for Hunter; she paused.

There was something very familiar about that figure. Walking closer to the French doors, she recognized Terminator and Hunter. Hunter was dressed in a T-shirt and sweatpants. He was tossing a baseball into a net-covered frame that bounced it back to him.

As soon as he threw the ball, Terminator would give chase, then the dog would bound back to Hunter.

She smiled at the sight. Hunter patted Terminator, then returned to tossing the ball.

She started to leave, but couldn't. Instead, she cracked open the door.

Hunter turned instantly. The forgotten ball rebounded and caught him on the head. He hissed as he rubbed his head and Terminator chased after the baseball.

'Did you need something?' he asked, his voice sharp.

I need you to kiss me.

She swallowed. 'I just didn't know where you were.'

'Now you do.'

The ice was back in his voice. This wasn't the Hunter who had been with her a short time ago, this was the Dark-Hunter who had awakened in the factory with her. Guarded. Distant.

And it cut through to her heart. It wasn't just the lump on his head from the baseball making him snappish; his old barriers were back in place. He was pushing her away.

Taking the hint, she nodded. 'Yeah, well, good night.'

Kyrian watched her leave. He'd wounded her. He could sense it and he hated himself for it.

Call her back.

But to what purpose?

There could never be anything between them. Not even friendship.

Grinding his teeth, he went back to his pitching. As he worked out, he tried to focus on Desiderius. Tried to will the Daimon into his grasp.

It was useless.

Amanda was still with him. It was her face he saw when he closed his eyes. Her scent that permeated his senses.

If he didn't banish her from his thoughts, he would get himself killed. And if he died, Desiderius would go after her.

Growling, he threw the ball against the net. He twirled around to catch it on the rebound, but before his hand made contact, a fierce pain slashed through his skull.

Kyrian cursed. He put the heel of his hand over his right eye, and as he struggled with the pain, an image tore through him.

It was Desiderius.

As the image sharpened, he froze. With amazing clarity, he saw Desiderius kill him.

And he heard Amanda weeping.

Chapter 8

After Amanda fell asleep, her dreams drifted for a time like a bizarre, twisting kaleidoscope coalescing without shape or form. Foreign images, people, and places twirled and tumbled in her mind until her head swam from them.

After a while, they became more focused and she could see them clearly. Unknown people greeted her as she walked past them.

It seemed so incredibly real; like a forgotten memory more than a dream. Even though she'd never seen these people before, she knew them by name. Knew things about them only a friend would know.

She heard the sound of men laughing and celebrating. Felt a strange mixture of joy and sadness as she became aware of a faded red tent filled with soldiers wearing ancient armor.

'You were brilliant,' an older soldier said, clapping her on the back. She recognized him as her second in command. A man she relied on and one who worshiped her. Dimitri had always looked to her for guidance and strength.

He had a fresh, open wound down the left side of his face, but his old gray eyes sparkled. Though his armor was covered in blood, he appeared remarkably unhurt. 'It's a pity Julian wasn't here to see this victory. He would have been proud of you today, Commander. I can guarantee all of Rome is weeping this night.'

At that moment, she realized the dream wasn't about her. She was Kyrian . . .

Kyrian's face was smudged with sweat, dirt, and blood, his long, leather-bound hair tousled. He had three long, thin braids that fell from his left temple down to the middle of his chest. The man was simply gorgeous and completely human.

His dark green eyes shimmered from victory and he had the carriage of a man who had no equal. Of a man destined for greatness.

Kyrian raised the goblet of wine in his hand and addressed the men in his tent. 'I declare this victory for Julian of Macedon. Wherever he is, I know he's laughing at Scipio's defeat.'

A loud cheer roared from the men.

Kyrian took a drink, then looked to the older soldier beside him. 'It's a pity Valerius wasn't there with Scipio. I was looking forward to facing him, too. But no matter.' He lifted his voice so that all the men gathered inside could hear him. 'Tomorrow, we march on Rome herself and we'll bring that bitch to her knees.'

The men shouted their agreement.

'On the battlefield, with a sword in your hand, you are invincible,' the old man said in an awed tone. 'By this time tomorrow, you will be ruler of the known world.'

Kyrian shook his head. 'Andriscus will be ruler of Rome tomorrow. Not I.'

The old man looked aghast, then he leaned close to Kyrian's neck and lowered his tone so that only Kyrian could hear him. 'There are those who think he is weak. Those who would support you if you decided—'

'No, Dimitri,' Kyrian said, cutting him off gently. 'I

appreciate the thought, but I swore to lead his army for
Andriscus and that I shall do until the day I die. I will
never betray him.'

The look on Dimitri's face showed his confusion. He
wasn't sure if he should applaud Kyrian's loyalty or curse
it. 'You're the only man I know who would turn down the
opportunity to rule the world.'

Kyrian laughed. 'Kingdoms and empires don't bring happiness, Dimitri. Only the love of a good woman and children
do that.'

'And conquest,' Dimitri added.

Kyrian smiled even wider. 'Tonight, at least, that appears
to be true.'

'Commander?'

Kyrian turned toward the voice behind him to see a man
cutting a swath through the men in the tent.

The soldier held out a sealed letter. 'A courier brought
this. It was discovered on a Roman messenger earlier today.'

Taking it from him, Kyrian saw the seal of Valerius the
Younger on the outside. Curious, he opened the vellum and
read it, and with every word, his panic swelled. His heart
beat faster. 'My horse!' he shouted, running out of the
crowded tent. 'Saddle my horse.'

'Commander?'

He turned to his second in command who had followed
him outside. A worried frown creased his tired old brow.
'Dimitri, you're in charge until I return. Pull the army back
into the hills, away from the Romans until you hear from
me. If I'm not back in a week, then lead the men to Punjara
and combine forces with Jason.'

'Are you sure?'

'Yes.'

A youth came forward with his black stallion. His heart
hammering, Kyrian swung himself up into the saddle.

'Where are you off to?' Dimitri asked.

'Valerius is riding to my villa. I'm going to head him off.'

Dimitri grabbed the horse's bridle, horrified. 'You can't go alone to meet him.'

'I have no time to wait for you. My wife is in danger. I will not hesitate.' Kyrian wheeled his horse about and spurred it through the camp.

Amanda twisted in bed as she felt Kyrian's rising panic. His need to protect his wife at any cost. The days ran together as he rode furiously, changing horses every time he happened upon a village. He never stopped to rest or eat. He was like a demon possessed, with only one thought on his mind. *Theone. Theone. Theone.*

He reached his home in the middle of the night. Weary and terrified, he leapt from his horse and pounded on the door for admittance.

An old man pulled open the heavy wooden door. 'Your Highness?' he asked in disbelief.

Kyrian pushed past the man, his gaze sweeping his grand foyer looking for signs of hostility. Nothing out of the ordinary met his fearful gaze. Still, he wasn't comforted. Not yet. He would not be calm until he saw her with his own eyes. 'Where's my wife?'

The old servant looked confused by the question. His mouth opened and closed like a fish. Finally, he spoke. 'In her bed, Highness.'

Starving, exhausted, and weak, Kyrian ran down the long, columned corridor toward the back of the house.

'Theone?' he called as he ran, desperate to see her.

A door at the end of the hallway opened. An incredibly beautiful and petite blond woman came to stand in the hallway. She closed the door behind her and swept a chiding glance over Kyrian's dishevelment.

She was alive and unharmed. And she was the most beautiful vision his adoring eyes had ever beheld.

Her long, golden hair was tousled, her cheeks bright pink.

She clutched a very thin white sheet over her nude body. 'Kyrian?' she asked sharply.

Relief rushed through him and tears filled his eyes. She was alive! Thank the gods. Blinking the tears away, he swept her up into his arms and held her close. Never had he been more grateful to the Fates for their mercy.

'Kyrian,' she snapped, bristling under his touch. 'Put me down. You smell so bad I can barely breathe. Have you any idea how late it is?'

'Aye,' he said through the tight knot in his throat as joy pounded through him. He set her down and cupped her face in his hands. He was so tired he could hardly stand or think, but he wouldn't sleep. Not until she was safe. 'And I must get you away from here. Get dressed.'

She frowned. 'Take me where?'

'To Thrace.'

'Thrace?' she asked incredulously. 'Are you mad?'

'No. I've received word that the Romans are headed this way. I'm taking you to my father for safekeeping. Now hurry!'

She didn't. Instead, her face darkened dangerously as fury snapped in her gray eyes. 'Your father? You've not spoken to him in *seven* years. What makes you think he'd shelter me?'

'My father will forgive me if I ask it.'

'Your father will throw us both out. He made his proclamation quite public. I've been embarrassed enough in my lifetime, I don't need to hear him call me a whore to my face. Besides, I don't want to leave my villa. I like it here.'

Kyrian disregarded her words. 'My father loves me and will do as I ask. You'll see. Now dress.'

She looked past his shoulder. 'Polydus?' she said to the old servant who had been waiting all that time behind Kyrian. 'Have a bath prepared for your master and bring him food and wine.'

'Theone—'

She stopped Kyrian's words by placing a hand on his lips. 'Hush, my lord. It's the middle of the night. You look dreadful and you smell even worse. Let us clean you, feed you, and put you to sleep, and then in the morning, we can discuss what needs be done to see me safe.'

'But the Romans—'

'Did you see any on your way here?'

'Well . . . no.'

'Then there can't be any danger at the moment, now can there?'

Too weary to argue, he conceded. 'I suppose not.'

'Then come.' She took him by the hand and led him to a small room off the main corridor.

The next thing Amanda saw was a room lit by a small fire and candles. Kyrian was leaning back in a gilded tub while Theone bathed him.

He captured her hand in his and held it to his whiskered cheek. 'You've no idea how much I've missed you. Your touch soothes me like nothing else.'

She smiled a smile that didn't quite reach her eyes and handed him a cup of wine. 'I heard you took Thessaly from the Romans.'

'Aye. Valerius was incensed. I can't wait until I march on Rome. I will have her yet, mark my words.'

Kyrian drained the cup, then set it aside. His body burning, he reached for his wife and pulled her into the tub with him.

'Kyrian!' she gasped.

'Shh,' he breathed against her lips. 'I would have a kiss from you.'

She acquiesced, but there was a coldness to her. He could feel it.

'What is wrong, my love?' he asked, pulling back. 'You seem so distant tonight. As though your thoughts are some-where else.'

Her face softened as she straddled his waist and took him into her body. 'I am not distant. I am tired.'

He smiled, then groaned as she moved against him. 'Forgive me for waking you. I just wanted to know you were safe. I couldn't live if anything ever happened to you.' He cupped her face in his hands and stroked her cheeks with his thumbs. 'I will always love you, Theone. You are the very air I breathe.'

Kissing her lips, he savored her taste.

She seemed to relax some in his arms as she slowly rode him. All the while her gaze watched him as if she were waiting for something . . .

As soon as he climaxed, Kyrian leaned back in the tub to watch her. He was as weak as a newborn whelp. But he was home, and his wife was his strength. His haven.

No sooner had that thought crossed his mind than a strange buzzing started in his head. A wave of dizziness swept through him.

And in an instant, he knew what she'd done. 'Poison?' he gasped.

Theone scrambled off him and left the tub. Hurriedly, she wrapped a towel around herself. 'No.'

Kyrian tried to get out of the tub, but another wave of dizziness gripped him. He fell back into the water. He couldn't breathe as thoughts wandered randomly through his drugged mind.

But foremost in his mind was the very treachery of the woman he loved. A woman he had given the world to.

'Theone, what have you done to me?'

She lifted her chin as she watched him coldly. 'I'm doing what you can't. I'm protecting myself. Rome is the future, Kyrian. Not Andriscus. He will never live to ascend to the Macedonian throne.'

Darkness fell.

Amanda groaned as she felt a severe pain lance through

her skull. When the light returned, she found Kyrian lying naked against a cold stone slab that was tilted at a forty-five-degree angle. His arms and legs had been secured with ropes to winches.

He glanced around the medium-sized room to an old table set in one corner, the top of which was covered with all manner of torture instruments. A tall, black-haired man stood looking over the table's offerings, his back to Kyrian.

Kyrian felt so alone and betrayed. So completely defenseless.

It was a terrifying sensation for someone who had never known vulnerability.

The room was stifling hot from the fire in the hearth. Somehow, Amanda knew it was early summer outside. The windows were open and a gentle Mediterranean breeze blew across the room, carrying the scent of sea, flowers, and olives. Kyrian heard laughter from outside and his stomach knotted.

It was too beautiful a day to die . . .

The man at the table cocked his head. Suddenly, he turned and pinned a menacing glare on Kyrian. Though the man was incredibly handsome, there was a cold sneer on his face that robbed him of his appeal. The man had the cruel, glittering eyes of a viper. They were soulless, calculating, and completely lacking in compassion.

'Kyrian of Thrace.' He smiled evilly. 'At last we meet. Though I'm sure this isn't quite what you had planned, is it?'

'Valerius,' he snarled as soon as he saw the banner on the wall over the man's shoulder. He would know that eagle emblem anywhere.

The Roman's smile widened as he crossed the room. There was no respect on Valerius's face. Only smug satisfaction.

Without another word, Valerius turned the winch that held the ropes to Kyrian's limbs. The ropes tightened, pulling at

Kyrian's muscles, tearing ligaments and popping his bones from their joints.

Kyrian clenched his eyes tight and ground his teeth at the agony that whipped through his body.

Tightening the winch even more, Valerius laughed. 'Good, you're strong. I hate to torture little boys who whimper and cry right away. It takes all the fun out of it.'

Kyrian said nothing.

After locking the winch into place to keep Kyrian's body painfully stretched, Valerius walked over to the table where a number of weapons and tools rested. He hefted a heavy iron mallet in his hands. 'Since you are new to my company, allow me to educate you on how Rome deals with her enemies . . .'

He sauntered back to Kyrian, offering Kyrian a goading smirk. 'First, we crush your knees. This way, I know you won't be tempted to leave my hospitality until I'm ready for you to.'

Valerius brought the mallet down over Kyrian's left knee, shattering the joint instantly. Unimaginable pain ripped through him. Biting his lip to keep from crying out, Kyrian gripped the ropes binding his hands. He could feel the warm blood from his cut wrists trail down his forearms.

Once he'd shattered Kyrian's other knee, Valerius picked up a hot iron from the hearth and brought it over to him. 'I only have one question. Where is your army?'

Kyrian narrowed his eyes, but said nothing.

Valerius laid the hot iron against his inner thigh.

Amanda lost track of the wounds as Valerius tortured Kyrian. Hour after hour, day after day with resolute vigor.

She'd never known a person could suffer so much and continue to live.

She gasped as water was thrown into Kyrian's face.

'Don't think you can pass out to escape me. Nor starve until I will it.'

Valerius grabbed Kyrian's hair and pulled his head

viciously, then poured broth down his throat. Kyrian hissed as the salty liquid stung the cuts on his face, his lips. He choked on the broth, but still Valerius poured it into his mouth.

'Drink, damn you,' Valerius snarled. 'Drink!'

Kyrian passed out again, and again the cold water brought him back awake.

Days and nights blended together as time went by while Valerius assaulted him, again and again. Always asking the same question. 'Where is your army?'

Kyrian never uttered a single word. Never once cried out. He kept his jaw so tightly locked that Valerius had to pry it open to force-feed him.

'Commander Valerius,' a soldier said as he came into the room while Valerius again turned the winches against Kyrian's arms and legs. 'Forgive my interruption, my lord, but there's an emissary from Thrace wanting an audience with you.'

Kyrian's heart stopped beating. For the first time in weeks, a sliver of hope swept through him, overwhelming him with joy.

His father . . .

Valerius arched a curious brow at his underling. 'This should be quite entertaining. By all means, show him in.'

The soldier vanished.

A few minutes later, an older, well-dressed man entered the room with two Roman soldiers trailing him. The man looked so much like Kyrian that for a moment, Amanda thought it was his father.

As soon as the man was close enough to recognize Kyrian's bloody, misshapen form, he gasped.

His dignity forgotten, his uncle ran to his side. 'Kyrian?' he breathed in disbelief, gingerly touching Kyrian's broken arm. His blue eyes were filled with pain and concern. 'Dear Zeus, what have they done to you?'

She felt Kyrian's tremendous shame and grief at seeing his uncle's sorrow. She felt the need inside Kyrian to relieve the guilt that swam in Zetes's eyes and to beg him to ask his father to forgive him.

When Kyrian opened his mouth to speak, all that came out was a hoarse croak. He hurt so badly that his unclenched teeth chattered from the weight of his physical suffering.

Kyrian's throat was so sore and parched that he choked, but by sheer force of will, he finally spoke through trembling lips. 'Uncle.'

'Can it be, he can actually speak?' Valerius asked, joining them. 'He's said nothing in four weeks. Nothing other than this . . .'

Again he laid a hot brand to Kyrian's thigh.

Clenching his teeth, Kyrian jerked and hissed.

'Cease!' Zetes cried, pushing Valerius away from his nephew.

He tenderly cupped Kyrian's bruised face in his hands. Tears fell down Zetes's cheeks as he tried to clean the blood away from Kyrian's swollen lips.

He looked up at Valerius. 'I have ten wagons of gold and jewels. His father promises even more if you release him. I have been authorized to surrender Thrace to you. And his sister, the Princess Althea, has offered herself to you as a slave. All you have to do is let me take him home.'

No! She heard Kyrian's inner scream, but the word was lodged in his burning throat.

'Perhaps. I'll let you take him home . . . After he's executed.'

'No!' Zetes said. 'He is a prince, and you—'

'He is no prince. Everyone knows he was disowned. His father was quite public with his decree.'

'And he has recanted it,' Zetes insisted. He looked back at Kyrian, his eyes kind and soothing. 'He wanted me to tell you he didn't mean what he said to you. He was foolish and blind when he should have trusted and listened to you. Your father loves you, Kyrian. All he wants is for you to come home where he can welcome you and Theone with open arms. He begs you to forgive him.'

Those last words burned through Kyrian more painfully than Valerius's iron brands. It wasn't his father who should apologize. His father wasn't the one who had been a fool.

It was Kyrian who had been cruel to a man who had never done anything other than love him. The agony of it swept through him anew.

Gods have mercy on them both, for his father had been right all along.

Zetes glanced to Valerius. 'He will give you anything for his son's life. *Anything!*'

'Anything,' Valerius repeated. 'How very tempting, but how stupid would I have to be to release the one man who has come close to defeating us?' He glared at Zetes. 'Never.'

Valerius took the dagger from his belt. Roughly, he grabbed the three long, thin commander's braids at Kyrian's temple and sawed them off.

'Here,' he said, handing them to Zetes. 'Take those to his father and tell him that is all of his son he'll ever get from me.'

'No!'

'Guards, see to it *His Highness* is taken away.'

Kyrian watched as his uncle was seized and dragged from the room.

'Kyrian!'

Kyrian struggled against his restraints, but his body was so sore and broken that all he succeeded in doing was hurting himself more.

He wanted to call Zetes back. He wanted to tell him how sorry he was for all he'd said to his parents.

Don't let me die without their knowing.

'You can't do this!' Zetes screamed an instant before the doors slammed shut, cutting him off.

Valerius turned to his servant. 'Fetch my mistress.'

As soon as the servant was gone, he returned to Kyrian. He sighed as if greatly disappointed. 'It appears our time together has ended. If your father is so desperate for your return, then it is only a matter of time before he marches against me. I certainly can't take a chance on him actually rescuing you, now can I?'

Kyrian closed his eyes and turned his head away from Valerius's triumphant sneer. In his mind, he saw his father on that last, fateful day as the two of them stood, toe to toe, in the center of the throne room. Julian had dubbed that day the Clash of the Titans. For neither he nor his father had been willing to listen or to yield.

He heard the words he'd said to his father. Words no son should ever utter to a parent.

The agony of it was a hundred times more severe than anything Valerius had dealt him.

While he grieved over his actions, the doors of his torture chamber opened to admit Theone. She walked into the room with her head held high, like a queen holding court. She stopped next to Valerius and gave him a warm, inviting smile.

Kyrian stared at her as the weight of her betrayal coursed through him. *Let this be a nightmare.*

Dear Zeus, please don't let this be real. It was more than his broken body and soul could take.

'You know, Kyrian,' Valerius said as he wrapped his arms around Theone and nuzzled her neck. 'I will commend you on your choice of wife. She is exceptional in bed, isn't she?'

It was the cruelest blow yet dealt him.

Theone met Kyrian's eyes without shame while Valerius circled behind her, cupped her breasts in his hands and kneaded them. There was no love on her face. No remorse. Nothing. She stared at him as if he were a stranger.

It cut him all the way to his battered soul.

'Come, Theone, let us show your husband what he inter-rupted the night he came home.'

Valerius removed the clip from her himation and let it fall to the floor. He pulled her naked body into his arms and kissed her.

Kyrian's heart splintered at the sight of Theone removing Valerius's armor. The sight of her eagerly welcoming his touch.

Unable to bear it, he closed his eyes and turned away. But still he heard them. He heard his wife begging for Valerius to fill her. Heard her moaning in pleasure. And when she climaxed in the arms of his enemy, he felt his heart wither and die.

At last Valerius had broken him.

He let the pain take him then. Let it wash over him until he felt nothing at all. Nothing but utter and complete deso-lation.

When they were finished, Valerius sauntered over to him. He wiped his wet hand across Kyrian's face and Kyrian cursed the scent he knew so well.

'Have you any idea how much I love the smell of your wife on my body?'

Kyrian spat in his face.

Enraged, Valerius pulled a dagger from the table and embedded it savagely in Kyrian's stomach. Kyrian gasped as the cold metal invaded his body. Maliciously, Valerius rotated his wrist and twisted the knife, pushing it in deeper.

'Tell me, Theone,' Valerius said, his eyes never leaving Kyrian's as he pulled the dagger out and left him weak and panting. 'How should I kill your husband? Should I behead him as befitting a prince?'

'No,' she said as she wrapped her himation around her and secured it with the brooch Kyrian had given her on their wedding day. 'He is the spirit and backbone of the Macedonian rebels. You can't afford to make him a martyr.

Were I you, I'd crucify him like a common thief. Let him stand as an example to Rome's enemies to know that there is no honor or glory in assaulting Rome.'

Valerius smiled cruelly, then turned to face her. 'I like the way your mind works.' He kissed her lightly on the cheek, then dressed himself.

'Say good-bye to your husband while I make arrangements.' He left them alone.

Kyrian struggled to breathe through his pain as Theone finally approached him. His body trembled from rage and agony. Still, her gaze was blank. Cold.

'Why?' he asked.

'Why?' she repeated. 'Why do you think? I was the nameless daughter of a prostitute. I grew up hungry and poor with no choice except to let any man use me as he saw fit.'

'I sheltered you,' he rasped through his split, bloody lips. 'Loved you. I kept you safe from anyone who would have hurt you.'

She narrowed her eyes at him. 'I am not about to let you war against Rome while I sit at home in fear of them tearing down my walls to get to you. I don't want to end up like Julian's wife, executed in my own bed, or sold into slavery. I've come too far to go back to scrounging for scraps, selling my body. I want my security and I will do anything to protect it.'

She couldn't have hurt him any worse. She had never seen him as *anything* other than a rich pocket.

No, he couldn't believe that. He refused to believe it. There had to have been a moment, just one, when she had cared for him. Surely, he couldn't have been *that* blind?

'Did you *ever* love me?'

She shrugged. 'If it's any consolation, you were the best lover I've ever known. I will certainly miss you in my bed.'

Kyrian let out an agonized bellow of rage.

'Damn, Theone,' Valerius said as he returned. 'I should

have let you torture him. I never once got that much pain out of him.'

The soldiers came in with a large cross. They laid it on the floor next to the table, then cut Kyrian down.

His limbs broken, he sank to the floor.

Roughly, they picked him up and dropped him over the wood.

Kyrian continued to watch Theone. Not even pity graced her brow. She merely looked on in morbid fascination.

Again, he saw his parents' stricken faces when he had left his home the day of the wedding. Heard Zetes's offer to Valerius.

Kyrian had betrayed them all for *her*. And now she couldn't even pretend to be sorry for what she'd done to him. What she had cost his family and his country.

He was Greece's last hope to stave off Roman tyranny. He was the only thing that stood between their people and slavery.

With one act of treachery, she had laid waste to all their dreams of freedom.

And all because *he* was a stupid fool . . .

His father's final, parting words rang in his ears. *She doesn't love you, Kyrian. No woman will ever be able to love you and you're a damned fool if you ever believe otherwise!*

A soldier placed a metal spike over his wrist and held it there as another drew back a heavy iron hammer.

The Roman guard brought it down on the spike . . .

Amanda came awake screaming as she felt the nail piercing her arm. Sitting up, she grabbed her wrist to make sure it had just been a dream.

She rubbed her arm, staring at it. She was just as she had always been and yet . . .

The dream had been real. She knew it.

Driven by a force she didn't understand, she left her room

to find Kyrian. She ran through the dark house, just after dawn, up the mahogany staircase and down a long hallway. She followed her instincts to a set of doors on the west side of the house.

Without hesitating, she threw open the double doors to a bedroom twice the size of her own. A single candle burned next to an old-fashioned, curtained bed, casting shadows against the far wall. The gold and brown curtains were pulled back and fastened to the posts while cream-colored sheers shielded the bed. Even so, she could see her Hunter writhing on the rust-colored sheets as if caught in the midst of the same nightmare she had seen.

Her heart hammering, she ran to the bed.

Kyrian woke up from his nightmare the very instant he felt Amanda's cool, gentle hand on his chest. He opened his eyes to find her sitting by his side, her gaze dark with horror, her brows knitted as she examined him.

He frowned while her hands roamed all over his chest. It was as if she didn't really see him at all, as if she were in some kind of strange trance.

He lay in complete silence, stunned by her presence.

She pulled back the silk sheet and touched the scar on his stomach, just to the left of his navel.

'He drove the knife in here,' she whispered, stroking the narrow scar.

Then she grabbed his wrist and tenderly traced the scars there. 'They hammered the spikes in here and here.'

Next she went to his hand and rubbed the pad of her thumb over his fingertips. 'They pulled your fingernails off.'

She reached up and cupped his stubbled cheek in her palm. Her eyes held a thousand emotions and the sight of those crystal-blue depths stole the breath from him.

No woman had ever given him such a look.

'My poor Hunter,' she whispered. Tears streamed down her face and before he knew what she was doing, she pulled the sheet away from him, baring his entire body to her questing gaze. He hardened instantly, his body throbbing at the sight of her concern for him.

She touched his scarred thigh where Valerius had once placed a hot brand to it.

'Oh God,' she gasped, her fingers brushing his puckered skin. 'It was real. They really did that to you . . .'

She looked up at him, her eyes swimming in tears. 'I saw you. I *felt* you.'

Kyrian frowned even more. Was that possible?

He'd been dreaming of his execution when she woke him. Could their powers have combined to allow him to reach out to her even while he slept?

It was a terrifying thought. If it were true, then it meant they were bonded together on a much higher level than the physical.

It meant . . .

He didn't finish that thought. There was no such thing as a soul mate, especially when one of them no longer had a soul. It just wasn't possible.

As Amanda stared at him, she ached all the way to her heart for the man before her. How had he borne such torture and betrayal?

He had carried it with him through the centuries. Alone. Always alone. Always hurting and wanting, with no relief.

No hope.

'So much pain,' she whispered.

How she wanted Theone's head for what she'd done to him. But most of all, she wanted to soothe Hunter. Wanted to ease the torment in his heart. Erase the pain of his past.

She wanted to give him something to hope for.

She wanted to give him his dream of children and of a woman who could love him.

God have mercy on her, but she wanted to be that woman.

Before she could stop herself, she leaned down and

captured his lips with her own. He moaned at the contact and cupped her face in his hands while he returned her kiss.

Amanda tasted him in a way she'd never tasted any man before. As their tongues danced, she could feel him all the way to her soul. She'd never in her life been bold in bed. But then she'd never wanted a man like this.

With the whole of her.

Tears welled in Amanda's eyes as she buried her lips against his collarbone, over the scar where Valerius had dragged his ring and left it bloody.

Such strength. Such love. She would give anything to have a man love her the way he had loved his wife.

More to the point, she wanted Hunter to love *her*. She wanted his heart. She wanted this man who knew what love was, who understood commitment and compassion.

Whether he would admit it or not, he needed her.

No man should walk eternity alone. No one should ever be hurt the way he'd been hurt. Not when his only crime was loving someone more than he had loved himself.

Her breath mixed with his as she climbed up his body and straddled his waist.

Kyrian groaned as he realized she wore nothing beneath his T-shirt. Her thighs were hot and moist as she slid herself against his bare stomach, igniting a fire deep inside him that needed her so much it terrified him.

Push her away.

But he couldn't. Not tonight. Not after the nightmare that was still fresh in his mind.

Right or wrong, he needed comfort. He wanted to feel loved again. He wanted to know the softness of a woman's hands on his body. The scent of Amanda on his skin.

Kyrian shook as she reached down and wrapped her hand around him. 'Oh gods,' he breathed against her lips. No one had touched him like this in over two thousand years.

His entire body throbbed and ached as she stroked his hot, rigid shaft.

Today, he would have her. There was no way he could push her away now.

His breathing ragged, he trembled from the feel of her fingers gripping him, her palm brushing up, along his shaft, then down to the base where she cupped him gently. Her fingers skimmed the underside of him, making him even harder, hotter, until he thought he would burst from it.

He trailed his hands slowly over her body, savoring every dip and curve. Savoring the feel of her soft skin and the T-shirt against his palms and fingers. He nuzzled her neck and for the first time since his Dark-Hunter incarnation, he felt an overwhelming urge to feed off a human.

The sound of her blood coursing through her veins filled his ears. Her raw energy beckoned him, making the Dark-Hunter in him long to sample her life force.

It was forbidden. No Dark-Hunter was supposed to puncture a human neck. And yet as he stroked the hollow of her throat with his tongue, the deep-seated need burned in him.

He grazed her neck with his fangs and it took every piece of control he had not to taste the blood he could feel rushing under his lips. He felt the chills spread over her body, making the nipple under his hand even tighter.

Pulling back with a growl, he latched onto her mouth and kissed her deeply as he slid his hand under the T-shirt, to the dark triangle between her legs.

He groaned at the feel of those tiny hairs teasing his fingers as he carefully separated them and touched her for the very first time.

She jumped in surprise, then moaned a welcoming murmur as she quickened her fairy strokes on his shaft.

Kyrian couldn't believe how wet she was already. Gods, how he wanted her. Wanted to taste every inch of her flesh. To drive himself deep into her fiery heat.

But he resisted because he wanted to savor the moment. Wanted to explore her tenderly, slowly.

He wanted this morning to last forever.

'You taste so good,' he whispered as he ripped the T-shirt from neck to hem, pulled it from her, and threw it to the floor. He nibbled a path from her neck to her breasts.

Amanda arched her back as he gently teased her nipple with his tongue and fangs. The feel of those sharp teeth on her skin made her burn like lava.

Once more he dipped his hand back down between their bodies and touched her where she ached most. His fingers swirled around her, teasing and soothing, delving and stroking, making her burn even more for him as he slid them deep inside her and made hot, sweet love to her with his hand.

'I want you, Hunter,' she breathed against his lips. 'I've never wanted anyone like this.'

He smiled, showing her his fangs as he rolled her over to lie beneath him with an ease of strength that awed her.

Amanda moaned at the feel of his hard, lean body on top of hers. His weight stole her breath and she wrapped her legs around his hips.

He was all sinewy power. It rippled from his body into hers.

Those sleek, honed muscles flexed around her with every graceful move he made. But even more captivating was the restrained power he showed. Like a fierce lion ready to strike.

She wanted more of him. She ached to feel him inside her. Ached to claim him in a way she knew no woman had claimed him in over two thousand years. She wanted this man's heart.

Even more, she wanted to claim him in a way no woman had *ever* claimed him before. She wanted to be everything he needed. His breath, his heart, but most of all his missing soul.

She wanted to give that back to him. To release him from his suffering. To free him from his past.

Arching her back, she kissed him deeply before she accidentally confessed her thoughts. Should he ever learn, she had no doubt he would pull away from her.

That was the last thing she wanted. So she summoned her repressed powers for the first time in over a decade and shielded her thoughts to hide her mind and her heart from him just in case he was still able to see inside her.

Today, she would be his comfort.

Kyrian growled at the sensation of Amanda's body beneath his. It had been so incredibly long since he had allowed himself to trust a woman like this.

Sweat broke out over his body as he left her breasts and nibbled her ribs, her hips, then he moved back up her body.

He wanted her with an inhuman need. Wanted things from her he dared not name. These thoughts of claiming her, of keeping her, should not be on his mind.

And yet they were.

Amanda ran her hand through his hair. She held him close as he nibbled his way from her lips to her throat, then down to her breasts where he took his time tasting her. His tongue circled her hardened nipple, teasing and stroking. He seemed insatiable as he devoured her like a starving man at a banquet.

Then slowly, carefully, he worked his way down her body. His long canine teeth scraped her skin with such tenderness that it amazed her. His hands burned her as he ran them beneath her hips. He slid his tongue down her hipbone, to her thigh.

He spread her legs wider and slowly laved his way up her inner thigh. She held her breath, writhing in anticipation of his touch.

When he hesitated, she looked down to find him staring up at her. The raw, possessive look on his face stole her breath.

His gaze held hers enthralled as he gently, slowly, ran his finger down her cleft, then back up. She shivered in response to his touch. He separated her tender folds, and took her into his mouth, all the while watching her.

Amanda cried out at the fierce ecstasy that ripped through her. No man had done that to her before.

He closed his eyes and moaned in a way that reverberated through her. His tongue slid in and around, making her entire body jerk and quiver with every sensuous lick he delivered.

Running her hand through his tousled curls, she arched her back, opening her legs wider to give him complete access to her.

Kyrian shook at the taste of her. He'd never wanted anything as much as he wanted this woman. There was something about her that drove him wild.

But he could feel his Dark-Hunter powers straining. Feel the animal in him awakening.

These were the powers he used when he fought or tracked. Powers that enabled him to sense his surroundings on a greater level. They made him aware of her heart pounding in her chest. Of the little tremors in her body that responded to his lips and tongue.

He felt the pleasure he was giving her and it made his body throb in time with the blood rushing through her thighs, which cradled his face. He closed his eyes as he fought the urge once again to sink his teeth into her thigh and taste her blood on his tongue.

Amanda clutched him to her as he continued to pleasure her. His fangs gently scraped her, sending a shudder through her. She opened her eyes and saw him intent upon his actions. It was as if he had zenned completely on her and nothing else.

He *was* sex, she realized. His very being was focused on her and her pleasure with the same intensity she was sure he only used to stalk the Daimons.

And when her release came, it was so fierce, so overwhelming, that she threw her head back and screamed out.

Still, he wasn't through with her. He growled as she released herself, but his licks never stopped. They became faster, stronger as he continued to feast on her body.

She hissed in pleasure.

It wasn't until she came twice more that he finally slowed. And even then he waited until the very last tremor had shaken her before he pulled away.

He rose up from between her legs and prowled up her body, slowly, methodically, like some hungry, powerful beast about to prey on its dinner.

His eyes flashed like jet, and his fangs were visible as he breathed raggedly.

'Look at me, Amanda,' he commanded as he ran his hand down to her thigh. 'I want to see your eyes when I take you.'

Swallowing, she did as he asked.

He cupped her face in his hand and kissed her deeply, then he took her hand into his and guided it to his swollen shaft.

Without being told, she knew what he wanted. Arching her hips, she led him inside her, slowly, inch by long, full inch until he filled her deeply. She moaned at the sensation of his power inside her. At the hungry, needful look in his eyes.

As she started to pull her hand away, he covered it with his and held it against him.

The hunger in his eyes intensified. 'I want you to feel us joined,' he said raggedly.

Amanda swallowed as he slid himself between her fingers and went even deeper inside her. In and out. It was the most erotic, incredible thing she'd ever known.

They moaned simultaneously.

Amanda saw the pleasure on his face as he rocked himself forcefully against her hips. 'Oh, Hunter,' she breathed.

He paused and looked down at her. 'It's not the Dark-Hunter inside you right now, Amanda. It's *me*, Kyrian.'

Joy exploded through her as she realized what he was offering her. He had let her inside him the same way she had allowed him to enter her.

Reaching up, she cupped his face in her hands. 'Kyrian,' she breathed.

He smiled. 'You feel even better than I thought you would,' he said as she felt a shiver run over his body.

He dipped his head down and took her lips in a tender kiss as he delivered fierce, fast strokes to her. Hard, long, and deep. They tore through her, spiking pure bliss through her body.

'Oh, Kyrian,' she moaned against his lips as she felt her pleasure building again.

No sooner had his name left her lips than something strange started happening to her. Something shifted inside her and she felt an erotic surge.

'Oh my,' she breathed.

Suddenly, she could feel him *feel* her.

It was as if they were really one person. She felt him inside her and she could feel herself around him.

Kyrian struggled to breathe as he felt it, too. They stared into each other's eyes.

Amanda ran her hand down his back. She felt the caress down her own spine. It was the most incredible thing she'd ever experienced.

He quickened his strokes, and she clung to him, both of them out of their minds with volcanic need.

They came together in one fierce moment of sublime pleasure. Kyrian threw his head back and roared as he buried himself deep inside her. Amanda cried out as he shook in her arms.

She held him close as he collapsed on top of her. She cradled him with her body while she floated back to herself.

Then, to her deepest regret, she could feel him receding from her.

'What happened?' he breathed.

'I don't know, but it was wonderful. Incredible. The absolute best.'

Laughing softly, he lifted his head and she frowned at the sight of his eyes in the dull candlelight. They were no longer black, but a strange hazel-green. 'Kyrian?'

He looked around the room, then grimaced. 'My powers are gone,' he whispered. And it was then she felt weakness overwhelm him.

He could barely move.

Worse, she felt intense agony invade his skull as he placed the heel of his hand over his right eye and hissed.

'Oh, my God,' she breathed as he lay beside her in complete misery. 'What can I do?'

'Call Talon,' he said between clenched teeth. 'Dial two and a pound sign on the phone.'

She rolled over to reach the nightstand and pulled the phone to her, then quickly dialed.

Talon answered on the second ring.

By the sound of Talon's voice, she could tell he'd been fast asleep. 'What's wrong?' he asked calmly after she told him who she was.

'I don't know. I've done something to Kyrian.'

'What do you mean?' he asked in a tone that told her he found it hard to believe she could do anything to his friend.

'I'm not sure. His eyes are a different color and he's doubled over in pain.'

'What color are his eyes?'

'Green.'

Talon fell silent for several rapid heartbeats before he spoke again. 'Let me talk to him.'

She handed the phone to Kyrian.

Kyrian gripped the phone as another wave of pain racked

him. He'd never felt anything like this before. It was as if his Dark-Hunter and human halves were at war with one another.

'Talon,' he breathed.

'Hey, buddy,' Talon said. 'You okay?'

'Hell, no. What's going on?'

'Offhand, I'd say you just found the way to drain out your Dark-Hunter powers. Congratulations, bud, you found your out-clause.'

'Yeah, and I feel peachy keen about it, too.'

'Don't be a smart-ass. The thing to remember is it's temporary. I think.'

Not comforted by the doubt in Talon's voice, he asked, 'How long?'

'I have no idea. I've never had my powers drained.'

Kyrian hissed against another wave of pain.

'Stop fighting it,' Talon snapped. 'You're only making it worse. Just relax.'

'Oh yeah, like you know.'

Talon snorted. 'Trust me, there are times to fight and this isn't one of them. Just go with it.'

'Go with it, my ass. It's not that easy. It happens to feel like I'm being cleaved in two.'

'I know,' Talon said, his voice thick with sympathy. 'What were you doing when you lost your powers?'

Kyrian cleared his throat as he cast a sheepish look to Amanda. 'I . . . um . . .' He hesitated with the explanation. The last thing he wanted to do was embarrass her.

But then, he didn't have to.

'Great *Diarmuid Ua Duibhne*,' Talon roared, 'you slept with her and it drained you, didn't it?'

Kyrian cleared his throat louder, then realized the futility of trying to hide something from a Dark-Hunter who could find out most *anything* he wanted to. 'Nothing happened until the end.'

'Ahhhh, I see,' Talon said, dragging the words out as if something had become clear to him. When next he spoke, he sounded strangely like Dr. Ruth. 'You know that moment you have after you come? When you're completely spent, sated, and helpless? Want to bet that's what sucked your powers out?'

Still, none of it made any sense to Kyrian. 'The rest of you sleep with women all the time without this.'

'Yeah, but every one of us has a different pressure point, you know that. In your mind you must equate that pinnacle moment with what made you a Dark-Hunter. Either that or maybe it was her powers. Maybe they fluxed with yours and sucked them out.'

'That's insane.'

'About as insane as the headache you have which is making my head hurt for you, by the way. Now hand me back to Amanda.'

Kyrian did. 'He wants to talk to you.'

Amanda took the phone.

'Listen,' Talon said, his voice stern and sharp. 'We have a serious problem here. Kyrian is down until his powers return.'

'How long?'

'I have no idea. But it'll probably be a while, and until then, he's human, and since he hasn't been human in over two thousand years, he's weak from it. Vulnerable.'

Panic gripped her as she looked back at Kyrian. He still had one hand over his eyes and she could tell by the tautness of his body how much pain he felt.

'Will he be back to normal by sundown?'

'I hope so. Because if he's not, the Daimons will have him.'

Her throat constricted as fear gripped her. The last thing she wanted was for him to be hurt because of her. 'Can't you help him?'

'No. It's against our Code. We hunt alone. I can't go after Desiderius until Kyrian is dead.'

'What kind of Code is that?' she shrieked.

'The kind that doesn't usually pierce my eardrum,' Talon hissed. 'Damn, girl, with that set of lungs, you have a bright future as an opera soprano.'

'You're not funny.'

'I know. None of this is. Now listen to me for a second. It's going to be embarrassing, can you handle it?'

His dire tone gave her pause. What was he going to say to her? 'I think so.'

'Good. Now, I think our problem stems from when Kyrian came. It's imperative that you not let him do that anymore. Because there's a real good chance it will drain his powers out of him again. You need to stay away from him.'

Amanda's heart ached at his words. She reached out and touched Kyrian. 'Okay,' she breathed.

'All right. It's a little after seven right now. Do us both a favor and watch over him until Nick gets there.'

'I will.'

Talon said good-bye and she hung up the phone, then returned it to the nightstand.

Kyrian looked up at her and the pain she saw in his greenish eyes tore through her. 'I only wanted to make it better. I never meant to hurt you.'

He took her hand in his and held it gently. 'I know.'

He pulled her into his arms and held her close, but still she could feel the rigidness of his body.

'You made it better, Amanda,' he breathed in her ear. 'Don't take away what you gave me by feeling guilty.'

'Is there anything I can do?'

'Just let me hold you for a little while.'

His words tugged at her heart. She lay cradled in his arms and felt his warm breath fall on her throat.

Kyrian buried his face in her hair and breathed the sweet

scent of her. He'd never felt as weak as he did just then and yet something about her presence gave him strength.

'*You have your out-clause.*' Talon's words rang in his head. Once a Dark-Hunter found something to drain their immortal powers, they could regain their soul. It was something he'd never thought about before. Something he'd never dared dream about.

He could be human again.

Permanently.

But to what purpose? He was what he was. An eternal warrior. He loved his life. Loved the freedom and the power it gave him.

Yet as he lay there with Amanda nestled in his arms, bare skin to bare skin, he began to think of other forgotten things. Things he had banished to the deepest crevices of his heart.

Closing his eyes, he saw her holding Niklos. She would make a good mother.

And as he drifted back to sleep, a part of him knew she'd make a wonderful wife.

Amanda came awake to someone tracing slow, scorching circles around her breasts. She opened her eyes and looked down to see Kyrian's hand gently kneading her. He had his thigh buried between her legs.

Her heart pounded as he slid his hand down, over her stomach, while he nibbled her neck with his long, pointed teeth.

'Are you going to bite me?' she asked.

His laughter vibrated down the column of her throat. 'No, love, I'm going to *devour* you.'

Rolling onto her back, she looked up and saw his eyes were even greener than before. They were a light, gorgeous, vibrant green. She reached up and ran her finger just below his right eye. 'Why did they change color?'

'When I lost my Dark-Hunter powers, my eyes went back to their human color.'

She frowned at him as she vaguely recalled the color from her dream. 'This was the color of your eyes before you lost your soul?'

He nodded, then dropped his head and suckled the hollow of her throat.

'Should you be doing this?' she asked as she ran her hand down his spine. 'Talon said you needed to rest.'

'I am resting.'

She sucked her breath in sharply as he separated the tender flesh between her legs and stroked her with his long, strong fingers. 'You're not resting, you're playing.'

His eyes searched hers. 'I *want* to play with you.'

'But won't this make you weaker?'

'I don't see how.'

'But what if—'

He stopped her words with a hot, scorching kiss. Amanda's thoughts scattered.

He nibbled her lips with his teeth and pulled back. His green eyes tugged at her heart. 'I can't feel what's inside you anymore, Amanda. Tell me you don't want me and I'll let you go.'

'I want you, Kyrian.' What an understatement that was.

He smiled at her, then drove himself deep inside her.

Amanda moaned at the strength of him filling her.

Kyrian's head swam at the warmth of her beneath him. If it were possible, she felt even better to him now than she had the hour before.

He stared at her face and took delight in her passion-drunk eyes. The flush in her cheeks. She was truly beautiful.

A wave of fierce possession tore through him. A feeling so intense that he had all but forgotten it.

He couldn't fathom where it came from, but it rocked his very being.

And it made a mockery of what he'd once felt for Theone.

He didn't understand it, and in truth, he didn't dare investigate it. Knowledge of his feelings could only hurt him more.

Amanda wrapped her legs around his as she savored each of his long, lush strokes inside her. She'd never dreamed lovemaking could be like this. Never dreamed of such intense pleasure.

And when her release came, she cried out.

Kyrian captured her open lips with his and with three more forceful strokes, he joined her.

His breathing ragged, he stared down at her. 'I think I'm addicted to you.'

She smiled a smile that made his heart skip a beat.

'Hey, Kyrian!'

Kyrian barely had time to pull the sheets over them before his bedroom door burst open to show a tall, handsome man in his mid-twenties.

Amanda froze as she met Nick's hazel-blue, wide-eyed stare. His dark-brown hair was long, and combed back from his face, and when he smiled, he displayed a deep set of dimples. 'I'll be damned, you got laid.'

'Nick,' he growled. 'Get out.'

'Yeah, but I have some news on Desiderius that you really want to know. Why don't you throw some clothes on and meet me in the office in a few minutes?' Unabashed, Nick swept another taunting look over them and sauntered out of the room.

'Remind me later, I really need to kill him.'

Amanda laughed, until she met his gaze. 'You look so different with green eyes,' she whispered, placing her hand against his whiskered cheek.

He responded by capturing her lips for another scorching kiss. His tongue taunted and teased hers in a possessive way that made her breathless and weak. 'What is it about you that I can't resist?'

'My charming personality?' she quipped.

Laughing, he kissed her lightly on the nose. Amanda watched him get out of bed. Her gaze feasted on his bare backside as he crossed the room to his bathroom.

She curled up in bed while he took a shower and just remembered the way he'd felt in her arms. His scent clung to her, and she reveled in it. It made her feel as if she belonged to him and yet she knew she never could.

He was a Dark-Hunter and she was an accountant. There had never been two more mismatched people born. Still her heart didn't listen. There was a part of her that wanted him on a level she'd never known existed.

And somewhere in the back of her mind, she couldn't help but wonder what it would take to free him of his Dark-Hunter oath.

Chapter 9

Kyrian walked down the hallway and opened the door to his office. Nick sat at the antique mahogany desk with his back to him. The black leather reclining office chair squeaked as Nick shifted in the seat while his fingers flew over the keys of the computer keyboard.

It was a familiar sight.

On the Internet, Nick was a demigod, which in hacker terminology meant he could pretty much infiltrate anything, no matter how secure the server. Because of that, Nick, Chris Eriksson, and Daphne Addams had been relegated to designing, maintaining, and securing the Dark-Hunter.com Web site where the Dark-Hunters and Squires kept all their records and communicated with each other.

It was nice to know Nick was picking up something other than women of questionable morals at school.

'So what had you barging into my room?'

Nick glanced over his shoulder with a devilish grin. 'Man, you got laid. It's about time.'

'Knock it off.'

Snorting, Nick turned his attention back to his instant message. 'You're the only man I know who can have sex with a woman who looks that good and be in this bad a mood ten minutes later. Damn, didn't you know sex is supposed to make you feel better?'

Kyrian rolled his eyes at his impudent Squire. Rules and regulations had never applied to Nick Gautier. Nor had the boy ever been intimidated by him. Not even on the night he had learned what Kyrian was.

'Nick . . .' he warned.

Nick opened a small window on the computer and read the message. 'Okay, okay. Here's the deal from the Oracles:

'*Of Apollite birth and of Daimon born, he is the one who will make you mourn.*

'*Through the wine god's blood and bath, he exists as pure wrath.*

'*To bring him under final control, you must find the Dark-Hunter with a soul.*'

Kyrian frowned at the riddle, which was the typical garbage given to them by the Oracles. Gods, how he *hated* them. Just once, couldn't they actually come out and say it in plain, simple language?

Oh no. Zeus forbid, the Oracles should actually *help* them protect the humans.

'What the hell does that mean?' he asked Nick.

Nick swung around in the chair to face him. 'Acheron interpreted it to say that only a Dark-Hunter with a soul can kill Desiderius. That's why no one has ever succeeded against him. It's simple prophecy, and you know how that works.'

'There's no such thing as a Dark-Hunter with a soul. Not a full soul, anyway.'

'Then according to the Oracles and Ash, Desiderius can never be killed.'

Kyrian let out a slow breath. 'That is *not* what I wanted to hear this morning.'

'Yeah, and all I have to say is I'm damned glad I'm not

in your boots on this one.' Nick frowned. 'Your eyes are green. What happened?'

'Nothing.'

Nick tilted his head and gave him a suspicious stare. 'Something's up.' He reached for his cell phone. 'Do I need to call Ash again?'

Kyrian took the phone from his hand and glared murderously at him. 'Leave Acheron out of this. I can handle it.'

'Yeah, you'd better. You get on my last nerve, but I'd hate to break in another Dark-Hunter.'

Kyrian snorted at him. 'What is that? A declaration of love?'

'It's one of loyalty. I don't want to see you go down like Streigar did.'

The thought sobered Kyrian. Streigar had been a fierce Dark-Hunter who had been trapped by vampire-hunting humans who exposed him to daylight. His death had upset all of them, Dark-Hunter and Squire alike.

'Don't worry,' he assured Nick, 'I'm not going to be a dawn-surfer. I can handle myself.'

'Want to bet that's what Streigar said, too?'

Kyrian growled. 'Don't you have class today?'

Nick laughed at that. 'Boy, I'm a backwoods Cajun, I ain't never got no class, cher.' He cleared his throat and dropped the thick Cajun accent. 'And no, today's registration. I've got to figure out what I'm taking next semester.'

'Fine, but I have a few things I need you to do today.'

'And that is different from any other day how?'

Sarcasm, thy name is Nick Gautier.

'I need you to take Amanda shopping for clothes. The Daimons burned her house down and she has nothing except the clothes on her back.'

Nick arched a brow. 'From what I saw, she had no clothes whatsoever on her back. Her front neither.'

Kyrian narrowed his eyes on his Squire.

'Don't have a hissy.' Nick held his hands up in mock surrender. 'I know she's yours and I would never encroach, but man, I'm not blind, either.'

'One day, Gator bait . . .'

'Yeah, right. That threat might actually carry weight if I didn't know how much you live to order me around. You'd go insane if you couldn't page me at all hours of the night.'

Kyrian couldn't deny that. The nights did have a way of getting long and boring when there were no Daimons to pursue. And bugging Nick at three A.M. did provide *some* entertainment.

Nick pulled out his Palm Pilot and made notes on it. 'All right, secret mission, take woman shopping.' He looked up at Kyrian. 'By the way, I want hazard pay for this. I seriously hate the mall.'

Kyrian laughed. '*That* I can tell by the way you dress.'

Nick gave him a fake wounded look. 'Excuse me, Mr. Armani. I happen to like the grunge look.'

'Sorry. I keep forgetting it's fashionable to look like you just rolled out from under a Dumpster.'

Stuttering in indignation, Nick pretended offense. 'Why don't you take your butt back to bed and save your oozing charm for your woman? 'Cause if you keep this up, *I'm* going to stake you . . .' then under his breath, he added, 'while you sleep.'

Kyrian crossed his arms over his chest. 'All right, you'll get your bonus, but play nice with her. Keep your sarcasm to a minimum.'

'Yes, O great Lord and Master.' Nick added another note – 'Be nice to woman, keep mouth shut' – then he looked up. 'By the way, is there a limit on what I'm to spend for her clothes?'

'No. Whatever she wants to spend.'

'Visit Needless-Markup and Lord and Taylor. All right, next?'

'Have her back here before dusk or I'm going to feed your Cajun hide to Talon's gators.'

A glimmer of fear flashed in his eyes. Nick *hated* alligators, but Kyrian had no idea why. 'All right, that scares me.'

'I also want you to go by Talon's and pick up a *srad*. Let's give Desiderius a surprise he won't see coming.'

Nick visibly cringed at the mention of Talon's circular daggers. It was an ancient weapon that made a Ginsu look like a butter knife. 'Do you even know how to use that thing?'

'Yes, I do.' Kyrian took a deep breath. 'Now, I need some sleep. Your primary job today is to take care of Amanda.'

Nick turned off his Palm Pilot and clipped it to his belt. 'You like her, don't you?'

Kyrian didn't answer. He didn't dare. Neither one of them needed to know that one.

Instead, he left Nick sitting at the computer and went back to his room.

After a quick shower, Amanda quietly stepped into the bedroom to dress while Kyrian slept in his large four-poster bed.

The room was completely dark with the only light coming from the bathroom. No one would ever be able to tell if it was day or night from in here, and yet Kyrian always seemed to know when the sun was up.

She stepped over to the bed to watch him lying there with the sheet draped over his middle to shield his nudity. Oh, that man had a body . . .

She could stare at him all day long and not grow tired of all that lush, tawny skin that she longed to explore some more with her lips and hands. What was it about him that was so addictive?

She ached to kiss those poetic lips and run her hands through the golden waves on his head, but she didn't want to disturb his sleep. He needed his strength.

Tiptoeing from the room, she headed downstairs to the kitchen.

Daylight sparkled against the white marble of the room, bright and cheerful. Rosa was frying bacon while Nick sat on a barstool looking through a college course catalogue.

Probably no older than twenty-four, Nick was lean and handsome. His shoulder-length dark brown hair could have used a trim, but somehow it suited his sculpted features. He was wearing a baggy sweater that had seen better days, and faded jeans with a hole in the knee.

'Hey, Rosa,' he said without looking up from his catalogue, 'if I take Spanish next semester, will you help me study for it?'

'*Sí*. I imagine Kyrian will, as well.'

'Great,' he said sarcastically. 'Between that and Ancient Greek Civilization, I'll have the friggin' time of my life.'

'Nick!' Rosa chastised. 'Such language you use. It is not becoming of a gentleman.'

'Sorry.'

Rosa set a plate of toast, bacon, and eggs down beside Nick, then turned and caught sight of Amanda in the doorway. 'There you are, señorita. Are you hungry?'

'A little.'

'Come,' she said, indicating the stool beside Nick. 'Sit and I'll make you breakfast.'

'Thank you, Rosa.'

Rosa smiled.

Amanda took a seat beside Nick. He brushed his hand off on his jeans and held it out to her. 'Nick Gautier,' he said with a charming, dimpled smile. 'Better known as "Nick, get your butt in here, I need you to . . ." Fill in the blank.'

She laughed. 'Bossy, isn't he?'

'You've no idea.' Nick pulled his cell phone off his belt and handed it to her. 'Speaking of, boss man said you'd need to call work.'

'Thanks.'

While Rosa made her breakfast, she called her boss and explained about her house. Luckily, her director was understanding and gave her a two-week leave of absence to take care of it.

As soon as she hung up, Amanda felt ill as she remembered her loss. 'I can't believe they burned down my house.'

'Your house?' Rosa asked. 'Who burned it down?'

'The authorities are looking into it,' Kyrian said from the direction of the living room.

Amanda turned around to see him standing in the doorway. He looked pale and uneasy.

Rosa smiled. '*M'ijo*, you are here today. Nick said you would be gone.'

'I'm not feeling well.' Even though his face was tender, he narrowed his gaze on Rosa. 'You came in on time this morning, didn't you?'

Rosa ignored his question. 'Come and sit. I'll make you something to eat.'

Kyrian cast a wary look to the sunlight spilling into the kitchen from the open windows. He took a step back into the dark living room. 'Thank you, Rosa, but I'm not hungry. Nick, I need to see you for a minute.'

Nick gave her a knowing smile. 'At least he didn't tell me to move my butt.'

'Nick,' Kyrian said. 'Move your butt, boy.'

While Nick went over to Kyrian, Rosa set a plate in front of her. 'Poor little one. What are you to do without a house?'

'I don't know. I guess I need to call my insurance company. Find a place to live . . .' Amanda's voice trailed off as she thought over all the things that needed to be done.

She'd have to replace her entire life. Everything. Toothbrush, shoes, books, furniture, phones. She didn't even have a pair of underwear.

Overwhelmed, she lost her appetite.

Whatever was she going to do?

Nick came back to the counter and picked up his catalogue, then went back to Kyrian in the doorway. 'I need a favor. I have to register at one o'clock, so if we're not back, can you sign up on-line for my classes? I know you need to sleep, but I really want to take Greek Civ next semester.'

'Why?'

'Dr. Alexander is teaching it and he's supposed to be really good.'

'Julian Alexander?' Amanda asked.

'Yeah,' Nick said, looking back at her. 'You know him?'

She exchanged a knowing look with Kyrian. 'Not half as well as Kyrian does.'

Nick shuddered. 'Ah, man, not another one of *you*. Great. Shoot me now and put me out of my misery.'

'Don't tempt me.' Kyrian took the catalogue. 'One o'clock. Anything else?'

'Yeah, do something about those eyes, they're creeping me out.'

Kyrian arched a warning brow at Nick's commanding tone. 'You two have fun.'

'Fun?' Amanda asked as Kyrian left them.

Nick returned to sit on his stool. 'We're going *shopping*.' He curled his lips and shuddered at the word.

'For what?'

He took a drink of orange juice. 'Whatever you need, my lady. Furs, diamonds, whatever.'

'Diamonds?' she asked, laughing at the outrageous thought.

'It's on Kyrian, so I say go for broke. Literally.'

She smiled. 'I can't do that. I have my own money.'

'Yeah, but why spend it? You have no idea how rich the man is. I promise you, buy the mall and he won't even notice.'

Amanda had no intention of doing that. Still, she did need

something else to wear. 'All right, can we also stop by my mother's?'

'Sure. My assignment for the day is to serve you any way you want me to.'

She shook her head at his devilish smile.

After she called her insurance company about the fire, Amanda let Nick take her shopping. But what frustrated her was Nick's inability to let her pay for *anything*.

'I'm under orders,' Nick said for the fifth time. 'You shop, I pay.'

She growled good-naturedly at him. 'Do you always follow orders?'

'I do so complainingly always.'

She laughed yet again as they left the store and headed back out into the mall with Nick carrying her bags. 'How long have you worked for Kyrian?' she asked as they got on the escalator.

'Eight years now.'

She gaped. 'Really, you don't look that old.'

'Yeah, well, I was barely sixteen when I started.'

'You can be a Squire at that age?'

Nick turned his head to ogle an attractive young woman in a tight, short skirt going up the escalator beside them, then he turned to flash a dimpled smile at her before he answered the question. 'I didn't know what he was for a long time. I just thought he was some whacked-out rich guy with a "pity the poor kid" complex.'

She frowned as they left the escalator and walked through the downstairs level. 'Why would you think that?'

Nick adjusted the bags he carried. 'You see beside you, my lady, the son of a career felon. My father died in Angola eleven years ago during a prison riot.'

Amanda winced at the thought of losing a father like that. 'And your mother?'

'She was an exotic dancer down on Bourbon Street. I grew up in the back room of the club where she worked, helping the bouncers hustle clients.'

Amanda cringed at the life he was describing. 'I'm sorry.'

He shrugged nonchalantly. 'Don't be. My mother might have her faults, but she's a good mom, and a terrific lady. She did her best with what little we had. My father knocked her up when she was fifteen and her father threw her out. So it was just the two of us while my dad hit the revolving door in and out of the penal system. We never had much, but she's always loved me.'

Amanda smiled at the love she heard in his voice. It was obvious he worshiped his mother. 'So how did you meet Kyrian?'

He paused for a second as if gathering his thoughts. 'When I hit my teens, I was sick to death of watching my mom hang her head in shame. Of her doing without food so I could eat a little bit more. I can remember walking to work with her and watching the way her gaze would stare longingly into store windows.' He sighed. 'She had such hungry eyes.'

His stare was hard, penetrating. 'My mother is the best-hearted woman God ever put on this planet. And I couldn't stand watching her degrade herself to feed me. Men groping her all the time. Or seeing the look on her face whenever she saw something she wanted and she couldn't afford it. At thirteen, I couldn't take it anymore, so I started stealing.'

Amanda's throat tightened. She didn't condone it, but she wouldn't judge him for it, either.

'One night, the gang I was in decided to mug a couple of tourists and I drew the line. It was one thing to shoplift and break into rich people's houses, but I wasn't about to hurt someone.'

So, even as a thief, Nick had honor.

'What happened?' she asked.

'The guys were furious at me and decided to get a little practice in by beating the crap out of me. One minute, I was under their feet, getting bludgeoned to death, and the next thing I knew there was this guy holding his hand out to me, asking me if I was okay.'

'Kyrian?'

Nick nodded. 'He took me to the hospital and paid for them to stitch up my head and knife wounds. He stayed with me until my mom got there. While we were waiting, he asked me if I wanted to go to work for him, running errands after school.'

She could just imagine Nick as a smart-mouthed teen. It said a lot about Kyrian's character that he had seen through Nick's caustic personality to find the goodness beneath it all. 'You agreed?'

'Not at first. I wasn't sure I wanted to be anywhere near some guy who had all the money in the world. Plus, my mom was very suspicious of Kyrian. She still is. She can't imagine why on earth he pays me so much money to do practically nothing.' He laughed. 'She's still half convinced I deal drugs for him.'

Amanda scoffed at the thought. His poor mother. 'What do you tell her?'

'That he's Howard Hughes with a God complex.' He sobered and gave her a harsh stare. 'I owe Kyrian my life. There's no telling where I'd be if he hadn't found me that night. One thing's for sure, I wouldn't be a pre-law student at Loyola, driving around in a Jag. I know he's a major asshole, but he's really a good guy underneath it all.'

Amanda thought about his words as they left the mall and stowed her purchases in the trunk of Nick's silvery-black Jag.

They got in the car and she buckled up. 'When did Kyrian tell you what he was?'

Nick started the car, then backed out of the parking space.

'When I graduated high school. He offered me a permanent job as his Squire.'

'And what exactly is a Squire?'

He pulled out into traffic, and as he shifted gears, she noticed a strange spiderweblike tattoo on his right hand. It held some kind of odd Greek design and she wondered if all Squires held such a mark.

'We were set up to protect the Dark-Hunters during the daylight hours and to procure whatever they need. Food, clothes, cars, maintain their homes, whatever. At one time, we literally stood guard over the special crypts they slept in, which is what started the whole vampires-sleep-in-coffins myth. Since sunlight is deadly to them, they used to sleep in caves or isolated chambers where there was no possibility of sun exposure. In return for our service, they provide financial support to us.'

'So each Dark-Hunter has a Squire?'

'No. Some Dark-Hunters prefer to go it alone. I'm the first Squire Kyrian has had in over three hundred years.'

She flinched at the thought of Kyrian being alone all that time. She could just imagine him walking the floors of his mansion like some restless spirit in search of comfort and finding none.

'And if you want to quit?' she asked Nick.

He sucked his breath in between his teeth. 'It's not really that easy. The Squires have a whole detailed organization that's kind of like the Hotel California – you can check out anytime you want, but you can never leave. Once you get out, they will monitor you until the day you die. If you ever betray them or the Dark-Hunters, you won't live to regret it.'

His ominous voice sent a chill down her spine. 'Really?'

'Oh yeah. Some of these guys come from a long family history of Squirehood that goes back thousands of years.'

'Is it like slavery?' she asked.

'No. I can leave at any time I choose, I just can't breach my Squire's oath. Once taken, the oath is unbreakable and eternal. When I get married, my wife won't ever know what Kyrian is, or what I do for him, not unless she's a Squire, too. After my children reach adulthood, I can decide to let them in on it or not. If I choose to let them in, they have to go before Acheron and Artemis, who will review and hopefully approve their application.'

Now that was truly scary, because as he spoke those words, a horrible thought occurred to her. 'What about me? Wouldn't they think I pose a threat?'

His face turned deadly serious as he paused at a red light and turned to face her. 'If you do, one of the Squires *will* kill you.'

She swallowed. 'That's not comforting.'

'It's not meant to be. We take our duties very seriously. The Dark-Hunters are all that stand between the human race and slavery or extinction. Without them, the Apollites and Daimons would own us all.'

Kyrian lay in bed, trying his best to sleep, but over and over he felt Amanda inside him. She was at the remains of her house. He knew it. He felt her tears, her rage. Her despair.

And he ached for her.

How he wished he could be there with her right now. Comforting her. Never before had the loss of daylight freedom bothered him, but now it did. If he weren't a Dark-Hunter, he would be able to stand by her side and offer her his strength. His support.

Closing his eyes, he breathed deeply, trying to stave off the pain. In a fit of anguished rage, he had chosen this course. Now, there was no way out. Artemis guarded her army zealously and had set the bar so high that in all this time, Kyrian had only known three Dark-Hunters to ever regain their souls.

All the others had died trying.

'What do I need with a soul, anyway?' he breathed as he opened his eyes to stare up at the brown and gold canopy over his bed. 'All it does is make a man weak.'

His life had meaning. It had purpose.

Then why did something within him actually hurt in desperate need for Amanda?

It was a feeling he hadn't experienced in centuries and it was a feeling that had once caused him to betray everyone who had loved him.

'I won't be weak again,' he whispered. It wasn't that he thought Amanda would hurt him intentionally. It was himself that he feared, for once he gave his heart or his loyalty, he never revoked it.

It came down to one basic fact. He was scared of himself and the lengths he would go to keep her safe.

After they visited the remains of Amanda's house and her mother's home, Nick drove into the heart of the French Quarter and parked on a side street so that they could walk over to Chartres. He led Amanda down the semicrowded retail area until they reached a small boutique called Dream Dolls and Accessories.

Amanda frowned. They were going to a doll store? How weird was that?

'What are we doing?' she asked as he opened the door for her.

'We're going to see the dollmaker.'

Okay, ask a stupid question . . .

She looked skeptically at Nick. 'You know, I don't think they make life-sized Barbies.'

He snorted at her as she walked into the shop with Nick one step behind her. 'I'm not looking for a Barbie and this trip isn't for me. I'm here for Kyrian.'

Now she really was worried. 'Why?'

Before he could answer, an elderly lady looked up from her workbench beside the door and caught Amanda's full attention. She held a Barbie doll whose face she was repainting.

The woman wore a strange orange headpiece with a light and a bifocal eye shield. It covered her stark white hair, which was pulled back into a tight bun. Her old, brown eyes were bright and friendly.

'Little Nicky,' she said in a motherly tone. 'What brings you here this afternoon and with such a beautiful guest? Why, I do believe this is the first time I've ever seen you with a woman.' She gestured at him with the tiny paintbrush in her hand. 'One worth being seen with, anyway. Why, she's plum nice-looking and I'm not talking about her looks, if you know what I mean.'

Nick raked a hand through his hair and shot Amanda an embarrassed glance.

'Liza, my love,' he said in a loud tone, flashing her a devilish, charming grin. 'Do I really need a reason to come see your shining face?'

She laughed at that. 'I may be old, Nicholas Gautier, but I ain't stupid yet.' She tapped her head, making her head-gear shake. 'My old noodle is still up to snuff and it's been more years than I care to remember since a man like you came by to see me for a social call. Now come whisper in my ear and tell me what you be needing.'

Nick went to whisper and it was then she realized Liza was a touch deaf. In fact, Nick ended up speaking so loudly, Amanda heard every word clearly.

Even when he ordered plastic explosives.

'Now, remember,' he said. 'Kyrian wants one just like Talon's.'

'I heard you, Nicky,' Liza said good-naturedly. 'What, you think I'm deaf?' She winked at Amanda.

'When should I come back?' Nick asked.

Liza pursed her lips. 'Give me a day or two. Can you?'
She held up the doll in her hands. 'Barbie waits for no Dark-
Hunter.'

Nick laughed. 'Sure, Liza, thanks.'

As they headed for the door, Liza stopped them. 'You
know,' she said to Amanda as she tottered up to her. The
old woman barely cleared five feet. She patted Amanda on
the arm. 'You have a graceful look to you. Like a pretty
little angel.'

Amanda smiled in gratitude. 'Thank you.'

Liza tilted the lenses up on her headgear and walked to a
shelf by the door. She stood up on her tiptoes and took a
custom-crafted Barbie off the shelf. It was all white, with
long, curly black hair, and it had faint, wispy angel wings
and a beautiful white beadwork gown.

Never had Amanda seen anything more beautiful or delicate.

Liza handed it to her. 'Her name is Starla. I painted her
face like a lady I know who comes in here all the time.' She
held the doll to her ear as if the doll were talking to her. She
nodded, then handed the Barbie to Amanda. 'She says she
wants to go home with you.'

Amanda's jaw dropped. Especially when she saw the four-
hundred-dollar price tag on the doll. 'Thank you, Liza, but
I can't take this,' she said, trying to give it back.

Liza waved her hand, refusing. 'It's yours, hon. You need
an angel to watch over you.'

'But—'

'It's all right,' Nick said, inclining his head to the door.
Then in a low tone, he said, 'Don't hurt her feelings by
refusing it. She loves to give them away.'

Amanda hugged the old woman. 'Thank you, Liza. I will
treasure her always.'

They were almost out the door when Liza stopped them
again. She took the doll back. 'I forgot something,' she said.

'Starla is very special.' Liza put the doll's legs together, then pressed her head down.

Two pencil-thin, three-inch blades shot out of her feet.

'It's for Daimons,' Liza announced, pulling the head up until the blades retracted. 'Beauty is sometimes best when it's lethal.'

Okay, Amanda thought slowly. She wasn't quite sure what to make of all this.

Liza handed her the doll and patted her arm again. 'You two take care.'

'We will,' Nick said and this time they made it all the way to the street.

Amanda stared at the doll in her hands, not sure what to think.

Nick laughed at her the whole way to the car.

'Liza's a Squire, isn't she?' Amanda asked as she got into the Jag and placed Starla *very* carefully in her lap.

'She's retired, but yes. She was a Squire and an Oracle for about thirty-five years until she turned Xander's care over to Brynna.'

'Is Liza the one who makes the boots for Kyrian?'

He shook his head as he started the engine. 'Another Dark-Hunter makes the big weapons. The swords, boots, and such. Liza makes the small weapons like the pendulums that carry plastique. She's an accomplished artist who likes to make jewelry and other innocuous items lethal.'

Amanda let out a deep breath. 'You guys are scary.'

He laughed at that, then checked his watch. 'It's almost three. We still have to go to Talon's and I have to get you back before dark, so we need to rush.'

'Okay.'

They drove for a good forty minutes, out of the city and into the deep bayou.

Down at the end of a long, winding dirt road, they came to a large, old shed/houselike structure. If not for the new locks on it, she wouldn't have believed anyone had used it in a hundred years. Well, that and the peculiar mailbox in front of it. It was black with what appeared to be giant silver spikes going through the box both diagonally and horizontally.

'Talon is weird,' Nick said as he caught her staring at it. 'He thinks it's funny that he staked his mailbox.'

Nick opened the garage door with the remote in his car. She gasped as they pulled inside and Nick parked the Jag.

Inside, the shed was tile and steel and housed a Viper, a collection of five Harley-Davidsons, and a small catamaran docked in the rear, over the swamp.

'Wow,' she breathed as she spotted one Harley that stood apart from the others. Sleek and black, it gleamed in the dim light. It was obviously a prized possession and she remembered Talon riding it last night.

Nick paid no attention to the car or motorcycles as he headed for the docked catamaran.

'Talon lives all the way out here?' she asked as she joined him on the crisp, clean dock and noticed that they had left enough room for another boat beside the first one.

He helped her into the catamaran, then moved to open the garage door that led out to the swamp. 'Yeah, being an ancient Celt, he loves nature. Even when it's gruesome.'

Amanda arched a brow. 'Is he really an ancient Celt?'

'Oh yeah. From the fifth or sixth century. He was a chieftain. His father was a druid high priest and his mother the leader before him.'

'Really?'

He nodded as he untied the boat, then jumped inside it. Once she was seated, he started the whirring engine.

'How did he become a Dark-Hunter?' she shouted over the roar.

'His clan betrayed him,' Nick said, steering the boat out into the swamp. 'They told him they needed to sacrifice someone of his blood. It was either him or his sister. He agreed, but as soon as they had him tied down, they killed his sister in front of him. He went nuts, but since he was tied down, there was nothing he could do. As they turned to kill him, he swore vengeance on all of them.'

Jeez, did *none* of them have a happy life?

'He killed his clan members?' she asked.

'I would imagine so.'

Amanda sat in silence while she thought about that. Poor Talon. She couldn't imagine what it would be like to watch one of her beloved sisters die before her eyes. They might annoy her a large portion of the time, but they meant the world to her and she would kill anyone who hurt one of them.

The horror that man must have felt that day. It must still haunt him.

Nick navigated deep into the swamp until they came upon an incredibly small cabin. She doubted it was even eight hundred square feet. It looked even more rundown on the outside than the shed where they had left Nick's car. The rough wood was a light, sun-faded gray and it looked as if it would crumble under the slightest breeze.

As they approached it, she saw a dock behind the cabin with two large generators and another catamaran.

'What does he do during hurricane season?' she asked as Nick turned off the boat.

'Nothing really. One of Talon's powers is that he can control the weather so it's not that big a danger. But there's always the possibility the place could blow apart in the daylight while he's sleeping and not aware of weather conditions. In which case, he's toast.'

'They like to live dangerously, don't they?'

He laughed. 'It takes a certain breed to do what they do. Flirting with disaster is pretty much a basic requirement.'

Nick got out of the boat first with a warning for her to

stay put. He carefully walked along a narrow, old walkway that led from the makeshift dock to the cabin door, then motioned for her to join him.

'Back off, Beth,' he snapped as an alligator approached her.

Amanda jumped back onto the boat.

'It's okay,' Nick assured her. 'They protect Talon in the daylight. As long as you're with me, they're harmless.'

'I don't know about this,' she said, reluctantly leaving the boat again.

Four massively huge alligators kept a vicious eye on her and followed her all the way to the door. Amanda's throat constricted in fear as the largest alligator climbed up on the porch behind them and swished its tail.

It hissed at them.

'Shut up, Beth,' Nick snapped. 'Or I swear I'll make luggage out of you.' Nick knocked on the faded old door.

'It's not dark yet, Nick,' Talon's thickly accented voice snapped from inside, making her wonder how he knew it was them. 'What do you want?'

'I need your *srad* for Kyrian before it gets dark.'

Amanda heard rustling on the other side of the door. A few seconds later, the lock clicked and the door opened the tiniest of cracks. Nick opened it wider and let them in.

She tried to see in the darkness, but had no luck until Nick turned on a small desk lamp.

Amanda froze as soon as she saw the interior. The walls were painted black and the place looked like a military control room. There were computers and electronic equipment everywhere. Though the location and-outside of the cabin would deny it, the man was a techno-junkie.

When her gaze touched on Talon, her jaw dropped wide open. The man was *completely* naked.

And he looked really good.

She stared at his perfect body, which was covered with

strange red and black Celtic tattoos over the left side of his torso, front and back, and all the way down his left arm. His large, dragon-headed torc gleamed in the dim light. And though the man was sinfully handsome, she was strangely unmoved by him.

She appreciated him for the incredible picture he cut, but he didn't make her heart race like Kyrian did. Nor did she feel even a hint of sexual desire toward him.

And Talon was totally unabashed by his state of undress.

Nick gave her an amused grin. 'I should have warned you, ancient warriors tend not to think much about nudity. Clothing is a modern hang-up none of them seem to have.' He looked at Talon. 'Celt, put some clothes on before you shock her.'

Talon growled at him. 'Why? I'm going back to bed. Take what you need and lock the door behind you.' He paused at his futon in the back corner and raked a hungry look over Amanda. 'Of course, if you want to leave Amanda, I might be persuaded to stay up for a bit and be sociable.'

Nick scoffed. 'Damn, Talon, can't you go an hour without a woman?'

'One is no problem. It's when I get to two or three that I get antsy.' Talon returned to lie down on the black futon. He rolled over on his side and closed his eyes.

At least until his phone rang. Talon cursed, rolled over, and answered it while Nick went to the huge weapon cabinet and picked up two nasty-looking round dagger things.

'Wulf, I'm not even awake yet,' Talon growled. 'And I don't really care, and why would you ask me something about ancient Greece anyway? Did I live there? The answer is *hell* no . . . Don't know, don't care . . . Hang on.' He turned over and looked at Nick. 'Nick, ever heard of Cult of Pollux?'

Nick looked over at him. 'You'd have to call Kyrian or one of the other Greeks.'

'Did you hear that?' Talon listened a sec, then turned back to Nick. 'Ash is walkabout, Brax, Jayce, and Kyros are MIA, and Kyrian isn't answering his phone. Wulf says it's *really* important.'

The significance of that sentence seemed to hit both men at once.

Talon spoke into the phone. 'When did you last try to reach Kyrian?'

Nick pulled his cell phone out and dialed.

'He might be in the shower,' Amanda suggested.

Nick shook his head. 'Even if he was, Rosa would answer.'

After a minute, Nick turned off the cell phone. 'Something's seriously wrong.'

Chapter 10

Kyrian woke up the instant his bedroom door opened.

Not fully conscious, he sensed Rosa entering his room and wondered why she would disturb him. She'd never done so before.

He rolled onto his back. 'Is something . . .'

The sentence died when a light, shimmering web covered him, pinning him to the bed. Kyrian froze as fury welled up inside him. He couldn't stand being trapped, especially flat on his back. Blood lust surged through him with a murderous frenzy.

Until he saw Rosa.

She stood by his bed, her brow covered in sweat as she stared at him with lost, dazed eyes. Over and over, she whispered the Spanish words, *'Debe matarle, debe matarle.'*

Must kill him, must kill him . . .

She raised the cleaver in her hand.

'Rosa,' Kyrian said as calmly as possible. 'Put the cleaver down.'

'Debe matarle . . .' She stepped closer to the bed.

'Rosa, *no haga esto*. Don't do this. Let me up. *Déjeme para arriba, por favor.'*

She was shaking so badly, Kyrian feared she'd have a stroke or coronary at any moment. Her frail body couldn't sustain this amount of stress.

'Desiderius say you are bad, *m'ijo*. You must die.'

Kyrian tried to think of some way to reach through her hazy madness and bring her back to reality. 'Rosa, you know me better than that.'

She lifted the cleaver higher.

Helpless beneath the net, Kyrian stared at the shining steel, waiting for it to slice into him. He wanted to implore her, to shout at her until she listened, but he didn't dare for fear of what it might do to the older woman. She was under enough stress without his adding to it. He would die before he harmed her.

His cell phone rang.

'I know, Desiderius,' she whispered in Spanish. 'I know. He must die.' She placed a hand on Kyrian's chest as if to keep him still. Not that he could move. The net held him completely immobile. 'Must be cut into pieces.'

Kyrian tensed as she brought the cleaver down.

It missed him by a hairsbreadth.

'*M'ijo,*' she whispered. Life returned to her eyes a second before they rolled back into her head.

She fell to the floor.

Terrified she was hurt, and panicking over his own vulnerability, Kyrian fought against the net with all his strength. It was no use. It was one of Artemis's nets, and once captured beneath it, any prey was completely trapped.

How in the gods' names could Rosa have gotten hold of it? Not even Desiderius should have had access to it. Only a god or demigod could claim an immortal weapon from its sacred resting place, and Artemis in particular guarded her weapons well.

And how could the Daimon reach out and control Rosa from a bolt-hole? No Daimon was that powerful.

Just what the hell was going on here?

Even though he knew it was futile, Kyrian fought against his confinement. As every minute passed, memories surged through him.

'How does it feel, Commander?' Valerius's voice taunted him from the past. 'You are completely under my control. Totally powerless. Defenseless.' He could still see the evil smile on the Roman's face, feel the agony of his torture. 'I'm going to enjoy watching you squirm for me. Hearing you beg for my mercy.'

Kyrian's sight dimmed as he relived every moment. He struggled to breathe. He would not be trapped again. Not like this.

Like a man possessed, he fought the net with every shred of strength he had.

An hour after dark, Nick entered the house first with Amanda and Talon only one step behind.

'Rosa?' Nick shouted, rushing through the kitchen and living room, toward the stairs. 'Kyrian?'

No one answered. The eerie silence rang in Amanda's ears as they ran up the stairs toward Kyrian's bedroom. Nick threw open the doors so forcefully that the breeze stirred the bed's sheers.

The room was empty.

Amanda hesitated in the doorway as she surveyed everything. Nothing was out of place, except for the bed's covers. Yet . . .

She *felt* something wrong. Something deep within her stirred her dormant powers and allowed her to connect with Kyrian. She sensed his concern. His fury.

Talon moved to the bed and cursed as he lifted a shimmery, silver web. 'This is unbelievable,' he snarled, balling it up into his fist.

'What is it?' Amanda asked.

'A *diktyon*. One of Artemis's nets.'

Amanda had absolutely no idea what that was, but she could tell by Talon's face it wasn't good. Nor should it be in Kyrian's bed while Kyrian was nowhere to be found. Panic sliced through her even more ferociously than before. 'Why is it here?'

'I have no idea, but if Kyrian was under it, I would say he's been taken by whoever tossed it on top of him.' Talon leaned over and picked a cleaver up from the floor.

Amanda's panic increased, and against her will, her powers surged, searching for Kyrian. She hated the thought of letting her psychic abilities have control of her, but she needed to know he was all right. She had to know *something*.

Closing her eyes, she saw him in a sterile environment. He was worried, but she didn't sense any danger from him. 'Try calling his cell phone,' she said to Talon.

He gave her a 'duh' stare. 'I've tried a dozen times.'

'Try a dozen and one.'

His expression told her he didn't appreciate her commanding tone one iota. 'All right,' he reluctantly agreed. 'What the hell? Futility has its purposes in life.' Talon pulled his cell phone out of his jacket pocket and dialed.

'There's no sign of a struggle,' Nick said, looking around.

'Kyrian,' Talon snapped, giving Amanda an odd look. 'Where the hell are you?'

Amanda took a step closer, her heart hammering as she realized that she had been right.

'You stay put until we get there.' Talon hung up and looked at Nick. 'He's at the hospital. Rosa had a heart attack.'

'Oh, my God,' Nick gasped. 'Is she all right?'

'He didn't go into it since he's not supposed to be on the cell phone in the hospital. Said he'd fill us in when we get there.'

*

Kyrian paced the waiting room anxiously. Anger and fear warred inside him. He wanted Desiderius's head for this. One way or another, he would make the Daimon pay.

'Just let Rosa be okay,' he breathed for the millionth time.

'Kyrian?'

He turned at the sound of Amanda's soothing voice. An inexplicable joy and relief tore through him at the sight of her approaching him.

Before he realized what he was doing, he pulled her into his arms and held her so tightly that she protested. But he couldn't help himself. His relief at seeing her alive and unhurt was too great. Now that he knew just how easily Desiderius could enter someone's home, nowhere was safe for her.

Desiderius could reach her anywhere. Use anyone to kill her.

That thought terrified him, and somewhere in the back of his mind was a little voice that warned him Desiderius might use her against him.

If they gave him the chance.

Kyrian cupped her face in his hands and kissed her deeply. He was going to kill the Daimon. As soon as Desiderius emerged from his bolt-hole, the Daimon would live no more. And for the first time in his existence, he would relish taking a life.

He looked up and caught Talon's censuring gaze and knew what thoughts were on the Celt's mind. Dark-Hunters weren't supposed to become romantically tied to anyone. It was the first, and most necessary rule of the Code. No one could ever think clearly when their heart was involved. Of all men, Kyrian knew that for fact.

Still, it didn't change what he felt for her.

'I need you to keep Amanda safe,' Kyrian told Talon.

Talon narrowed his eyes. 'Tell me what happened.'

'Desiderius used Rosa to trap me. He had complete

control of her. If he can do that to Rosa, he can do it to *anyone*.'

Talon let out a slow breath. 'And you wonder why I live alone.'

Kyrian ignored his warning tone and the meaningful look Talon gave Amanda.

Kyrian met Amanda's gaze and gently stroked her cheek with his thumb. 'Amanda, I need you to call your sister. Tell her to guard her back and to not be alone. Have one of your sisters raise a cone of protection or whatever it is they do to protect her from Desiderius. We've no idea what other powers he might have.'

He sensed her worry and fear. Her heart was pounding in her chest.

'I take it these aren't normal Daimon powers?' she asked.

'No. We've never encountered anything like it.' He looked back at Talon. 'I spoke to D'Alerian and he said Desiderius is messing with the human subconscious in order to weaken their resistance to his power. D'Alerian should be able to provide some help, but he can't guarantee absolute protection. Call Acheron and tell him I think we have a rogue god on the loose. One of them has to be helping Desiderius. There's no other explanation. And it would help if we knew who and why.'

Talon nodded. 'What are you going to do?'

'I'm going to do my damnedest to finish this tonight. If I can find his bolt-hole, I'm going into it.'

Talon's eyes were harsh. 'Kyrian, you're not a Were-Hunter. If you go in, you won't be able to come back out. You'll kill yourself trying, or worse, you'll be stuck between dimensions forever. Let me call Kattalakis—'

'I told you, we don't dare let a Were-Hunter near this guy. I'm more convinced of that now than ever. God help us all if Desiderius claims one of *their* souls. It's a risk we can't take.' He glanced to Amanda and the concern on her face.

He would protect her, no matter what. 'Second rule of the Code, you've got to do what you've got to do. If I die, you're up next. And if you are, *don't fail*.'

Talon nodded even while Amanda grabbed Kyrian's arm. 'Kyrian,' she whispered, 'I don't want you out there alone.'

'I know, Amanda. But he's too powerful and dangerous to go unchallenged. He almost killed Rosa.' Kyrian left out the part about how she'd almost killed him. They didn't need to know that.

Thank the gods D'Alerian had sensed Rosa's subconscious turmoil and come when he had. If not for the Dream-Hunter's intervention, Kyrian would still be trapped in his bed.

And trapped in his bed without Amanda was not something he wanted.

'Nick,' he said, looking past her to his Squire. 'Call me the instant you hear from the doctor.' He started to leave, but Amanda stopped him.

Before he realized what she intended, she pulled him to her lips and kissed him blind. Her lips tugged at his while her tongue stroked his. He felt her hands clutching the lapels of his coat. Felt her fear for him, and it scorched his wounded heart with pure bliss. 'You be careful,' she said in a stern voice.

He touched her lightly on the chin. 'I will.'

Amanda watched him walk off with a sick feeling in her stomach. 'Talon, are you sure you can't help him?'

'Believe me, I hate the "no help" rule as much as you do. But if I tried to help, I'd only weaken him.'

Nick handed her his phone. 'Call Tabitha and warn her.'

As Amanda dialed the first number another thought struck. 'Who is D'Alerian and how can he guard our subconscious?'

'He's one of the Dream-Hunters we told you about,' Talon said.

She frowned. 'So do you guys get to pick which one you are?'

Talon shook his head. 'Dream-Hunters are a whole other species. They're born of the gods and not made from humans.'

'And the Were-Hunters? Where do they come from?'

'They are half human, half Apollites who got a hold of some seriously bad mojo.'

She swallowed the fear that rose up to choke her. That didn't sound good at all. 'I thought they were good guys.'

'Some of them are, but some of them are slayers.'

'With the powers of a sorcerer who can walk through time and space,' she said, her stomach knotting.

'And occasionally dreams,' Nick supplied.

Amanda laughed nervously. 'You know, I was a whole lot happier when I didn't know about any of this.'

'Which is why we do our best to keep this silent,' Talon said. 'Believe me, humans would never be able to sleep at night if they knew what was out there waiting for them.'

Amanda nodded, wondering if she'd ever be able to sleep again.

Terrified, she finished dialing her sister's number. Now that she knew more about what they were dealing with, she needed to get her sister to watch out for Lord King Badass, and the Dark-Hunter who was their only hope.

Kyrian spent the entire night hunting the streets of New Orleans to no avail. Desiderius was still in his bolt-hole and there was no sign of him or any other Daimon anywhere. It may have been that his powers still weren't up to their full capacity or that the Daimon had some way of shielding his location. Whatever it was, Kyrian couldn't find a trace of him. Not even his electronic tracker helped.

He cursed his luck.

Never in his Dark-Hunter existence had he been so uncertain.

He didn't like the feeling one bit. Especially not when Amanda's life balanced on whether or not he could find the fiend and stop him.

Disgusted and weary, he made his way into his house. Everything was dark and silent. Amanda was upstairs in the house. He could feel her presence like a touch and it soothed him in a way he didn't want to contemplate.

Just knowing she was here . . .

Happiness surged through him.

But he didn't seek her out. He had too many things on his mind. Things he needed to sort out. Think through.

He entered the billiard room and grabbed his glove and baseball, then went to pitch it. Focusing on the ball, he let his mind wander. Wander through his painful past, and to the doubts that still lingered.

Why couldn't his wife have loved him?

Since the day Theone had betrayed him, he had been suspicious of anyone who came near him. He had given his wife everything he had, and still it hadn't been enough. If he couldn't win her love, then he could win no one else's. He knew it.

Over the centuries, Kyrian had convinced himself that it didn't matter. That he needed no one at all.

Until Amanda. She had breached his defenses and now he felt naked before her.

She, alone, had opened his heart and touched him deep inside it. He wanted her. Mind. Body. Soul. There was no part of her he didn't want to claim.

A movement to his left caught his attention.

Turning his head, he saw Amanda coming through the doorway, dressed in sweats. He couldn't believe how sexy he found them on her. She had her hair in two braids down the side of her face. There was something innocent and almost childlike in the way she was dressed, but there was nothing girlish about the woman approaching him.

She shook the man in him all the way to his foundations. 'How long have you been home?' she asked.

Kyrian would have answered, but she chose that moment to walk up to him and kiss his cheek. A strange sensation ran through him. Her actions were those of true affection.

'What are you doing up?' he asked. 'It's after four.'

'I couldn't sleep.'

She left his side to walk to the other end of the atrium room. When she turned to face him, he saw Nick's baseball glove on her hand. Like a pro, she held the glove up to catch the ball.

He smiled and tossed the ball gently to her.

She caught it, then fired back a fast ball that hit his glove with a resounding smack and burned his palm beneath the leather. 'Ow!' he teased at the sting on his hand. She threw better than Nick did. 'I'm impressed.'

She winked at him. 'I was the closest thing to a son my poor father had. He taught me to play.'

Kyrian tossed the ball back to her. 'He taught you well.'

Her smile widened. They tossed the ball for several minutes in silence. Gods, he had never thought to find a woman willing to do this with him at such an unholy hour. Even Nick complained, but Amanda seemed content just to be with him.

'How did it go?' she asked. 'Did you find him?'

'No.' He sighed. 'I just can't figure it out.'

'You will.'

He hesitated as he heard the utter confidence in her voice. 'You have no doubts?'

'None. I know you won't let him hurt us.'

'I couldn't help Rosa.'

'I'm sorry,' she said as she caught the ball and returned it. 'It must be hard for you to accept that fact, but it wasn't your fault. You did your best to protect her.'

Kyrian clenched his teeth. 'It hurts. More than I thought possible. I can't believe he got to her.'

Her eyes were sympathetic and warm as she smiled sadly at him. 'I guess it explains how he got into our houses to start the fires.'

He nodded. 'He probably used Allison. I found her passed out in her room, much like Rosa. I think the human mind can't handle the stress of it.'

'If it helps, Tabitha said Allison is fine and back home now, so Rosa should heal and be back to normal without any lasting damage.'

'That's good to know.' Kyrian watched her as she played ball with him. And with every toss of the baseball, he felt himself slipping more and more.

He knew he was falling for her and he was powerless against it.

In fact, the longer they played, the more he wanted her. He watched her shirt pull tight when she drew back to toss the ball. And he loved the way tendrils of her hair swept onto her face and she had to brush them back. Her lips were parted and her breathing heavy.

He found himself purposely throwing the ball over her head to watch her reach up to catch it. Every time she did, the sweatshirt rode up, baring a portion of her stomach to his hungry gaze. Then she would run after the ball, her breasts bobbing, her hips swaying. But the best part was seeing her well-proportioned backside when she bent over to retrieve the ball. Gods, but that woman had the best derriere . . .

Unable to stand it anymore, he tossed the glove to the ground.

Amanda froze as Kyrian took long, determined strides toward her. Before she could figure out his intent, he picked her up in his arms and kissed her fiercely.

Those wonderful, hard muscles flexed around her while he held her feet off the ground. Due to her size, no man had ever been able to pick her up, and yet Kyrian did it with such ease that it made her heart pound. She loved the way he made her feel. So feminine. So petite.

She wrapped her legs around his waist as his tongue ravished her mouth. Oh, the heaven of those hard, developed abs flexing between her thighs . . . The man was perfection.

Growling, he nipped her lips with his fangs while his hand cupped her bottom.

He left her lips and nuzzled her neck, nibbling his way under her chin. Her entire body melted at the feel of his hot breath on her skin. Oh yes, this was what she had wanted all day. Just to feel his arms holding her. To have him in her arms where she could give him all the love she felt for him.

She throbbed, needing him to fill her again.

Kyrian shook from the force of his want. Over and over, he remembered the way she had felt as he slid himself into her. The look on her face as she came in his arms.

He burned for her, and yet he dared not take her.

Not now. Not when he needed his strength to fight Desiderius.

Still, his body didn't listen. He had to touch her. Had to feel her skin.

Before he could stop himself, he sank to his knees and laid her down against the cold tile floor.

Amanda swallowed at the raw hunger on his face. He removed her clothes so fast that she barely felt his hands on her at all. But once he had her naked, it was another story entirely.

Only then did he slow down.

Fully clothed, he stared at her naked body in the moonlight as he ran his hands over her breasts, tracing them, teasing her hard nipples with his palms. 'You are the most beautiful woman I've ever seen,' he said, his voice low.

Amanda knew better than that. She'd seen the beauty of his wife, but the knowledge that he felt that way about her sent a shiver through her. He was definitely the best-looking man she had *ever* seen. Period.

As he leaned down to kiss her passionately, she reached to unbutton his shirt.

Kyrian caught her hands in his and shook his head no. If he let those graceful, soft hands touch his skin, he knew he would be lost.

Instead, he kissed each palm in turn, then returned to her throat, her breasts. He sampled her body with his lips, his tongue, his fangs.

As Kyrian tasted her, he felt his honed powers surging. Desperate and hot, he trailed his mouth from her breasts down to her satiny stomach, then to her thighs. He heard her gasps of pleasure as she opened her legs to him.

Right then, he wanted to possess her with a ferocity that overwhelmed him. It was primitive and all-consuming. And all he could think of was Amanda.

Her blood pounded in his ears.

Shaking from the force of it, he closed his eyes and took her into his mouth to taste the sweetness of her body that he craved most.

Amanda moaned at the feel of his tongue inside her. Burying her hands in his hair, she lifted her hips to him. He was so wild as he tasted her. So ferocious and thorough that she hissed at the incredible feel of him making love to her with his mouth.

He was absolutely relentless with his hot caresses, and when she came, it tore through her, making her scream and writhe with the most blissful orgasm she'd ever experienced.

Still he tasted her. Again and again. His tongue and mouth swirled and teased, stroking her, coaxing her until she was lost in the throes of another orgasm even more intense than the first one. Her head spun from it and every single nerve ending in her body tingled.

Kyrian pulled away from her then, and crawled up her body like a hot, panting predator. His eyes were even blacker than they'd been before as he parted his lips and stared at her neck with a hunger so intense it startled her.

'Kyrian?' she asked.

Kyrian could barely hear her through the haze in his mind. All he could smell was her scent. Her body pressed against his as he throbbed and ached for more.

Take her. Taste her. Claim her.

Make her yours . . .

He ground his teeth as he watched the vein in her neck pulse. *Just one taste . . .*

One taste . . .

But it would be against her will.

'Is something wrong?' she asked.

He struggled against his hunger that demanded he take her regardless. His groin was on fire for her. His needs out of control.

Her scent was all over him. She was all he could focus on. All he could think of.

And it made him dangerous. Lethal.

Growling, he summoned up the last of his willpower and forced himself away from her. 'Run, Amanda,' he snarled.

Amanda didn't hesitate. Something was wrong with him. Grabbing her clothes, she ran to her room.

Kyrian heard her footsteps recede as he lay on the cold floor. He buried his hand against his burning erection as he writhed in pain.

This was unlike anything he'd ever experienced. Dear Zeus, another minute and he would have sunk his fangs into her.

Closing his eyes, he shook as he fought down the beast inside him. The beast that demanded he take her over and over, no matter the consequences.

*

Amanda didn't stop shaking until she reached her bedroom. She would never forget the feral look on Kyrian's face when he had told her to run.

She'd never feared him before, but right then she had seen the Dark-Hunter in him that she was sure made the Daimons wet themselves in terror.

Breathing deeply, she tried to calm herself. All she'd ever wanted was a normal relationship.

But then normality with a vampire was asking a lot.

Her heart pounding, she paused as she saw herself in the mirror. Her lips were swollen from his kisses, her neck red from where his whiskers had rubbed against her.

'Amanda?'

She paused at the sound of Kyrian's voice through the door. 'Yes?' she asked hesitantly.

He nudged the door open, but didn't come inside. 'Did I scare you?'

'Honestly?'

He nodded.

'Yes.'

His heated gaze bored into her. 'I'm sorry.'

She knew he meant it. Could see the guilt in his eyes.

'Why haven't you asked to go home?' Kyrian asked, his low tone cutting across the quiet stillness of the room.

She tensed at his question. 'You want me to leave?'

He was silent so long she didn't think he would answer. Finally he whispered, 'No, I don't.'

There was so much heartfelt emotion in those three words that she couldn't have been more stunned had he declared his love.

She started for him and he took a step back. She realized he still wasn't in full control of himself. Even so, she wanted him.

'Then I won't leave until I wear out my welcome.'

Kyrian froze at her words. In the back of his mind was

the thought that the earth would surely cease to exist before Amanda wore out her welcome in his house. And it was quickly followed by the knowledge that when the earth ceased to exist, he would still be alive and Amanda . . .

He winced at the truth of immortality and the knowledge that for the two of them there could never be a happily-ever-after.

Chapter 11

The next night, Kyrian was haunted by what had happened with Amanda.

He'd come so close to losing it with her. So close to . . .

He forced it from his mind as he walked the rooftops of the French Quarter at midnight. The frigid winds whipped at his leather coat while he walked along the roof's edge, looking down into the alleys below.

Like a cat, he often prowled high above where no one could see him coming. At least not until it was too late.

He paused as he heard something.

'Don't hurt me.' The frightened voice was faint on the wind and came from several blocks over.

Twice as fast and as surefooted as a cheetah, he glided over the rooftops until he found the one who had spoken. To most, it would look like a poor man being mugged in a dark alleyway, but the four blond Daimons were highlighted by Kyrian's Dark-Hunter vision.

He arched a brow at the ordinariness of the scene. For some reason, Daimons liked to travel in fours or sixes.

They had the poor human man cornered against an old, rundown building.

Something about the human seemed strangely familiar to him.

The stench of the garbage was pungent as the man tried to hand the Daimons his wallet. 'Take it,' he said, his voice wavering. 'Just don't hurt me.'

The tallest Daimon laughed. 'Oh, we're not going to hurt you, little human. We're going to *kill* you.'

Kyrian stepped off the roof with his arms spread for balance. His black coat fluttered in the wind as he fell three stories down to the alley below.

He landed in a silent crouch behind them.

'Did you hear something?' one of the Daimons asked, looking around.

'Just the sound of a human heart pounding.' The tallest Daimon grabbed the man.

'Or,' Kyrian said, rising slowly to his full height. He pulled his coat back and placed his hand over the hilt of Talon's *srad*. 'The sound of four Daimons about to die.'

As they stepped away from their victim, he recognized the human. It was Cliff.

Cliff recognized him at the same instant.

'You!' he roared. 'What are you doing here?'

Damn you, Fates, Kyrian thought. The last thing he wanted to do was help the man who had hurt Amanda. She had told him the whole story of her ex-fiancé. Right down to Cliff's harsh criticisms of her family. The man didn't deserve his help.

Damn you, Code.

Out loud Kyrian said, 'It would appear I'm saving your life.'

'I don't need your help.'

The four Daimons turned to look at Cliff, then burst out laughing.

'You heard him, Dark-Hunter,' the Daimon leader said. 'He doesn't need your help. So, go on. Go away.'

More tempted to leave than he ought to be, Kyrian let out a slow breath. 'Yes, but you know, sometimes you just have to save them even when they don't want to be saved.'

The tallest Daimon attacked. Kyrian tossed the *srad*, but before it could make contact with the Daimon, Cliff grabbed the Daimon and whirled him away. 'Now, I'll show you who's bad.' He punched the Daimon who just stood there, laughing at him.

The *srad* bounced off the wall, breaking into two pieces. *Moron!* If not for Cliff's bullshit heroics, the Daimon would be dead.

Forcing himself, Kyrian ran to get between Cliff and the Daimon before the Daimon struck. He barely made it. As it was, he ended up being kicked into Cliff's flabby body.

The two of them fell to the ground. Rolling with the fall, Kyrian got to his feet in one swift move while Cliff struggled on the ground.

Kyrian fought the urge to roll his eyes at the weakling. 'Would you run already?'

Cliff blustered as he gained his feet. 'I'm just as capable of fighting them as you are.'

Kyrian growled low in his throat at the imbecile. For one thing, Cliff was barely six feet tall while the Daimons were Kyrian's height and over. Cliff had the body of a couch-warrior and the Daimons were well-honed and ready to kill.

Oh yeah, Cliff was a big threat.

Before he could move, two Daimons rushed him. Kyrian caught the first one with his boot and obliterated the Daimon into dust. The other slashed out at him with a sword.

Kyrian flipped up and backward, coming to rest on the fire escape above them.

'Hey!' Cliff said. 'How did you do that?'

He didn't have a chance to answer before the other three Daimons started up the ladder after him. Kyrian jumped back to the alley.

The Daimons followed.

Kyrian braced himself for them. As soon as the leader drew near, Cliff came running up beside him with a long two-by-four. He swung to hit the Daimons at the same time the Daimons moved for Kyrian.

Caught between the two, Kyrian couldn't maneuver. As a result, Cliff's board caught him across the back of his head.

Pain shot through his skull as he staggered back.

With a shake of his head, Kyrian recovered his senses a second before two Daimons grabbed his waist and knocked him to the ground. They grabbed his arms and spread him out. Panic set in the instant they held him there as his old memories surged through him.

'We found his vulnerability,' one of the Daimons said. 'Tell Desiderius that with his arms spread out, he goes nuts.'

They might have found it, but none of them would live long enough to reveal it.

Roaring with rage, Kyrian brought his legs up over his head and flipped himself up between them. His fangs bared, he stabbed one Daimon and then the other.

The remaining Daimon took off toward the street. Kyrian tossed the other *srad* straight into the Daimon's back. He evaporated.

Kyrian turned to see Cliff gaping at him.

His face ashen, Cliff's eyes rolled back in his head an instant before he passed out.

Disgusted, Kyrian went to check on him. His pulse was fast, but stable. 'What did she *ever* see in you?' he asked as he pulled out his cell phone and called an ambulance.

Hours later – once he was sure Cliff would live – Kyrian made his way into his house.

Still no Desiderius to be found. Anywhere.

Damn.

He stopped at the kitchen door to watch Amanda curiously. It was almost five A.M. and she appeared to be making soup and sandwiches.

How very odd is this?

She moved around the kitchen like a graceful nymph, completely unaware of his presence. She hummed a gentle tune, 'In the Hall of the Mountain King' by Grieg if he wasn't mistaken. What a strange choice.

He'd never seen a more beguiling woman in his life. She wore a silk dorm shirt that gave a hint of transparency, yet completely concealed her body from his view. The light blue color was a perfect complement for her pale skin and auburn hair.

His body reacted instantly to the sight of her, growing hard and hot.

The more he watched her, the more he wanted her.

She poured the soup into mugs, then dipped her finger into the soup to test the warmth.

It was more than an immortal man could take.

Moving like a shadow, he came up beside her and caught her hand.

She looked up with a gasp until she registered his identity. Smiling at her, he guided her finger into his mouth where he swirled his tongue around it, tasting the soup and the woman.

'Delicious,' he breathed.

A blush covered her cheeks. 'Hi, honey, how was work?'

He laughed out loud at her Donna Reed impersonation. 'Been watching *Nick at Nite* again?'

She shrugged coyly. 'I thought you might like to come home to a hot meal for once. It must get lonely to have nothing but an empty, dark house to greet you.'

More so than she would ever know. He stared down at her, at those parted lips that beckoned him. It had been centuries since anyone greeted him when he returned. Centuries of untold loneliness and solitude.

Loneliness and solitude that had vanished the instant he woke up in that abandoned factory and had looked into those wide, intelligent blue eyes that seared him.

Amanda was completely unprepared for Kyrian's next actions. He kissed her like a man possessed. His tongue stroking and delving as his hands roamed her back, then cupped her derriere.

It still amazed her that she allowed him to handle her like this, and yet she didn't mind it in the least. She'd never thought of herself as a particularly sexy person. Not until she met him.

When it came to Kyrian, she couldn't get enough.

She wanted him around her all the time. Wanted to hold him, touch him, be with him.

If she could, she would handcuff herself to him forever.

Without breaking from the kiss, he slid his hand beneath the bottom of her shirt, seeking her wet heat that throbbed for him. She moaned as he touched her, as his fingers slid and teased her mercilessly. Heaven, how this man made her yearn for him.

'Kyrian, your soup,' she said breathlessly.

He pulled back, his breathing ragged, his lips swollen from tasting her. 'It'll wait.'

There was something more untamed than usual about him tonight. Something wild and wicked. He carried her to the table and laid her across the top of it.

His eyes hot and hungry, he stood between her legs and looked down at her. 'Now here's a banquet fit for a king.'

And then he fell on her. Amanda gasped at the fury in his questing hands that seemed to be all over her at once. His touch electrified her. Satisfied her and left her craving more.

As he kissed her insane, she reached down between their bodies and unzipped his pants so that she could touch him. He was already rock-hard and throbbing and when she cupped him in her hands, he moaned against her lips.

He amazed her. This immortal warrior who needed no one and yet he was so tender in her arms. This man who trembled as she stroked his shaft and cupped him gently in her palm.

Kyrian couldn't think with her hands on him. All he could do was smell her, taste her.

He wanted her completely.

Wild with desire and unable to think past the moment, he pulled her hands away from him and drove himself into her.

Amanda groaned at the incredible feel of him deep inside her. He was so thick and hard. She felt so wonderfully full. She wrapped her legs around his waist as he rocked his hips hard and slow against hers.

'Oh yes, Kyrian,' she moaned, arching her back.

He ran his hand over her gauze-covered body, and cupped her breasts in his hands as he continued to thrust into her.

They made love without any hurry. Amanda writhed at the power of his thrusts as he nibbled her throat, scraping her skin with his fangs. Closing her eyes, she again felt that incredible bonding with him. They were one.

He trembled in her arms and whispered her name against her lips, making her quiver with desire.

And when the world shattered, she swore she could see colors everywhere.

Kyrian watched her climax, felt her body clutching his. Gods, how he yearned to satisfy himself, but he didn't dare. Already he felt his powers waning. Powers he needed to keep her safe.

Grinding his teeth, he reluctantly withdrew from her.

He straightened his clothes in silence, but his entire being ached. Pressing the heel of his hand against his jeans, he tried to loosen the fabric that bit into his erection.

It was useless.

Amanda felt sympathy for him as she watched his stiff,

awkward movements. How could he satisfy her and not take pleasure himself? It had to be sheer torture for him.

Yet he said nothing about it.

As he ate in silence, her heart wept for him. Her poor warrior.

And in the back of her mind came the little voice warning her that no matter how much she might want him, they could never have a relationship.

Amanda woke up a little after three in the afternoon. She got up, showered, and dressed while Kyrian continued to sleep.

Goodness, the man was handsome. He had one arm raised up around his head and looked more like a little boy as he slept than an immortal dark warrior.

Impulsively, she leaned over and kissed his parted lips. He reached for her, catching her about the neck. He held her so tightly that she could barely breathe.

'Kyrian?' she whispered, trying to get loose. 'Honey, you're making me turn blue.'

He paid no attention. It took her a full three minutes before she was finally able to extricate her head from his arms.

'Okay,' she breathed as he turned onto his side. 'Remind me not to do that again.'

Amanda pulled the covers over him and tiptoed from the room.

She found Nick in the living room downstairs wearing a pair of Rollerblades as he zipped from one end to the other, sorting papers.

'What are you doing?' she asked.

He paused and shrugged. 'Kyrian gets pissed when I use my skateboard in the house.'

Amanda laughed. 'Okay. But I imagine he's not fond of the skates, either.'

'Probably not, but damn, this place is huge and I need

to get from point A to point B without wearing my legs out.'

She laughed again. Nick was infectious once you got used to him.

He turned a tight circle and skated to the kitchen. Before she could get halfway through the living room, he returned with a glass of orange juice for her.

'Thanks,' she said, taking it from him. 'What's the word on Rosa?'

'Miguel said she's better. She was up watching *Wheel of Fortune* when I called.'

'Good.'

'Yeah, Kyrian will be happy.'

Suddenly, a loud crash sounded behind her. Terrified it was Desiderius bursting in, she whirled around to see a huge pile of gold and diamonds on the floor where a twelfth-century hand-carved table used to be.

'Oh man,' Nick said with a disgusted look. 'Kyrian really liked that table, too. Boy, is he ever going to be pissed.'

'What is *that*?' Amanda asked, getting up to go look at the king's ransom in gold bars and diamonds.

Nick sighed. 'It's payday.'

'Excuse me?'

He shrugged. 'Artemis hasn't caught on to the fact that she could just wire the money into her Dark-Hunters' accounts. So, once a month we end up with a wad of gold and diamonds somewhere weird. It was a real bitch the time it landed in the pool.'

'No kidding,' Amanda said, awed by the amount. 'Someone could get hurt.'

'That ain't no lie. It's what killed Kyrian's third Squire.'

She turned to look at him and quickly learned he wasn't joking.

'So, what do you do with all that?' she asked.

He smiled. 'I get to play Saint Nick. There's a Squire in

town who will convert it into currency. From there most of it goes to charities. Two percent of it is funneled into a Squire's fund that takes care of the families of Squires who die in the line of duty or Squires who retire, and another two percent goes to a research facility that makes nifty toys for the Dark-Hunters.'

'How much does Kyrian keep for himself?'

'None. He just lives off the interest of the money he had from when he was human.'

'Really?'

He nodded.

Wow. The man had been seriously loaded as a mortal. 'Okay, can I ask a really nosy question?'

Nick smiled. 'You want to know how much I make?'

'Yeah.'

'Enough to make me a very happy man.'

The phone rang.

Nick skated off while Amanda took her juice to the couch and sat down to read the paper. She set her juice on the black coffin coffee table.

A few minutes later, Nick came rushing back in, his brow furrowed. He didn't speak to her as he moved to the armoire against the far wall. He opened the locked door to display an entire arsenal of weapons.

Dread consumed her. 'What's going on? Who was on the phone?'

'That was Acheron calling with a full-alert warning.'

She frowned. By his frenzied movements, she knew it wasn't good. 'What does that mean?'

The look on his face chilled her. 'You know the phrase "All hell's breaking loose"?'

'Yes.'

'It was invented for full-alert. For some reason, there is a high concentration of Daimons leaving bolt-holes in this area, and when that happens, the Daimons reach their full power and they feed whether they need it or not. The only thing worse than a full-alert is a solar eclipse. Tonight, things will get ugly.'

At seven o'clock, Amanda learned firsthand what he had meant by that.

She was cleaning up Kyrian's 'breakfast' while Nick briefed him on what Acheron had said.

Kyrian had chosen twice the weapons he normally went out with and he was on his way out the door when the phone rang. Amanda answered it.

'Mom?' she asked as she recognized the crying voice. Her heart stopped. 'What is it?'

Kyrian went rigid at the door, then rushed to her side.

'Mandy,' her mother said through her sobs. 'It's Tabby . . .'

Amanda didn't want to hear anything more. She choked on her sob and dropped the phone. The next thing she knew, Kyrian held her in his arms while Nick talked to her mother.

Kyrian's sight dulled as he listened to her hysterical mother talking to Nick while Amanda trembled in his arms. Her tears soaked him, and as they fell, he vowed to kill Desiderius.

'It's all right,' he whispered against Amanda. 'She's just hurt.'

She pulled back and looked at him. 'What?'

Kyrian wiped the tears from her cheeks. 'He didn't kill her, sweeting.' Though she was in bad shape, from what he could gather from her mother, Tabitha would survive.

Desiderius, however, would not.

'Tabitha is in the hospital,' Nick said, hanging up the phone. 'Luckily, there were only two Daimons and her group was able to fight them off.' He looked to Kyrian. 'You know, it sounds to me like Desi was just toying with her to make you mad enough to lose your head in a fight. There's no other reason why he would send only two Daimons and not more.'

'Nick, shut up!' Kyrian snapped. The last thing he wanted was for Amanda to be any more upset. He kissed her lightly on the lips. 'Nick will take you to the hospital.'

He pulled out his cell phone and called Talon, who was already on his way into the city. He told the Celt to get over to his house and escort Amanda just in case Desiderius was waiting for them.

'Kyrian,' Amanda said as he hung up. 'I don't want you to go out tonight. I have a really bad feeling.'

So did he. 'I have to go.'

'Please, listen to me—'

'Shh,' he said, placing a finger over her lips. 'This is what I do, Amanda. It's what I am.'

As soon as he could, Kyrian had her in Nick's car with Talon tailing them while he headed downtown to find that bloodsucking, soul-stealing pig and do what he should have done the night they met.

Hours went by as Kyrian scoped out the French Quarter, looking for Desiderius. The Daimons would replenish their strength tonight, and sooner or later, he knew they would make an appearance in their prime feeding ground.

Desiderius, much like the rest of his brethren, preferred to haunt the French Quarter where unwary and often drunk tourists could be found.

So far, there was nothing.

'Hey, baby,' a prostitute called as he passed her. 'You want some company?'

Kyrian turned to face her, then pulled out all the money, about five hundred dollars, he had in his wallet and handed it to her. 'Why don't you take the night off and go get a good meal?'

Her face stunned, she grabbed the money and ran.

Kyrian sighed as he watched her dodge through the crowd. Poor woman. He hoped she put it to good use. Even if she didn't, she could certainly use the money a lot more than he could.

Out of the corner of his eye, he saw a flash of silver. Turning his head, he found two young men in the crowd. They were definitely human.

At first, they appeared to be the typical kind of street-gang youths Nick had once been, tough as nails and wearing black jackets, until he noticed the way they watched him.

As if they knew what he was.

His instincts alert, Kyrian returned their stares. The tallest, who appeared to be in his early twenties, crushed out his cigarette and crossed the street, his eyes never leaving Kyrian.

He raked a cold look over Kyrian's body. 'You the Dark-Hunter?'

Kyrian arched a brow. 'You the flunky?'

'I don't like your tone.'

'And I don't like you. Now that we've dispensed with the introductions and have declared our mutual distaste for one another, why don't you take me to the one who holds your leash?'

The man narrowed his eyes on him. 'Yeah, why don't I do that?'

It was a trap. Kyrian knew it. So be it. He wanted this confrontation. Was more than prepared for it.

Willingly, he followed after them.

They led him down the back alleys into a small, enclosed courtyard. Shrubs obscured most of the walls and tall plants blocked the streetlights from the area.

Kyrian didn't recognize any of it. But it didn't matter.

As they rounded a large hedge, he caught sight of Desiderius waiting. His smile evil, the Daimon held a panic-stricken pregnant woman in his arms with a knife at her throat.

'Welcome, Dark-Hunter,' he said, his free hand stroking the woman's distended belly. 'Can you believe what I was

lucky enough to find? Two life forces for the price of one.'
He bent his head and rubbed his nose against the woman's
neck. 'Mmm, just smell the strength.'

'Please,' the woman begged, her voice hysterical. 'Please
help me. Don't let him hurt my baby.'

Kyrian took a deep breath as he fought the fury inside him
that demanded Desiderius's blood on his hands. 'Let me
guess, you'll trade her life for mine?'

'Exactly.'

Trying to rattle his opponent, Kyrian let out a tired breath
as he surveyed the six Daimons and two human criminals
around him. If not for the woman, he could have taken them
easily. But one move against any of them and he had no
doubt Desiderius would cut her throat. Indeed, Daimons
valued very little more than taking the soul of a pregnant
woman.

'Couldn't you think up something a little more original
than this?' Kyrian taunted him, knowing Desiderius was
pompous enough to take insult. 'I mean, push your limits.
You're supposed to be a crazed mastermind and this is all
you have to offer?'

'Well, since you're unimpressed, let me kill her.' He
pressed the knife against her throat.

The woman screamed.

'Wait!' Kyrian snapped before the Daimon could draw
blood. 'You know I'm not going to let you hurt her.'

Desiderius smiled. 'Then drop your *srads* and move to
stand against the fence.'

How did he know about those?

'Okay,' Kyrian said slowly. 'And why?'

'Because I said so!'

Trying to figure out his reasoning, Kyrian pulled Talon's
weapons out from under his coat and moved slowly toward
the fence. Once he stood in front of it, the two human men
grabbed his wrists and placed ropes around them.

Suddenly, he was pulled backward, his arms spread out against the fence. Kyrian fought wildly. His heart pounding, he jerked at the ropes holding him pinned. All his calm, cool Dark-Hunter rationale evaporated, leaving him in the throes of panic. He fought his restraints like a wild animal caught in a trap.

He had to get out of this. He would not be tied helpless. Not like this. Not ever again.

He fought against the ropes, tearing the flesh around his wrists. He didn't care. All he wanted was his freedom.

'I told you I knew your weaknesses,' Desiderius said. 'Right down to the fact you would never let me hurt a pregnant human.' He leaned down and kissed the girl on her cheek. 'Melissa, be a good girl and thank the Dark-Hunter for his sacrifice.'

Kyrian froze as she left Desiderius's embrace and moved to stand by the oldest human male.

She'd been in on it all along.

Son of a bitch, when would he learn?

'Are you ready to die?' Desiderius asked.

Kyrian bared his fangs at him. 'I wouldn't be so cocky. You haven't killed me yet.'

'True, but the night is still young, isn't it? I have plenty of time to play with Artemis's errand boy.'

Kyrian gripped the ropes and pulled with all his strength as another wave of panic threatened to consume him. He had to calm down. He knew it, and yet those old, haunting memories of his torture in Rome tormented him.

'What's the matter?' Desiderius asked, stepping forward. 'You look a bit pale, Commander. Are you remembering the humiliation of your defeat? The touch of the Roman executioners as they prepared you?'

'Go to hell!' Kyrian toed the release for his boot and kicked out at Desiderius.

Desiderius jumped back out of range. 'Oh yes, I forgot

about those boots. After you, I shall have to go find good old Kell as my next Dark-Hunter target. With him out of the way, what would all of you do without your weapons expert?' He inclined his head to the girl. 'Melissa, be a dear and rid the commander of his boots.'

Kyrian ground his teeth as the girl came forward. Dark-Hunter law allowed him to protect himself against humans who sought to do him harm, but he couldn't bring himself to hurt her, especially while she was pregnant. Though she didn't know it, she was still a little girl. 'Why would you mess up your life with him?' he asked her as she pulled his boots off.

'Once my baby comes, he's going to make me immortal.'

'He doesn't have that power.'

'You're lying. Everyone knows vampires can take or give life. I want to be one of you.'

So that was how Desiderius was enlisting his human helpers. 'You could never be one of us. He'll kill you once he's finished.'

She laughed at him.

Desiderius clucked his tongue. 'Still trying to protect her even while she prepares you for your slaughter. How sweet. Tell me, were you so considerate of your Roman brothers?'

Kyrian threw his body toward Desiderius.

A Daimon came out of the shadows with a large hammer. Kyrian froze the instant he recognized it. He hadn't seen one in over two thousand years.

'Yes,' Desiderius said as he moved closer to Kyrian. 'You know what this is, don't you? Tell me, do you remember the way it felt when Valerius used it to break your legs?' Desiderius cocked his head. 'No? Then let me refresh your memory.'

Kyrian clenched his teeth as Desiderius brought the hammer down across his left knee, instantly splintering the bones. Once he had delivered a like blow to his right leg, the Daimon dared to stand before him.

Kyrian held himself up with his hands. He tried to put weight on his legs, but the pain made it impossible.

Desiderius smiled at him as he handed the hammer back to the Daimon. Then he pulled something out of his pocket.

Rage filled Kyrian as he recognized the ancient Roman spikes they had used for crucifixion.

'Tell me, Dark-Hunter,' Desiderius said with a smile, 'would you like me to put you up for the night?'

Chapter 12

Amanda came awake with a start. It took a full minute to realize she had fallen asleep in Tabitha's hospital room, lying against Nick. Her mother was asleep on the cot they had rolled in a short time ago, and she and Nick had taken the two uncomfortable chairs by the door.

Tabitha was still asleep on the bed where the doctors wanted to monitor her until morning. A Daimon had viciously cut a line down her sister's cheek that would leave an ugly scar. Bruises and cuts lined her body, but the doctor had assured them that Tabitha would heal.

Their sisters had gone home at their mother's urging, but Amanda had stayed just in case either of them needed anything. Her heart pounding, she looked up as her father returned to the room with two cups of coffee in his hands. He handed one to Nick. 'You want mine, kitten?' he asked Amanda, holding his cup out to her.

Amanda smiled at her father's kindness until she remembered her vision.

'You okay?' her father asked.

She looked at Nick, her heart pounding. 'Kyrian's in trouble.'

Nick laughed before taking a drink of coffee. 'You were dreaming.'

'No, Nick. He's in trouble. I saw him.'

'Just relax, Amanda, you've had a really bad day and you're worried about Tabitha. It's understandable, but Kyrian never gets in over his head. He's fine. Trust me.'

'No,' she insisted, 'listen to me. I'm the first to admit I hate my powers, but I know they're not lying to me. I can feel his panic and pain. We have to find him.'

'You can't go out there,' her father said. 'What if this Desiderius is waiting for you? What if he sends someone to hurt you like he did Tabby?'

She met her father's pale blue eyes and offered him a small smile. 'Daddy, I have to go. I can't let him die.'

Nick sighed. 'Amanda, come on. He's not going to die.'

She dug at his coat pocket. 'Then give me the keys to your car and I'll go myself.'

Nick playfully captured his keys from her hand. 'Kyrian would have my head.'

'He can't have your head if they kill him.'

She saw the indecision on his face. Nick set his coffee on the floor, then picked up his cell phone and dialed it.

'See,' she said. 'He's not answering.'

'That doesn't mean anything this time of night. He could be in the middle of a fight.'

'Or he could be seriously hurt.'

Nick pulled his PDA out of its cradle on his belt and turned it on. After a few seconds, his face paled.

'What is it?'

'His tracer's off.'

'Meaning?'

'I can't track him. No Dark-Hunter turns their tracer off. It's their lifeline if they get into trouble.' Nick shot to his feet and shrugged his coat on. 'Okay, let's go.'

Her father stepped between them and the door. He stood

even in height to Nick and had his entire body braced for a fight. 'You're not taking my baby out there to get hurt. I'll kill you first.'

Amanda stepped around Nick and kissed her father on his cheek. 'It's okay, Daddy. I know what I'm doing.'

By the light in his eyes, she knew he doubted her.

'Let her go, Tom,' her mother said from her cot. 'There's no danger to her tonight. Her aura is pure.'

'Are you sure?' he asked her mother.

She nodded.

Her father sighed, but still he looked doubtful. He glared at Nick. 'Don't you let her get hurt.'

'Believe me,' Nick said, 'I won't. I answer to a much scarier person than you for her welfare.'

Reluctantly her father let them leave.

Amanda rushed through the hospital, to the parking lot, then ran over to Nick's Jag.

Once they were in Nick's car, Amanda did her best to remember where she had seen Kyrian in her vision. 'It was a small, dark courtyard.'

Nick snorted. 'This is New Orleans, chère. That doesn't tell me anything.'

'I know. I think it was in the Quarter. But I don't know. Dammit, I just don't know.' She scanned the dark streets as they passed them. 'Is there a Dark-Hunter we could call who might be able to help find him? Maybe we should get Talon back?'

'No, Talon is hunting his own target.' He handed her his cell phone. 'Push redial and keep trying to call Kyrian.'

She did, repeatedly, but there was still no answer.

As dawn approached, Amanda became desperate. If they didn't find him soon, he'd be dead.

Terrified, she did what she had never dared before. She leaned her head back on the seat and purposefully reached down deep inside herself to touch the full strength of her untested powers. A terrifying surge went through her, making her warm and throbbing.

Images swam in her head, some old, some undefinable.

Just as she was sure her powers would tell her nothing, a clear image came to her. 'St. Philip Street,' she whispered. 'We'll find him there.'

They parked on St. Philip and got out of the car.

Amanda didn't know how, but she guided Nick down the alleys, straight to a dark courtyard. They rounded the buildings and saw nothing.

'Dammit, Amanda, he's not here.'

She barely heard him. Following her instincts, she rounded a tall hedge, then stopped dead in her tracks.

Kyrian hung against a fence, his entire body slumped.

'Oh, my God,' she breathed as she ran to him.

Gently, she lifted his head and gasped as she saw his bloodied face. They had beaten him so severely that he could barely open his eyes.

'Amanda?' he whispered. 'Is it really you, or am I dreaming?'

Tears filled her eyes. 'Yes, Kyrian. It's me.'

Nick cursed as he stopped beside her and reached to touch one of the nails in Kyrian's arm. He drew his hand back sharply before it made contact and hurt Kyrian more. She saw the rage in Nick's eyes as he cursed again. 'My God, they nailed him to a board.'

Amanda wanted to throw up at the thought. She could tell by the wounds exactly what Desiderius had done. He had reenacted Kyrian's execution.

'We've got to get you out of here,' she said.

Kyrian choked, then coughed up blood. 'There's not enough time.'

'He's right,' Nick concurred. 'It'll be dawn in five, maybe ten minutes. We'll never get him home before the sun rises.'

'Then call Tate.'

'He couldn't get here in time.' A tic appeared in Nick's jaw as he touched Kyrian's hand where someone had embedded a nail into the center of it. 'I'm not sure how we could get him loose even if Tate did make it in time.'

'It's all right,' Kyrian said, his voice strained. He swallowed and met Nick's tormented gaze. 'Take Amanda to Talon and have him protect her and Tabitha.'

Nick took off running.

Ignoring Nick, Amanda focused on Kyrian. 'I'm not going to let you die,' she insisted, her tone high-pitched and sharp. 'Damn it, Kyrian, you can't die like this and become a Shade. I won't let you.'

The tender look in his eyes stole her breath. 'I'm only sorry I failed you. I wish I could have been the hero you deserved.'

Amanda took his face in her hands and made him look at her. Her hands shook as she wiped the blood away from his lips and nose. 'Don't you dare give up. Do you hear me? If you die, who's to say Desiderius won't get Talon, too? Fight for me, Kyrian. Please!'

Kyrian grimaced. 'It's all right, Amanda. I'm just glad you found me. I didn't want to die alone . . . again.'

Her heart lurched at the words as tears fell down her face. No! The scream reverberated through her soul.

She couldn't let him die. Not like this. Not after he had protected and cared for her. Not after he had come to mean so much to her.

Over and over in her mind, she pictured her precious Dark-Hunter roaming the earth trapped between worlds. Forever hungry. Forever alone.

She couldn't allow that to happen.

Nick returned with a crowbar in his hands.

'What are you doing?'

Nick gave her a hard stare. 'I'm not going to let him die like this. I'm going to get him free.' He tried to pry the nail out of Kyrian's hand.

Kyrian drew rigid from the pain.

'No!' Amanda shouted.

Nick went flying. 'What the hell?'

Before she knew what she was doing, she felt her powers well up inside her. They surged forward like a waterfall, out of her control.

In that instant, the nails came free of Kyrian's body and he fell into her arms. 'Help me, Nick,' she breathed, trying to stay on her feet and hold him up.

Nick was aghast.

Shaking off his stupor, Nick picked Kyrian up in his arms. He staggered from the weight of him, but made his way to the car as fast as he could. 'We still don't have enough time to get him home before sunrise,' he panted out in broken syllables.

'We can take him to my sister's. She only lives a block over.'

'Which sister?'

'Esmeralda. You met her earlier, the one with the long black hair.'

'The voodoo high priestess?'

'No, the midwife.'

Without another word, Nick drove them to Essie's house in record time. It took some doing, but they managed to get Kyrian to the porch just as the sun started to rise over the roof opposite them.

Amanda pounded on the door to her sister's narrow Victorian home. 'Esmeralda? Hurry! Open the door.'

She saw her sister's shadow through the Victorian lace curtain an instant before the doorknob turned. Amanda shoved the door open and Nick carried Kyrian into the foyer without a second to spare.

'Pull the shades down,' Nick ordered Esmeralda as he laid Kyrian on the dark green contemporary sofa.

'Excuse me?' Esmeralda asked. 'What is this?'

'Just do it, Essie, I'll explain in a minute.'

Reluctantly, Essie followed Nick's orders.

Amanda touched Kyrian's face. 'They made a terrible mess of you.'

'How's Tabitha?' Kyrian asked weakly. Amanda was touched by his concern for her sister when he was so hurt himself.

'I'm calling an ambulance,' Esmeralda said, picking up the phone from the end table.

Nick grabbed the phone from her hands. 'No.'

The look on Esmeralda's face would have quelled most men. Nick just glared back at her without flinching.

'It's all right, Essie,' Amanda assured her. 'We can't take him to a hospital.'

'He's going to die if you don't.'

'No,' Nick said, 'he won't.'

Esmeralda cocked a disbelieving brow.

'He's not human,' Amanda explained.

Esmeralda narrowed her eyes suspiciously. 'What is he, then?'

'He's a vampire.'

Rage suffused her face as she railed against them all. 'You brought a vampire into my house? After what happened to Tabitha? My God, Amanda, where was your brain?'

'He's not going to hurt you,' Amanda insisted.

'You're damned straight. I'm going to call—'

Nick stepped between Esmeralda and the phone. 'You call anyone and I'll rip the phone out of the wall.'

'Boy,' Essie said in a warning tone, 'don't think for two seconds you—'

'Stop it!' Amanda shouted. 'Kyrian needs your help, Esmeralda, and as your little sister, I'm begging you for it.'

'Do you—'

'Essie, please.'

She saw the indecision warring in Essie's eyes and knew

the thoughts in her mind. On the one hand Esmeralda didn't want to help the evil undead; on the other, she couldn't really say no to her sister.

'Please, Es, I've never before asked a favor of you.'

'Not true. You borrowed my favorite sweater in high school to wear to that game where Bobby Daniels was playing.'

'Es!'

'All right,' she relented, 'but if he bites anyone in this house, I'm staking him.'

Kyrian lay still while Esmeralda and Amanda peeled his bloodied clothes from him. He hurt so badly he could barely breathe. Over and over, he saw the Daimons attacking him and he wanted blood.

'Let the sun have him.' Desiderius's mocking voice rang in his ears.

That bastard would pay. Kyrian planned to make sure of it.

Amanda's heart wrenched at the wounds on Kyrian's body. His forearms and hands were covered with nail holes.

Never in her life had she hated anyone, but right then she hated Desiderius with so much passion that if he were here, she'd rip him apart with her bare hands.

She left Kyrian only long enough to call her parents and check on Tabitha.

While Essie bandaged Kyrian, Nick paced the floor.

'What do you want me to do about Desiderius?' Nick asked Kyrian.

'Stay away from him.'

'But look at you.'

'I'm immortal. I will survive this. You wouldn't.'

'Yeah, well, had we taken another three minutes to get there, you wouldn't have survived it, either.'

'Nick,' Amanda warned. 'You're not helping. He needs to rest.'

'I'm sorry,' he said, raking a nervous hand through his

tousled dark brown hair. 'I attack when I'm worried. It's a defense mechanism.'

'It's all right, Nick,' Kyrian said. 'Go home and get some sleep.'

His jaw rigid, Nick nodded. He looked at Amanda. 'Call me if you need *anything*.'

'I will.'

As soon as he was gone, Esmeralda finished tending Kyrian. 'That really must hurt. What happened?'

'I was stupid.'

'Okay, Stupid,' Esmeralda said pointedly, 'we're going to have to set those legs and I don't have a splint.'

'Can I borrow the phone?' Kyrian asked.

Frowning, Esmeralda handed it to him.

Amanda carefully bathed the blood from his face as he dialed. 'How can you be so lucid?' she asked him. 'This has to be excruciating for you.'

'I was tortured by the Romans for over a month, Amanda. Believe me, this is nothing.'

Still, it made her ache for him. How could he stand it?

She listened while he talked to whomever he'd called.

'Yeah, I know. I'll see you shortly.'

Amanda took the phone from him.

Kyrian closed his eyes and rested while Esmeralda motioned her into the kitchen.

'Now I want an explanation. Why is there a wounded vampire on my couch?'

'He saved my life; I'm just returning the favor.'

Esmeralda glared at her. 'Have you any idea what Tabitha would do if she *ever* found out?'

'I know, but I couldn't let him die. He's a good man, Es.'

Her cheeks paling, Esmeralda's jaw dropped. 'No, not *that* face.'

'What face?'

'That weepy, Brendan-Fraser-is-on-the-screen face.'

'Excuse me?' Amanda asked, offended.

'You're infatuated with him.'

Amanda felt her face turn red.

'Mandy! Where's your brain?'

She avoided her sister's probing stare by looking back to the couch where Kyrian lay. 'Look, Essie, I'm not stupid and I'm not a child. I know there can never be anything between us.'

'But?'

'What but?'

'You look like there should be a "but" on the end of that sentence.'

'Well, there isn't.' Amanda pushed her gently toward the stairs. 'Now go on back to bed and get some sleep.'

'Yeah, right. Are you going to make sure Mr. Vampire doesn't snack on one of us while I sleep?'

'He doesn't suck blood.'

'How do you know?'

'He said so.'

Essie folded her arms over her chest and gave her a piqued stare. 'Oh well, that makes it official, then, doesn't it?'

'Would you stop?'

'C'mon, Mandy,' she said, gesturing toward the couch. 'The man is a killer.'

'You don't know him.'

'I don't know any alligators, either, but I sure as hell wouldn't leave one in my house. You can't change the nature of a beast.'

'He's not a beast.'

'Are you sure?'

'Yes.'

Still she saw the skepticism in her sister's eyes. 'You damn well better be, little girl, or we'll all pay a foul price.'

While Esmeralda dressed for work several hours later, Amanda made a small breakfast for Kyrian.

'I appreciate the thought, but I'm really not hungry,' he said gently.

She set the plate on the coffee table. Tenderly, she traced her hand down the bandage on his arm where blood had already seeped into it. 'I wish you had listened to me and stayed home.'

'I can't do that, Amanda. I have an oath and a duty to fulfill.'

The job. It was all that mattered to him and she wondered if he protected her because he cared, or if she were just part and parcel of what his duty entailed. 'Still, you tell me you believe in my powers and then when I tell you—'

'Amanda, please. I had no choice.'

She nodded. 'I hope you kill him.'

'I will.'

Amanda squeezed his hand. 'You don't sound quite as sure as you did before.'

'That's because I spent the night nailed to a board and I don't feel very well this morning.'

'You're not funny.'

'I know,' he said. 'It just bothers me that he really did know where to strike to do the most damage. Right down to—'

She waited several minutes, but he didn't elaborate. 'To?' she prompted.

'Nothing.'

'Kyrian, talk to me. I want to know how he got you into this condition.'

'I don't want to talk about it.'

Before she could press him, someone knocked on the door.

'Please,' he said quietly, 'go let D'Alerian in.'

'The Dream-Hunter?'

He nodded.

Curious, she got up and opened the front door, then stepped back. The man on the porch was nothing like she'd expected.

Towering over her, the Dream-Hunter had hair as black as night and eyes so colorless and pale, they seemed to glow. Dressed all in black like a Dark-Hunter, the man before her would command attention if not for the strange tendency of her eyes to want to look away from him. It was weird. Really weird. She had to force herself to look at a man who should make any woman gape in lustful awe.

Without a word, he stepped past her and went to Kyrian. The door jerked itself out of her hands and slammed shut to keep the daylight out of the room.

D'Alerian had a sleek, graceful walk as he moved toward the couch where Kyrian lay. He shrugged his leather jacket off and pulled the sleeves of his black shirt back on his arms.

'Since when do you knock?' Kyrian asked.

'Since I didn't want to scare the human.' D'Alerian swept a gaze over Kyrian's body. 'You're a mess.'

'That's what people keep telling me.'

There was no humor in D'Alerian's face. Nothing. He was even more serene and calm than Talon. It was as if he had no emotions whatsoever.

D'Alerian held his hand out and one of the armchairs moved to rest beside the couch.

Without paying her any heed, he touched Kyrian on the shoulder. 'Sleep, Dark-Hunter.' And before he finished the words, Kyrian fell soundly asleep.

Amanda watched as the Dream-Hunter kept his hand on Kyrian's shoulder and closed his eyes. Only then did she see emotions cross D'Alerian's face. He gasped and tensed as if he were the one being tortured. In fact, he showed all the pain she would have expected from Kyrian.

After a few minutes, D'Alerian pulled his hand away and leaned forward in the chair, his breathing labored. He covered his face with his hands as if trying to banish a nightmare.

When he looked up at her, the intensity of his stare made her jump.

'I've never, in all eternity, seen anything like that,' he whispered hoarsely.

'Like what?'

He let out a deep, ragged breath. 'You want to know how Desiderius got to him?'

She nodded.

'His memories. I've never felt such agonized pain in anyone. When they come upon him, they weaken him. And so long as they do, he will always lose his battle calm.'

'Is there anything I can do?'

'Not unless you can think of some way to erase those memories. If they continue to plague him like this, he's doomed.' D'Alerian looked at Kyrian. 'He will sleep until tonight. Don't disturb him. When he wakes, he'll be able to walk, but he will still be weak. Try not to let him go after Desiderius for a few days. I will speak to Artemis and see what can be done.'

'Thank you.'

He nodded and was gone in a golden flash of light. Two seconds later, his jacket evaporated, too.

Taking his vacated seat, Amanda looked up at the ceiling and laughed nervously. All she'd ever wanted in her life was normality. Now she had a vampire lover and a Dream-Hunter, whatever that was, poofing in and out of her sister's house while yet another vampire was trying to kill her.

Life was nothing if not ironic.

She turned her head to watch Kyrian. His breathing was easier than it had been before and the stern frown had faded from his features. The marks on his body were horrendous, but even they appeared to have faded out some.

Just what had Desiderius done to him?

Kyrian came awake to the moonlight streaming through the open windows. At first, he couldn't remember where he was, until he tried to move and pain sliced through him.

Clenching his teeth, he sat up slowly and found Esmeralda

standing with a huge cross in front of her and a garlic neck-lace around her neck.

'You stay right there, buster. And don't try any of that mind-meld stuff.'

In spite of himself, Kyrian laughed. 'You know, crosses don't work on us and neither does garlic.'

'Yeah, right,' she said, inching closer to him. 'Would you still say it if I touched you with it?'

When she came close enough, Kyrian grabbed the cross out of her hand. 'Ow, ow, ow!' he feigned, then he held it to his chest. 'Really,' he said seriously, handing it back to her. 'It has no effect. As for the garlic, well, it's garlic and it stinks, but if it doesn't bother you, I can live with it.'

Esmeralda pulled the necklace off. 'So what is your vulnerability?'

'Like I'm going to tell you.'

She cocked her head. 'Mandy was right, you are infuri-ating.'

'You should have talked to my father before I ate him.'

Esmeralda paled and took two steps back.

'He's teasing you, Es. He never ate his father.'

Kyrian turned to see Amanda standing in the doorway behind him. 'Are you sure about that?'

She smiled. 'Very much so, and you must be feeling better to taunt us.' Amanda came forward and checked the bandages on his arms. 'Good Lord, they're practically healed.'

He nodded as he reached for one of the shirts Nick had dropped off that afternoon while he slept, and put it on. 'Thanks to D'Alerian. After another few hours, they'll be gone completely.'

Amanda watched as he slid off the couch. Only the slow-ness of his movements betrayed the fact he was still re-covering. 'Should you be up?'

'I need to move, it'll help with the stiffness.' As he walked past her, he mumbled under his breath, 'Some of it anyway.'

She helped him into the kitchen. 'Essie, is there any spaghetti left?'

'He eats spaghetti?'

Amanda looked up at him. 'Do you?'

He cast a menacing glare at Esmeralda. 'It's not as good as sucking the necks of Italians, but it's not bad.'

Amanda laughed at the horrified look on her sister's face. 'You better leave her alone or she might stake you while you sleep.'

He took a seat at the kitchen table and cast a hot, longing stare at her body. 'Personally, I'd rather *stake* you while we're awake.'

She smiled at his double entendre as she fixed a plate of spaghetti. 'I'm so glad to have you teasing me again. I was terrified I'd lost you this morning when we found you.'

'How's Tabitha?'

'She's fine. They're sending her home even as we speak.'

'Good.' By his expression she could tell he was deeply troubled.

'What is it?' she asked as she set the microwave timer.

'Desiderius is out there and he will kill again. I can't just lie down and—'

Amanda stopped his words by placing her hand over his lips. 'If you get yourself killed, what good would it do anyone?'

'It would help Nick since he would inherit all my property.'

'You're not funny.'

'You say that to me a lot.'

She smiled tenuously. 'Before you go after Desiderius again, we need to think this through. Right now, he believes you're dead, so we have one shot at surprising him.'

'We?'

'I'm not going to let you fight him alone again. He threatens me and mine and I'm through sitting on the sidelines waiting for him to strike.'

Kyrian reached up and cupped her face. 'I don't want you hurt.'

'Then teach me what I need to know to help you kick his butt.'

He smiled at that. 'I haven't fought with anyone else in over two thousand years.'

'Well, you're never too old to learn.'

He snorted. 'You can't teach an old dog new tricks.'

'There's no time like the present.'

'Time is of the essence.'

'God helps those who help themselves.'

He laughed. 'You're not going to let me win this, are you?'

'Nope. Now let me get you fed, then I'll show you the research I did while you were sleeping.'

Kyrian watched as she dribbled cheese over his spaghetti. He'd never in his life come across a woman like her.

After Desiderius had left and he'd been waiting to die, he had spent the last moments with his eyes closed, remembering the way she looked in his bed. The way she felt in his arms.

It had given him more comfort than he had a right to ask for.

What if you fail again to kill Desiderius?

The idea horrified him. Amanda would be alone. He closed his eyes and thought of her lying in the hospital like Tabitha. Or worse.

No, Amanda was right, he needed to teach her to protect herself.

Desiderius was too dangerous. Too crafty. Worse, the bastard had delivered on his promise. He knew exactly where to hit.

'Kyrian?'

He looked up at Amanda.

She brought the plate of spaghetti and salad over to him and set it on the table, then placed her hand against his brow. 'Don't think about it.'

'Think about what?'

'Desiderius. You were thinking so hard, I swear I could hear your thoughts.'

Esmeralda stuck her head in the kitchen. 'I'm headed out to deliver Cara's baby. Are you sure you're all right alone with him?'

'I'm fine, Essie. Go, shoo, begone.'

'All right, but I'll call later.'

Amanda growled at her sister and looked at Kyrian. 'Have you ever tried to live with nine mothers?'

'No, I can't say that I have.'

After he had finished eating and called Nick, Amanda took him upstairs to bathe.

Kyrian stood completely still as she unbuttoned his shirt and removed it, then she undid his pants. He hardened as her fingers brushed against him. 'You know, I haven't had an actual bath in decades. I always shower.'

'Well, this will be more fun – I promise.' Rising up on her toes, she kissed him lightly on the lips.

Kyrian followed her lead as she placed him in the tub. The hot water felt wonderful against his skin as she lathered a washcloth. He traced the line of her jaw with his fingers.

Amanda removed her clothes, then joined him in the tub.

Kyrian wrapped her in his arms, but as she moved against him, old memories assailed him.

All of a sudden, he was in his old home and he could feel Theone against him. See her cold face.

Amanda felt him stiffen. 'Did I hurt you?'

'Let me up,' he said, pushing her away.

Something was wrong with him. Something bad. 'Kyrian?'

He wouldn't meet her eyes and suddenly she understood what D'Alerian had meant earlier.

Determined to rid Kyrian of his demons, she grabbed his face in her hands and forced him to look at her. 'Kyrian, I am not Theone and I will never betray you.'

'Let me—'

'Look at me!' she insisted. 'Look into *my* eyes.'

He did.

'I fed you, I didn't drug you. I would never hurt you. Never.'

Kyrian frowned.

She moved higher up on his stomach, her body sliding against his. 'Love me, Kyrian,' she said, placing his hand on her breast. 'Let me erase those memories.'

He didn't know if it were possible, but as he felt her bare, wet skin against his, her hot breath on his neck, he realized he didn't want to push her away. He had been so long without a woman's comfort. So long without a caring touch.

She slid herself against him, banishing his thoughts. 'Trust me, Kyrian,' she whispered in his ear an instant before she swirled her tongue around the sensitive flesh of his earlobe.

Fire shot through him. 'Amanda,' he breathed, her name a prayer for salvation on his bruised lips.

He had tried so hard to let go of his past, tried so hard to banish it, and yet it was always there just under the surface waiting to stab him when he least expected it.

But not now. Not with her in his arms.

Amanda saw the veil in his eyes fall. For the first time, she saw the soul of the man who had no soul. Better still, she saw the heat and the yearning. The need he had for her.

Smiling, she gently kissed his lips, careful not to hurt him any more.

To her surprise, he deepened the kiss and slid his arms around her. He buried his hand in her hair and held her so tight against him that it stole her breath. His tongue stroked hers with a hunger that fired her own.

Amanda reached down between them and took him into her hand, then led him slowly, inch by wonderful inch, into her.

She rode him slow and easy, careful of his injuries.

Kyrian leaned his head back and watched the satisfied look on her face as she stroked his body with hers. Reaching out, he cupped her chin in his hand. 'You are so much more than I deserve.'

Amanda took his lips with hers and kissed him hard, tugging at his lips with her teeth. Goodness, but the man could kiss. Her tongue grazed his fangs as she quickened her strokes. His moan reverberated through her.

He cradled her head with his hands as he deepened his kiss. Overwhelmed by her emotions, she came fiercely in his arms. He kissed her even harder.

'That's it, Amanda,' he whispered, taking her breast into his hand and gently squeezing it. 'Come for both of us.'

Amanda opened her eyes and saw the raw hunger in the midnight depths. 'This is so unfair to you.'

He smiled. 'I truly don't mind. Just being inside you is enough.'

Not believing it for a minute, Amanda helped him from the tub and toweled him off. She tucked him into the bed in the guest room, then carefully sealed the windows to make sure no daylight would leak through in the morning.

She watched as Kyrian slept, his ravaged body healing so fast she could almost see it.

If only she could heal his damaged heart as easily.

Damn his wife for her cruelty.

She heard a knock on the door downstairs.

With one last look at her guest, she crept to the hallway and went downstairs to open the door and found Nick standing on the porch with a small suitcase.

'I thought he'd need some more clothes and a few other things.'

Amanda smiled at his thoughtfulness and let him into the house. 'Thanks. I'm sure Kyrian will appreciate it.'

Nick set the suitcase by the couch. 'Where is he?'

'Upstairs, sleeping, I hope.'

'Listen,' Nick said sternly. 'Talon's dogging Tabitha on the way back to your mother's to make sure she's okay and I have a couple more Squires looking after Esmeralda and the rest of your family. Now that Desiderius thinks Kyrian is dead, there's no telling what he might do, or which one of you he might go after. Tell everyone in your family to watch their backs.'

Kyrian listened to them as he lay in bed. He could hear the fear in Amanda's voice. The anxiety. And he knew one way to dispel it.

If Desiderius knew he was still alive, he would wait to go after Amanda's sisters. Kyrian was the prime target to the Daimon; they were merely bonuses.

Slowly, painfully, he rolled out of bed and dressed.

Chapter 13

'Kyrian, I hate to disturb you—' Amanda broke off as she opened the bedroom door and found the bed empty.

'Where is he?' Nick asked, moving into the room behind her.

'I don't know, he was here a second ago.'

Cursing, Nick pulled his phone out, then stopped. 'Dammit, he doesn't have a phone with him.'

'Surely he wouldn't leave.'

She started to go check the bathroom, but he stopped her with a 'duh' stare.

'Surely he would.' He went to the window and they watched as Kyrian pulled Nick's Jag out of the driveway.

Kyrian's first stop was the doll shop. His intention was to find one of Desiderius's flunkies and the last thing he needed was to be unarmed when he met him.

It was just after eight when he swung open the door and heard the little bell tinkle above his head. Liza came immediately from the back, her wrinkled face warm and friendly until she caught a look at the healing bruises on his face.

'General,' she said, her voice chiding. 'Are you all right?'

'I'm fine, Liza, thank you. I just came to pick up my order.'

She frowned. 'I gave it to Nicky yesterday, didn't he tell you?'

Kyrian cursed silently. It figured. The *one* time Nick had remembered to pick up something would be the one time Kyrian wanted him to wait.

Then, Kyrian heard a faint rustling sound in the back of the shop, behind the burgundy curtains. Kyrian felt a strange stirring. One he hadn't felt in a long time.

No sooner had the chill gone down his spine than the curtains parted of their own accord. Cast in shadows, the figure emerging dominated the small shop. At six feet eight inches, and dressed all in black, he was a man who made all life-forms either quiver in fear or straighten in respect.

Or in Kyrian's case, it made him glare.

A wide smile broke across Acheron's roguish face. Though his black Ray-Ban Predator sunglasses obscured his eyes, he was still able to make women swoon when they saw him. Arrogant and tough, he took no prisoners and showed little mercy on anyone.

Acheron was a creature of many idiosyncrasies, the most peculiar one being his ever-changing hair color. He changed it so often, many of the Dark-Hunters made bets on what color he was going to dye it for the week. Tonight, he wore his long, dark green hair pulled back in an old-fashioned queue with one thin braid falling loose from the nape of his neck, over his chest.

'Acheron,' Kyrian greeted him irritably. 'Come to check up on me?'

'Never, little brother. I'm here to sightsee. Can't you tell?'

'Yeah. You look like a tourist. That dark green hair passes every time.'

Ash laughed at the sarcasm. 'Well, I figured since Talon

is protecting what's her name . . . Tabitha? And you're after Desi-do-wrong, the two of you could use a hand.'

'The last time I asked for a hand, Artemis sent me a disembodied one.'

Ash grinned. 'You know that when dealing with the gods, you have to be specific. Besides, I have information.'

'You could have e-mailed it.'

Ash shrugged. 'My presence here means nothing. You know I won't interfere with you and Desiderius.'

Now, why didn't he believe that?

Oh yeah, because Acheron Parthenopaeus had never minded his own business when it came to badass Daimons. 'Seems I've heard that one before.'

'Fine,' he said, shrugging nonchalantly, 'I'll take my unwanted information and—'

'I've already heard what the Oracles said.'

'But you don't know the rest of the story,' Liza interjected.

Acheron frowned at her.

'What story?' Kyrian asked.

Acheron took a piece of gum out of his coat pocket and unwrapped it. Meticulously. 'You said you didn't want to know.'

'Fine, I'll go after him without it.'

As Kyrian reached the door, Ash's voice stopped him. 'Don't you find it odd that Desiderius has powers beyond anything you've seen from a Daimon?'

'Oh,' Kyrian said, turning back to face him. 'Let me think. Yeah.'

Liza sniggered until Acheron gave her a sideways glare. She straightened up, then burst out laughing. Excusing herself, she ran to the back of the store, and cackled.

Acheron watched her leave, then turned to face Kyrian. He sobered. 'All right, here are the facts. It seems old Bacchus got horny one night and made out with an Apollite babe. Nine months later, she had Desiderius.'

'Shit.'

'Yeah,' Acheron concurred as he picked up one of Liza's dolls she had fashioned to look like Artemis. He frowned at the startling likeness, then set her back on her shelf. 'The good news is old Daddy Bacchus couldn't care less since he has bastards strung out all over history. The bad news is Desiderius was just a little ticked off that Daddykins doesn't care about the twenty-seven-year time limit on his life. Since he's half-god, he thought he should have a little longer life span than that. One, say, that reaches immortality.'

'So, he turned Daimon.'

Acheron nodded. 'And with those added demigod powers, he is equal to us in speed, strength, and skills. And unlike us, he has no Code.'

'That explains a whole lot, doesn't it? If you can't get back at the gods themselves, then go after those who serve them.'

'Exactly. And we are prime Desi bait.'

'One question.'

'Answer.'

Kyrian ignored his sarcasm. 'Why does it have to be a Dark-Hunter with a soul who defeats him?'

'Because that is the prophecy, and you know how prophecy works.'

'How do you know all this?'

Acheron looked back at the doll he'd picked up. 'I talked to Artemis last night. It took a while, but I wormed it out of her.'

Kyrian considered that for a minute. Acheron had always been the goddess's favorite Dark-Hunter. Her preference for Acheron had been a long-standing grudge in the hearts of many Dark-Hunters. But Kyrian didn't mind. He was grateful for the Atlantean's ability to find out information from Artemis and give it to them.

'You know,' he said to Acheron, 'one day you're going

to have to explain to me this relationship the two of you have and why you're the only Dark-Hunter who can be in a god's presence and not get fried.'

'One day, I might. But it won't be tonight.' Acheron handed him a retractable sword and a throwing dagger. 'Now get your ass back to bed. You have a job to finish and you need your strength.'

Kyrian started away from him.

'Oh and Kyrian?'

He turned to face him.

'Don't go home alone.'

'Excuse me?'

'Desiderius has your number. It's no longer safe there.'

'I don't give a damn if—'

'Listen to me, General,' Acheron said, his voice menacing. 'No one here doubts your ability to make Desi the next menu item at the Road Kill Diner; however, you have other people to protect, including a headstrong Cajun who listens about as well as you do, and a sorceress with virtually untapped powers. So, for once, could you just do as I ask and not argue?'

Kyrian smiled tightly. 'Just this once, so don't get used to it.'

Acheron watched as Kyrian left the shop. No sooner had he gone than Liza came from the back.

'Why didn't you tell him that you got his soul from Artemis?' she asked.

Ash slid his hand into his pocket where the medallion rested. 'It's not time yet, Liza.'

'How will you know when it's time?'

'Trust me, I will.'

She nodded, and held the curtains open for him. 'Now, speaking of people who should tend their wounds, you need to come back here and let me help you. Goodness, but I've never seen anyone with their back in worse shape than you. Why on earth you let anyone beat you like that is beyond me. And I know you had to let them. A Dark-Hunter with your powers would never take something like that unless he wanted to.'

Ash didn't answer, but he knew the reason. Artemis never willingly let go of one of her Dark-Hunters. The price of their freedom was a high one.

He had agreed to sacrifice some of his flesh in order to gain Kyrian a chance to kill Desiderius.

Most of all, his torn and bruised back had bought the General a chance for happiness. It was a bloody ritual he willingly underwent every time a Dark-Hunter wanted his or her soul back.

A ritual none of them knew about.

What went on between him and Artemis was private. And he would always keep it that way.

Kyrian eased his way over to Bourbon Street where he'd found the punks before. The pain in his side was lessening, but still excruciating. It took him a full half hour before he found what he was looking for.

And the look on the punk's face was priceless.

'Holy shit!'

Kyrian grabbed him before he could run. 'Tell Desiderius we're not finished.'

The kid nodded.

Kyrian released him and watched as he tore down the street at a dead run.

He knew the first rule of war was that a surprise attack virtually guaranteed a victory, and he had just blown his best surprise. Still, he refused to keep his advantage at the risk of Amanda or one of her family members being hurt. Desiderius wouldn't go after them so long as he had a Dark-Hunter to contend with.

Limping, he returned to Nick's car and finally headed back to the one thing that gave him peace.

*

'Where have you been?' Amanda asked as soon as Kyrian returned.

'I had something to do.'

Nick cursed. 'You went to find Desiderius, didn't you?' He cursed again. 'You sent word to him that you were alive.'

Kyrian ignored him as he headed to the couch and sat down.

'Are you okay?' Amanda asked.

He nodded as he stretched out.

Nick glared at him. Rounding the sofa, he clenched and unclenched his fists at his sides. 'Dammit, Kyrian, why would you—'

'Nick, lay off me. I'm not in the mood.'

Nick's nostrils flared. 'Fine, go and get yourself killed. What do I care anyway? I get the house, the cars, everything. So you go right ahead and tell him you're wounded and half-dead. Tell you what, why don't I just leave the door unlocked and invite him on in here?'

'Nick, you're not helping,' Amanda said gently.

She saw the agony in Nick's eyes. The filial affection he had for his Dark-Hunter. 'You know what?' he said through gritted teeth. 'I don't give a damn. 'Cause I don't need anyone.' He pointed at Kyrian. 'I don't need you, your money, or a damn thing. I've never needed anyone but myself. So you go right on and die, 'cause I don't care.'

Nick turned to leave.

Faster than she could blink, Kyrian was on his feet in front of Nick.

Nick glared at him. 'Get out of my way.'

Kyrian's face showed the patience of a father with a rebellious teen. 'Nick, I'm not going to die on you.'

'Yeah, right. How many times do you think Streigar said that to Sharon before he was turned into an extra crispy fried Dark-Hunter?' Nick shrugged Kyrian's hold off his arm and stormed out of the house.

A tic started in Kyrian's jaw as he pulled his cell phone off his belt and dialed it.

'Acheron,' he said after a brief pause, 'I have a renegade Squire who is no doubt headed out to the Quarter in a new anthracite Jag XKR convertible. Can you catch him before he does something stupid?'

His brow creased with worry, Kyrian met her eyes as he listened. 'Yeah, thanks.'

He looked extremely peeved at something Acheron was saying. 'Yes, O great lord and master, I'm resting.'

A shocked look came over his face. 'How do you know I'm standing?'

After a brief pause, he snorted. 'Bite me, Ash. Good luck with Nick.' He hung up the phone.

Even though she didn't know exactly what Acheron had said, she caught the gist of it. 'He's right, you need to lie down.'

Kyrian's black eyes flashed. 'I don't need to be coddled.'

'Fine, *Nick*. Want to tell me how you need nothing and no one too and then storm out of the house?'

Kyrian offered her a sheepish smile. 'Now you know why I tolerate him. Two peas in a pod.'

Amanda laughed, even though her heart felt for both of them. 'Let me guess, you were just like him at his age?'

'Actually, he's a lot more tolerable than I was. Not quite as stubborn, either.'

Amanda stepped into his embrace and wrapped an arm around his waist. 'Come on, let's go upstairs.'

To her amazement, he allowed her to take him back to the guest room and put him back to bed.

As she undressed him, she saw his pink, healing wounds. Taking his arm in her hand, she touched the small nail holes. 'I can't believe you're up so soon after what happened.'

He sighed. 'You can't keep a Dark-Hunter down for long.'

Amanda barely heard his words. As she touched the

wounds, images flashed through her mind. She felt Kyrian's rage, his pain. Then she saw a flash of the future. Of Kyrian spread out against a wall and at Desiderius's mercy.

Of Kyrian dying.

Gasping, she let go and stepped back.

Kyrian frowned at her. 'What is it?'

Amanda patted her chest as panic swirled through her. She fought her anxiety attack as hard as she could, but inside she was screaming over what she'd seen.

She couldn't let him die. Not like that.

Forcing herself to calm down, she stared at Kyrian. 'You have to let go of your past. So long as you hold on to it, Desiderius will be able to destroy you.'

He looked away. 'I know.'

'What are you going to do? If you don't stop remembering it, he'll have you again.'

'I can handle it, Amanda.'

'Can you?' she asked, her throat tight as she saw him dying again. Oh, dear Lord, please not that. She couldn't bear to lose him. The thought of going a single day without feeling his arms around her, hearing his voice . . .

His laughter.

It was unimaginable. The pain unbearable.

'I can control myself,' he insisted.

But she knew the truth. She had experienced his execution firsthand. Worse, she knew he had never dealt with it. Not really. He had only pushed it out of his mind.

All of a sudden, she had an idea how to purge it from him.

At least she hoped it would work.

'I'll be right back.'

Kyrian watched her leave, his emotions churning. Better than anyone, he knew his weaknesses. All Desiderius had to do was spread his arms out and he was lost to panic. Lost to memories so painful that he was powerless against them.

He ran his hands over his eyes. There had to be some way

to push it all out of his mind. Some way to face the Daimon with a clear head.

The minutes ticked by as he considered possible solutions. Kyrian became aware of someone watching him.

He rolled over in the bed to see Amanda in the doorway holding a tray and dressed in a long, flowing white satin robe. A warm smile on her face, she entered the room and set the tray on the dresser.

Kyrian frowned.

She approached the bed gracefully, then bent one knee. It peeked out from the slit in the robe. Bracing her leg against the bed, she rolled him over, onto his back. Still he stared at her stockinged leg and the hint of a garter belt underneath the robe.

Her smile grew wider as she reached into her pocket and pulled out a long silk scarf.

Kyrian's frown deepened as she wrapped it around his wrist. 'What are you doing?'

'I'm going to make it better.'

'Make what better?'

'The past.'

'Amanda,' he growled as she pulled his arm toward the bedpost. As soon as he realized she intended to tie it there, he jerked away from her. 'No!'

She grabbed his arm and held it between her breasts. 'Yes.'

Amanda watched the panic in his eyes. 'No,' he reiterated firmly.

Licking her lips, she lifted his hand to her lips. Opening her mouth, she gently suckled the pad of his forefinger. 'Please, Kyrian? I promise you won't regret it.'

Desire coiled through his stomach as he watched her. Her tongue flicked across his skin, down between his fingers. Then, she scraped the inside of his wrist and forearm with her fingernails, raising chills the length of his body.

She led his hand from her lips, to the parting of the robe, then inside to her bare breast. 'Pretty please?'

His breathing ragged, he closed his hand over her. It was all he could do to remember what she was asking him.

She was asking for his complete trust. Something he hadn't been able to give to anyone in more than two thousand years.

Terrified of what had happened to him the last time he'd made that mistake, he met her gaze and felt his will crumble. Would she one day betray him?

Dare he take the chance?

This time when she guided his arm to the post, he ground his teeth, but didn't move as she secured it to the carved wood. Still, his heart pounded.

Amanda knew she had just won a small victory. Smiling, she tied the scarf loosely. 'You can get loose at any time,' she told him. 'Just say the word and I will release you, but if you do, it will stop immediately.'

'What will stop?'

'You'll see.'

Amanda took his other arm and tied a scarf to that wrist. Kyrian watched her, his breathing sharp and unsteady. To her amazement, he said nothing as she tied him down. Sweat beaded on his forehead.

He pulled against the scarves, his muscles rippling and bunching. 'I don't like this.' He moved to free himself.

Climbing up on his body, Amanda caught his wrists in her hands and held him there. She dipped her head down and touched his lips with hers.

Kyrian tensed as he felt her tongue darting along the seam of his lips, begging for entrance. Opening his mouth, he welcomed her inside. He moaned at the way she stroked his tongue with hers, at the taste of her.

Her mouth was as close to heaven as a soulless man was likely to ever come. Her rose scent invaded his head, making him dizzy and hot. Breathless. Time stood still as her hands stroked his chest and he felt her breasts pressing against him.

It wasn't until he reached to hold her that he remembered she had him tied down.

Growling in frustration, he yanked at the silk.

At the sound of tearing fabric, Amanda pulled back from her scorching kiss. 'Remember,' she said huskily, 'if you get free, you'll get nothing but a cold shower.'

He stopped moving instantly.

To his chagrin, Amanda pulled back from him.

She ran her hands slowly down her robe, over her breasts, until she reached the belt. Taking her time, she unknotted the belt and parted the robe to show him her bare breasts.

His body burned as she let the robe flutter to the ground at her feet.

To his delight, she wasn't naked. She wore the dark blue garter belt he'd bought for her.

His mouth watered at the sight.

Slowly, seductively, she walked to the bed and climbed up his body again like a sensuous cat as her breasts trailed from his stomach to his chest. Kyrian hissed at the feel of her stretched out over him, of her breasts caressing him.

'How are we doing, General?'

He swallowed. 'Fine.'

Smiling, she traced the line of his jaw with her lips and tongue.

'I'm better when you do that,' he whispered, his body on fire from her touch.

She pulled back with a laugh. 'How about I make you blind with ecstasy, then?'

He strained against the ties. 'It would appear I'm all yours, sweeting.'

How she wished that were true. Amanda left the bed and moved to the tray. As she picked up the warm honey, she remembered the boiling oil the Romans had used on Kyrian.

Remembered the look on his face as they poured it over his skin, scalding him.

Her heart constricting, she moved back to where he lay at her mercy. She held the bottle over his chest and saw the shadow pass across his eyes as he too remembered.

Kyrian involuntarily cringed as the warm honey first touched his bare skin. But there was no scalding pain. No blisters forming or skin burning. It actually felt good.

Relaxing, he watched as Amanda drew small circles in the honey, smearing it around his nipples where she dragged her nails, sending chills over him, and then down to his stomach.

She set the honey aside, then slowly licked every bit of it from his skin. He writhed in blissful pleasure as she laved him. Her tongue delved into his navel, making him even harder for her.

She laughed low in her throat as she looked up at him from his lower abdomen. Then she moved up his chest with one long lick that culminated at his Adam's apple. Hissing, he leaned his head back to give her greater access to his neck, and when she lightly bit his skin, chills shot through him.

'Amanda,' he breathed.

Smiling at him, she left the bed and grabbed a small bowl.

Amanda didn't know where her boldness came from. Never had she behaved this way, but she wanted to save Kyrian at any cost. Besides, something strange was happening to her as she did this for him. It was as if some part of her were gaining its freedom.

Shaking the thought off, she dipped her fingers into the bowl of whipped cream, then brought them to his lips. She traced the outline of that poetic mouth with her thumb.

Kyrian licked the whipped cream from his lips as Amanda straddled his waist. Oh, the feel of her wetness on him. It drove him wild. And when she moved, grinding herself against his swollen shaft, he thought he would die from the pleasure of it.

'Let me feed you, Commander,' she whispered, then slowly she used her finger to feed him the whipped cream.

Kyrian swallowed as his emotions swirled. She was re-enacting Valerius's cruelty. But there was no pain from her. Only an ecstasy he'd never known before.

Locking gazes with her, he offered her a tentative smile.

'Why are you doing this?' he asked.

'Because I care for you.'

'Why?'

'Because you are the most wonderful man I have ever known. Granted, you're stubborn and infuriating, but you're also kind, strong, and giving. And you make me feel so . . .'

He arched a brow.

Amanda sat back and eyed him. 'Now what's that supposed to mean?'

'What?' he asked innocently.

'That look.'

Kyrian frowned. 'What look?' He tried to reach for her, then remembered his restraints. How odd that he could have forgotten them.

Amanda dipped her head down to kiss him.

Kyrian moaned at the feel of her lips on his, of her tongue darting in and out of his mouth, carrying with it the taste of whipped cream.

She pulled back. 'Do you like that?'

'Yes, I do.'

'Then you're going to love this.'

He watched as she scooted down his body, then took the whipped cream and made him a loincloth with it. Her fingers grazed his erection as the cool cream coated him.

Kyrian moaned at the sensation that sent heat all over his body.

Amanda nudged his legs apart and stared down at her handiwork.

She locked gazes with him, then laid her body down at his feet and took his sac gently into her mouth.

He growled at the feel of her tongue licking the tenderest part of his body. Her mouth closed around him as her tongue swirled, licking and delving as she worked her way to the other side, where she sucked him in tenderly and rolled her tongue around him.

Kyrian clenched the ties on his hands as waves of pleasure racked him. Nothing had ever felt better than her mouth on him or her tongue darting over his skin.

When she was through licking the cream from his sac, she started on his shaft. Kyrian strained against the ties as she closed her mouth around him, all the while watching him watch her.

She dropped her head down to tease the tip of his shaft with her tongue. His breath caught as she swirled her tongue around the tip, then took his entire length into her mouth. His head swam from pleasure while her hand stroked him from underneath.

He hissed and jerked at how incredibly good she felt. Instinctively, he arched his back, sending himself deeper into her mouth. She didn't protest.

Kyrian moaned as he felt the animal in him awaken. He craved her with blind obsession. 'Amanda,' he said, his voice hoarse and ragged. 'I want to taste you.'

She lapped at him, then raised her head to look at him. 'Taste me how?'

His breathing intensified as she scaled his body.

She straddled his waist, braced her hands on his ribs, and looked down at him. 'Tell me what you want to do to me,' she said, her cheeks blushing at her words.

As he looked at her, he felt her emotions. She was scared and unsure, but wanted to help him at any cost. Touched more deeply than he should be, Kyrian licked his lips. 'I want to feel your breasts,' he said raggedly.

'Like this?' she asked as she cupped them for him.

The sight of her hands on herself, clutching her breasts, made him moan. 'Yes,' he gasped. 'And I want to taste them.'

Smiling at him, she held her breast to his parted lips.

Kyrian strained against the ties as he took her swollen nipple into his mouth and tasted her. Her blissful murmurs of pleasure filled his ears, spurring him on.

He pulled at the ties, shredding the fabric more.

She laughed evilly. 'If you free yourself, Kyrian, then I get dressed and we stop. Is that what you want?'

He shook his head and relaxed his arms.

'Then what else do you want?'

'You.' The heartfelt word poured out of his lips before he could stop it.

'Me?' she asked, her face hopeful.

Unable to lead her on when he knew there was no future for them, he added, 'I want to be inside you.'

He felt her pang of disappointment and it cut him deeply. 'Amanda—'

'Shh,' she said, placing her hand over his lips. 'I am all yours,' she whispered as she impaled herself on his swollen shaft.

Kyrian closed his eyes at the incredible feel of her wetness sliding down the length of him.

Amanda leaned forward and captured his lips with hers as she rode him hard and slow. She nuzzled his neck with her lips and felt his moan against her tongue as she quickened her strokes.

She could feel him writhing as she rotated her hips against him.

He leaned his head back and growled like a caged beast. He braced his feet against the mattress and pressed his hips up, driving himself even deeper into her.

When Amanda came, she screamed from the force of it.

She felt Kyrian go ramrod stiff.

'Don't move,' he hissed.

She obeyed without question as he clenched his eyes shut and ground his teeth. His body trembled beneath hers and she saw more sweat beading on his forehead.

After a minute, he let out an elongated breath. He opened his eyes and stared at her. 'Now can I get free?'

She nodded as she realized he still hadn't come. He had fought it with all his strength.

Even though she understood why, a part of her was hurt to realize he didn't trust her enough.

Stop that! she snapped at herself. *What kind of selfish stupidity is that? He needs his powers.*

Now more than ever.

Startling her, Kyrian easily ripped the fabric of the ties and freed his hands. Immediately, he gathered her into his arms and held her close. 'Thank you, sweeting,' he said, kissing her softly.

She smiled at him. 'My pleasure.'

He laughed at that and settled her down to lie by his side. He spooned up behind her and held her as if he were afraid to let go.

It wasn't long before he fell asleep. His hot breath fell against her bare shoulder.

Amanda reveled in it and hoped that because of what she'd done tonight, he would survive his next confrontation with Desiderius.

Amanda came awake to the sound of the phone ringing. Pulling back from Kyrian, she realized they were lying entwined. Her face flamed as she recalled what she had done with him. Never had she been so unabashed and yet with him she didn't mind.

Sliding out of his arms, she grabbed the phone in Esmeralda's room. 'Hello?'

It was Esmeralda. 'Mandy, thank goodness you're still there. My car broke down. I'm on the side of the road. Any chance you can come pick me up?'

'Sure.'

She jotted down the location, then took a quick shower and went back to the guest room to dress.

She leaned over Kyrian and kissed his cheek. As she pulled away, he grabbed her. 'Where are you going?'

'To pick up Essie.'

'It's not safe.'

'It's broad daylight. I'm fine.'

She saw the reluctance in his eyes. 'How long to sundown?'

'Hours still.'

'All right, but come right back.'

'Yes, sir, Commander, sir.'

'You're not funny.'

She kissed him on the lips and left.

Kyrian woke up a short time later. Getting up, he saw his wounds were almost all gone.

He unwrapped the bloody bandages and tossed them into the small wastebasket by the door.

'Amanda?' he called at the door.

No one answered. He listened for sounds in the house and only silence greeted him.

She must not be back yet.

Grabbing his clothes, he went to the bathroom.

It didn't take long to shower, shave, and change. Once clean, he made his way slowly back to the room. He paused at the door as he caught sight of Amanda. She was dressed in a pair of tight jeans and a black sweater that hugged those curves he loved to feast on.

Her hair down, she looked luscious.

He walked up behind her silently while she was examining the trash can.

Without speaking, he dipped his head down to nibble her neck. No sooner had he brushed her skin with his lips than he caught her scent.

This wasn't Amanda.

It was Tabitha.

Chapter 14

Kyrian took a step back as Tabitha whirled to face him. Her battered face was still bruised from the beating she had taken from Desiderius's minions and she wore a bandage over one cheek to cover the sutures. She dropped into a wobbly, tough fighting stance.

Anguish swept through him that he had failed to protect one of the people Amanda loved best in the world.

He swore it wouldn't happen again.

'Who are you?' she demanded. 'Where's Esmeralda?'

Kyrian glanced to the mirror to see his missing reflection and quickly took a another step back before Tabitha noticed it, as well. 'Her car broke down on her way home. Amanda went to pick her up.'

He realized too late that he should have kept his mouth closed because recognition flared in her eyes as she registered his unique accent.

'*You!*' she screamed. 'What have you done to my sisters?'

'They're safe.'

'Like hell!' She rushed him.

Unwilling to hurt her, Kyrian pivoted on his feet and ran down the hallway.

'Vampire!' she screamed.

He heard rustling downstairs and realized she wasn't alone in the house.

'Pull open the curtains.' As she screamed out the order, Tabitha grabbed the curtain cord in the upstairs hallway that shielded the line of windows there, and gave a yank.

Kyrian hissed as the daylight touched him. Leaping over the banister, he landed in the living room below.

Two pairs of eyes widened as they took in his size. The dark-haired man turned pale, but the blond woman reacted quickly, running to the window to open more shades.

Before Kyrian could move, Tabitha was on him. She kicked out and caught him right in his sore side. 'Die, vampire scum!'

Kyrian hissed, baring his fangs at her, then back-flipped away from her, and started for the kitchen. He slid to a halt in the doorway as he saw the sunlight streaming through the room. There was no place to go in there that wouldn't kill him.

Something hard and sharp bit into his shoulder. Growling, he turned to see Tabitha with a long dagger. She drew back to stab him again.

Kyrian caught her wrist at the same time her two friends rushed him. The four of them stumbled back. Kyrian slung one of them off and broke free. He tried to run back to the living room, but Tabitha somehow managed to get in front of him.

Hatred burned in Tabitha's eyes as she swung the dagger in a way meant to slice open his stomach.

Kyrian jumped back into a ray of light. Pain lacerated his back. Hissing again, he dodged her and ran for the living room, trying to stay in the shadows.

They rushed him at the door, slamming him against it. Desiderius's words rang in his ears as they tackled him to the floor.

'They'll take you down like a pack of wild dogs.'

Tabitha sat on his chest, her hand on his throat as her two friends grabbed his arms and held them down. Had they attacked him like this yesterday, he would have gone mad with panic. But today he felt a strange lucidity as he remembered Amanda restraining him last night.

'What did you do to my sister?' Tabitha demanded.

'Nothing.'

'Don't you lie to me! I saw the blood in the trash can.'

Trying his best not to hurt her, Kyrian brought his legs up and wrapped them around Tabitha's upper body and pulled her away as the dagger slashed, barely missing his throat.

He caught the man on his right in the stomach with his fist, then sent the woman flying over them, onto the couch. He cursed as Tabitha sank her teeth into his thigh.

Kyrian pulled the knife from Tabitha's hand and embedded it deep into the hardwood floor. 'Listen to me.'

'No!' she shrieked, squirming and punching.

Kyrian rolled over with her, pinning her to the floor. Instinct demanded he knock her unconscious, but as he caught sight of the face so close to Amanda's he realized he could never hit her.

That moment of hesitation cost him as her friends grabbed him again. Kyrian rolled with them, rising to his feet at the same time the door opened, spilling more light into the room.

Cursing, he barely made it into a corner.

Amanda's shrill tone rang out. 'Stop!'

The humans froze when they heard Amanda's voice, while Kyrian tried to catch his breath. His new wounds throbbed as blood oozed down his back. Amanda rushed to his side and slid her hands over him to inspect the damage.

Tabitha pulled the dagger from the floor. She approached him with a determined stride, her angry eyes never leaving him. 'Out of my way, Mandy. I'm going to kill a vampire.'

'Wrong,' Esmeralda inserted, closing the door and moving

to stand between him and Tabitha. 'You're about to kill your twin sister's *boyfriend*.'

Tabitha gaped and paused mid-stride. She looked from Kyrian to Amanda. 'Excuse me?'

Amanda ignored her. 'Are you all right?'

He rubbed his hand over his bleeding arm. 'Never better.'

'Him?' Tabitha asked in disbelief. 'What about me and the guys? I don't see you asking about us. He almost tore our heads off.'

Amanda glared at her sister. 'I don't see any of you *bleeding*. Believe me, if he had really wanted you hurt, none of you would be standing.'

Tabitha raked them with a disgusted sneer. 'You're defending a vampire?'

'I'm defending Kyrian,' she said emphatically.

Curling her lip even more, Tabitha looked back and forth at them. 'What are you? Insane? You want a boyfriend who drinks blood, lives forever, kills for fun, and can't go outside in the daylight? Why, Mandy, I do believe you've finally found the King of the Losers. Congrats. I didn't think anyone could top Cliff's loserness.'

That set off a whole deluge of insults and shrillness.

'Loser? I don't want to hear it from a woman who dates a man who hasn't worked more than two weeks in the last three years.'

'At least Eric has a soul.'

'Kyrian has a heart.'

'Oh, please. You think that makes up for it? Tell me, Mandy, are you willing to give up everything for him? Your life, your future? What can a *vampire* offer an accountant? You want kids. Can he give you those?'

Kyrian's heart sank as he listened to them fight. With every word out of Tabitha's mouth, he became more and more aware of just how right she was.

He looked at the daylight streaming into the house.

Daylight that was lethal to him and vital to Amanda. Humans needed sunlight as much as they needed to breathe. As long as she was with him, Amanda would never have peace. She would have to sacrifice all her dreams for him.

It was something he could never allow her to do.

Heartsick, he crept along the shadows, toward the stairs.

'Would you two stop fighting!' Esmeralda shouted.

Kyrian paid them no more heed as he went up the stairs.

Several minutes and a truckload of insults passed before Amanda realized Kyrian was gone. 'Kyrian?'

'He went upstairs,' Esmeralda told her.

Amanda started for the stairs, but Tabitha stopped her. 'You can't do this to yourself.'

'You know nothing about him, Tabby. He's a Dark-Hunter, not a vampire.'

'Yeah, and Julian Alexander said there's no real difference between them. They both have animal qualities and are *killers*.'

'I don't believe Julian said that.'

'I don't care if you believe it or not, it's true. And while you're mulling that one over, let me tell you another thing Julian said. Artemis will kill your *boyfriend* before she ever lets him walk free.'

Her heart screaming a denial, Amanda pulled away and went upstairs. She found Kyrian in the bedroom gathering up his things.

'What are you doing?'

'Leaving.'

'You can't go outside. It's just after noon.'

His face was blank, cold. 'I called Tate.'

'Kyrian . . .' She reached out to touch him.

'Don't touch me,' he snarled, baring his fangs to her. 'You heard what Tabitha said. I'm an animal, I'm not human.'

'It wasn't an animal I slept with last night.'

'Wasn't it?'

'No.' She laid her hand on his cheek.

She saw him savor her touch for only an instant before his face went rigid. He removed her hand from his cheek. 'You say that, Amanda, and yet do you know how many times I've had to pull back from sinking my teeth into your neck? How many times I have felt your blood under my tongue and have craved a taste of it?'

She swallowed in fear. But she refused to give in to it. He was only trying to scare her off. 'You have never hurt me and I know you would die before you did.'

He said nothing as he grabbed his suitcase and left her.

She followed him down the hall, to the top of the stairs. 'You can't leave like this.'

'Yes I can.'

She pulled him to a stop before he could descend down to the foyer. 'I don't want you to leave me.'

Kyrian paused at her words. Words that tore him apart. He didn't want to leave her, either. He wanted to toss her over his shoulder, carry her back to the room, and make love to her for the rest of eternity.

He wanted the right to claim her. The right to have her.

But it wasn't meant to be. He was a servant to the goddess. His life wasn't his own.

'Go back to your world, Amanda. It's safe there.'

She cupped his face in her hands. Her bright blue eyes searched his with such an aching need that it made him hurt all the more. 'I don't want safe, Kyrian. I want you.'

He pulled away from her tender touch and headed down the stairs. 'Don't say that.'

'Why not?' she asked, following him. 'It's the truth.'

'You can't have me,' he said between clenched teeth as he whirled on the stairs to face her. 'I'm already owned.'

'Then let me love you.' The plea in her voice ate at his

will. Gods, how easy it would be to open himself to her. To take her into his arms and . . .

Watch her grow old while he stayed the same. Hold her in his arms when she died of old age and left him to live out eternity. Alone.

The pain of the thought was enough to cripple him. Life without her was not something he wanted to contemplate. And if it hurt this much to let her go after only a couple of days, how much worse would it be in a few decades?

It was more than his wounded heart could bear.

'You can't.'

'Why?' she asked.

'Some things are not meant to be.'

She touched his arm, her eyes begging him to see her side of things. But he couldn't. He didn't dare.

'Maybe this *is* meant to be.'

'You're wrong.'

A knock sounded on the door.

Amanda watched as Esmeralda opened the door. Tate wheeled his stretcher in.

The resigned, pained look on Kyrian's face as he saw the body bag would be forever etched in her heart.

'Don't leave, Kyrian,' she begged one last time, praying this time he would listen.

'I have no choice.'

'Yes you do. Damn you, you stubborn man. You do have a choice. Don't leave me.'

He rubbed his hand over his eyes as if he had a throbbing headache. 'Why do you want me to stay?'

'Because I love you.'

Tabitha's angry curse rang from the kitchen and was followed by silence so loud, it was deafening.

Kyrian closed his eyes as agony assailed him. He'd waited an eternity to hear a woman say that to him and mean it.

But now it was too late.

'The last time I believed a woman loved me I gave up an empire for her and watched her laugh while I was crucified. Don't be a fool, Amanda. Love isn't real. It's an illusion. You don't love me. You can't.'

Before she could argue, he flipped gracefully into the body bag and zipped it closed.

'Don't you leave me!' she shouted, grabbing his arm through the thick plastic.

'Get me home, Tate.'

Tate gave her a sad smile as he pushed the stretcher through the door.

Amanda growled her frustration. 'Damn you, Kyrian Hunter. Damn you.'

Kyrian heard her muffled words. They tore through him. He was such a godless fool.

Don't leave her, his heart begged.

But he had no choice.

This was the path he had chosen. His decision had been made with full knowledge of the consequences and sacrifices.

Amanda belonged to the light and he belonged to the darkness. Somehow, he would find a way to reclaim his soul without her, and once he did, he would kill Desiderius.

Amanda and Tabitha would be free and he would return to the life he knew. The life he had sworn himself to.

But deep in his heart, he knew the truth. He loved her, too. More than he had ever loved anything else in his life.

And he had to let her go.

Chapter 15

It was just after five o'clock and nearing dusk when Amanda reached Kyrian's. She parked her dark blue Taurus in front of the house and walked up to the grand front door, then knocked.

She expected Nick to answer; instead, the door swung open slowly to show her no one at all.

Frowning, she walked inside.

The door instantly slammed shut behind her, making her gasp in startled alarm. Now that she thought about it, the front gates had done the same thing. Only then she had assumed Kyrian had seen her car on the video monitors and had opened the gates before she had a chance to buzz the house.

Now she wasn't so sure.

Her heart hammering, she still didn't see anyone about. The silent house appeared completely empty. 'Hello?' she asked, entering the foyer slowly. 'Nick? Kyrian?'

'So you're Amanda Devereaux.'

She froze when she heard the voice coming from the living room. It was deep and provocative, with an accent unlike anything she'd ever heard before. The rich sound reminded her of quiet thunder.

For an instant, she feared it might be a Daimon, until her eyes adjusted enough to where she could see the stunningly gorgeous man on the sofa. He was lying on his back with his legs dangling way over the arm of the sofa and his hands behind his head as he watched her from the darkness.

Shirtless and barefoot, he wore a pair of tight leather pants. He had long, dark green hair and a stylized small birdlike tattoo on his left shoulder, the tail of which curled down and around his biceps. His skin was the same golden tone as Kyrian's and it set off to perfection the small gold necklace he wore around his neck.

'And you are?' she asked.

'Acheron Parthenopaeus,' he said in that steady, deep voice. 'Pleased to meet you.' His words were devoid of any warmth or emotion.

Okay, this was no Yoda. Well, except they both had green heads.

The man on the sofa looked to be no more than in his early twenties and yet there was a hardness to him that belied his youthful appearance. It was as if he had seen hell first-hand and had returned from the journey forever wiser.

Even while lying down, he commanded awe, and a shiver of fear went down her spine. Something about Acheron was truly frightening, but she couldn't put her finger on what it was.

He just made her greatly uneasy.

'So you're the infamous Acheron.'

A smile played across his devastatingly handsome face. 'Lord and master of the great barbarian horde that roams the night.'

'Are you truly?'

He shrugged nonchalantly. 'Not really. I would have better luck harnessing the winds.'

She laughed nervously.

He rose slowly to his feet and approached her like a great,

stalking beast. As he drew near, the force of his presence and the sheer size of him overwhelmed her.

At least six-foot-eight, he towered over her with an indescribably powerful essence.

'My God,' she breathed as she craned her neck to look up at him. 'Is there some unwritten law that you guys have to be giants?'

He laughed, showing her a glimpse of his fangs. 'What can I say? Artemis likes her Dark-Hunters tall. Short men need not apply.'

As he stopped before her, she saw his eyes.

Her jaw went slack. Unlike Kyrian's, they shimmered. There was no other word for it. As she watched him, his eyes shifted through an entire blue and silver spectrum. Like quicksilver, the colors changed and blended. It reminded her of a turgid sea with shifting waves.

'Off-putting, aren't they?' he asked as he watched her watch him.

'Are they supposed to do that?'

He smiled a tight-lipped smile, but didn't respond as he pulled a pair of black opaque sunglasses from his back pocket and put them on. Now that his eyes were covered, she noticed the strange scar on his neck. It looked as if someone's hand print had been burned into his throat while he was being throttled. Very, very strange.

'What brings you here, little human?' Acheron asked.

'I've come to see Kyrian.'

'He doesn't want to be seen.'

'Well,' she said, stiffening her spine to stand strong against this Dark-Hunter she was sure could splinter her in a nanosecond. 'We don't always know what's best for us.'

He laughed at that. 'Very true. So you think you can save him?'

'You doubt me?'

He cocked his head as if assessing her mettle and walked

a small circle around her. As he passed, she saw the healing wounds on his back. They overlapped and crisscrossed like some twisted river map. But the most peculiar part was that they seemed to form an intricate pattern that was as beautiful as it was horrifying.

Her heart lurched at the sight. He must have endured untold hours of agony for each visible welt.

Dropping her gaze from his lean, muscular back, she found the bow mark of Artemis that was identical to the one Kyrian had on his shoulder. Only Acheron's was located over his right hipbone.

'You know,' he said in a low, ominous tone. 'I've walked this earth for over eleven thousand years, my lady.' He paused and leaned to whisper in her ear. 'I have seen things in my life that are unimaginable to you, and you ask if I doubt you?'

He took a step back so that he could watch her face before he finished his sentence. 'Lady, I doubt the very air you breathe.'

'I don't understand you.'

He ignored her confusion. 'You want his soul.'

'Excuse me?' she asked as a nervous tremor went through her.

'I feel you, lady. I hear you. Your mind is a whirlpool of feelings and fears: Can you have him? Does he love you? Could he *ever* love you? Do you honestly love him? Is there even the tiniest chance that the two of you can find a way to be together? Or are you just fooling yourself?'

She shivered as he laid bare the very thoughts and doubts in her heart.

He stopped in front of her and tilted her chin until she looked up at him. She could sense him probing her soul through her eyes, but she could see nothing of his liquid silver gaze. All she saw was herself reflected in the black lenses of his sunglasses.

When he spoke, his voice seemed to be coming from inside her head. 'The one question that bothers you most is how to save him without killing your sister in the process.'

'How do you know all that?'

He gave an odd half-smile. 'My powers are unfathomable to you.'

'Then why don't you kill Desiderius before he hurts Kyrian again?'

He dropped his hand from her chin. 'I can't.'

'Why not?'

'For the same reason Kyrian can't. I have no soul with which to fight him. He would kill me, and given the sins of my past, I shudder to think of the means he would use.'

She thought about that for a moment. Desiderius had tried to kill Kyrian the same way Kyrian had died as a mortal, which meant Acheron must have suffered something even worse than crucifixion.

Just what had killed this fearsome Dark-Hunter?

And hard on the heels of that thought was another. 'How does a Dark-Hunter get his soul back?'

He backed her against the wall like a lion cornering its prey. The very air around him seemed to sizzle with mystical energy and power. 'Souls are strange things, lady. They can only be passed by free will. The one who owns it must willingly let it go.'

'So I need to summon Artemis since she holds Kyrian's soul?'

He laughed evilly at that. 'She would eat you alive, little girl.'

His tone set her anger off. He might be Mr. Badass, but she wasn't a child. 'Don't patronize me.'

'Oh, I'm not patronizing you. I am only warning you. You are incapable of taking on the goddess. She is the wind. The mistress of our destinies and you, little girl, are nothing more than a tiny morsel she would gobble up and spit out for fun.'

'Thank you for that vivid imagery,' she said, her stomach turning at the thought.

He smirked at that. Then his harsh features softened. 'You do want to save him, don't you?'

Again she had the feeling he was eavesdropping on her thoughts. 'Of course I do. He means everything to me.'

He nodded. 'You are pure of heart. This might actually work.'

Now that scared her more than anything else he'd said or done. Something in his tone told her his idea was the worst kind of risky. 'What might work?'

Acheron moved to a black backpack that rested on the coffin coffee table. He reached inside and pulled out a black carved wooden box. Silver symbols and classical Greek writing covered it. 'What you seek is in here.'

He opened the box to show her rich black velvet lining that cradled a red medallion. Like Acheron's eyes, it shimmered. But its colors turned from red to yellow to orange. Colors that seemed to lick the center carving that looked like a swirling wind.

'How beautiful,' she breathed as she reached to touch it.

Acheron pulled it from her reach. 'Touch it and it will burn you like the very fires of hell.'

She dropped her hand instantly. 'What is it?'

'Kyrian's soul.'

Her heart stopped beating when she heard his blasé tone. Swallowing, she stared at the medallion. Could it really be his soul?

No, it wasn't possible. 'You're lying to me.'

'I never lie,' Acheron said simply. 'I have no need to.'

Still, she wasn't ready to believe he had possession of what she wanted more than anything. 'What are you doing with it?'

'I was hoping you might help me return it to him so that he could kill Desiderius.'

'Return it how?'

Acheron picked the medallion up, cradled it in his palm, and closed the box.

'It doesn't burn you?' she asked.

He gave her a sly smile. 'I told you, my powers are beyond your imagination.'

'Then why don't you return it to Kyrian?'

'Because he doesn't trust me and, unlike you, I have no heart, pure or otherwise.' He turned the medallion over as if studying it. 'You see, there is only one way for a Dark-Hunter to regain his soul. A pure, loving heart must take the medallion into his or her palm and hold it while the Dark-Hunter is drained of his supernatural powers. Only when the human part of him remains can a Dark-Hunter die a normal death.'

'I beg your pardon?'

He looked at her, and even though she couldn't see his eyes, she knew he was staring at her. 'The only way to give his soul back is to stop his human heart from beating. When it beats for the last time, the medallion must be placed against the mark where the soul was captured. It will leave the medallion and reenter his body.'

Her head throbbed as she tried to come to terms with what he was saying. 'I don't understand. How do you stop his heart from beating?'

'You drain his Dark-Hunter powers, then you stake him through the heart.'

She stepped back, her mind whirling. 'No! He'll vaporize like a Daimon. You're trying to get me to kill him, aren't you?'

'No,' he said earnestly. 'The Dark-Hunters are my children and I would sooner damn myself to a Shade before I ever let one be hurt. You asked how to return his soul to him and I've answered you. If you want to free him, you have to drain him and kill him.'

Before she could say another word, Acheron took her hand and brought it over the medallion in his. The heat from it was excruciating. It was like holding her hand over a propane torch.

'Now imagine touching it,' he whispered. 'Then think of holding it. You will have to keep the medallion in your hand from the moment he is staked until his heart stops beating and you release it back into his body.'

His grip tightened on her wrist and she could feel his hidden gaze boring into her. 'Do you love him enough?'

'I . . .' Amanda hesitated. 'How long do I have to hold it?'

'As long as it takes. I can't tell you that. It is different for every Dark-Hunter.'

'And if I let go of it before the soul is free?'

'Then Kyrian is doomed for eternity to walk as neither Dark-Hunter nor Human. He will be trapped between this world and the next as a Shade. He will yearn for food and never be able to eat. He will thirst and never drink. He will suffer eternally.'

Amanda stared at the medallion in horror. 'I can't chance it.'

Acheron released her hand, then returned the medallion to the box. 'Then he will die anyway when he faces Desiderius.'

'There has to be another way,' she whispered.

'There isn't.'

Her chest tight, she tried to imagine draining Kyrian's powers and leaving him vulnerable. Could she do that to him?

Acheron moved to return the box to his backpack.

'Wait,' she said, stopping him. 'You said the medallion must be placed exactly where the soul was captured.'

'Yes.'

'How would I find that?'

He gestured to the bow mark on his hip. 'The brand will

always show you where Artemis was touching us when she captured our souls.'

Amanda opened her mouth to speak, but a booming voice silenced her.

'What are you doing here?'

Amanda whirled to find Kyrian behind her.

He looked to Acheron. 'Why did you let her in?'

Acheron passed a warning look to her. *Say nothing*, his voice whispered through her mind. 'It suited me to,' he said aloud.

Kyrian's face hardened. 'I told you not to.'

Acheron smiled, his fangs flashing for an instant. 'And I listen to you since when?'

Kyrian glared.

Amanda's gaze drifted down Kyrian's body and she noted he was dressed again in his black jeans, shirt, and boots. 'You're not going after him *tonight*, are you?'

'I have no choice.'

She looked over her shoulder at his boss. 'Acheron . . .'

Acheron shrugged nonchalantly. 'It's his decision.'

'He's wounded,' she insisted.

'He's a Dark-Hunter. He knows his strength and weaknesses. It's for him to decide.'

Frustration welled up inside her and she wanted to kill them both. 'You would let him die?'

'This has nothing to do with Acheron,' Kyrian said, cutting her off. 'As he said, it's for me to judge.'

'Yeah, well, your judgment sucks.'

'Yeah, well, Tabitha says the same about yours.'

She glared at him.

He glared back until she broke eye contact with him. Then he glanced to Acheron. 'Watch over her for me.'

'Is that an order?' Acheron asked in disbelief.

'Don't be an ass.'

He cocked a taunting brow. 'I'm an Ash, not an ass.'

A tic appeared in Kyrian's jaw. 'And I have an appointment to keep. Later.' He turned around and stalked out of the room.

Amanda stood frozen in the living room.

And her heart shattered at the sound of the garage door opening and Kyrian's car starting. The man was so damned stubborn!

'He was wrong, Acheron. You're not the ass, he is.'

Acheron laughed.

Amanda rubbed her hands over her eyes as she tried to think of what she should do. But in her heart she knew. Kyrian was going to die one way or another.

At least if she killed him, he stood a chance. 'Give me the medallion.'

Acheron handed her the box. 'Are you sure?'

'Absolutely not.'

She tried to take the box, but he held on to it. 'Whatever you do, *don't* change your mind after you take this into your hand. It would be the cruelest thing you could do to him. I would rather he die fighting Desiderius than die by the hand of the woman he loves. Again.'

Her hand trembled under his. 'I would never hurt him.'

'No offense, but the last time I heard that, the woman dropped the medallion ten seconds after she picked it up. Don't make me wrong again.'

'I won't.'

He nodded grimly and released the medallion to her. 'Remember, you have to take it into your hand the moment he's staked. Hold it until he's dead, then place the medallion over the bow mark.'

'How will I know when it's done?'

'Trust me, you'll know.'

Amanda placed the medallion in her backpack purse next to the box with the Barbie doll Liza had given her. She'd started carrying the doll the night Tabitha had been attacked.

It was probably stupid, but knowing the doll was there just in case comforted her. Besides, it was better than carrying a gun, and even with the spikes in the legs, she was sure it was safer.

As she closed her purse, her cell phone started ringing. Digging it out of the side pouch, she answered it.

'Mandy, is that you?'

She wrinkled her nose when she heard Cliff's nasal voice. 'I thought—'

'Listen,' he said, interrupting her. 'Something terrible has happened . . .'

He sounded as if he'd been crying. Even though they were over romantically, she couldn't help feeling concern for him. He might be a jerk, but up until a couple of weeks ago, she had intended to marry him. 'What?'

'It's my mother,' he said, choking on a sob. 'Look, I know we're not on the best of terms, but I have no one else to call. Could you please come over here? I don't want to be alone.'

She hesitated. A strange, sick feeling clenched her stomach. Attributing it to the fact she couldn't stand the thought of seeing Cliff again, she realized just how selfish denying him would be. He needed her. She would go for a few minutes, then return here to wait for Kyrian. 'All right, I'm on my way.'

'Thank you.'

Acheron cocked a brow at her. 'Something wrong?'

'A friend in need.'

He nodded. 'You go and I'll find your sister and watch over her.' Acheron pulled on a black T-shirt. 'By the way, be careful.'

'Of?'

'It's nighttime and evil things are roaming out there.'

Another ripple of fear went through her. 'Should I be afraid?'

'Follow your gut, little girl. Do what you have to do.'

She hated the way he referred to her as 'little girl' all the time, and yet she couldn't seem to get ticked off about it. 'You like being vague, don't you?'

'It was a choice of being a Dark-Hunter or a prophet. Personally I like the slash-and-kill stuff much more than prayers and the lotus position.'

Acheron Parthenopaeus was a very odd individual.

Amanda fished her keys out and made her way back to her car. As she drove out of the driveway, toward the expressway, it dawned on her how strange that Acheron would send her out alone . . .

Why would he do that when Kyrian had asked him to watch over her?

Because Tabitha is far more likely to get into trouble walking the streets than you are going to Cliff's.

Oh yeah. That explained it. The only danger at Cliff's would be him boring her to death.

It didn't take her long to get there.

Amanda walked up to Cliff's first-floor apartment, then knocked on the door and waited for him to answer.

He opened the door. He was wearing a pair of Levi's and a yellow button-down shirt. 'What?' he asked, looking over her shoulder. 'No friend driving you this time?'

She glared at the jealousy she heard in his voice. How dare he! 'What's that supposed to mean?'

He shrugged and opened the door wider. 'Nothing. I'm just upset tonight. Thanks for coming on such short notice.'

Again she heard that voice in her head telling her to leave. Like a fool, she ignored it and stepped inside.

He shut and locked the door behind her.

'Well, well,' a familiar voice said from the kitchen. 'What have we here?'

Amanda froze as Desiderius stepped out of the shadows.

Chapter 16

'You!' Amanda screamed and started for the door.

Cliff caught her. 'Not so fast.'

'How could you?' she asked Cliff. Then she turned to glare at Desiderius. 'I don't understand why you're here. How?'

Desiderius sighed. 'Please don't make this any more cliché than it has to be. It's bad enough that I had to stoop to such a primitive ploy to trap Kyrian. Now you expect me to dump my entire plan on you so you can escape and kill me?' He shook his head. 'You know, I watch bad movies, too.'

Suddenly, she felt Desiderius in her thoughts. Felt him goading and prying into her memories. Her head ached and swam as bizarre images played through her mind. Images of Desiderius embracing and caressing her. Of his breath on her neck.

Worse, Amanda felt the barriers of her mind collapsing under the pressure of his fierce mental onslaught.

'She is as you promised, Cliff.' His voice came at such a faint distance. Like a vague whisper on the wind. 'Her powers are pure, virtually untouched.'

'I know. It's what drew me to her the first time I met her.' Cliff smiled. 'And with the information we gathered on how

Kyrian fights from that night in the alley, we should have no trouble defeating him.'

Desiderius paused as he looked upon the lesser beast. He considered humans to be the lowest of low. They were, after all, only food for the gods.

The only thing below them were mongrels such as Cliff. Half Apollite, half human, the sniveling coward had served his uses.

All in all, he should be grateful that Cliff's Apollite father had died before he could impart the real truth of the boy's heritage to him.

As for Cliff's human mother . . .

Well, she had been a tasty morsel.

Desiderius had always known having a mongrel for a pet would one day pay off. All the years of having to rear the vile creature didn't seem so repulsive now.

And when Cliff had found this little sorceress in his own office, Desiderius had bided his time waiting for Cliff to expose and develop her psychic powers before Desiderius took her soul and her powers along with it.

But she had been resistant.

Who could have guessed the outcome of all this? After Cliff had panicked and broken up with Amanda over her sister's behavior, Desiderius had known he would have to act quickly to claim the sorceress before she escaped their clutches.

As soon as Cliff told him how close the twins were and how often Cliff had been inside Tabitha's home, Desiderius's plan had formed.

When he had handcuffed Amanda to the Dark-Hunter, he had pretended to confuse her with her sister, hoping Amanda would panic and use her powers to kill the Dark-Hunter to protect Tabitha. He'd never dreamed she would reach into her powers to protect the Dark-Hunter.

Not that it mattered.

Now with the channel open, she was ripe for the plucking.

'You will bring me over now?' Cliff asked. 'Make me immortal, too?'

'Absolutely.'

Amanda barely registered the sight of Desiderius walking over to Cliff and taking him into his arms. She saw his fangs flash an instant before Desiderius sank them into Cliff's willing neck.

Her head swimming even more, she felt herself floating toward the floor. Too late, she realized her thoughts were no longer her own.

Kyrian paused in the heart of the French Quarter looking around as his long black leather coat billowed around his legs. Tourists lined Bourbon Street, walking around, oblivious to the danger. Some of them paused as they caught sight of him dressed in black, wearing his sunglasses because the garish lights hurt his eyes.

He could hear the cacophony of jazz, rock, and laughter mixing in the cool winter winds.

Numbing his mind to the distractions, he reached out with both his powers and his technology and still he had no sign of Desiderius.

'Dammit,' he snarled.

He rubbed his aching shoulder where Tabitha had attacked him.

As he massaged the pain, the image of Amanda replaced her sister's. He saw her laughing face the way she'd been last night draped over him as she made the tenderest of love to him. No one had ever touched him so deeply.

'Because I love you.'

Those words seared his heart. More so because he had heard her feelings in her voice. She meant them in a way no woman had ever meant them before.

She loved him.

And he loved her. Loved her so much that inside he wanted to die knowing he couldn't have her. The Fates were cruel bitches. He'd learned that centuries ago. And yet on this cold night, that one basic fact burned inside him.

Come to me, Amanda, I need you.

He flinched at the thought.

'Don't think about it,' he whispered, knowing it was futile. If he could have one single wish . . .

He forced the thought away. He had a mission to accomplish. He must stop Desiderius.

His phone rang. He pulled his cell phone off his belt and answered it.

It was Talon. 'Ash wanted me to tell you something weird is going down. The Daimons are attacking in droves tonight. I've nailed ten so far and he's on the tail of four more. He wants you on your toes.'

'Tell Gramps not to worry. Everything is quiet in the Quarter.'

'All right, just don't get jacked out there.'

'Don't worry. I can handle myself.'

'By the way,' Talon said. 'Eric is with Tabitha. He said she's loose in the Quarter, hunting Desiderius, too.'

'You've got to be kidding me.'

'I wish. Ash was tailing her in the Garden District, but had to let her go when he spotted a group of Daimons after tourists.'

Kyrian hung up at the same time his tracker hummed. It signaled that there were Daimons nearby. Grabbing his tracker from his coat pocket, he trailed their neural activity to a side alley a block away.

He entered the darkened area to find six Daimons attacking four humans.

'Hey!' Kyrian called, distracting them from their victims. He smoothed back the edge of his coat and pulled out his retractable sword. Pressing the stone on the hilt, he extended it out to its full five-foot length.

'Tell me,' Kyrian said to the Daimons as he twirled it around himself, 'have you ever seen a pissed-off ancient Greek general?'

The Daimons passed a wary look among themselves.

Kyrian fell into his crouch with his sword held in both hands as he sized them up. 'It's not a pretty sight. Really.'

'Get him!' the leader called and at once they rushed him.

Kyrian caught the first one with a parry that caused him to explode into powder. He twisted around like a graceful cat and caught a second one with an upper cut to the middle. The Daimon gasped and vaporized.

Before Kyrian could rebound from that attack, one of the Daimons caught his sore arm and clawed the sword from his grasp. Kyrian twisted and caught him with the toe of his boot. He too evaporated.

Another one caught him about the waist and rammed him back against the wall.

The other two closed in.

He kicked at the one on his waist at the same time the two approaching him vaporized.

He saw Tabitha standing on unsteady legs. 'Eat steel, you vampire dogs,' she said as she tossed a throwing star at Kyrian.

Stunned by the fact she had tossed it to him as protection and not to harm him, he caught it in his hand and used it to kill the last Daimon.

By the time he reached Tabitha, she was kneeling on the ground. Her neck was bleeding steadily, her face pale. Kyrian tore part of his shirt to make a compress, then dialed for an ambulance.

'Eric?' she asked, her voice strained as she tried to see into the darkness where the other victims lay. 'Is he dead?'

'I'm right here, baby.'

Eric staggered over to where they were. He fell down beside Tabitha and gathered her into his arms.

'She's not going to die,' Kyrian assured him.

Eric nodded. 'I tried to tell her not to come out tonight. That it was going to be bad. She doesn't listen.'

'It runs in the family.'

Tabitha touched Kyrian's arm while he gave directions to 911. After he finished, she stared at him, her brow dark with disbelief. 'Why did you save me?'

'It's what Kyrian does, Tabby,' Eric whispered.

While Eric held her, Kyrian checked on the other two people on the ground. They were the same ones who had attacked him in Esmeralda's house. Unfortunately, they weren't as lucky as Eric and Tabitha.

'Eric,' he said, returning to them, 'what happened?'

Eric shrugged. 'One minute we had them and the next, they turned on us.'

'Did they say anything?'

Erik looked sick as he held Tabitha close. '"I'll swallow your soul."'

Kyrian stared at him for a heartbeat, then clenched his teeth at their warped sense of humor. 'Daimons watch way too many B movies.'

Tabitha reached out and touched Kyrian's hand. 'Thank you.'

He nodded. 'I return the gratitude.'

'Man, Kyrian,' Eric breathed. 'You were right about them. I've never seen Daimons move like that before. I should have listened to your warning.'

Frowning, Tabitha looked between them. 'You two know each other?'

'My father used to work for Kyrian's friend Talon.' Eric met Kyrian's gaze. 'I've known Kyrian all my life, Tabby. Believe me, he's one of the good guys.'

Before she could say anything else, the ambulance arrived.

Kyrian waited until they were both inside and under medical care before he called Amanda to tell her the news.

She didn't answer her cell phone.

He called her mother, her sister, and his house. No one answered.

His stomach knotting with fear, he headed for his car. Maybe Amanda was still at his house waiting for him.

Or maybe Desiderius has her . . .

He imagined her being attacked like Tabitha. Saw her bloody and dead like Tabitha's friends. The terror and pain of the thought wracked him.

Amanda had to be all right. He couldn't live if anything happened to her.

Like a demon possessed, he drove home as fast as his Lamborghini would go.

His body shaking in fear for her welfare, he rushed through the garage and into the dark house, listening.

Please, gods, anything. Just don't let her be harmed.

He heard Amanda upstairs, humming her Grieg tune in his bedroom. Relief and gratitude rocked him so hard, he almost staggered. He had to see her to make sure she was fine and healthy. Taking a deep breath in relief, Kyrian sprinted up the stairs and opened the door.

He froze.

Amanda had lit the candles on his wall sconces. She wore the skimpiest, sheerest white nightgown he had ever seen in his life. Her long legs were encased in stockings and a lacy white garter belt. With her back to him, she was leaning over the bed, scenting his sheets with the rose oil she rubbed onto her skin after her bath.

The candlelight displayed the outline of her creamy body to perfection.

His entire body burned at the sight of her. Overwhelmed by his emotions, he went to the bed and pressed himself against her back. He held her tight in his arms, leaning his head against hers as he shook with relief.

Amanda was alive and unharmed.

She moaned in pleasure. The sound reverberated through him, heightening his desire even more.

'Touch me, Kyrian,' she breathed, taking his hands from her waist and leading them to her breasts. 'I need to feel you tonight.'

He needed it, too. After being so terrified that she was lost to him, he needed to feel her in a way that made his mind whirl.

Growling at the feel of her hardened, gauze-covered nipples in his palm, he dropped his head to taste the scented flesh of her neck.

She turned in his arms, reached up and removed his sunglasses from his face, then she claimed his lips with hers.

'Amanda,' he breathed as her rose scent encircled his head, beguiling him. 'What is it you do to me?'

She answered him by tracing her tongue along his jaw, then down under his chin to his neck. A thousand chills shot through him as she slid his coat over his shoulders and dropped it to the floor.

She untucked his shirt and ran her hands underneath it, branding his skin.

The voice in his head wanted to push her away, but he couldn't. In truth, he never could.

He loved this woman. There was nothing more to be said about it than that. She truly was his soul mate. He would deny it no more.

For this one tiny moment, he would revel in the love he felt for her. Revel in the way he craved her.

Her eyes hungry, she undid his pants and slid her hands over his swollen shaft. 'I love how you feel in my hands,' she whispered, stroking him. 'Tell me, Kyrian, can you read my thoughts?'

Kyrian closed his eyes as he savored her touch. When she cupped him, he shivered. 'No,' he breathed. 'I relinquished that power when you asked me to.'

Picking her up, he set her on the edge of the bed and stood between her knees. She smiled a smile that lightened his heart as she unlaced the front of her gown and bared her breasts to him.

His body burning, Kyrian nudged her legs farther apart so that he could look at her. Gods, how he loved looking at her. Dropping to his knees, he took her into his mouth.

She let out a strangled cry as he tasted her completely. Kyrian closed his eyes as he ran his tongue over her. Her thighs trembled around his face as he brought her to climax.

Her hand clutched at his hair and all the while she rocked her hips against his face.

'Oh yes,' she moaned.

Kyrian waited until she was completely finished. Only then did he stand up.

Her eyes were liquid and hot as she stared up at him. She rose up on the bed and finished undressing him, then she slid off the bed in front of him and offered him her back.

Without being told, he knew what she wanted. Growling low in his throat, he drove himself inside her with one forceful thrust.

She moaned in pleasure, rising up on her tiptoes and then dropping herself down to take him into her body all the way to his hilt.

Kyrian's entire body shook.

Kissing her shoulder, he slid his hand over her soft belly, then down through her nether curls so that he could touch her swollen nub. He stroked her tenderly with his hand while he kept his hips completely still. He let her take control of their pleasure.

Amanda milked him with her body until she came again, screaming his name.

Just as he felt their pleasure combining and his powers slipping from him, he pulled out of her. His breathing ragged, it was all he could do not to double over from the pain of his unspent lust.

For once, Amanda didn't take pity on him. Instead, she turned around and kissed him avidly.

'Amanda,' he said, trying to get away from her.

'Shh, Kyrian,' she whispered against his lips. 'Trust me.'

Against his instincts, he did. She laid him down on the bed, then climbed on top of him. Kyrian shook as she guided him back into her body.

She felt so incredibly good as he felt her inside him. Felt her pleasure as his as she rode him.

His ecstasy mounting, he let her roll him over until he was on top, cradled between her thighs. Feeling a little better, he rode her hard and fast.

This time when he went to pull out, she wrapped herself around him and held him tight.

Kyrian frowned as she rocked herself against him, drawing his shaft deeper into her body. She moaned as her body clutched at his.

'Amanda, stop,' he breathed raggedly. If she continued, he would be lost.

Again he tried to pull away and again she held tight, sliding herself against him. Kyrian ground his teeth, trying to stave off his orgasm.

It worked until he felt her climax again. The sound of her cry combined with her clutching him was more than he could take. Against his will, his body released.

Kyrian leaned his head back and shouted from the ferocity of his pleasure. There was truly nothing better than being in Amanda's arms. Her body.

For the first time in two thousand years, he felt at home.

And as those tender feelings swept through him, he felt his Dark-Hunter powers recede again.

No!

Amanda kissed him lightly on the lips and rolled over with him. He was too weak to protest. All he could do was stare up at her.

She left the bed and pulled on a robe.

'Amanda?' he called.

She returned a moment later with a glass of wine. 'Everything is all right. I'm here, my love,' she said.

She held the glass of wine to his lips. Trusting her completely, he drank it.

After a few minutes, the room began to swim. 'What are you doing?' he asked as a feeling of dread consumed him.

But he already knew.

Like Theone all those centuries ago, she had drugged him.

The last sight he had was of her opening the door to admit Desiderius into his bedroom.

Chapter 17

Kyrian came awake with his hands tied above his head. He was positioned against a dark, dank wall inside an unfamiliar house. The old-fashioned room was lit by candles that cast dancing shadows around him and he heard whispers surrounding him. By the looks of the place, he would surmise it was an older home probably not all that far from his own house down in the Garden District.

Scanning the room, he found Amanda and Desiderius standing a few feet away from him with Desiderius's arm draped around her shoulders.

Disbelief overwhelmed him.

Not again. Dear gods, not again.

How could he have been so damned stupid?

His mind had tried to tell him something had been wrong. He'd even known Desiderius would be able to get to Amanda. But he hadn't listened. He'd let his love for her, his need for her, blind him.

Kyrian clenched his eyes shut.

What hurt most was knowing what Desiderius would do to her once he killed him. Without him to protect her, Amanda was at Desiderius's utter mercy.

It really would be like Theone all over again. Once Valerius had executed him, the Roman had thrown Theone out, saying he didn't want a whore in his bed who might ruthlessly hand him over to his enemies someday.

Since Theone had betrayed the military leader of the Macedonians and caused their defeat, she'd been unable to return home. The villa she had loved so much had been burned to the ground. Everything she'd held dear had been confiscated.

Persecuted by his countrymen, she had fled Greece to Rome where she ended up a prostitute in a rundown stew.

She'd died of disease less than two years after him.

In the end, she had caused the very fate she had tried so hard to avert.

Opening his eyes, Kyrian saw Amanda a few feet away from him. She was dressed in a pair of jeans and a black turtleneck. With her hair pulled back, he could see her profile perfectly as she clutched a doll to her.

How could she do this to him?

But then, he knew. Desiderius's powers had been more than she could take. Somehow, in spite of D'Alerian's efforts, the Daimon had invaded her dreams and turned her mind.

Rage darkened his vision. He wouldn't let her die. Not like this. In spite of his weakness, he grabbed the ropes and pulled as hard as he could.

'So, you're awake.'

Desiderius and Amanda moved to stand before him. His eyes taunting, Desiderius placed one hand on Amanda's shoulder. 'It's painful, isn't it? Knowing I'm going to bed her before I kill her and there's nothing you can do to stop me.'

'Go to hell.'

Desiderius laughed. 'You first, Commander. You first.' He trailed one long, evil finger down the line of Amanda's jaw. She didn't react at all. It was as if she were in some kind of trance. 'I would take her in front of you, but I never could stand an audience. I was never *that* twisted.' He laughed at his own joke.

Kyrian felt the rope slacken a degree. Working it, he put all his attention into gaining his freedom.

The ropes drew tight again.

Desiderius laughed. 'Do you honestly think I'm so stupid as to let you get free?' He took a step forward and stood practically nose to nose with Kyrian. 'This time, I won't chance your survival.'

Kyrian smirked as if the Daimon were a little gnat buzzing by his head. 'Ooo, if I were wearing boots, I'd be shaking in them.'

Desiderius eyed him in disbelief. 'Don't you *ever* get scared?'

Kyrian gave him a dry look. 'I faced down an entire Roman legion with only a sword to protect me. Now, why would I be afraid of some two-bit, half-god Daimon with an inferiority complex?'

The Daimon hissed at him, baring his fangs. He grabbed the crossbow off the table and loaded a steel bolt into it. 'You will learn not to taunt me. I am not one you mess with.'

'Why not? What makes you special?'

'My father is Bacchus. I am a god!'

Kyrian snorted. The first rule of war: make your opponent lose his temper. Emotions clouded judgment and made one do stupid things, and it would give him the opening he needed to get free and save both of them.

Besides, he liked the way the throbbing vein stood out in Desiderius's temple. It let him know he hadn't lost his touch when it came to taunting his enemies. 'What you are is pathetic. You're a bully and a psycho. No wonder Daddy has no use for you.'

Desiderius screamed in fury. He brought the crossbow down hard against Kyrian's face.

Kyrian's entire head ached from the blow. He tasted blood on his lips. Running his tongue over the cut, he tsked the Daimon.

'You know nothing of my life, Dark-Hunter. You don't know what it's like being born to die.'

'We are all born to die.'

'Oh yes, the humans and their finite lives that are three times the length of ours. How I pity them.'

He grabbed Kyrian by the throat and pressed his head back against the wall. 'Do you know what it feels like to watch the woman you love decay before your eyes? Eleanor was only twenty-seven. Twenty-seven! I did everything I could to save her. I even brought a human to her and still she refused to take the soul that would save her. She was pure unto the end.'

Desiderius's eyes turned dull at the memory. 'She was so beautiful and gentle. I had begged my father for help and he turned his back on me. So I watched my beautiful wife turn old in a handful of hours. I watched her body age until it decayed in my arms.'

'I'm sorry for you,' Kyrian said quietly. 'But it doesn't excuse what you've done.'

Desiderius screamed his outrage. 'What I've done? I've done nothing except be born to a cursed race while I watch the humans squander the gift of life they have. I do them a favor by killing them. I alleviate their boring, insipid lives.'

His blue eyes darkening dangerously, Desiderius curled his lip. 'You know, I obtained a copy of your Dark-Hunter handbook when I killed one of your brethren ninety years ago. The entry that struck me most was the one where it said to always go for a Daimon's heart. To strike at his most vulnerable spot.'

He aimed the crossbow at Amanda. 'Your heart would be her, wouldn't it?'

Kyrian masked his terror. His fear. Even though he was weak, he tightened his grip on the ropes holding him and lifted his feet up to kick Desiderius with all his remaining strength before the Daimon had a chance to hurt Amanda. Desiderius staggered back, the crossbow dropping away from her to point toward the floor.

'Run, Amanda!' he shouted.

She didn't move.

Kyrian fell back against the wall. 'Damn it, Amanda, please run for me.'

She didn't appear to hear him at all. She merely stood staring into space as she hummed and gripped her doll.

Desiderius laughed as he righted himself. He licked the blood from his lips while he eyed Kyrian with malice. 'She's mine, Dark-Hunter. You can die with the knowledge that I will use her well before I take her soul and her powers.'

Desiderius smiled an evil smile a second before he shot the crossbow straight into Kyrian's heart.

The force of the bolt embedding itself into his body drove him into the wall. Kyrian gasped at the pain of the steel biting into his body.

Desiderius came forward to stand before him. His eyes amused, he ran his finger around the small amount of blood that seeped from the wound. 'What a pity Dark-Hunter blood is poisonous to drink. I'm sure it's richer and thicker than what I normally have to live on.'

Kyrian barely heard the words as his heart struggled to beat. His ears buzzed. It was the most painful thing he'd ever felt. His sight dulling, he turned to look one last time at Amanda.

Her features were pinched as she watched him and for a moment he could pretend that she remembered him. That she knew he was dying and that she cared.

Had she been herself, he knew she would run to him.

Unlike his wife, she would cry when she heard of his death. And in a strange way, that comforted him.

Desiderius left him and went to pat her on the shoulder. 'Go on, Amanda, kiss your lover farewell.'

Kyrian struggled to breathe as she approached him. He had so many things he wanted to tell her. So many things he wished he'd said to her while she'd been able to really hear his words.

At least he wouldn't die alone.

'I love you, Amanda,' he whispered, hoping that somehow she would later recall his words to her and know that he meant them.

Her eyes blank, she leaned forward and covered his lips with her own and pressed her hand to his shoulder.

He felt the blackness of death descend over him and as he died, he heard her last whispered words. 'I will love you for eternity, my dark warrior.'

Then everything vanished.

Amanda held her breath as she felt the heat seeping out of the medallion she clutched underneath the doll's dress, into Kyrian's lifeless body. Her hand shook as she waited for him to reawaken, and with every second that passed, she shook more.

It wasn't working . . .

Oh God, no! Acheron had lied to her after all!

Tears stung her eyes as the medallion turned icy cold and fell from her grasp.

Still, Kyrian didn't move.

He lay limp against the wall, his face pale. His body cold.

No!

It was over and Kyrian was dead.

No!

Desiderius's evil laughter rang out through the dark room and made her entire soul weep in anguish.

Right then, she wanted to die, too. This was all her fault. She had stood by and let Kyrian die and had done nothing to save him. Her grief welled up and lodged as an unreleased scream in her throat.

'I love you, Amanda.' His words would haunt her forever.

Sobbing, she wrapped her arms around Kyrian's body and held him close, willing him to wake up and speak. *Please, God, take anything from me, but please let him live.*

'Amanda?' Desiderius's voice was sharp as he commanded her back to his side.

She held tighter to Kyrian, laying her head on his chest, beside the bolt, and willing her life force into him.

Amanda froze as she heard something. It was a faint sound, but it made her soar.

She heard Kyrian's heart beating.

Pulling back, she watched as his eyes fluttered open.

Kyrian gazed into Amanda's dark blue eyes that sparkled from her tears. No longer blank, her eyes stared into his with a purpose. And with love.

Her face softening, she passed her hand over his chest and the bolt shot free.

In that moment, he knew she hadn't betrayed him. She had set him free.

'You have your soul back, Kyrian of Thrace,' she whispered as the ropes around his wrists unknotted. 'Now let's make this bastard pay.'

Desiderius screamed in fury as he realized what was happening. Kyrian didn't have his Dark-Hunter powers, but it didn't matter.

For the first time in over two thousand years he had his soul, and the feel of it and the knowledge that Amanda hadn't betrayed him invigorated him.

The Daimon was a dead man.

Desiderius ran for the door.

It slammed shut. 'I wouldn't want you to leave the party so soon,' Amanda said. 'Not after everything you've done to make us so welcome.'

'Amanda?' Kyrian said uncertainly.

She looked at him, her eyes shimmering ever so slightly

in a way that reminded him of Acheron's. 'Desiderius unlocked my powers for me,' she said quietly. 'He thought to use the telekinesis and telepathy for himself.' She looked at Desiderius and smiled. 'Surprise. When you unleashed them, you lost all control over me.'

Desiderius struggled to open the door.

Kyrian stalked him like a hungry panther after its prey. 'What's the matter, Desiderius, afraid of a mere human?'

He turned with a snarl. 'I can beat you. I'm a god.'

'Then do it.'

Cursing, Desiderius charged him. He grabbed Kyrian around the waist and drove him against the wall. Desiderius opened his mouth to bite him.

'Oh, like hell,' Kyrian snarled. 'I didn't just get my soul back to lose it to you.' He kneed the Daimon in the groin.

Desiderius stumbled away from him.

'Kyrian.'

He turned to see Amanda with his sword. She tossed it to him.

Extending the blade, he went for Desiderius. The Daimon dodged his swing and lifted his hand to astral-blast him. Kyrian cursed as the blast hit him in the chest right where the crossbow bolt had been. He staggered back.

Oh, it hurt.

Dazed, he couldn't defend himself as Desiderius rushed him. He braced himself in expectation of Desiderius's blow.

It never came.

Instead, Amanda popped the Daimon with a blast of her own.

Kyrian frowned at her. 'Baby, can I handle this, please?'

She poked her lip out at him. 'I was only trying to help. Besides, haven't you been battered enough?'

Before he could answer, Desiderius ran at him again.

Amanda held her breath as she watched them fight. Even weak, Kyrian was amazing. He flipped over Desiderius and retrieved his sword. Desiderius grabbed a sword from the table and charged him.

The sound of clashing steel echoed as the two of them engaged.

'Go, baby,' she whispered, clutching her doll in her hands.

Kyrian would win. He had to. She'd gone through too much to see him die now.

As she watched them fight, she realized the sun was rising. She could see it just peeping through the closed windows.

Desiderius saw it and cursed, then he landed an upper blow to Kyrian that knocked the sword free from his grasp.

She held her breath.

Desiderius smiled as he stalked Kyrian away from where his sword had fallen. 'Tell you what,' he said evilly. 'Why don't you give Hades my best?'

'Kyrian!'

Kyrian turned to see Amanda lob her doll at him. Instinctively, he caught it. He cursed as the blades in the doll's feet bit into his hand.

A smile broke across his face.

Laughing, he ducked Desiderius's blow, and caught the Daimon right in the heart with the doll's feet. 'Tell Hades yourself,' he said as Desiderius gaped.

Time stood still as Desiderius met Kyrian's eyes. The Daimon's face went through an entire array of emotions, disbelief, fear, anger, and pain.

Then, in the blink of an eye, Desiderius disintegrated.

Kyrian and Amanda stood frozen as the full impact of the moment hit them.

It was over. Desiderius was dead. Amanda and Tabitha were safe.

Kyrian had his soul.

And the woman he loved had saved his life.

His heart pounding, Kyrian dropped the doll to the floor and walked toward Amanda. 'You are a very accomplished actress.'

'No. I was terrified.' She reached a shaking hand out to

his chest. 'I almost screamed when he did that. You have no idea how hard it was. Acheron told me that you had to die in order to be free and I knew I couldn't kill you. I knew the only chance we had was to let Desiderius do it for me.'

Kyrian took her hand in his, and as his fingers brushed her palm, he felt the blisters. He turned her hand over to see the medallion symbols branded into her flesh. 'It must have been excruciating.'

'I'm all right.'

He swallowed at her nonchalant tone. How could she dismiss what she had done for him? He arched a brow in disbelief. For him, she had ruined her hand. 'You're scarred for life.'

'No,' she said, smiling. 'I think it's the most beautiful thing I've ever seen.' She leaned forward and whispered in his ear. 'Second to you, that is.'

Kyrian cupped her face in his hands and kissed her. 'Thank you, Amanda.'

As she watched him, the joy faded from her face and she gave him a scared look. 'Julian and Acheron said you could summon Artemis now and return your soul to her, if you chose to.'

'Now, why would I choose such a thing?'

She shrugged. 'You're a Dark-Hunter.'

He kissed her lightly on the lips. 'What I am is a man in love with a woman. I want *you*, Amanda. For the rest of my blessedly short mortal life. I want to wake at dawn with you in my arms and watch our children play and fight. Hell, I even want to hear them back-talk me.'

She smiled at him. 'Are you sure?'

'I have never been more sure of anything in my life.'

She took his hand and led him from the room.

Kyrian stopped dead in his tracks as he saw the early morning light in the living room. From habit, he stepped back as he stared at it.

The bright sunlight didn't hurt his eyes. There was no burning of his skin.

Tightening his hand on Amanda's, he forced himself to walk forward, through the door.

And for the first time in over two thousand years, he walked out into daylight. The feel of the sunshine on his skin was incredible. The warmth, the tingly early breeze. His heart pounding, he looked up into the light blue sky and saw the white clouds.

It was a glorious day.

One he owed to Amanda.

Scooping her up in his arms, he held her close. 'All hail Apollo,' he whispered.

Amanda smiled as she hugged him dearly. 'No. All hail Aphrodite.'

Chapter 18

Kyrian stared in amazement at the wedding band on his left hand. He still couldn't believe the good fortune that had brought Amanda into his life.

Seven months had passed since the day Amanda had returned him to the light. Seven wonderful months of being with her night and day. Of helping her to accept, develop, and harness her powers, which were now stronger than his own.

Not that it mattered to him. He still had more than enough of his Dark-Hunter powers left to keep her safe. And her safety was the most important thing to him.

That and waking every morning to see the smile on her beautiful face.

And now they were married.

Amanda grabbed him from behind and squeezed him tight. 'What are you doing out here alone?' she asked.

He turned to see her in her wedding dress. The milky-white color set off her skin to perfection. Her cheeks were flushed with excitement, and the moonlight glowed in her eyes.

'I was getting some fresh air.'

She smiled a smile that made him weak and strong at the same time. 'Want to ditch the party and run for it?'

He laughed. 'Only eight out of that gargantuan crowd are mine, the rest are *your* guests.'

'Oh,' she said, wrinkling her nose. 'Never mind. It could get really ugly. Besides, my Aunt Xenobia might curse us.'

He draped his arm over her shoulders as she led him back into the ballroom of his house.

The orchestra played while a hundred and fifty members of the Devereaux-Flora clan danced, ate, and talked. Miguel, Rosa, and Liza sat with Amanda's sister Selena at a table where they were laughing with Grace and her infant son.

Amanda left him to visit with her mother and father.

Talon, Nick, Julian, and Acheron closed in around him.

Julian congratulated him. 'This one's a keeper,' he said.

Kyrian nodded. 'Yes, she is.'

'Man,' Talon said wistfully. 'I'm going to miss our three A.M. bullshit sessions. Wulf's already climbing the walls because he's lost his Doom opponent.'

Kyrian smiled as he recalled the lonely nights he had spent with his Dark-Hunter brothers and sisters on-line. 'Tell the Viking not to worry. I'll sneak up every now and again and challenge him.'

Acheron took a drink of his champagne. 'So, what are you going to do with your short life?'

Kyrian watched Amanda grab three-year-old Niklos up and dance with him. She was going to make a wonderful mother someday. 'I'm going to live it. Happily.'

Nick had his hands in his pants pockets. 'Guess I have to start looking for another Dark-Hunter to serve . . .' He looked meaningfully at Talon.

'Like hell, Gator bait, don't cast those eyes at me. I don't have Kyrian's patience. Besides, there's only enough room in my cabin for me and my computer.'

'Don't worry,' Ash assured Nick. 'I'll find you someone to serve.'

Nick looked horrified. 'Please don't do me any favors. I have visions of you sending me up to Alaska to serve Zarek's psycho ass.'

Kyrian laughed until Amanda rejoined them with a severe frown on her face.

'What is it, baby?' he asked.

'There's, um . . . a, um . . .'

The men looked at her expectantly.

'Yes?' Kyrian prompted.

'There's a fleet of UPS trucks in the driveway.'

The men exchanged puzzled looks before they all headed out to the front of the house where seven UPS trucks were lined up.

One of the drivers approached Kyrian. 'Hi,' he said in greeting. 'I'm looking for a Mr. K. Hunter.'

'That would be me,' Kyrian said.

'Good. Any idea where you want this stuff?'

'What is all this stuff?'

The driver handed him a clipboard with the names of the people who had sent the items. 'Wulf Tryggvason, Zoe, Blade Fitzwalter, Diana Porter, Cael, Brax, Samia, Arien, Kyros, Rogue, Kell, Dragon, Simon, Xander St. James, Alexei Nikolov, Badon Fitzgilbert . . .' On and on the Dark-Hunter names went.

'You know, Kyrian,' Acheron said with a laugh, 'you're going to have to buy a bigger house.'

'Yeah,' Talon said, 'but just wait until you have kids. I'll bet you get twice as much as this.'

They all burst out laughing.

Amanda stepped into Kyrian's embrace and looked up at him. 'I think your Dark-Hunter cohorts are going to miss you. You sure you have no regrets?'

Kyrian kissed her lightly on the cheek. 'None whatsoever. You?'

'Never.'

Acheron watched as the two newlyweds headed into the house arm in arm.

'Wanna bet where they're going?' Talon asked.

Ash laughed. 'No bet. I already know.' He turned to the driver and told him to leave the gifts in the living room. 'I think my wedding gift will be to hire an unpacking crew in the morning.'

Nick laughed. 'Let me go show them where to stack it so Kyrian doesn't get ticked.'

'I'll help,' Talon said.

Ash watched Nick run ahead of the drivers with Talon following at a much more conservative pace. He listened to the darkness and to the sounds of the night that he knew so well. He felt a slight stirring behind him.

It was a presence he knew even more intimately than the night.

He drained the last of his champagne. 'What are you doing here, Artie? I wasn't aware you had an invitation.'

A long, gracefully tapered hand touched his shoulder. Even through the tuxedo, he could feel the warmth of her as she caressed him. Unearthly tall and statuesque, she moved like a sleek, sensuous wind. Soft. Elegant.

And capable of total destruction when stirred too vigorously.

'I'm a goddess,' she spoke, her Greek accent smooth and cultured. 'I don't need an invitation.'

Acheron turned his head to see Artemis standing to his left. Her rich light auburn hair glowed in the moonlight and her iridescent green eyes sparkled.

'I hope you've come to wish them well,' he said.

She glanced askance at him as she toyed idly with his newly dyed black hair. A sly smile curved her perfect lips. 'I do. But the real question is, do you?'

Ash stiffened at the implication. 'What kind of question is that? You know I do.'

'Just checking to make sure that little green-eyed monster wasn't making you have second thoughts.'

He narrowed his gaze at her. 'The only green-eyed monster I know is you.'

She sucked her breath in sharply at his words, but her smile never wavered. 'Oooo,' she crooned in a sexually charged tone. 'Acheron is getting nasty in his old age.' She leaned her chin to rest on his shoulder as she stroked his jaw with a well-manicured fingernail. 'It's a good thing I like you, otherwise you'd be baked bread.'

He sighed. 'Yeah, lucky me. By the way, the correct term is "toast."'

Artemis could never keep track of colloquial slang, yet she seemed to enjoy using it. Or misusing it, anyway. There were times he suspected she did it on purpose just to see if he would dare to correct her.

'Mmmm,' she said, playfully wrapping her arms around his waist. 'I like it when you get all feisty.'

Acheron stepped away from her. 'So who are you transferring to New Orleans to take over Kyrian's spot?'

She licked her lips impishly and mischief glowed in her eyes. But before she could answer, Julian approached them.

'Little Cousin Artemis,' he said in greeting.

'Julian of Macedon,' she said coldly. 'Didn't know you were here.'

'Same.'

'Well,' Acheron said. 'Nice to know no introductions are needed.'

Artemis passed a threatening glare to Julian. 'Yes, well, I wish I could stay, but I can't.'

Before she vanished, she leaned forward and whispered the answer in Acheron's ear.

He went cold with the news as she twinkled into mist.

There were times when Artemis could be the biggest bitch on the planet.

Julian cocked a brow at him. 'What did she say?'

'Nothing.' The last thing Acheron wanted was to drop that bomb on Julian and Kyrian. And he certainly wasn't going to do it in the middle of a wedding.

He turned to Julian. 'So, General, you have your best friend back. I'll wager the two of you are going to get into some serious trouble.'

Julian laughed. 'Not likely.'

Somehow Acheron had a hard time believing that. Just as he had a hard time believing that Artemis would leave well enough alone.

Epilogue

Amanda brushed Kyrian's hair back from his face as she kissed his lips. Her wedding dress and his tuxedo were piled in a heap on the floor while they were tangled in the silk bedsheets.

'We're being awfully rude, aren't we?' she asked.

Kyrian smiled. 'Yeah, but I like rudeness.'

She laughed. Then he kissed her and she forgot everything else in the world.

'So, tell me,' he asked as he nibbled below her ear with his human teeth. 'Do you miss being an accountant?'

'Not at all. You?'

'I never was an accountant.'

She nipped his nose. 'You know what I mean. Do you miss being a Dark-Hunter?'

He licked her ear, sending chills over her. 'At times, yes. But I'd rather have you.'

'Do you really mean that?'

He pulled back to look into her eyes. 'With every piece of my heart and soul.'

'Good,' she whispered, kissing him. 'Because now that you're mortal again, the baby and I need you to be careful.'

Kyrian froze. 'What?'

She smiled down at him. 'We're pregnant, Mr. Hunter. About six weeks along.'

Kyrian kissed her deeply and held her close in his arms. 'That, Mrs. Hunter, is the best news I've ever heard.'

Amanda cupped his face in her hands. 'I love you, Kyrian of Thrace. And I never want to lose you.'

'I love you, Amanda Devereaux-Hunter, and I swear to you, you never will.'

Amanda kissed him again, knowing for the first time in her life that there really was such a thing as happily ever after. Even if it did mean marrying a vampire.

Still hungry for more?

Turn the page for a sneak peak
at another thrilling
Sherrilyn Kenyon novel

Night Embrace

Welcome to the dark side . . .

Prologue

A.D. 558, GLIONNAN

The roaring village fires burned high into the night, licking at the dark sky like serpents twining through black velvet. Smoke wafted through the misty darkness, pungent with the scent of death and vengeance.

The sight and smell should bring joy to Talon.

It didn't.

Nothing would ever bring joy to him again.

Nothing.

The bitter agony that welled inside him was crippling. Debilitating. It was more than even he could bear and that thought was almost enough to make him laugh . . .

Or curse.

Aye, he cursed from the excruciating weight of his pain.

One by one, he had lost every human being on earth who had ever meant anything to him.

All of them.

At age seven, he'd been orphaned and left the heavy responsibility of caring for his baby sister. With nowhere to go and unable to provide for the infant himself, he had returned to the clan that had once been led by his mother.

A clan that had banished both his parents before his birth.

His uncle had been in his first year as king when Talon had forced his way into his hall. The king had grudgingly accepted him and Ceara, but his clan never had.

Not until Talon had forced them to.

They might not have respected his parentage, but Talon had made them respect his sword arm and temper. Respect his willingness to maim or slay any and all who insulted him.

By the time he'd entered manhood, no one dared to mock his birth or impugn his mother's memory or honor.

He had risen through the ranks of warriors and learned all he could about weapons, fighting, and leadership.

In the end, he had been unanimously voted his uncle's successor by the very people who had once mocked him.

As the heir, Talon had stood by his uncle's right side, protecting him relentlessly until an enemy ambush had caught them off guard.

Wounded and in physical agony, Talon had held his uncle in his arms while Idiag died from his injuries.

'Guard my wife and Ceara, boy,' his uncle had whispered before his death. 'Don't make me regret taking you in.'

Talon had promised. But only a few months after that, he'd found his aunt raped and murdered by their enemies. Her body desecrated and left for the animals to prey upon.

Less than a full year later, he'd cradled his precious wife, Nynia, to his chest as she, too, drew her last breath and left him all alone, forever bereft of her gentle, soothing touch.

She had been his world.

His heart.

His soul.

Without her, he had no longer wished to live.

His spirit as broken as his heart, he had placed their still-born son into her lifeless arms and buried the two of them together by the loch where he and Nynia had played as children.

Then, he'd done as he had been taught by his mother and uncle.

He had survived to lead his clan.

Laying aside his grief as best he could, he had lived only for the clan's welfare.

As a chieftain, he had spilled enough blood to fill the raging sea and had taken countless wounds on his own flesh for his people. He had led his clan to glory against all the mainlanders and northern clans who had sought to conquer them. With most of his family dead, he had given his clan everything he had. His loyalty. His love.

He had even offered them his own life to protect them from the gods.

And in one heartbeat, his clansmen had taken the last thing on this earth he had loved.

Ceara.

His cherished little sister whom he had sworn to his mother, father, and uncle he would protect at any cost. Ceara with her golden hair and laughing amber eyes. So young. So kind and giving.

To satisfy one man's selfish ambition, his clan had slain her before his eyes while he lay tied down, unable to stop them.

She'd died calling out for him to help her.

Her horrified screams still rang in his ears.

After her execution, the clan had turned on him and ended his life as well. But Talon's death had brought no relief to him. He had felt only guilt. Guilt and a need to right the wrongs done to his family.

That vengeful need had transcended everything, even death itself.

'May the gods damn you all!' Talon roared at the burning village.

'The gods don't damn us, we damn ourselves by our words and deeds.'

Talon turned sharply at the voice behind him to see a man clothed all in black. Cresting the small rise, this man was unlike any he'd seen before.

The night wind swirled around the figure, billowing out his finely woven cloak as he walked with a large, twisted warrior's staff held in his left hand. The dark, ancient oak wood was carved with symbols, the top decorated with feathers fastened by a leather cord.

Moonlight danced upon hair that was an unearthly jet-black which the man wore in three long braids.

His silvery, shimmering eyes seemed to swirl like phantom mists.

Those glowing eyes were eerie and haunting.

Standing to the height of a giant, Talon had never before had to look up at anyone and yet this stranger seemed the size of a mountain. It wasn't until the man drew nearer that Talon realized he was only a few inches taller and not as ancient as he'd first seemed. Indeed, his face was that of a perfect youth who stood on the precious threshold between adolescence and maturity.

Until one looked closer. There in the stranger's eyes lay the wisdom of the ages. This was no lad, but a warrior who had battled hard and seen much.

'Who are you?' Talon asked.

'I am Acheron Parthenopaeus,' he said in a strange accent that spoke Talon's native Celtic tongue flawlessly. 'I was sent by Artemis to train you for your new life.'

Talon had been told by the Greek goddess to expect this man who had roamed the earth since time immemorial. 'And what will you teach me, Sorcerer?'

'I will teach you to slay the Daimons who prey upon hapless humans. I will teach you how to hide during the day so that the rays of the sun don't kill you. I will show you how to speak without revealing your fangs to the humans, and all else you need to know to survive.'

Talon laughed bitterly as blinding pain swept through him once more. He ached and he hurt so much that he could scarcely breathe. All he wanted was peace.

His family.

And they were gone.

Without them, he no longer wished to survive at all. Nay, he couldn't live with this weight in his heart.

He looked to Acheron. 'Tell me, Sorcerer, is there any spell you have that can take this agony from me?'

Acheron gave him a hard stare. 'Aye, Celt. I can show you how to bury that pain so deep inside you that it will prick you no more. But be warned that nothing is ever given freely and nothing lasts forever. One day something will come along to make you feel again, and with it, it will bring the pain of the ages upon you. All you have hidden will come out and it could destroy not only you, but anyone near you.'

Talon ignored that last part. All he wanted for now was one day when his heart wasn't broken. One moment free of his torment. He was willing to pay any cost for it.

'Are you sure I will feel nothing?'

Acheron nodded. 'I can teach it to you only if you listen.'

'Then teach me well, Sorcerer. Teach me well.'

Chapter 1

'You know, Talon, killing a soul-sucking Daimon without a good fight is like sex without foreplay. A total waste of time and completely un . . . satisfying.'

Talon grunted at Wulf's words while he sat at a corner table at the Café Du Monde, waiting for his waitress to return with his black chicory coffee and beignets. He had an ancient Saxon coin in his left hand that he rolled between his fingers as he scanned the dark street in front of him and watched the tourists and locals drift by.

Having banished most of his emotions fifteen hundred years ago, there were only three things Talon allowed himself to enjoy anymore: loose women, hot chicory coffee, and phone calls with Wulf.

In that order.

Though to be fair, there were times when Wulf's friendship did mean more to him than a cup of coffee.

Tonight, however, wasn't one of them.

He'd awakened just after dusk to find himself pathetically low on caffeine, and though the theory went that immortals couldn't have addictions, he wouldn't wager on it.

He'd barely taken time to pull on a pair of pants and his leather jacket before he came seeking the goddess Caffeina.

The cold New Orleans night was uncommonly calm. There weren't even many tourists on the street, which was unusual this close to Mardi Gras.

Still, it was prime Daimon season in New Orleans. Soon the vampires would be stalking the tourists and preying on them like an open banquet.

For the moment, though, Talon was glad it was quiet, since it allowed him to deal with Wulf's crisis and feed the one craving that wouldn't wait.

'Spoken like a true Norseman,' Talon said into his cell phone. 'What you need, my brother, is a mead hall filled with serving wenches and Vikings ready to battle their way into Valhalla.'

'Tell me about it,' Wulf agreed. 'I miss the good old days when Daimons were warriors and combat trained. The ones I found tonight knew nothing about fighting, and I'm sick of the whole 'my gun will solve all' mentality.'

'You get shot again?'

'Four times. I swear . . . I wish I could get a Daimon up here like Desiderius. I'd love a good down-and-dirty fight for once.'

'Careful what you wish for, you just might get it.'

'Yeah, I know. But damn. Just once, can't they stop running from us and learn to fight like their ancestors did? I miss the way things used to be.'

Talon adjusted his black Ray-Ban Predator sunglasses as he watched a group of women walk past on the street nearby.

Now there was one challenge he could sink his fangs into . . .

Under his closed lips, he ran his tongue over his long left canine tooth while he watched a beautiful blond woman dressed in blue. She had a slow, seductive walk that could make even a fifteen-hundred-year-old man feel underage.

He *so* wanted a piece of that.

Damn Mardi Gras.

If not for the season, he'd be hanging up on Wulf and running after her to fulfill his first comfort.

Duty. How it reeked.

Sighing, he turned his thoughts back to their conversation. 'I tell you, what I miss most are the Talpinas.'

'What are those?'

Talon cast a wistful look at the women who were quickly drifting out of his line of sight. 'That's right, they were before your time. Back in the better part of the Dark Ages, we used to have a clan of Squires whose sole purpose was to take care of our carnal needs.'

Talon sucked his breath in appreciatively as he remembered the Talpinas and the comfort they had once provided to him and his Dark-Hunter brethren. 'Man, they were great. They knew what we were and they were more than happy to bed us. Hell, the Squires even trained them how to pleasure you.'

'What happened to them?'

'About a hundred or so years before you were born, a Dark-Hunter made the mistake of falling in love with his Talpina. Unfortunately for the rest of us, she didn't pass Artemis's test. Artemis was so angry, she stepped in and banished the Talpinas from us, and implemented the oh so wonderful you're-only-supposed-to-sleep-with-them-once rule. As further backlash, Acheron came up with the never-touch-your-Squire law. I tell you, you haven't lived until you've tried to find a decent one-night stand in seventh-century Britain.'

Wulf snorted. 'That's *never* been my problem.'

'Yeah, I know. I envy you that. While the rest of us have to pull ourselves back from our lovers lest we betray our existence, you get to cut loose without fear.'

'Believe me, Talon, it's not all it's cracked up to be. You

live alone by choice. Do you have any idea how frustrating it is to have no one remember you five minutes after you leave them?'

Wulf expelled a long, tired breath. 'Christopher's mother has come over here three times in the last week alone just so she can meet the person he works for. I've known her for what? Thirty years? And let's not forget that time sixteen years ago when I came home and she called the cops on me because she thought I had broken into my own house.'

Talon grimaced at the pain in Wulf's voice. It reminded him why he no longer allowed himself to feel anything except physical pleasure.

Emotions served no purpose in life and he was much better off without them.

'I'm sorry, little brother,' he said to Wulf. 'At least you have us, and your Squire, who can remember you.'

'Yeah, I know. Thank the gods for modern technology. Otherwise I'd go insane.'

Talon shifted in his fold-up chair. 'Not to change the subject, but did you see who Artemis relocated to New Orleans to take Kyrian's place?'

'I heard it was Valerius,' Wulf said in disbelief. 'What was Artemis thinking?'

'I have no idea.'

'Does Kyrian know?' Wulf asked.

'For an obvious reason, Acheron and I decided not to tell him that the grandson and spitting image of the man who crucified him and destroyed his family was being moved into the city just down the street from his house. Unfortunately, though, I'm sure he'll find out sooner or later.'

'Man, human or not, Kyrian will kill him if they ever cross paths – not something you need to cope with this time of year.'

'Tell me about it.'

'So, who got Mardi Gras duty this year?' Wulf asked.

Talon dropped the coin in his hand as he thought about
the ancient Greco-Roman slave who would be temporarily
moved into the city tomorrow to help combat the Daimon
explosion that occurred every year at this time. Zarek was
a known Feeder who preyed on human blood. He was
unstable at best, psychotic at worst. No one trusted him.

And it was just Talon's luck to have Zarek here, especially since he'd been hoping for a Dark-Huntress to come
visit. It might drain his powers to be in the presence of another
Dark-Hunter, but he would still rather have an attractive
woman to look at than deal with Zarek's psychosis.

Besides, for what he had in mind, he and a Huntress didn't
need their Dark-Hunter powers anyway . . .

'They're importing Zarek.'

Wulf cursed. 'I didn't think Acheron would ever let him
leave Alaska.'

'Yeah, I know, but word came from Artemis herself that
she wanted him here. Looks like we're having a psycho
reunion this week . . . Oh wait, it's Mardi Gras. Duh.'

Wulf laughed again.

At last the waitress brought his coffee and a small plate
of three beignets that were heavily covered with powdered
sugar. Talon sighed appreciatively.

'Coffee arrived?' Wulf asked.

'Oh, yeah.'

Talon took a whiff of his coffee, set it aside, and reached
for a beignet. He'd barely touched the pastry when he saw
something across the street, on the right side of Jackson
Square down the Pedestrian Mall. 'Ah, man.'

'What?'

'Friggin' Fabio alert.'

'Hey, you're not too far from the mark either, *blondie*.'

'Bite me, Viking.'

Peeved by the timing, Talon watched the group of four
Daimons stalking the night. Tall and golden blonde Daimons

who possessed the godlike beauty of their race. They strutted around like punkish peacocks, drunk on their own power as they scoped out tourists to kill.

By nature, Daimons were cowards. They only stood their ground and fought against Dark-Hunters when they were in groups and only then as a last resort. Because they were so much stronger than humans, they preyed openly on them, but let a Dark-Hunter near them and they ran for cover.

There had been a time once when it wasn't like that. But the younger generations were more careful than their ancestors. They weren't as well trained or as resourceful.

However, they were ten times cockier.

Talon narrowed his eyes. 'You know, if I were a negative person, I would be seriously annoyed right now.'

'You sound annoyed to me.'

'No, this isn't annoyed. This is mild perturbance. Besides, you should see these guys.' Talon dropped his Celtic accent as he invented a conversation for the Daimons. He raised his voice to an unnaturally high level. 'Hey, Gorgeous George, I think I smell a Dark-Hunter.'

'Oh no, Dick,' he said, dropping his voice two octaves, 'don't be a dick. There's no Dark-Hunter here.'

Talon returned to his falsetto. 'I dunno . . .'

'Wait,' Talon said, again in the deep voice. 'I smell tourist. Tourist with big . . . strong soul.'

'Would you stop?'

'Talk about inkblots,' Talon said, using the derogatory term Dark-Hunters had for Daimons. It stemmed from the strange black mark that all Daimons developed on their chests when they crossed over from being simple Apollites to human slayers. 'Damn, all I wanted was a drink of coffee and one little beignet.'

Talon glanced wistfully at his drink as he debated what should take priority. 'Coffee . . . Daimons . . . Coffee . . . Daimons . . .'

'I think in this case the Daimons better win.'

'Yeah, but it's *chicory* coffee.'

Wulf clucked his tongue. 'Talon wanting to be toasted by Acheron for failure to protect humans.'

'I know,' he said with a disgusted sigh. 'Let me go expire them. Talk to you later.'

Talon stood up, zipped his phone into the pocket of his motorcycle jacket, and stared longingly at his beignets.

Oh, the Daimons would pay for this.

Taking a quick drink of coffee that scalded his tongue, he skirted through the tables and made his way toward the vampires, who were stalking toward the Presbytere building.

His Dark-Hunter senses alert, Talon headed to the opposite side of the square. He would head them off and make sure they paid for their soul-stealing ways.

And for his uneaten beignets.

Chapter 2

It was one of *those* nights. The kind that made Sunshine Runningwolf wonder why she bothered leaving her loft.

'How many times can a person get lost in a city where she's lived the whole of her life?'

The number seemed to be infinite.

Of course, it would help if she could stay focused, but she had the attention span of a sick flea.

No, actually she had the attention span of an artist who seldom stayed focused on the here and now. Like an out-of-control slingshot, her thoughts drifted from one topic to the next and then back again. Her mind was constantly wandering and sifting through new ideas and techniques – the novelty of the world around her and how best to capture it.

To her there was beauty everywhere and in every little thing. It was her job to show that beauty to others.

And that neat building they were constructing, two or three, maybe four streets over, had distracted her and got her thinking up new designs for her pottery as she wandered through the French Quarter toward her favorite coffeehouse on St. Anne.

Not that she drank that noxious stuff. She hated it. But the retro-beatnik Coffee Stain had nice artwork on the walls and her friends seemed partial to drinking gallons of the tar-liquid.

Tonight she and Trina were going to go over . . .

Her mind flashed back to the building.

Pulling out her sketchbook, she made a few more notes and turned to her right, down a small alley.

She took two steps, and ran into a wall.

Only it wasn't a wall, she realized, as two arms wrapped around her to keep her from stumbling.

Looking up, she froze.

Ay, Caramba! She stared into a face so well formed that she doubted even a Greek sculptor could do justice to it.

His wheat-colored hair seemed to glow in the night and the planes of his face . . .

Perfect. Simply perfect. Totally symmetrical. Wow.

Without thinking, she reached up, grabbed his chin and turned his face to see it from different angles.

No, not an optical illusion. No matter the angle, his features were perfection incarnate.

Wow, again. Absolutely flawless.

She needed to sketch this.

No. Oils. Oils would be better.

Pastels!

'Are you all right?' he asked.

'I'm fine,' she said. 'I'm sorry. I didn't see you standing there. But do you know your face is pure eurythmy?'

He gave her a tight-lipped smile as he patted the shoulder of her red cape. 'Yes, I do. And do you know, Little Red Riding Hood, the Big Bad Wolf is out tonight and he's hungry?'

What was that?

She was talking about art and he . . .

The thought faded as she realized the man wasn't alone.

There were four more men and one woman. All insanely beautiful. And all six eyed her as if she were a tasty morsel.

Uh-oh.

Her throat went dry.

Sunshine took a step back as every sense in her body told her to run.

They moved in even closer, penning her between them.

'Now, now, Little Red Riding Hood,' the first one said. 'You don't want to be leaving so soon, do you?'

'Um, yes,' she said, preparing to fight. Little did they know, a woman who made it her habit to date mean biker types was more than able to deliver a swift kick when she needed it. 'I think it would be a really *good* idea.'

He reached for her.

Out of nowhere a circular something whizzed past her face, grazing his outstretched arm. The man cursed as he pulled his bleeding arm to his chest. The thing ricocheted like Xena's chakram, and returned to the opening of the alley where a shadow caught it.

Sunshine gaped at the outline of a man. Dressed all in black, he stood with his legs apart in a warrior's stance while his weapon gleamed wickedly in the dim light.

Even though she could see nothing of his face, his ever-changing aura was mammoth, giving him a presence that was as startling as it was powerful.

This new stranger was dangerous.

Deadly.

A lethal shadow just waiting to strike.

He stood in silence, looking at her attackers, the weapon held nonchalantly, yet somehow threateningly, in his left hand.

Then, total chaos broke out as the men who surrounded her rushed the newcomer . . .

Talon fingered the release for his srad and folded its three blades into a single dagger. He tried to get to the woman, but the Daimons attacked him en masse. Normally, he'd have no trouble whatsoever obliterating them, but Dark-Hunter

Code forbade him to reveal his powers to an uninitiated human.

Damn.

For a second, he considered summoning a fog to conceal them, but that would make fighting the Daimons more difficult.

No, he couldn't give them any advantage. So long as the woman was here, he was fighting with his hands tied behind his back, and given the superhuman strength and power of the Daimons, that wasn't a good thing at all. No doubt that was why they'd attacked.

For once they actually stood a chance against him.

'Run,' he ordered the human woman.

She started to obey him when one of the Daimons grabbed her. With a kick to the groin and a whack across his back after he doubled over, she dropped the Daimon and ran.

Talon arched a brow at her move. Smooth, very smooth. He'd always appreciated a woman who could watch out for herself.

Do you love fiction with a supernatural twist?

Want the chance to hear news about your favourite
authors (and the chance to win free books)?

Keri Arthur
S. G. Browne
P.C. Cast
Christine Feehan
Jacquelyn Frank
Larissa Ione
Sherrilyn Kenyon
Jackie Kessler
Jayne Ann Krentz and Jayne Castle
Martin Millar
Kat Richardson
J.R. Ward
David Wellington

Then visit the Piatkus website and blog
www.piatkus.co.uk | www.piatkusbooks.net

And follow us on Facebook and Twitter
www.facebook.com/piatkusfiction | www.twitter.com/piatkusbooks

piatkus